One night, after I turned eight, I heard her sneaking out of our room. A real pretty dress the color of the ink on my school papers hovered above shoes with heels whittled down to little dots at the bottom, the kind that look as though you could kill somebody with them if they were giving you trouble.

So from my spot in the bed, the spot next to the sea foam green wall, I asked her, "Where you goin', Mama? Who you going with?"

And Mama said, "Don't even ask, Myrtle Charmaine."

PRAISE FOR LISA SAMSON'S *Songbird*

"A stylish novel that will make readers alternately laugh and cry for more than four hundred pages."
—Terry Mapes, Mansfield, Ohio, *News Journal*

"Written with a hint of a southern twang, SONGBIRD draws its characters with such singularity that readers may forget they're fictional."
—Elizabeth Wisz, *CBA Marketplace*

"When I want to smile, when I want my heart to be touched, when I want an honest look at life as we live it, I pick up a book by Lisa Samson and I'm never disappointed. Don't miss SONGBIRD."
—Robin Lee Hatcher, bestselling author of *Firstborn*

"SONGBIRD is simply superb! A beautifully written tale of one woman's remarkable journey. If you haven't yet discovered Lisa Samson, don't waste another moment!"
—Marlo Schalesky, author of *Cry Freedom* and *Freedom's Shadow*

"Lisa Samson's SONGBIRD reads like a southern folk poem or road movie with explosions of insight. It's edgy and honest, and it rings like a haunting melody. The author pulls you into a waif's world and makes you care what happens to her . . . Lisa Samson's an up-and-coming writer who gets downright nosey with her characters—probing inner nits and anatomy to discover what really makes them tick."

> —Janet Chester Bly, author of *Hope Lives Here* and *The Heart of a Runaway*

"Lisa Samson's consummate skill as a storyteller shines through her latest work, SONGBIRD. Woven among insights of pure honesty, the story sparkles with hope, encouragement, and healing. I loved this book!"

> —Lois Richer, author of *Inner Harbor* and *Blessings in Disguise*

"As usual, Lisa Samson delights us with SONGBIRD! Her distintive writing voice is compelling, lively, and irresistible. A must-read."

> —Nancy Moser, author of *The Seat Beside Me* and *The Sister Circle*

"With a unique style of prose, Samson's writing is as warm and quirky as ever . . . She brings SONGBIRD to vibrant life."

> —Liz Curtis Higgs, bestselling author of *Bad Girls of the Bible*

Songbird

LISA SAMSON

WARNER
Faith

NEW YORK   BOSTON   NASHVILLE

Copyright © 2003 by Lisa E. Samson
All rights reserved. No part of this book may be reproduced in any form or by any electronic or mechanical means, including information storage and retrieval systems, without permission in writing from the publisher, except by a reviewer who may quote brief passages in a review.

Cover design by Charles Brock, The DesignWorks Group, Inc.
Photo of girl by © Darrell Lecorre/Masterfil

The Warner Faith name and logo are registered trademarks of Warner Books.

Warner Faith

Time Warner Book Group
1271 Avenue of the Americas New York, NY 10020
Visit our Web site at www.twbookmark.com

Printed in the United States of America

Originally published in Trade Paperback by Warner Faith
First Mass Market Paperback Printing: May 2005

10 9 8 7 6 5 4 3 2 1

For my niece,
Melissa Chesser,
Family songbird
And my dear friend.

I love you,

—*Aunt CeeCee*

"None can cure their harms by wailing them."

—William Shakespeare, *Richard III*, Act II

Songbird

Prologue

Good morning, merry sunshine,
How did you wake so soon?
You've scared the little stars away,
And shone away the moon.
I watched you go to sleep last night,
Before I stopped my play,
How did you get way over there,
And, pray, where did you stay?

I never go to sleep, dear,
I just go 'round to see
My little children of the East,
Who rise to watch for me.
I waken all the birds and bees,
And flowers on my way,
Then last of all, the little child
Who stayed out late to play.

I could be digging graves. That's definitely worse.

It's a cold, drizzly Wednesday night in late November. Gravediggers work out in the eight P.M. rain. So off I haul myself to the 7-Eleven, pour up a couple of hot chocolates, slip in a little half-and-half, and slide on back to that small church cemetery right there on Route 29. Imagine my surprise when the fellow down there in the grave, dug only about three feet deep so far, looks up with a smile brighter than the generator-powered light that shines down into the crisp-edged rectangular hole. Now, I don't know much about much, really, but I say when you take the trouble to stop and buy a couple of hot chocolates at the 7-Eleven, and one of the men you hand them to happens to look like Mel Gibson's younger brother, right there's your reward from the Almighty.

I present them the hot chocolates for "When you want to get a little warm," and accept their "Thank you, now"s. I realize I should say, "God bless you" or something, you know, to fill them in on the fact that my kindness was due to the kindness Jesus bestowed upon me, but I only manage this crazy little salute before I wheel around and almost get plonkered by a hitherto unseen pickup truck backing toward the gravesite.

Thank the good Lord I am able to bite back, "Goodness gracious, you almost had to dig an extra one for me!" And give the fabled grandma Min yet another reason to roll over in the grave I have no idea whether or not she occupies? No, thank you.

So I drive along home to our RV, practicing my new solo, "Beulah Land, Sweet Beulah Land," and tell my husband, Harlan, all about it and we laugh ourselves a good one. Harlan's bald with flimsy hazel eyes, but his pulpit voice, the main attraction of the Harlan Hopewell Evangelistic Crusade, I imagine tints even the angel Gabriel a light shade of green. And I love him.

And you know how they say, "No good deed goes unpunished"? Well, I drag red clay from the gravesite all over our carpet. See? That's when I know I've done something right, because the Devil has to get the last word. I know this because each day I have to talk myself out of bed and into the hum of life, and old Scratch does his darndest to win that battle, too.

The great thing about God is that He'll always answer your prayers. One day, oh, years ago after I turned sixteen and had run away from my second foster home, I just prayed to the Lord. I prayed, Lord, help me to see ways to make folks feel like they're worth something. Because I can tell you this, when you feel like you're worth nothing, the thought of living with that for the rest of your life feels like looking down a hole dug clear through to China. Only there's no China at the end. And you know what? God answers that prayer all the time! So many chances greet me out there every day, I force myself to pick and choose which ones to act on! God is so good.

Just like the song says.

Back in 1960 my mama, Isla Whitehead, thought otherwise. At least I guess so. My birth occurred on a night in December so warm I broke my first sweat at the ripe old age of one hour. It hit eighty that day. A record-breaker for sure! And I don't know why I broke a sweat, other than maybe somehow I envisioned the road before me. And my mama went and named me Myrtle. Myrtle Charmaine Whitehead. Now you just tell me if that isn't a name a girl will do her solemn best to slough off right out of the starting gate?

One time Mama said she recognized the trappings of something special built right into me: fame, fortune, notoriety, she never did say. The Lord only knows how someone can tell that by looking at a newborn. Mama claimed infallibility about such matters. Mama claimed the powers of ESP. Of course, she also used to say she knew enough dirt about Queen Elizabeth II to dethrone the poor woman!

Oh, my lands! However, my few memories of very early childhood: sunny days in the park near Lynchburg College, cheese sandwiches by the river, Easter dresses, and cat's cradle, I force myself to recall for my own sake, not for Mama's. I remember the song she always sang when she woke me up, "Good Morning, Merry Sunshine," but when she stopped singing it to me, I can't say.

Mama wore no golden band from the time I could remember. So far as I know, marriage and Mama never crossed paths. Isla Whitehead was the Woman at the Well but without any marriage certificates to fall back on. If Jesus struck up a conversation with her down by the drinking fountain at the market downtown, He wouldn't ask her the question, "Woman, have you a husband?" because, back then, Mama would have said "yes," and that would have just been a flat-out lie. Nothing like the Woman at the Well who told the truth, part of the truth, and nothing but part of the truth. As my little King James Bible says, "God cannot be tempted with evil, neither tempteth He any man." So He might just have asked her how many men she had, and Mama might have said two, to which He would have replied, "You rightly say. You've had two men, and another twenty to boot." Although, I can't quite picture my Lord and Savior using the phrase "to boot."

I can, however, picture the expression of love in His eyes for Mama. It's the same one He has for me, too. "Jesus Lover of my soul, let me to Thy bosom fly."

Just like the song says.

Oh, I like all the songs.

As far as I know, Lynchburg never labeled Mama as the local strumpet or some such derision-filled title. I never knew about her nights out until I'd aged a bit. And the proverbial train of "uncles" never hokey-pokied through our little rented room. She just lucked out that I slept like Gulliver and never knew she'd flown our sad little life for however brief a time.

In fact, I knew nothing of Mama's dark, insatiable penchant for men and that her life of dates, clandestine love affairs, and dangerous caterwauling had been so widespread until I reached maturity and assembled the puzzle years after she discarded me.

Even now, I have many unanswered questions. But isn't that life?

Anyway, we all have only one tale to tell, our own. And usually questions remain and all we can do is be glad we're alive to field them right on into eternity.

Part One

1

*M*ama waited tables down at
the Texas Inn, right where Route 29 dipped back up from
its sojourn across the bridge that spanned the James
River. Now, coming down the big hill before the river
you can get the prettiest view of the city of Lynchburg,
Virginia. The streets are layered in tiers downtown as
though some building farmer decided to employ the Inca
method. Beginning with Main Street, jumping up to
Church Street, then Court, and finally Clay, downtown
just sort of hovers there, the steeples sometimes piercing
the morning mist from the river, sometimes glowing like
holy swords of fire in the afternoon sun. Now that I'm an
adult I appreciate this view, but back in the late '60s and
early '70s, it wasn't so well lit and some folks thought
downtown would never bounce back to the glory days.

The Texas Inn, serving chili and barbecue and egg
sandwiches and the like, drew in all manner of truckers
back in those days. Guys with names like Norman and Al
and Bobby-Jay gathered from far and wide just to steal a
glimpse of the saucy waitress with the pearly teeth. See,
Mama, well, she was flat-out the prettiest waitress there.

I grew up hunched awkwardly at the counter, penciling schoolwork, weighed down by the red frizzy ponytail I usually gathered myself thereby accidentally achieving a topsy-turvy effect. Listening to the jukebox blurt out country-western music and the occasional rock 'n' roll tune like "Sweet Home Alabama," I watched as Mama worked her magic on the customers. She never introduced me to her customers, even the regulars.

I guess I couldn't blame her.

"Ask for Isla. She'll treat you right," folks leaving informed those just walking through the doorway. I just didn't know how right she treated them! I just thought she was sassy and smart and daring and removed, as if humans wasted her time unless they were admiring her and even then, she met compliments with snappy derision.

"That Isla is something else!"

"Isla darlin', you just come on over here and refill my coffee and we'll talk about *things*."

She'd say, "Stuff it in your pants, Joe, there's plenty of room down there."

And they'd just laugh.

"That Isla sure ain't hard on the eyes, is she, Stanley?"

And Mama wasn't. I disappointed her that way, I know. We looked nothing alike, this harsh white and red, bloodshot eye of a child and her black-eyed Susan mama. Mama's brown hair radiated a golden warmth and she always wore it straight down, its waves curving around her sweet, valentine face. Olive complexioned with reddish brown lips, she talked smart to the men, hands on hips, chin pointed high as though she really had no business waiting tables at the Texas Inn. Mama's way of answering questions without really answering them kept them at bay, yet happy, and when a rare jovial mood visited her, all sorts of crazy stories from sparkling lips entertained them, tales of escapades filled with phrases like, "And then he took out his," and she'd lean far forward, exposing her bosoms all the while keeping my little ears from hearing her words.

She never seemed to inhabit her eyes. Not really.

I only knew this about her: Mama came to Lynchburg in 1956 as a freshman at Randolph Macon Women's College and never left. She told me she grew up in Suffolk, Virginia, and had planned on never seeing the place again.

"It's the most boring, stuffiest old place you've ever seen. And your grandma Min is the most boring, stuffiest old woman you've ever seen. Who needs the 'peanut capital of the world'? We can have lots of fun right here in Lynchburg. So don't ask to go there, Myrtle," she said.

And I didn't ask. Because when fun and Mama collided, the party lasted for weeks! But most times, Mama distanced herself from me and everyone else, it seemed, and when she didn't want to talk about something, she wouldn't. She'd just sip on her glass of "medicinal gin" and pretend you never asked a thing. Sometimes she stared out between the blinds and talked about Queen Elizabeth.

She'd go on vacation usually after one of those times. Somehow Mrs. Blackburn always knew when Mama really needed a vacation. And I'd spend those days with Mrs. Blackburn, sitting on her porch overlooking the street. And I'd watch all those college girls and realize I'd never walk in their shoes. I knew that then, somehow, as well as I knew when looking at *National Geographic*s at school that I'd never be living by a mud hut, wearing a thousand necklaces above bare breasts.

One particular student named Margie would take me out for milk shakes when Mama was on vacation. She'd say, "Rich or poor, it doesn't matter. This sort of thing hits women of all walks and ages. Believe me, my mother goes at least once or twice a year, so I know firsthand." I really thought she was talking about vacations so I said, "How nice for her," and she'd say, "You don't get it yet, do you, Myrtle?"

"Get what?" I'd ask.

She'd just smile and say, "Good for you."

One night, after I turned eight, I heard Mama sneaking out of our room. A real pretty dress the color of the blue ink on my school papers hovered above shoes with heels whittled down to little dots at the bottom, the kind that look as though you could kill somebody with if they were giving you trouble.

So from my spot on the bed, the spot next to the seafoam green wall, I asked her, "Where you goin', Mama? Who you going with?"

And Mama said, "Out. Don't even ask, Myrtle Charmaine, because you're old enough now to be here for a couple of hours by yourself." But she couldn't hide the sparkle in her eyes.

"What if there's a fire or something?"

"You just find Mrs. Blackburn. She'll take care of you; you know that. But it had better only be because there's a fire or something. I'm so excited, Myrtle."

"But what about if I get sick?"

"Your towel's hanging right there." She pursed her lips.

"But—"

She shook her head and finger and grabbed my ear with a twist. "I mean it, Myrtle. If I find out you went out of this room while I'm out, you'll wish you hadn't!"

"Oh, Mama!"

"Shut up, now, Myrtle." She let go. "Let this be a nice time for me."

And so I said nothing else, because when Mama really exploded it was like a ball of blue lightning circling down the chimney to what had seemed like a fine party only a moment before. A blue ball skirting about the room like the Tazmanian Devil. And when she exploded she said some cruel things. I kept a list so I wouldn't say them to my own kids someday.

1. You ruined my life.
2. You don't appreciate anything I do for you.
3. How did I end up stuck with you?
4. Get out of my face, Myrtle, I can't bear to see you for one more second.

She called me the name of a female dog a lot. Even now I can't speak that word or write it, and people use it so flippantly it makes my teeth ache.

And Mama never *asked* me to do anything.

"Get over here."

"Go away."

"Fix that hair of yours, Myrtle. You look like a clown."

Now, a lot of the kids at school had parents that spanked them good. But Mama always gave me the silent treatment after her tirades. I'd rather have been walloped and been done with it. One time, when I brought Vicki Miller home with me from school, Mama rewarded me with a two-hour lecture I could barely comprehend and an icy silence for three days afterward. We ate some lonely meals together over at the soda fountain in the drugstore by the college for a while and I figured if I ever crossed her again, only something big and worth more than Vicki Miller would do.

My nosebleeds started around then. Mama jumped on that, telling me not to come down to the restaurant after school anymore, saying, "Nobody wants you to bleed all over their corn dog, Myrtle. And I wager the sight of you caused them to lose their appetites anyway."

Mama sure was right, though, about bringing Vicki home because before then, nobody knew much about me and where I lived. And Vicki told everybody about our little rented room, saying, "Imagine that! Myrtle White-head doesn't even live in a house! She just lives in a little room near the college, with lots of other college girls in the house." And then, just so she didn't indisputably prove herself the Devil incarnate she had turned out to be, she added a, "Poor Myrtle."

See, Mama made sure my clothes looked nice because she was proud like that and I think she tried to do the best she could with the Raggedy Anne daughter she found herself responsible for. She skimped on issues of lodging, food, and transportation. It didn't matter what the weather, Mama always walked down to the Texas Inn to save bus fare. And I can't even begin to tell you how many leftover egg sandwiches rolled up in three layers of napkin I ate for breakfast before school.

I never knew life could be any different.

I looked out the window that night Mama left in such excitement. The man down there, he looked like a no-good. With golden rings, bracelets, and patent leather shoes for company, his overall appearance gave off more shade than the oak trees lining Rivermont Avenue.

I sure didn't like the way he laid a hand on Mama's rear end.

Pretending I slept, I felt Mama climb into the bed beside me hours later. "See, Minerva Whitehead? I can make out just fine on my own," she whispered with a drunk laugh.

I felt a movement in the bed and winked open my eye and she lay there fluttering a wrist encircled by a new gold bracelet. Slim, and light. I'd seen them in the jewelry store window downtown. They cost next to nothing.

"Real gold," she giggled.

I felt reasonably sure Minerva Whitehead, the grandma I'd never known, didn't think that going out on dates with shady guys like that no-good counted as making out just fine at all.

2

$\mathcal{I}$ began singing at five years old. Mama would drop me off at First Baptist Church right on Rivermont Avenue at nine o'clock on Sunday mornings and she'd continue on toward downtown and heaven knows what. This Sunday school teacher named Mrs. Evans taught us little songs like, "Shadrach Meshach and Abednego," "Dare to Be a Daniel," "My Lord Knows the Way Through the Wilderness," and my favorite one about the Devil sitting on a tack. Mrs. Evans approached me one day just as we finished singing "The Happy Day Express" and said, "Myrtle, the Lord has given you a gift."

And I looked around for a bright package somewhere in the room. "I don't see nothin', Miz Evans."

Mrs. Evans laughed and her dark, straight hair swung back and forth like wind chimes in the breeze, and her pretty blue eyes scrunched up like pansies before they bloom. "It's not in a box, Myrtle, unless you count your voice box."

Then she told me that God's gift to me was my singing voice. "You never forget who gave you your pretty voice,

Myrtle. Some gifts God blesses us with because we've taken the time to work hard at them, but some of them, special ones like you've got are just flat-out free."

I hugged her then and she felt so warm. When she hugged me back I cried. Her warmth, her sweetness, her joy ran like waters in the desert. I look back on that moment now and I realize that Mrs. Evans saved my life right then. And even to this day, when I imagine my larynx I picture a little gift box there in my throat, given to me by God so that I can return the favor. It's wrapped in dark blue paper with gold stars. And gold ribbon—the real fabric kind, that shimmers and glows with each note that comes from beneath the lid—holds it all together.

3

*M*y relationship with Mama
had its redeeming times every so often, like shopping together for school clothes or my Easter dress. One year
when I was nine I tried on a lavender dress and coat, the
kind with the little silk bouquet of flowers pinned at the
collar. I slowly slid the latch of the dressing room door to
the right, anticipating her displeasure upon the revelation
of my person. You see, I'd swung a lot the day before at
recess, creating a tangle of auburn thicker than a bed of
sea kelp, and my scalp still hadn't recovered from the
brushing she'd given my hair. I'd screamed and cried, but
that one crack of the brush to the side of my head cured
that. I looked like a blotched piece of chicken in a dress.

She sat there on an upholstered fold-out chair near the
dressing room door. "Turn around, Myrtle." Her index
finger up to her mouth, she looked me over, nodding
slowly. "Yes, ma'am, that will do." And that year, she
knelt down and pulled me close and said, "You really are
a pretty thing, Myrtle Charmaine. And someday, we'll
just put a little permanent wave in that hair of yours to

calm things down, but for now, you're little, and it works just fine."

I never knew what to believe.

I hid the rest of my nosebleeds from her. But she never let me come back to the restaurant except for dinner a few times. And the nosebleeds only surfaced with greater frequency as though my body tried in any way possible to release what had become pent up inside of me.

She met him the December before she threw off the mantle of motherhood. The snazzy guy from Washington, D.C. Nothing like that no-good Lynchburg fellow she traded up for years before, this man reeked of savior faire. He topped quite a list:

1. Old Guy. Nothing distinct about him.
2. Salesman Guy. He always shook her hand and said, "Hi, good to see you."
3. Bald Guy. My favorite. I swear he used to be a friar or something. Hardly a man inclined to caterwaul with a woman like my Mama.

A woman like my mama.

If that isn't a too tight shoe I don't know what is.

There were more. Cowboy Guy. Trucker Guy. And lots more Old Guys. Oh, my lands, more than any woman's fair share of Old Guys bobbed their way down Mama's list.

"Don't go near that window when you hear the horn blow, Myrtle."

I watched her get ready. Just like most little girls do, I guess, I found my mother fascinating. Now, when she went to work at the Texas Inn, she wore her hair real simple, either straight down, or back in a headband or a low ponytail. But that night, I'll never forget the way she pulled it up into a French twist, and how the golden streaks in the brown of her hair shimmered like a hundred glowing rivers back into the whirlpool of hair at the crown of her regal head.

Her long neck gleamed white in the light of the small, frilly lamp on the school desk that performed double duty as my place of study and her vanity. So there she sat, her elbow bent against the wooden surface, an eyebrow pencil in her slim clutch, and she worked it so smoothly, first on her eyelids, then in quick little strokes on her brows. "And I'm not sure when I'll be home, so don't even ask."

"You look so pretty, Mama."

"I do? You really think so, Myrtle?"

"You're the prettiest lady in Lynchburg, Mama."

"Let's hope Jeremy thinks so."

Jeremy! That sounded like a classy name.

"Why are you being so nice, Myrtle? You get in trouble at school today?"

"No, ma'am."

She rooted in the drawer for the lipstick brush. Sometimes when I'd get home from school, I'd sit there and pull the cap off her lipstick brush. I'd twist the bristles into view and do my own lips with the residue left from when she'd painted on her lipstick before work. One day I forgot to wipe it off before she came home and she said, "Myrtle, you look like a tramp. Wash your mouth right now."

But that night, Mama seemed so excited. "Myrtle, things might just change for us. I feel like good luck is in the air." She shook as though a little engine puttered inside of her.

Despite Mama's warning, I watched her slip into the man's car and was thankful she didn't look up at the window, because a nosebleed gushed. When it stopped, I walked down to First Baptist for the Christmas pageant rehearsal.

Mrs. Evans sat in the sanctuary with the rest of the kids and she waved real big and motioned me over, as if her arm said, "Now, just you get on over here, you sweet thing."

And I ran down the aisle, no thoughts of nosebleeds or Mama's dates. Mrs. Evans basted everybody together as though an invisible thread passed through each body and then stitched me in right between her left side and the end of the pew. She curled her arm around me and squeezed a little.

"We're singing 'Away in the Manger,' the one with that pretty tune you don't hear too often."

I shook my head. "I don't know which one you mean."

So she hummed it in my ear. "You got that?"

I nodded.

"Sing it back, with the words."

And so I did, and Mrs. Evans's eyes grew. "You're a peach, Myrtle Whitehead. How about singing a solo?"

"I've never sung a solo."

"It'll be fine."

Since Mrs. Evans said it, I believed it.

"That settles it, then." She squeezed again. "You'll sing the song, and James'll be Joseph, Ida will be Mary and have you seen the Stuarts' brand-new baby?"

I nodded.

"He'll be the Baby Jesus."

And you know, Mama sat right there the night we put on the pageant, right on the fourth row, on the center aisle, and when I began to sing, she cried. She just cried and cried and I felt so bad.

"Why were you crying, Mama?" I asked afterward. "Were you sad?"

"Not really, Myrtle." She held my mittened hand in hers and we walked slowly down Rivermont Avenue toward home. Mama seemed so normal that night.

"Then why were you crying?"

"Don't even ask."

It was the last important question I'd ask her for the next fifteen years or so.

4

That December brought a change in her that I still don't understand. Perhaps it was designed to give me more cause for regret upon her desertion, or perhaps it served as something to cling to in those subsequent years when all I really had was memories.

That Christmas morning, we decided to attend Rivermont Presbyterian, closer to home, and the prettiest church you've ever seen. My how those ladies decorated that year. Candles flickered in hurricane lamps on each windowsill, their tiny spark of glow a twin of the picture of the little oil lamps pieced together in the stained glass of the windows above. The lacy screen up front supported feathery fir garlands and velvet bows and fresh fruit.

I sniffed the lush, yuletide perfume of the hushed, candle-softened sanctuary as we tiptoed in that morning. Mama did, too, and she took my hand and whispered, "There's nothing like the smell of fresh pine, is there, Myrtle?"

And I shook my head. "I do believe they should bottle it, Mama."

Isla Whitehead awarded me one of her few chuckles. "They do, Myrtle Charmaine. It's called Pine-Sol."

And we had ourselves a laugh as I fingered the soft wool of my new scarf, noticing, for the first time, a tiny little bluebird embroidered in the corner of one end. Mrs. Evans knitted scarves while she watched TV at night. And that Christmas, she gave one to me. Even Mama thought it pretty though she didn't have much of a heart for "homemade things" in general. But now, years later, whenever I take the winter things out of storage, there it sits in the box, shimmering baby blue and silver and cream. I do believe I'll have it dry-cleaned one day and wear it for the season.

None of the nearby restaurants turned on their lights that Christmas Day, and all of the college girls had traveled far and wide, and were now snug at home in Connecticut with fireplaces, or Atlanta or Richmond with their spacious warm kitchens decorated with hanging brass pots and the finest in cutlery, or even Los Angeles with clear swimming pools, sparkling plastic beverage holders in a wide variety of colors, and palm trees cha-chaing with ocean zephyrs. The girl with the room next to ours hailed from California and her parents named her LaFontaine, a name much preferable to Myrtle, I can say with utter conviction. Nobody knew how she kept that tan all year round, but me and Mama suspected the two battered Chinese screens and three disposable pot roast pans we found one day up on the flat roof of the house had something to do with it.

To our surprise, however, when we returned from church a wide basket perched right in front of our doorway. Now Mama had been planning on us having squirt cheese on Ritz crackers, Vienna sausages, Slim Jims, and a variety pack of Frito-Lay products for our Christmas dinner. She'd even placed four Yoo-Hoos and a pint of High's eggnog outside on our window ledge.

"Look!" Mama cried, and she bent down and read the pretty card.

"Who's it from, Mama?"

"Don't even ask, Myrtle."

So much for a nice Christmas.

I figured that snazzy man from Washington, D.C. figured into the whole mysterious equation.

"Can I see what's inside of it?"

"Of course, Myrtle, don't be a fool! Let's quick get inside before anybody sees."

Well, what a basket, is all I can say! Fancy stuff in there. Crackers, caviar, cream cheese, a half bottle of champagne made up our first course. Next came cheese straws, a cute little Danish canned ham, pâté, and some grapes. And by then we were so stuffed we couldn't eat the dessert.

I fell asleep on the bed. Mama stayed there with me that evening and her happy mood increased. We'd eaten fancy food and nobody was taking her off on a date that night. Mama just sat at the window drinking champagne. Before I drifted off she said, "Myrtle, what would you think of us having a house someday?"

I said I'd like that just fine. And after I woke up from my nap, we ate pecan tartlets, fine chocolates, and drank up the eggnog. For the first time I realized why people said, "Merry Christmas." In fact, until that day, I never really thought much about the salutation at all, what people really said, or why they even said it.

"Merry Christmas, Mama."

And Mama only smiled and sipped some more.

5

$\mathcal{D}$own at Mrs. Evans's house she draped those new little twinkly kind of lights on almost every bush. At least they shone new back then and so different from those big, pasty, colored lights people clipped onto the branches of their firs, yews, and azaleas. The first Christmas she used them, Mrs. Evans's lights blazoned intense colors, the filament of the bulbs standing staunch behind a thick coating of sheer pigment. The second year, they shone a bit paler, and by the end of that season, with all the rain that fell, the color had cracked some, flaked off some. White light beamed through the fissures.

I loved those lights.

I loved them more when the white shone through because her yard glowed brighter, happier. But I remember most the day after the big-basket Christmas when Mama took me for a walk after dark to look at the decorations. It was the first year for Mrs. Evans's twinkly little lights and I thought, "How beautiful!" In fact, I said just that.

"I think so, too, Myrtle," Mama said above my head.

"Maybe one day we'll have lights like that on a house of our own."

Now, Mama never talked like this even three months before. She'd never muttered hopeful sentiments, someday wishes, or even regretful what-ifs. Many times Mama said to me, "Myrtle, life is what it is. You've either got to deal your own cards, or take what comes. But if you choose the latter, then don't bellyache."

Well, we stood there in rapt pleasure at Mrs. Evans's lights when her green door opened, splaying light across the brown grass like a searchlight on a field of desert troops in close formation. "Is that you, Myrtle?" she hollered.

"Yes, ma'am."

"Come on, Myrtle, let's go," Mother whispered.

But I broke free and ran up to the porch. Silent treatment or no silent treatment, nosebleeds or no nosebleeds, I wasn't going to hurt Mrs. Evans's feelings to save myself from Mama. I experienced a panic, as though an unseen hand drew battle lines and I'd better get myself on the winning side quickly.

Mama's explosions came and went, but Mrs. Evans's love never waned.

Of course, Mrs. Evans hugged me tight and acted like seeing me was akin to the news that World War II ended. And I hugged her back.

"Is that your Mama out there, Myrtle?"

"Yes, ma'am."

"Well, come on up!" Mrs. Evans hollered. "I just put the kettle on." And she waved her arm like usual, the plump length of it encased in a tan woolen, hand-knit sweater, the kind with a metal zipper running up the front.

I eyed Mama, praying my heart out that the good mood would continue somehow. I knew better than to open my mouth and cloud her mood.

Mama walked up the drive with a strained smile, obviously controlled by something deeply ingrained. The woman who waited tables at the Texas Inn became, I suspect, the young woman from Suffolk with a mother named Minerva. "Thank you. But we only have a minute."

I didn't say a *word*. One thing we always had was time.

"Well, we'll take what we can get, right Myrtle?" Mrs. Evans said to me.

And I still didn't say a thing, I just nodded and let her usher me into her warm little white rancher at the end of Rowland Drive.

"That's a beautiful magnolia you have out there," Mama said. "And I so enjoyed the pageant! I never knew Myrtle could sing like that."

"Isn't she a peach?"

"Well, she sure didn't get the talent from me. I can't carry a tune in a bucket."

"Must be from Myrtle's father."

And Mama didn't say a *word*. She just nodded. Because believe me, I asked the father question long before that day and, well, it doesn't take a genius to imagine her response.

"Let me get that tea. How do you like it?"

And we told her. Nothing in it for Mama, a little milk and some sugar for me.

Mrs. Evans produced a plate the size of a truck tire supporting sugar cookies she and her teenage children must have baked. They gathered with us, too, two girls with long brown hair and a nice-looking black-haired boy who towered over the rest of them. Laughter and crumbs mixed together there with the smell of our tea, the Christmas tree, and the fire going on the grate in the living room.

Mama sat like a fence post, and even when one of the girls sat down at a Miles Kimball-type piano and played Christmas carols, the music tinny and bright, she looked as though her thoughts were landed in Alaska or Zimbabwe.

Who are you? I suddenly remember**ed the woman** who used to sing me awake each morning.

When the music started, an old lady inchwormed into the room with an aluminum walker. She wore her white hair piled high like a dollop of Cool Whip and the makeup that overlaid her wrinkles appeared somewhat clownish, the way too much makeup does on old people, but she smiled and bared these big yellow teeth and her eyes sparkled just like her daughter's. The whole family waved her over the way, I know now, all the Evanses do, and she plopped down in a lounger. The cute boy pulled the wooden handle at the side to make good use of the footrest.

"That's my mother," Mrs. Evans said. "Mama! This here is Myrtle, the little girl I told you about. My Sunday school class's little songbird."

"Hey," I said.

"And this is her mother, Isla Whitehead."

"Nice to meet you," the older lady said with a bright smile. "My name's Sara Jaffrey."

Mama greeted her.

So we sat and drank our tea, ate some cookies, sang some songs, and had the first real family moment I could ever remember.

These days, I look back to that night and I try to re-create it at least once during the holidays. I made the mistake one year of going stylish with my lights. White lights everywhere. But it wasn't the same. So I dragged out the old-fashioned colored ones the next year, went to Wal-Mart to make sure I had enough bulbs to replace the burnouts, and baked more cookies than usual. I think people weigh themselves down in the aim of achieving effect. We ride by folks' houses with blinking lights, flashing spirals of color waltzing in bare branches, and I think to myself those people know a little something extra. They know what they like and well, that's enough.

"Don't think of yourself more highly than you ought," the New Testament says, and I think that includes things like Christmas decorations. I've met the folk that have the perfect garlands and sprays and wreaths, the folk that live in Williamsburg-style houses. And I've met the folk that live at the edge of town in two-bedroom ranch houses that have Frosty the Snowman, lights playing tag around the roof, and a Rudolph stuck askew somewhere on the lawn. I'd rather sit in the home of the latter with an errant couch spring poking my derriere because, truthfully, they're glad to have me, and they never look at my shoes and wonder where I'd been before I got there.

6

*T*he day Mama left was the worst day of my life. I've had some rough patches since then, but no other day sticks its thorns into my memory like that day.

When I got off of the bus that Friday, I pulled my hood up over my ears and ran right up onto the porch. Now, our boarding house, long and narrow, had porches up at the front. One porch upstairs, one down. Of course, we didn't live in a porch room, but Mrs. Blackburn did, the lady who owned the place and took care of me from time to time. She lived upstairs in an apartment with two bedrooms, a living room, a private bathroom, and a kitchen.

January had hit hard for Lynchburg, the temperatures barely making it above freezing the entire week. Usually Mrs. Blackburn sat outside on her porch watching the kids walk home from school and the college girls arrive back from their day of classes at Randy Mac.

Not today.

After spidering up the steps inside using both arms and legs, I dug for the key that hung on a chain around my neck and rested beneath my blouse against my flat chest.

I scooped it out, bent over some, and shoved it into the lock.

"I'm home!" I yelled, knowing that Mama's shift at the Texas Inn ended around 3:30, but every once in a while Mama arrived home early and so I tried to holler just in case.

No answer.

Oh, well.

I pulled the key out of the lock, scooped my schoolbag up higher on my shoulder, and shut the door behind me.

The bed lay before me, bare, just a pile of mattresses and a brown frame. The linens nowhere in sight, I figured maybe Mama decided to go down to the washateria.

The drawers gaped open in geriatric smiles, dark recesses evident behind their grin.

No clothes?

I ran over and peered in.

Huh?

And then, I saw it. On the white vanity desk an envelope lay, bleeding white sterility into its blanched surroundings. I almost didn't even notice it except for the one word scribbled on the front.

"Myrtle."

Okay, this seemed odd, but every once in a while Mama could surprise you.

Nevertheless, my hands shook as I tore the envelope with my thumb. The ragged edge sliced into my finger, a deeper than normal paper cut. I quickly pulled my pointer up to my mouth and sucked hard as though each slice of one's skin had a proper allotment of blood bestowed upon it and if I sucked it out quickly the whole thing would be over and done with in a much more efficient manner.

Finishing the task, I noted an orange-red smear on the envelope.

"Oh, no!"

But I pulled out the sheet of notepad paper, watched as four twenty-dollar bills wafted to the floor, then filled my lungs with air that felt needy and hot and deficient. I allowed my eyes to do their job.

"Dear Myrtle Charmaine," it said. "I've gone away for a spell. Nothing you should worry about, though."

Away? Not worry? What was going on?

"I know you're probably wondering how I can just leave town like this, but Myrtle, I'm so excited! I'm going off to prepare a better life for us. And it won't take long."

How long was long?

"Just go on up to Mrs. Blackburn's like usual and hand her the rent money here in this envelope. I'll be back in a couple of weeks."

I calculated. Sixty dollars for Mrs. Blackburn. Twenty for me, I guessed. I read on.

"The new little fridge is packed full with a half gallon of milk, some butter, and as much lunch meat as I could get inside. There's four boxes of cereal in the closet, two loaves of bread, a jar of peanut butter and . . . oh . . . well, you just see for yourself. I even left a couple boxes of Little Debbie treats for after school that I think you'll enjoy. I washed up the bed linens but didn't have time to put them on. They're in the closet as well."

It was right then that fear pounced upon me. And I'm not talking some cute little kitten pounce. This was a pounce a big load of bricks might make if it possessed the wherewithal.

Two weeks?

"Now just go to school as usual. Study hard and you make sure you still go to church. DON'T TELL ANYBODY ABOUT THIS! I'll be home soon enough, Myrtle Charmaine.

"Get to bed early. I don't want you staying up all night just because you think you can get away with it."

Oh, yeah, right, Mama!

"And don't let *anyone* in the door. Not even people you know. And please don't forget to wash your hair once a week and take a bath twice. I left an extra can of my spray deodorant in the desk. I noticed this morning you should probably start using it."

I shook my head. Deodorant. Now this was just the icing on the cake!

"Be careful. I'll be home in two weeks. And by then we'll probably be able to move away from this little town to a real house.

"Sincerely, your mama, Isla Jean Whitehead."

7

        I've lived inside of days where I've only known I was alive because of the toenail clippings I saved in a sandwich Baggie.

Nobody has a right to be happy. We earn it. Plain and simple. We earn it by learning, by being alone. And we learn through experience.

Maybe that's what the whole "pursuit of happiness" means.

Sometimes, even now, especially when polishing my toenails, I remember how God deserted me when I was only eleven years old. Only a month of desertion, but more desperation, more fear, more loneliness and anxiety had been packed into that month than most people experience in a lifetime.

When Mama left and I still lived in our room, I saved all my toenail clippings. I did that for the next six years. Because when I looked at that bag, I knew for sure I was really alive. That Myrtle Charmaine Whitehead still existed and wasn't a figment of my imagination or anyone else's.

8

I waited out the two weeks as Mama said and as the money was lasting longer than planned I waited another two just to give her some leeway. I figured buying big houses in Maryland or someplace up north took time.

I went to school as usual, guarding my secret not only for Mama but for myself. Everything seemed magnified. The math numbers got bigger on my page. My signature looked all wrong, too loopy and ill-defined. Every day, as I sat doing spelling tests, looking up the definitions to vocabulary words, and swinging on the swings ever so slowly, I just knew that it would be the day Mama returned. I read the note a thousand times, searching for clues, claiming promises.

But time never feels inclined to stop. The cereal was gone, the milk, too. I'd scraped every last smear of peanut butter from the jar until I could see my room clearly through the curves of its sides. The money was gone. I became hungry enough to act.

So I did what any eleven-year-old would do when

faced with a dilemma. I called on the one person I trusted to take matters into good hands.

The Christmas lights, though unplugged, still hung from the boxwoods, and I walked up the drive and around the side to the kitchen door.

Mrs. Evans already stood there, shaking out a tea towel. "Myrtle? What a nice surprise!"

"Can I come in? I think I got a problem."

So she waved her arm, said, "Of course," and helped me take off my slicker. "Come sit right here in the living room. You want a snack or something?"

"No, ma'am."

And then my nose started bleeding again. Doggone it! As if things weren't bad enough!

Mrs. Evans, who nursed down at Virginia Baptist Hospital, jumped up and came back with a clean dish towel.

"You sure you want me to bleed all over this?" I asked with my hand cupped under my nostrils, picturing a little white nurse's cap on her dark hair.

"Who wants to bleed into a paper product?"

So I held it on up there.

She took my other hand. "Mama's asleep but she won't be for long. You have that look about you like it's a private matter."

"It is." The towel snuffed my tones.

"Why don't you pinch up there on the bridge of your nose? And hold your head back, honey. That should help."

I obeyed, noticing the cobwebs in the corner, the way the wall near the fireplace lost its hold on the ceiling just a tad, the way the light from the corner windows feathered against the graying paint. I noticed how sickening it is to feel your own blood sliding down the inner surface of your throat.

It worked though. Like a charm. Now why didn't Mama ever tell me to do that?

"So what is it you have to say?" she asked as my sight regained its normal vista.

"It's Mama, Missus Evans. She left."

"Are you sure she's not down at the restaurant?"

I shook my head and handed her the ragged note.

There are times when life stands still. I know, we all experience those moments. But just then it seemed every little dart of her eyes over Mama's handwriting took minutes. And I heard Mama voicing words, but not the words there on the stationery.

Nobody wants you bleeding all over their corn dogs, Myrtle.

Myrtle, wipe that lipstick off right now, you look like a tramp.

Don't even ask, Myrtle.

Don't even ask, Myrtle.

Don't even ask, Myrtle.

Mrs. Evans looked up and tears filled and spilled over those pansy eyes all in one go. "Oh, sweet pea. Oh, honey. Oh, you poor sweet lamb."

Sweet lamb.

And her arms spiraled around me and her love filled up the spaces that people like grandmas and sisters and aunts and uncles were supposed to fill.

"My poor little songbird."

I couldn't cry. I know she expected that, but I couldn't. I stayed right there in the circle of tan woolen knit, though. Finally I muttered, "I didn't know where else to go."

"You came to the right place. You know a peach like you is welcomed here anytime. And I'm so glad you picked me to come to."

As if my life overflowed with thoughtful, sweater-girded fairy godmothers who lived on quiet cul-de-sacs in real houses with things like stoves and toilets. Thoughtful women just waiting for me to ask them to take care of me!

"Now, I've got a package of butter cookies. You want some Kool-Aid or a milk?"

"Milk, please."

"All right."

"Are they the kind of cookies that look like flowers with holes in them?"

"Yep. I'm going to make a couple of phone calls, then we'll go on back to your house and get your things."

"We don't have a house."

That didn't phase Mrs. Evans. "Well, we'll go to your home, then."

Didn't she hear me?

Well, she'd see soon enough that Myrtle Charmaine Whitehead was nothing more than boarding house trash.

9

$\mathcal{A}$t fourteen years of age I had just begun to menstruate. The nosebleeds cleared up within two months of moving in with the Evanses. My nickname became Peach. In all my life up until that time I never thought I'd have a nickname.

Now I don't know much about much, really, but I say, when people care about you enough to shorten your name, or give another one altogether, well, what a blessing.

One time, after Harlan and I got married I met the sweetest little family at a church in Spartanburg, South Carolina, where the crusade was going full swing. A newborn baby named Stephanie graced their arms. And I said, "Hey, little Stephie-boo."

"Her name is *Stephanie*!"

Well, that just shocked me. I felt my eyes go all round at the father's tone and do you know I just cried? Like an idiot, I just let 'em flow right there in the vestibule, I felt so hurt. Didn't they realize? Didn't they know? Was their love for their child that taken for granted? Was others' love for that baby taken for granted, too?

Should love ever be taken for granted?

Some people would say that yes, it should, but they can only say that because they've been loved so thoroughly for a very long time.

While the Evanses failed to fill up the empty place Mama left, they filled up all the others. And wouldn't you know, about a year after I came to live with them I waved my arm like the rest of them?

The cute boy, James, became my brother and moved down to the basement to his own room. So he was thankful for my presence. The eldest daughter, Frances, already twenty and working over at the shoe factory, got James's room. And I went in with Stacy who said, "You're a whole lot easier to live with than Frances, especially after dinner!" Then she held her nose because poor Frances was not blessed with a satisfactory digestive system.

Despite our age difference, Stacy became my best friend and as much of a sister as an only child deserted by her philandering mother could hope to have. Stacy, sophomore cheerleader over at E.C. Glass High School, spent hours with me listening to popular rock 'n' roll groups with geographical names: Kansas, Boston, Chicago. Stacy and I sang duets at church, too. We'd practice at home, Mrs. Evans at the Kimball stabbing out the alto part again and again with Stacy.

"Why don't you just let Peach sing the harmony?" Stacy complained every practice. "She gets it right away."

"Because she needs to sing the higher notes, honey. When you go above a high C you sound like an air hose." And then she'd turn around on the revolving piano stool, pull Stacy in close and say, "A good alto range is nothing to sneeze at."

"But I don't *hear* the part, Mama!"

"That's what practice is for."

And so on and so forth.

Stacy just sighed, shook her head, and rolled her eyes.

And that describes the way life turned out at the Evanses. And you know what? Mrs. Evans never even blinked when, every single day after school (I actually got to skip the seventh grade), I ran down the hill and I hollered, "You hear anything today?" Never once. She'd just shake her head and say, "Sorry, Peach. Maybe tomorrow will be different."

Mrs. Evans always had something to report after her shifts at the hospital. And we'd come to know the patients that stayed on a little longer than most. I do believe this is when I learned to care for the nameless and the faceless.

When my first menstrual period trickled onto the scene, I felt Mama's absence with a dentist-chair pain. It hit me at that moment there in the bathroom as I stared down at the bloody spot on my underwear that the important firsts had just begun. I held out hope for Mama's return for my various graduations, my wedding day, the birth of my someday children, but I had forgotten about that first passage into womanhood.

The fact that I was the last girl in my class to get "it" didn't help matters any. I carried the same maxipad, taken from communal stash of women's hygiene products in the linen closet, around in my purse for a year, pretending I was just like the rest of them.

I knew I wasn't like the rest of them.

Not even close.

I considered not telling Mrs. Evans about it. No need, though. Mrs. Evans is like one of those wise old Chinese women. She just knew.

"Myrtle, honey?"

I remained in the bathroom. Had already flushed and all. And now I sat on the floor with my back up against the tub, feeling that thick mattress of a thing between my legs. Nobody prepares you for that feeling. That foreignness. That walk through a previously unknown portal where paper products end up in hitherto lonely territory.

It felt lonely. See, nobody can menstruate for you. You're just plum on your own with that one.

"Yes, Miz Evans?"

"You all right in there, Peach? You been in there a while."

"Yes, ma'am."

"What're you doing?"

"Just sitting here on the floor."

"On all that cold tile?"

"Yes, ma'am."

I could hear her feet shuffling on the hardwood floor. "Can I come in?"

"Okay." And I got to my knees and reached up to disengage the lock.

She stood there in her sweater. That fall day, my second month of ninth grade, a light breeze whispered in through the bathroom window. It rustled through my hair and across my eyes.

Mrs. Evans's gaze slid to the little wicker trash can where the cardboard box to the maxipad belt stood on end. "Oh, Peach."

And she sat right down next to me and put her arm around my shoulders. "You okay?"

"I guess so. My stomach hurts a little. Actually it's around the back some."

"Those are cramps."

"Why do you get them?"

And she explained the entire thing. The sloughing, the bleeding, the ramifications of this monthly womanly activity.

My eyes inflated. I already knew about sex and all that. I mean, a kid doesn't reach the ninth grade without learning a thing or two from a dirty joke they failed to understand. But the reality of all that sickened me, because I remembered Mama. Mama was a woman. Mama had periods. Mama had a baby. Therefore Mama had sex with . . . who? There it was again. That father business.

It always amazes me how the mind travels like a jet plane. One second you're thinking about periods and the next you're wondering who your father is.

"Well, Peach. You know where the stuff is. You need any help?"

"Oh, no ma'am!"

And I got one of her hugs. "You'll be okay."

"I suspect I will."

She smiled. "Every female that's made it past the age of thirteen or fourteen survived it."

I sure knew about surviving.

"I've got a surprise for you." She grabbed hold of the lip of the square porcelain sink and levered herself to her feet. Her excitement pulled me to mine and she took my hand and dragged me to the kitchen table. "Now just sit down right there, Myrtle, and listen to me."

She clasped her hands in front of her ribs. "Guess what?"

"What?"

"You'll never believe this."

"What?"

I sat on the edge of my chair.

"Mr. Evans and I have decided to get you voice lessons!"

"Really?"

I hardly knew how to react. Lessons. Real lessons. Like piano lessons. Or art lessons. Or ballet lessons. Only voice lessons. Lessons like Vicki Miller's flute lessons.

"You excited?"

I nodded.

But at the same time. Lessons. Permanence. But hey, Mama'd sure be excited once she came home to find me singing even better than before!

Isn't that right?

I thought about *The Brady Bunch* right then. Stacy and I watched *The Brady Bunch* after school every day. And, oh, how I loved those episodes where the kids performed! All dressed up in white outfits with fringes and rhinestones! Or a rainbow theme, each boy and girl in a different color.

Sha, na, na, nah, na, na, na, nah!

Sha, na, na, na, nah.

Maybe I'd sing even better than Marsha Brady! Maybe I'd join up with some snazzy group like that, where we'd twirl around to choreography, hold microphones, dig the air with bent elbows, and end on an upward note with hands to match.

10

*O*ne day I found out that there are actual people out there that never even had a birthday cake! Not once did someone say to them, "I'm so glad you were born that day eight, or however many years ago, that I'm going to make you a cake!"

I once read a book about a preacher who threw a party for a prostitute at an all-night donut shop. Cake. Decorations. Other prostitutes. The bakery guy. And this preacher.

She said, "I've never had a birthday cake before. Can I just take it home?"

So that's one of those "count my blessings thoughts." Thank You, God, the Evanses didn't give me just one birthday cake a year, but two.

In the winter of 1973, two years after Mama left, I asked Jesus into my heart. Now, I'm still not sure where that phrase "ask Jesus into your heart" ever came from 'cause it's not in the Bible.

Jesus says, "Lo, I stand at the door and knock."

But He didn't say "the door to your heart."

He also said, "He that believeth in Me, though he were dead, yet shall he live."

Although, I doubt He said "believeth" as He was Jewish and not a fancy-pants English fellow.

It was a December Sunday, my conversion. It wouldn't have made headlines in *Sword of the Lord* or even *Christianity Today*, for that matter. It was a quiet occurrence between me and God with Mrs. Evans in attendance.

The pastor at First Baptist preached about the Woman at the Well, which by now is known by all who have attended one of our revival meetings as my favorite story. How many times I wished Jesus awarded Mama the same chance He gave that lady. But I realized that day, at thirteen years old, that the Lord whispered my name.

Myrtle Charmaine! You need to get on over here now with Me. Drink of My living water. 'Cause it goes with you wherever you are. Lo, I am with you always even unto the end of the age.

I pictured Him waving His arm just like Mrs. Evans did.

After the service, we ate chicken an' Jiffy dumplings there in the kitchen at the Evanses' house, and I drank three glasses of water. I cleared the table while Stacy washed the dishes and Frances dried. James was away at college that year getting his master's degree in anthropology.

"Mrs. Evans?"

"Yes, Peach?" She looked up from the kitchen table where she sat with the Sunday crossword from the *News and Daily Advance.*

"I was thinking about that living water Pastor Fred was talking about in his sermon."

Stacy and Frances froze.

"Was a fine sermon, wasn't it?"

"Yes, ma'am. Have you drunk that water?"

"Uh-huh."

"What about Stacy and Frances?"

"Why don't you ask them?"

They restarted their chore with a vengeance.

"Well?" I set a bouquet of silverware into the soapy depths at the kitchen sink.

"I asked Jesus into my heart when I was five," Stacy said.

Frances adjusted the stream of water. "I was eleven."

"What about James?"

Mrs. Evans nodded. "A few years ago. He was longer in coming to the Lord. Had to sow some wild oats first." She turned to her mother. "Right, Mama?"

The old lady nodded and scratched her limber cheek. "Some do, Peach. And that's a fact. But some don't. Some just believe and that's that."

I thought for a moment, wondering if Mama ever heard about living water, because she sure as anything knew about wild oats, if wild oats were what I thought!

"Well, I might as well get it over with," I sighed.

The entire kitchen erupted in laughter and all those arms, so good at waving, went around me. Mrs. Evans led me through a prayer and I told the Lord how much I loved Him, how I believe He died and rose again and took all my sins to the cross. The hatred I felt for Vicki Miller came clearly to mind just then. And I asked His forgiveness, expressing my thankfulness in advance for His guidance in my life.

Mrs. Evans thought of that.

And then I said "Amen."

"Well, hallelujah!" Grandma said.

"Amen to that!" Mrs. Evans agreed.

And Stacy looked at Frances and then her mother. "The Lord brought her to us for this moment, Mama."

"Yes, He did, Stacy. He certainly did."

In February of 1974, two months after my fourteenth birthday, I came home from voice lessons on a Monday evening. Right there on the kitchen table sat a large cake with white icing, and on the icing, in feeble Grandmotherly handwriting, lay the words "Happy First Birthday Myrtle!!!!"

Just like that. Four exclamation points.

At first I felt confused.

Then Grandma shuffled in with her walker. "You like the cake I made you?"

"It's beautiful. But—"

"It's not your birthday and you're a lot more than one year old." Then she laughed and leaned forward. "Oh, Peach. Don't be alarmed. Today's your spiritual birthday. See there?" And she pointed to the calendar on the wall. Right there two cross beams intersected and the words "Myrtle, one year," shouted their way off the page to land right inside my heart. She pulled out the chair next to her. "That's the day you gave your heart to Jesus."

"And you made me a cake for that?"

"It's what we do here."

I sat down.

"You want a piece?"

"Uh-huh."

"Well, all right, then."

There was no song, no party. Grandma didn't even call

the others to the table. We just sat together. Her and me. And we each ate two pieces of red velvet cake.

We ate off Grandma's old willowware pattern plates. And I gazed on the two doves flying above the wedding pagoda wondering what love feels like. To escape death and dismay and fly away to a place called love.

"I love these plates, Grandma."

"I've always loved willowware."

Grandma didn't have much, but what she had she loved.

I asked Stacy about the birthday cake that night as we lay in blankets and moonbeams.

"Oh, that's Grandma's thing," she said.

"It's nice."

"It sure is. What kind of cake did she make?"

"Red velvet with cream cheese icing."

"Is there any left?"

I nodded.

"Wanna sneak into the kitchen and have a midnight snack?"

"Okay."

In the dark, swallowing giant gulps of milk from cavernous brown mugs, we ate together. Like sisters do, I guess.

"You know, Mama never let me drink big glasses of milk," I told Stacy.

"There's nothing like a big old swallow, is there, Peach?"

"Nope."

Stacy straightened some hairpins in her soup-can rollers attached to the back of her head and she screwed up her pansy eyes, looking just like her mother. "Do you know how glad we are you came to live with us?"

I nodded.

"Why won't you become an Evans, Myrtle? Mother and Daddy want to adopt you so badly. I heard them talking about it on the phone last night."

The reason I don't mention Mr. Evans all that much is because he was a traveling salesman for a children's clothing line. I saw a play years later about a traveling salesman for a clothing line, but Mr. Evans acted nothing like that guy. A real cracker, he sold clothes like preachers sold hope. Every Saturday night he took us over to Billy Joe's for burgers and ice cream. And every Monday morning he kissed my cheek before he slid into his Buick and drove south, or north, or west, or wherever he headed that week. Any kid would have been thrilled to have this kind man for a father. And Frances, James, and Stacy loved Mr. Evans.

"I don't know what's wrong with me," I said.

"Well, it's okay. You act like an Evans now, even if you don't have the last name. And you'll always be my little sister. I prayed for a little sister for years and you were God's answer."

"But you all know I love you. Don't you?" Didn't they? The thought alarmed me.

"Of course we do, Peach."

I climbed back up to the top bunk a few minutes later and I folded my arms behind my head and lay back, angry at myself.

Just why are you being so loyal to that woman, Myrtle? You're just a big old fool. She's been gone for a long time now, Myrtle Charmaine Whitehead. Mama's gone. And she ain't never coming back.

11

_T_hat same spring, I arrived early at the school auditorium, well before the start of the performance. In the front-row, I laid out six programs. My hands shook, the papers vibrating like an autumn leaf as I gently laid them on the tops of the padded movie-theater-type seats.

The spring play, and I received a part.

West Side Story!

No, I wasn't Maria. Not Myrtle Charmaine White-head! But Vicki Miller wasn't either, because Vicki Miller still haunted junior high school.

Ha-haaah.

Sometimes good things do happen to good people.

Nevertheless, I sang my heart out as one of the Shark girls. Stomping and clapping and happy to be "free in Amadeeca." I twirled my skirt, kicked up my foot and jerked my head back and forth.

New York City, here I come!

I realized I might even run into Mama up that way.

Every time I twirled toward the front of the stage there they were. My family.

Grandma smiled with the sweet, placid face of a china doll. Mrs. Evans sat comfy and satisfied. Mr. Evans just smiled and the Evans kids looked ready to erupt in an-end-of-the-game, one-point-ahead cheer.

North. South. East. West. Myrtle Charmaine, she's the best! Goooo Peach!

We celebrated that night at Billy Joe's. Mr. Evans even let us order hot fudge sundaes. "What a great evening!" he said, tipping his water glass to me.

"It was your night to shine, Myrtle!" Mrs. Evans reached over and gave me hug.

"I wasn't the star, Mrs. Evans."

"You were to me."

I held the embrace longer than usual and I wanted so badly to tell her I loved her. To let her know that, just in case.

But I didn't.

I look back now, all these years later and hold that moment with more regret than any other in my life. Lost opportunities affect us all and we promise we'll make up for it someday, redeem the time, make it right.

But sometimes you can't.

And that pain never leaves. All you can really do is push it from your mind and propose to make as few mistakes like that as you can in the future.

I hugged her tightly and didn't let go until she made the first move.

12

$\mathcal{D}$on't get too comfortable with your life.

If there's one thing I've learned after all I've seen, done, and heard, it's that. God uses bad circumstances for His good. Just ask Joseph. Just ask Noah. Just ask:

Mary.

Joshua.

David.

Abraham.

Jacob.

Rahab the harlot.

All those Bible people.

But God gives "more grace when the burdens grow greater."

Just like the song says.

Near the end of ninth grade, during April of 1974 when the trees had lost their froth of color but their leaves still shone tender, the principal of the school called me out of class.

Sometimes you just know that something's wrong. But something could have been right, too. Maybe Mama came back and maybe Mr. Jackson felt sad for Mrs. Evans because that meant I'd be leaving her house.

He ushered me into the inner sanctum of the school offices and set me in one of the two chairs in front of his desk. He eased his skinny self down into the other one then set an earth shoe atop one wine-colored polyester clad knee, truly tipping me off that I wasn't in trouble. The authority of the desk didn't separate us. He was going to talk human to human.

"Myrtle, you need to get your book bag together. Your brother is coming to pick you up."

I shook my head. "Why?"

"Well, there's been an accident."

"What happened, Mr. Jackson?"

"I think James should tell you."

"Is everybody all right?"

"Well, no, honey."

He whipped his head around at the knock on his door. "Yes?"

It opened a crack and I saw his secretary's nose peep through. "James is here, Mr. Jackson."

"Thank you, Pat."

He turned to me, took my hand and tried to stretch his mouth into some sort of reassuring smile. "Go ahead, Myrtle. Go get your things."

He stayed in his seat, his forehead now in his hand, as I left the room.

What a moment. That spiked heartbeat. That clammy skin. That thickening inside me. That horrible, burning claw of inevitability sticking in my throat.

And there stood James.

"James!" I cried out and ran over to where he stood in front of the secretary's desk.

I haven't really described James yet. Tall, and just an average-looking guy, he sported black hair and Mrs. Evans's pansy eyes, but darker blue, and he wore his clothing as neatly and comfortably as an orange wears its skin.

His face just then bore a far different look than his pressed khakis and blue button-down shirt called for. Something had swept across him earlier, leaving red eyes and blotched skin. James hugged me to him tightly and just cried and cried.

"It's Mama," he said a minute later.

Then he pulled away.

"There was an accident out on Fort Avenue, Myrtle. This little Datsun pickup pulled out of the cemetery drive. He pulled out in front of a dump truck that swerved into the oncoming traffic."

"Right into Mrs. Evans?"

He nodded.

"Is she all right?"

"Well, the ambulance has taken her to Lynchburg General. But it doesn't look good, Peach." He cleared his throat and shoved his hands in his pockets. "Go on and get your stuff," he said again.

I ran out of the office and down the hall as though my head and hair burned with an intense fire. I had to get there. To the hospital. I had to tell her. I had to tell Mrs. Evans I loved her. I had to tell her.

Please God, I prayed and prayed. Please, please, please, please, please.

13

$\mathcal{M}$rs. Evans died before I made it to the hospital. Even all these years later I'm still upset at the Lord for not answering that prayer. How much would it have taken for Him to have let my foster mother hang on just a few more minutes, regain consciousness in a miraculous manner as I drew up close to the gurney? Just for a few minutes so I might have lifted her dying hand to my breast and said, "I love you, Mrs. Evans. You loved me more than anybody ever did. I know that. I want you to know I know that."

I just wanted to tell her.

Would that have been so hard?

Was that too much to ask?

Mr. Evans sat there in a nearby lounge, holding a can of Sprite and not sipping. He stared down into the can, just shaking his head. The girls cried together. James sat next to his dad, wiping his eyes with the back of his left hand again and again, his right hand limp, curling upward on his knee.

I pleaded with the nurses tending to Mrs. Evans. "Please let me go in! Please let me see her."

Nobody came to my aid, so lost in their own sorrow. Nobody heard my pleas, the hurricane winds of grief drowning out all sound.

"We can't honey. We're tending to the body."

"Please!"

Every bit of tissue in my body wailed, beating itself blue with frustration and anger and loss, bursting all my capillaries, but instead of blood, tears exploded out.

So I sat by the door of her room, hunched like a mouse into a little ball, listening to the hushed voices of the nurses. I watched Pastor Fred approach, I saw his brown wingtip shoes stop in front of me, felt his hand smooth my hair, watched his feet move on toward the Evanses.

I sat by the door as the morticians came.

I sat by the door as the gurney rolled by, the sheet falling down from the square frame like a tablecloth.

I sat by the door as the gurney rolled back out, the sheet falling in graceful scallops from the pressure points of Mrs. Evans's dead body.

I sat by the door and watched the Evans family shoes shuffle by. Stacy's Keds stopped in front of me.

"Let's go, Peach, honey."

I arose. "Where's Grandma Sara, Stacy?"

"She stayed home to make phone calls."

"She didn't want to see Mrs. Evans one last time?"

"Grandma knows better than to think that body is really Mama."

I felt rebuked in a small way.

"Are you okay, Peach?" Stacy and I caught up with the others.

I nodded, still unable to speak my heart.

I hope Mrs. Evans knew how I felt. I hope that somehow she could tell because she was so wise. But I can't be sure. And now, I'll have to entertain regret for the rest of my life. Trying to get things right the first time.

When we came home to the house after the funeral I sat with Grandma. The ladies from church laid out the food for the guests and I heard their gentle hum of conversation in our kitchen.

Women like Mrs. Evans are supposed to live forever because they're the ones the earth needs. They're the food, the water, the sun, and the air to regular humans who just haven't gotten it yet. They're the ones that show us, in human form, how it's done.

No one could believe it.

"What's going to happen to you now, Grandma?"

Her frizzy beehive hair vibrated as she shook her head. "I guess I'm going to have to go into the home up there on Langhorne Road."

"What about the others?" What about me?

"I don't know, Peach. I just don't know."

So, after Stacy graduated from E.C. Glass in June, Mr. Evans put the house on Rowland Drive up for sale. When it sold in August, he bought one of those apartments up near the Cavalier Grill. James returned to UVA, found a job for Frances near the campus, and she moved in with him. Stacy left for Word of Life Bible Institute in upstate New York at the end of August and they shuffled me into the foster care system.

"I can't take care of you with my traveling, Peach," Mr. Evans said that day he told me the news, "and the others are too young to do it."

I drew blood on the inside of my lip as I looked down. "When will they come to get me?"

"Tomorrow."

I nodded and turned to Grandma, who stood there crying. "Well, I don't have too much to gather, I guess." I looked up. "Can I take a willow plate with me? Just one?"

She nodded. "That would make me happy, Peach."

"And my pillow?"

"Of course," Mr. Evans said.

That fast, it all fell apart.

I was back to eleven years old. Only now, I had a life worth losing. And it was gone.

Part Two

1

*S*trike up the band. Get out the baton. Find your seat, the parade is about to begin.

The thing about parades is that usually the features and floats get better and better. Take the Tournament of Roses Parade, for example. Just when I think I've beheld the most beautiful sight I've ever seen, along comes some lacy, white float, with twirly flowers and a real waterfall. Unfortunately, real life seems to go downhill. At least sometimes. Nobody ever quite compared with Mrs. Evans. Even now, all these years later, I still talk to her.

I know that sounds crazy. But Mrs. Evans didn't really die. She's just with Jesus, probably leading a choir of little children that died early, taking care of them as they grow to whatever kind of maturity we reach in heaven.

"Mrs. Evans!" I called sometimes. "You'd understand about this. This boy in my class . . ." I never talked to my mother after she left the way I talked to Mrs. Evans.

Ten months in foster care at the Campbells' began my circus train of homes. Then the missus had a baby and didn't want to take the chance I'd cause trouble and harm her real daughter. We never bonded anyway. I didn't want to.

At all.

And then the three months at the Wagners' practically wore my fingers to the bone as they merely wanted a maid they could actually get paid to work like a dog. However, I did learn the value of a clean bathroom, and if I scrubbed in there, I didn't have to listen to Mrs. Wagner's incessant bellyaching about ridiculous matters like the new carpet in the family room, which began pilling on day one, or that large crack down the middle of the patio out back. Oh, she was a sight, too, in her platform shoes and tight jeans and pale lipstick. She chain-smoked all day, sitting there on the screen porch reading true crime books and magazines. Mr. Wagner worked all the time, and who could blame him? They ended up moving back home to California.

Then came the Biggs. Let's just say I knew how to keep a bedroom door closed without a lock. I lasted three days there because it wasn't hard to see what was coming. I may sound cavalier about it all these years later. I just choose to remember my God-given strength at that time and am quite proud of the fact that man ended up in jail without my virtue in his pocket.

End of story, okay?

May of 1975 brought me, my willowware plate, and my pillow to the fourth stop on the post-Evans rail line. The home of Mrs. Cecile Ferris and her husband Clarke. Now Clarke, independently wealthy with some long-dead ancestor's money, spent his mornings eating breakfast over at Bill's Country Kitchen, his lunchtimes at the Cavalier just down the street from his three-story, pillared

Greek temple of a house, and his cocktail hour right at the Oakwood Country Club up the road. Dinner usually saw him back at home with his wife, after another cocktail hour, of course, in the game/music room at the side of the house. Clarke Ferris could play the piano like Liberace and we had us some good times. They were more than happy to get my voice lessons going again and he taught me all sorts of tunes. Cole Porter. The Gershwin boys. Hoagie Carmichael. Rodgers and Hart. Rodgers and Hammerstein. Louis Armstrong and Count Basie. Lerner and Lowe.

Oh, the music from *Camelot* just spoke to me! I can't imagine being Guenevere and having a man like Lancelot singing that "If Ever I Would Leave You" song to me. Even though it's hopeless, and their love is forbidden, I get the feeling that he'd lie across train tracks for her, or more to the point, swim an eel-infested moat.

Cecile Ferris, swathed in buttercup or robin's-egg blue chiffon, her mother's jewels, and real silk stockings, hair pulled straight back, always sat on the sofa. She sipped on Harveys Bristol Cream and hummed along.

I filled the role of showpiece. And made the Ferrises feel good about themselves. Grandma Sara and I still enjoyed each other when I visited Wednesdays after school talking about Cecile's clothing and the Ferrises' funny ways.

2

Cecile found me in my room on an evening early in December just before my fifteenth birthday. The rain had been sluicing Lynchburg for over a week. Cold, winter rain that flowed like Rio Grandes of depression, clearing out the delusion with which I normally consoled my aching heart. I found myself getting irrationally angry at inanimate objects, hurling them against the wall. My nose, bleeding again, did so with greater frequency and I found myself oversleeping more than I should have. Life felt so imposing and important. Too important, if that makes sense. Too serious. Too overwhelming.

Head in my math book, I had been thinking just how ridiculous geometry was for a girl who only wanted to sing. Unless I decided to go into acoustics, I saw no value in all of those angles and theorems. I did however appreciate being on the honor roll, and since I had skipped a grade I realized that I did have some sort of reputation to uphold. Even if it was just for myself.

Right then, more than ever before, I kept to myself at school. Tenth-grade schoolwork was hard enough without all the social dilemmas. I doubted anybody would have wanted to hang out with me anyway. I had nothing to offer them.

See, what I had realized that past year at the Wagners' and the Biggs' was this: Mama really wasn't coming home. I thought I had realized it earlier, but then I fell back to my old habit of hope like a dog to an old, familiar vomit, a vomit that had stopped tasting bad a while before because that's all it had fed upon for years.

Some days it seemed the Evanses had never existed at all.

So a nocturnal pastime developed that I dubbed, "The Disappearance Theory Hour." The latest sign of my inner distress was insomnia. Now, I don't know much about much, but I say insomnia is truly a trial! I've heard of people not getting a wink of sleep for years on end. Of course, I believe in the traditional theory of Hades as hellfire and brimstone or else why would God make His precious Son go through all of that pain on the cross for nothing? That would be a monstrous thing, I believe. And you know, I think even some of those radio preachers would agree with me. My husband Harlan does. And he's even been to Bible college. But I think that persecution by insomnia should entitle you to skip hell altogether, because lying there night after night, watching the moon, each car that slips down the avenue, each tiny feathering of the leaves by an errant wind, lying there like that—it's misery, pure and simple.

But I'd lie there in my room, the green room with a distinct guest-bedroom feel (except for the framed pictures of the Evanses, my own pillow, and my willow plate), looking out at the night sky through the leaves of

the big sugar maple tree outside the window and I'd
theorize.

I made a list of the possible happenings of Isla Jean
Whitehead.

1. She just plumb forgot about me.
2. She didn't forget, but figured I'd be all right one
   way or the other.
3. She was having so much fun she hadn't realized
   how the time had flown.
4. She had other children by now and to bring me into
   the big, beautiful house in Washington, D.C. would
   just be confusing for everyone involved.
5. She tried to come back to get me but that snazzy
   man wouldn't let her, and so she'd been checking
   up on me in secret all of these years for her own
   sense of satisfaction. She'd known I was doing all
   right.
6. She was dead.

That's why I didn't want to admit anything beforehand, before I really gave her enough time. Because I
knew that any mother who really loved her daughter
would come back when she said. So Mama either didn't
love me anymore, an evil thing to do, or she was dead.

Either one, take your pick, broke my fourteen-year-old
heart. I decided that day dead was better than evil.

Isla Jean Whitehead died that day.

And my goodness, almost four years after her disappearance, it was time for me to let her go. At least for a
while. I had things to do. A life to get on with. I had
breasts, small ones, but breasts, nonetheless, menstrual

periods, and hopes for a scholarship to William and Mary someday. Isla Jean Whitehead, just go on and die, and leave me to grow up without your ghost getting in the way.

Not that you were even all that nice when you left.

So when Cecile Ferris breezed into my room around 10:15, drink in hand, chiffon fluttering, I was trying to memorize theorems.

"Myrtle, dear. How is your homework coming along? Isn't it late? Shouldn't you be in bed?"

Cecile always asked questions in threes. Like some people sneeze three times, every time.

"Just memorizing theorems for a geometry test tomorrow. It is late, yes ma'am, but I couldn't sleep, so I decided I'd redeem the time and study a little."

"What a good child. Now, guess what? Did you know we always have a big Christmas party here? And would you like to sing for us that evening, with Clarke on the piano, of course?"

Immediately, I thought of what a party here might be like. I pictured an old movie. Lots of swirling gowns, waiters hoisting trays of little foods, the pop of corks, and an underpinning of laughter and conversation.

"Okay. I will. I like singing with Mr. Ferris."

"Perfect! I'll have my seamstress come and fit you for a gown tomorrow after school. You don't mind, do you? What's your favorite color? And would you be opposed to having it full length?"

"That sounds fine. I like yellow, and I've never had a full-length gown, but I've always wanted one."

"Perfect, then. Clarke says he'll practice with you after school each day. Do you mind learning some new songs?

Will your voice teacher mind? Do you think you can learn enough new old tunes to fill an hour?"

"It all sounds fine to me."

That was the thing about Cecile. All of her questions kept her from being overbearing. She never wanted to force me to do anything I didn't want to do. I sometimes think wealthy charity-minded folk who would even consider taking in a foster child don't quite know how to handle the situation. So they don their kid gloves and hope for the best.

Lucky for her she got me, a generally genial teenager with a focus on greater things, 'cause she could have ended up with some horrible girl who'd sneak out and take the car night after night, and poor Cecile wouldn't have possessed the hardware needed for a do-it-yourself project like that!

The next day I sat next to Clarke at the piano and sang "That Old Black Magic."

I liked Clarke. A boyish quality still lightened his overall demeanor, putting an innocent twinkle into his eye, enabling him to appreciate a meal around a breakfast booth with farmers, truckers, and mechanics and still hang out with the bluebloods at Oakwood Country Club.

I'm suspicious of most rich people, I'll say that right up front. Not a good thing for someone in the business of living off others' donations. Harlan many a time has said, "Look, Charmaine. It's the only way we can minister to all the regular folk. Just because they've got a lot to give doesn't make the gift any less valuable to us or their motives any less pure."

So Clarke and I sat there together, that gentry musty smell clouding around us. But I didn't mind. He set his hands on his knees and turned toward me. "What about doing a couple of the more modern tunes?"

"Like what?"

"Oh, I don't know. Like 'Feelings' or something? Or 'The Shadow of Your Smile.'"

"Okay. And how about 'Sing'?"

"I don't know that one."

"It's by the Carpenters. I love the Carpenters."

Clarke stood up. "Let's get on over to the record store at the Plaza."

So we went and bought a Carpenters album.

"Can we go by Billy Joe's for ice cream?" I asked.

But he shook his head and drove the other way.

When we pulled up to the house he hurried into the music room, opened up the lid to the hi-fi player, and put on the music. We listened to "Sing."

"What do you think, Mr. Ferris?"

"Don't like it. Doesn't have that classic feel."

And "Feelings" did?

Well, you just never know. I could give him "Shadow of Your Smile," picturing a movie starlet singing that while dressed in unimaginable finery. But "Feelings"? Still, maybe there was something to what he said. Maybe there was something to hanging on to the old standards.

After we practiced, the seamstress arrived to measure me. She didn't smile much, but then again, her mouth was pinched down on a bunch of pins.

When she finished, she took out a pad and wrote down the numbers. "Mrs. Ferris says you like yellow. And with that red hair, I'd say it's not a bad choice."

"It's cheerful."

"Never mind that, it's what looks good that matters. Black would really be the best, now that I think about it."

I thought about number six on my list of Mama's possibilities and refused.

"All right. I'll get started. I'll consult with Mrs. Ferris from here on out."

And so began my professional career.

Trudging up the stairs, the strains of "It's Very Clear, Our Love Is Here to Stay" piggybacked my steps. And I considered the words, thinking it the most ridiculous song ever written.

3

*T*wo weeks later I was a hit. The hairdresser dolled me up. I wore a little makeup for the first time, other than the school plays. My yellow dress, a pale shade in brushed silk with antique ecru lace "befit my tender years," as Mrs. Ferris said, yet displayed an elegance. But not a stuffy elegance. I looked like a very proper singer. I looked at least twenty years old.

I shook a lot of hands that night, my own hands enveloped in full-length evening gloves.

"You'll go far."

"That's a set of pipes you've got there, little missy!"

"My goodness, isn't Cecile quite the lucky one to have you here to sing for her?"

I waved to a little old man who patted my hand as he held it, tears in eyes. He'd just said, "'Fly Me to the Moon' was my late wife's favorite song."

But one comment stood out among the rest. "You're quite a woman, Myrtle."

I turned to the source of the new voice. And there he stood, a rugged young man with saucy, impertinent eyes, the kind of eyes I'd read about in those little romances

Grandma Sara used to read. But his weren't dark and brooding. They were blue, as bright a blue as you can imagine. A blue like a pansy, a blue just like Mrs. Evans's blue.

Now, I'm short. I'll tell you that straight away. And this fellow wasn't all that tall, maybe 5'10", but next to my bitty old 5'2", he towered.

My heart raced. I was thankful for the gloves that drank in the sweat from my palms. Beautiful, he exhibited a freedom such as I'd never seen, with his overly long hair, his casual dress and, could that be an empty earring hole in the left lobe? Yes, wild and free and beautiful. And that night, so was I, the pretty singer with golden tones, fluid arms, and talent. I wasn't like the rest of them.

We had that in common.

"Thank you."

"When will you be singing again?"

I shook my head. "I'm the Ferrises' foster daughter. It's not like I have paying gigs."

He raised his brows, highlighted by hours in the sun, I supposed. His tanned face seemed to point in that direction as well. Wild and free.

Free.

My very first rush of power hit me. I felt like I finally had set my feet upon the earth. I was free, wasn't I? No parents to tell me what to do. No real guidance of any sort. I was free.

4

On Sunday afternoon, he came to call. His voice filled the entry hall like a valentine in Charlie Brown's mailbox.

"Yes, it's me again, Aunt Cecile. I didn't get a good chance to visit with you at the party. You don't mind my stopping in do you?"

"Of course not, Richard."

Richard.

Come to think of it, he did look like a Richard. I'd call him Rich, though. I really would.

She strolled arm in arm with him into the living room. So I snuck down to the bottom of the wide, curving staircase, tucked my knees under my chin and listened.

His father was doing fine after the death of his mother. Yes, ma'am, UVA was going splendidly, he was going to get to room in the Jeffersonian part next year, a real honor even if the rooms were only heated by a fireplace and you had to drag your own wood over from the woodpile. "And don't get me started on the bathrooms." Yep, still planning on going overseas during the summer to work on a well-digging project in Africa.

Hmm. That seemed interesting, very noble and all.

"No, Aunt Cecile, let's not get started on politics! Come now, you know better, you yellow dog Democrat. Yes, I'm a Democrat, too, but for different reasons, important reasons."

Politics? Oh, who cares? Get on with more interesting discussion.

"Oh, yes! I didn't tell you about that? Are you sure? Not even during our visit to UVA? Clarke and I decided with this big old house and no ability to have children of our own, we'd try helping out a needy young person."

A needy young person. Yes, that would be me.

And then I heard words that sent shivers through me. "She's extraordinary!"

"Yes, she is, isn't she?"

"Has such presence. A very natural thing."

"Oh, yes. Utterly herself, I believe. I mean, she's been taking voice lessons for years, but no one can teach that sparkle. What is it they call it out in Hollywood? You know that expression, don't you? Help me out, please?"

"The 'it factor'?"

"Heavens, yes. That's it exactly."

"Can I meet her today?"

Oh, just those voices and nothing more, and I didn't give a hoot! It was all I needed. Someone wanted to talk to me. Myrtle Charmaine Whitehead.

"Of course! Will you stay for supper? You like pork, don't you? Can I get you a drink?"

"Be delighted. Do you think she'll sing for me?"

"I don't see why not. Now tell me more about this trip of yours," Mrs. Ferris began, and I beat it on up to my room. I had to get ready! I had to shower, shave my legs and underarms—even though I'd be wearing a long-sleeved dress, but let's face it, you feel better with your underarms shaved—pick out something to wear. Something simple, not school-girlish, but not as though I'm trying to look mature. It's one thing to look mature. But to look like you're trying to look mature is, well, immature. Kinda pathetic, too. I got enough sympathy without going looking for it.

The whole time I readied myself I heard his words, "Do you think she'll sing for me?"

For me.

Oh, my lands! Sing for him.

And then it occurred to me that never once had I really had a crush on a boy in school. But here this young man comes along, well, a bonafide man, actually, and I turn into a big bowl of whipped cream, nothing but air and sugar.

Sing for me.

The blue eyes, that windy hair. I wanted to look at his hands, get a good, long look at them, and I wanted to wonder what they'd feel like caressing my face.

Yes, I'll sing for you, Richard. I'll sing like you've never heard before. I'll shine under your chin like a spring buttercup.

5

*T*hat seamstress seemed to think of black as my "quintessential" color. But when I walked into the dining room for dinner, wearing the emerald dress Grandma Sara had made for me the year before, I banished black forever!

His eyes descended on me, first to my hair, which I'd gathered up with a few hairpins to lie on top of my head, then they examined my face—I just smiled with a relaxed little grin, acting, acting, acting like I did in the school plays—and then they stared at my chest.

No one ever stared at my chest before. But at fourteen, I wasn't what even a compulsive liar would call voluptuous, because even a compulsive liar would get no thrill in the lie. It would be like pointing to a blade of grass and saying, "That there's a pot roast." Or plunging a hand into ice water and saying, "Reminds me of that hot tub Aunt Evaline bought last year."

But I was sweet enough looking, I guess. Enough for Richard the Adventurous, anyway, to see me as more than a little kid.

They stood by the table, almost ready to be seated,

drinks in hand with musical ice that accompanied each lift to their mouths.

"Myrtle, this is my nephew, Richard."

He came forward and took my hand in his left hand, covered it with his right. "It's good to see you again. Aunt Cecile has been telling me a lot about you."

"There's not much to tell."

"You've had quite a life, I hear."

"I guess so."

And then the housekeeper came in with a big tureen of soup. She set it at Clarke's place, put a stack of bowls next to it, and quietly left the room.

"Shall we?" Clarke asked.

"Of course, darling." Cecile sat down at the other end of the table and Richard and I sat across from each other.

I'd like to say, all these years later, that I remember the conversation, but I don't. They talked about family members I felt no connection to. See, even then, I viewed that house as just a layover in my life, a little stop in a purposeful journey. I didn't know the reason then, but I know now. Richard was why. And I count it a good thing that I hadn't heard about *Lolita* by then because I would never have left with him. I would have been wise about men obsessed with young girls.

6

That evening after Richard left I snuck out and walked up to the nursing home. Good old grandma sat right there in the TV lounge.

"I was just praying for you, Myrtle."

"I guess I can use all the prayers you've got."

I sat down on the aqua-blue vinyl chair across from her. The TV blared *The Gong Show*.

"I'm sorry, Peach. I'm sorry you're over there without family around every day."

"Yeah, well." I shrugged. "Nothing's ever going to feel like home again, anyway."

And Grandma turned toward me and she laid her gnarled old hands atop the flames of my hair. She closed her eyes. "A hedge of protection, Jesus. I'm praying for that now with all the faith you've ever given me. Amen. A hedge of protection, Lord. That's what I'm asking for."

I realized all of a sudden, I'd gotten what I came for. So we sat and watched Gene Gene the Dancin' Machine and the more alert folks in the room just blew out their wheezy laughs or squealed their cackles.

After the show, Grandma said to this fellow in denim

overalls and a kelly-green cardigan sweater buttoned up beneath the bib, "Get out your accordion, Gerald."

So he shuffled down the hallway to his room, brought back one of those little European kind of accordions, not the Lawrence Welk kind. "What'll it be, Sara?"

"Let my granddaughter here sing, 'Redeemed How I Love to Proclaim It.'"

So he started off with a bellowy blow of the instrument, playing the last line of the chorus. And I jumped right in finishing up with "His child and forever I am!"

Just like the song says.

We sang some more and nurses wheeled patients in. We sang "Glory to His Name." "Blessed Assurance." "Calvary Covers It All." "In Times Like These." Old women smiled to "Trust and Obey." Old men wiped their eyes during "I'd Rather Have Jesus." The real crazies danced some wonderful little jigs but I didn't mind. People worship like they worship. I learned that there at the home.

When I left, one of the orderlies, a black man the size of a chess piece, said, "You got the gift, child. Yes, you do."

And I remembered the woman who had told me that years and years before. And I thought about that little gift-wrapped package in my throat, the one in blue paper with gold stars. And for the first time since Mrs. Evans died, I wept. I ran out of the home, down Langhorne Road and I cried and I cried and I cried and I didn't care who saw. The sun had died long since. The stars fused their light behind my eyes and I wondered what in heaven God thought He was doing.

"You tell her, Lord! You tell her I loved her!" I cried

into the blackness as I cut through Cecile and Clarke's backyard and laid myself down on the frigid grass.

Blood flowed warm from my left nostril, running down the side of my face to burrow deep into the soil.

7

I think about Richard Lewellyn now and a wolf comes to mind. But not a bad wolf, like a fairy-tale wolf or a big bad wolf. Just a wild, canine creature without the majesty of a lion, but with more gusto than, say, a fox or a bobcat. Nothing feline outlined Rich, but a doglike cast hallmarked his overall description as a free running winter wolf with a great mane of feathery hair blowing in the breeze.

We left together three days after he came to dinner. During those days we walked the grounds, the avenue, and when Cecile and Clarke declared they had a dinner date with a couple from the club, Rich ushered me down to the Cavalier. He never took my hand. He only ventured but one small kiss, and that on my cheekbone.

I prayed the entire time I wouldn't see Mr. Evans. Not only did I not want to explain that I'd given my heart to a twenty-one-year-old world traveler, I didn't think I could.

But he never even walked by the dingy plateglass window of the restaurant. I use the term "restaurant" quite loosely. Pretty much a beer-and-hot-dog joint, but that night, it might have been some swanky place in Paris for all the magic it conjured.

My heart kept pounding in my chest, never letting up, filling my head with the wine of new emotion.

"You seem older than fourteen," he said. And I really must credit him with gentlemanly conduct up until this time.

"Well, I'm almost fifteen and I've been through a lot, I guess."

His large blue eyes, drooping down a bit at the corners, were like vacuums, sucking my soul from between my lips as I told him my life story.

I don't know much about much, but I say, when you have an incredible life story at the age of fourteen, something's just not right.

I had more in common with a juicy peach than was good for me. A lot of people don't understand this. Well, how could this be? Didn't she find God there in the Evanses' kitchen that day? Did she turn down the voice of the Holy Spirit?

I'm no theologian, but I know that God never lets anything go to waste. I still believe that Jesus became my Lord and Savior in the Evanses' kitchen that day. But I knew nothing about God as my Father. Nothing. Mr. Evans, the only father I ever knew, stayed away most of the time. So fathers became people who carted you off for ice cream and if their schedule allowed, sat in hard metal chairs at the school plays. And then, when times got rough, they sloughed you off onto somebody else because they had a job to do. Mr. Evans wouldn't have done that to Stacy or Francie.

I don't blame him. It's just the way life works. Mr.

Evans never loved me like a real daughter. He only did what he did for his wife. And I guess that makes all the sense in the world, but it left a mark under my skin. Nothing anybody would see as they walked by, but I knew it was there.

As the words flowed out to Richard, I knew I'd been dealt a raw hand. I'd tried to play the cards right, as Mama always said, and I believe I succeeded. But now, what did it all matter, anyway? Here I sat in a beer-and-dog joint with a stranger, telling a tale of woe that would inspire even a country singer.

Yes, I could have been abused.

Yes, I could have been foraging on the street.

Yes, yes, yes, yes, yes!

I could have also been in a home with a mother who loved me, my own father who worked all day and came home at night with a sucker in his pocket for me and my brother and maybe even a baby sister.

Real brothers. Real sisters.

I knew, biologically speaking, someone sired me, but here I sat in the traffic of life waiting for someone to pick me up in his car and spirit me away from the boring mayhem.

So, if the rest of my story offends, all I can say is, you had to have been there to understand.

8

I ran away with Richard, sud-
denly enveloped in the world of Sandinistas and NPR,
and the aftermath of Watergate. On and on he'd blabber
there in his big Mercedes, obviously a cast-off family car,
about that blankety-blank Richard Nixon and his cronies.
Oh, my lands! I just heard "Blah, blah, blah—curse,
curse—blah, blah, blah, blah," and watched the passion
in his profile as he spoke, negotiating the roads out of
Virginia and up to Vermont. We slept in the car that night,
lucky for me, I guess. No room for fooling around, and
we still did no more than kiss a little bit. He kept asking
me to sing for him. But only for so long. "Shh, for a
minute, sweetie pie. *Morning Edition*'s coming back on."

I didn't mind that show one bit. It bored me, of course,
but I didn't mind. The little musical interludes, the self-
important Eastern accents, the stories about the environment. So different from anything I'd ever heard before.
An entire world opened up before me like a beautiful scal-
lop. Pretty on its face, but the real meat a bit mysterious.

That was it exactly. Lynchburg was fine and all, but I
never really knew much else existed before that time with

Richard. Places became more than just black moles on the veiny skin of a map. Sights worthy of picture post-cards or magazine photos belonged to me. People lived and died in these places, raised families, ate popcorn on Friday nights, snuck cigarettes out back, and shopped for necessities like toilet paper, deodorant, mousetraps, shoelaces, or even yards of yellow rickrack and notions like that.

It took us two entire days to get to Vermont because Richard, always talking about his desire to be a journal-ist, kept stopping to take pictures. I didn't mind. The colder it grew the more apt I was to stay in the car and flip through the buttons on the radio, always making sure, however, to get it back to the lower public radio portion of the dial because Richard had a look about him that told me I shouldn't mess with stuff like that.

Driving north, eating peanuts from long plastic sleeves, Richard started going on and on about the horri-ble inequality between the classes in our country.

"Take somebody like you," he said. "You're so bright and beautiful and talented, and I'll bet you've never thought about what it would be like to attend college, have you, baby?"

"Well, actually—"

"You've been too busy *surviving* to dream, sweetie pie."

He sounded so sure of himself.

"Right?" he said.

"Well, I don't know. I'd like to be a singer. Maybe even an actress. I've dreamed about that."

"But what about *education*? What about expanding your mind, leading others in the world of knowledge, im-pacting society?"

Oh, my lands!

I looked over at this guy and realized he didn't have a clue! He thought he cared about "somebody like me" but not even a ghost of self-doubt haunted his upper crust. So I decided to play along with him.

"Of course not. A girl from the wrong side of the tracks like me? What could a girl like me know about anything? What could someone like me offer all those smart people at college? And society? Well, even the very word scares me silly." I poured my accent on thicker than syrup straight from the maple tree.

"My point exactly, sweetie pie!"

There had been no point. And certainly no constructive idea, just a stupid, condescending observation based on what he thought it must be like to be "someone like me."

We stopped for a few hours in a rest area in Pennsylvania and he took me in his arms. But things changed. I was only an experiment, and this only a research trip, and he'd return to UVA and write some fancy paper as if he knew what it was like to be alone and without any hope other than what you have in God, and so far He'd pretty much stuck to the bare bones. He would go back to his lodgings and his keg parties and think he'd really done something for mankind, figure he'd given some waif a better turn than anyone else would give, and what would happen to me? I'd left no note for the Ferrises. I'd just disappeared.

By the time we reached Vermont, we were rounding our way from second base and zooming like a race car into third.

9

$\mathcal{T}$he snow piled up a good two feet on either side of the walkways, and drifts that looked like miniature, frozen-lipped mountains towered around.

"It's beautiful!" I cried out. "I've never seen anything like this."

"There are a lot of things you'll never see, sweetie pie, if you stick with me." Richard smiled.

"Why do you call me 'sweetie pie'? Why don't you ever call me Myrtle?"

"I've never been fond of the name Myrtle."

"Me, either. I don't why Mama named me that. If you'd have known her, you wouldn't think her the type."

"What's your middle name?"

"Charmaine."

"Now, that's pretty."

We got out of the car and headed for the cabin. Tendrils of smoke wove themselves up into the crisp sky, only to be unraveled by the icy breeze.

"I think I'll call you Charmaine, then."

"Okay."

"I'll introduce you around as Charmaine."

"Okay."

I entered the cabin with him.

A smoky haze heavied the air. Cigarette smoke and something smelling sweetish. Kind of cloying, really, but I didn't analyze it then, because the prettiest woman I'd ever seen sat on the couch. And she held hands with two men.

"Hey, y'all, this is Charmaine," said Richard.

"Hallo." From the girl.

"Hi." From the thin guy with running shorts, a torn T-shirt, and bare feet.

"Hey." From the heavyset guy with jeans and a plaid flannel shirt.

The woman's outfit suggested all manner of escapades. European travel. Asian nights. African markets. "Jingle, jangle, jingle," you could hear her jewelry sing. Copious ebony ringlets piled like a sheep shearer's finale atop her small head. And

Then . . . these bangs, pencil straight bangs caught on her lashes.

So, with my barely pubescent body, my frizz cloud of orange hair, my stick arms and legs (which thankfully hid themselves in my coat and pants), my big teeth, and breasts with a lot more to look forward to than their present situation, I wondered what crazy person took over my brain and steered my naive body into the car of Mr. NPR. A nice warm bed, two crackpot foster parents, a voice teacher, and a cookie jar on the counter always stuffed with either peanut butter kisses or snickerdoodles, or if luck smiled, chocolate chip cookies with walnuts, waited for me in the only town I'd ever known.

Not to mention a willowware plate on my nightstand.

Thank the Lord I thought to bring my pillow!

I took a deep breath and clasped my hands in front of me.

"Beer's in the fridge," said flannel man. "My name's Lou, Charmaine."

"Hey."

"Oh, she's darling, Rich!" The exotic lady spoke with an English accent.

Goodness gracious, I am an idiot! What was I thinking just going on the road with a college boy?

"I'm Lady Andrea Gault."

"Oh, *please*, Ands," said Richard, who decided just then to help me off with my pea coat and expose to the world the fact that he'd brought nothing more to the party than a spindly teenager. "Cut the nobility garbage. You're not in London. And believe me, Charmaine's the last person you need to impress."

Well, how about that? What did *that* mean? And an English lady? I mean, if I was Lady Something, I don't know what would be so exciting about a cabin in Vermont with three sloppily dressed college guys and an underage red-haired foster child from Lynchburg, Virginia. But then I remembered the truth and said to myself, "You don't know nothin', Myrtle Charmaine. You don't know nothin' about nothin'. So just keep your big mouth shut and your big eyes open and try not to let anyone surprise you or you'll wind up hurt."

You see, Mama gifted me with suspicion. That day when I realized she wasn't coming back, a bare lightbulb turned on in my head. Wanting to see the world in a romantic light wasn't enough anymore. The rosy hues of trust and that perennial hope-for-the-best we humans are born with, dissipated a little more with each day Mama failed to return.

I wasn't bowled over by these people the way most young teens would've been. Because if a mama could leave her child forever, a *mama*, then this collection of oddballs was capable of just about anything.

Dinner consisted of wine, beer, and cocktails, accompanied by bar snacks. Pretzels, peanuts, little sour onions, pickles, and olives. I found a bottle of Yoo-Hoo in the back of the fridge. I hate Yoo-Hoo, but it sure beat the stuff they were drinking. Although I knew all about developing palates for alcohol due to the burp-laden explanations of drunk middle-schoolers beneath the bleachers ("You gotta give it more than one sip, Myrtle!"), this was neither the place nor the time. Around nine I said, "Y'all got any real food in the house?"

"Nope," said Lou, and downed the last of his beer. "There's a little store a quarter mile down the main road if you want something."

Nobody said another word, so I pulled my coat on and took a solitary walk in the brilliant light of stars and moon on snow. The wind chilled me, but being out of the smoky air, feeling my lungs freshly painted with second-hand tar and nicotine, I smiled like a widemouth bass, breathed in through my nose and hurried forward. With just a few dollars in my pocket I only bought a premade chicken salad sandwich, a Coke, and a small bag of barbecue potato chips. I sat right there with the old lady, a Guinea-pig-type woman with skitterish, yet kind eyes and a snub nose, who ran the register with squat little fingers and we talked us a good one. She told me about her four grandchildren and I said I did well in school, but was here on a little family vacation for Christmas break. I lied. I know I did. And I've no excuse other than at this time, I was so disappointed in my own stupid self, I didn't see any reason to make it worse. I'd fallen into a second-rate den of iniquity and I did it all on my own!

But sitting there with that lady whose name I'll never know now, well, it was the first time I felt like myself in three days.

"You take care now." I threw out my trash, feeling a lot better having eaten real food, and buttoned my coat back up.

"You too, honey. Bring your family on by if you get a chance."

"I'll do that."

"And make sure you keep that hood on tight. Temperature's already dropping."

Dropping? How cold can it go? "All right. 'Bye, now."

I thought about that as I walked home. How cold can it really be? I mean, it's easy to think of time as going on and on, never ending, on and on and on. But what about temperatures? Are they infinite? Does cold get so cold it turns into something else? Does hot get so hot it cannot burn one degree higher? Or do they go on, intensifying, clarifying, and insisting on that one step further? Was that what had happened to Mama?

I let myself into the cabin to find Johnny Dangerous and the gang all sitting around the fireplace smoking marijuana and did I want a hit? No, not really. Not if it makes me look all droopy and stupid like you all. They began to annoy me.

"Sing us something, then, Charmaine," Richard said after he tied on a couple of shots of whiskey.

"She sings?" said running shorts man, who I found out was named Jonesy, short for Bartholomew Jones which sounded to me like some sea-faring type of name. "I'll get my guitar."

Guitar? Oh, my lands!

"What do you want to sing, honey?" he asked me.

"You know the old tunes?"

"Lay it on me, baby. My parents were singers."

"Really?"

"I grew up all over the country at folk festivals and all. Anyway, what do you want to sing?"

I loved the way he fingered the strings with hands so much prettier than Richard's. Richard suddenly got up, announcing his need to use the bathroom, only he didn't say it half so nice. I caught Jonesy's eyes and he rolled them. "I'll bet he acted real gentlemanly before he got here, didn't he?"

I nodded with an apologetic smile, apologizing for being found up here with this whole sorry group of humans. That's the thing that got me about this gaggle. They sat around and talked about society and humanity and the horrible machine of the free enterprise system and capitalism, but what was their reaction when all I wanted was some supper? All these lofty ideals obviously had no practical, one-on-one application. I guess it was right then that I realized if these people were what you found at universities, I'd gladly remain in ignorance with the ignorant.

He shrugged. "Too bad I'm already in love with Andrea."

I felt my smile go sideways and sad. Boy, did men just assume things when the girl was young.

"Not that that really matters," he said. "I mean, the others will fall asleep sometime, right?"

What a jerk!

So I sang to Jonesy's guitar, our first number being "Turn, Turn, Turn." He thought he was being "retro" (a term I had to ask Richard to explain later), but I suddenly remembered Mrs. Evans and I hoped she couldn't see down from heaven. Especially later that night when Richard took me into the back room and laid me down on his cot.

Drunk and high, he pawed and nuzzled and slobbered, oblivious to my sobs of fear and embarrassment. We had rounded all of third base and home plate was coming soon, and darn it all, only a man would come up with the analogy of a baseball game! Stupid, stupid, stupid, Myrtle Charmaine Whitehead, the tramp with her mama's lipstick. The tramp.

And the night got colder still.

Oh, Lord, please! I prayed. Make him stop. Make him stop. And tears overflowed and I sang to myself, whimpering, "Good morning merry sunshine, why did you wake so soon?" The words puttered out of me in a vibrating whisper a note puffing out every third word. My eyes closed against his form and then I remembered Grandma Sara back in Lynchburg, maybe even praying for me that very moment and I pushed at him hard, his naked body a wall above me that suddenly came crashing down.

Oh, Grandma Sara! I cried as I rolled him off me to slink down the side of the bed and onto the floor. Oh, Grandma! I cried as I shivered back into my clothing, covered Richard with the blanket and stepped out into the main room of the cabin.

I felt her prayers about a hedge of protection being answered. I almost saw the words themselves in the glimmer of the coals in the fireplace.

I sat on the couch alone.

Enough to put the fear of God right where it should have been, back in Lynchburg. That weird bunch at the cabin had me shaking like an unbalanced washing machine by five o'clock the next morning. There they all were, lying around with messy clothes and breath so bad it soured the general atmosphere of the interior.

Stale and stewy, like people cooking away in a ragout of irresponsibility, of thinking we're just so wonderful, and in-the-know, so on-the-edge, so lah-dee-dah when all we're doing is exchanging the same juices and flavors, back and forth, trading the same old ideas and expressions, over and over and over. The night before told me everything I needed to know, because surely Richard wouldn't always be drunk and Jonesy might find he could get away from Lady Andrea and then where would I be?

Torn between two jerks. Feelin' like a fool.

I zipped up the fur-lined boots Richard bought for me somewhere in Pennsylvania, put on as many of my clothes as possible to lighten my bag.

And then I did something I'm still ashamed of to this day. I dipped into everyone's wallet and took out ten dollars from each. Forty dollars plus one of my own. Would that get me back home? But then again, where was home? Really? Where was home? Where had home ever been?

I stuffed my pockets with cocktail snacks and thanked

God I was leaving with my virginity intact. Barely. But still hanging there like a possum by the tip of its tail.

Slipping into the purple chill, I secured my hood tightly, wrapped my scarf so that only my eyes showed, and started off in the direction of the little store.

I imagined the conversation that would ensue when consciousness tickled them awake like a feather down a throat.

"Where's Charmaine?" Andrea would say.

"Gone. Stuff's gone." That would be Richard.

"Pity," Lou would say as he rebuttoned his flannel shirt after his turn, I presumed, with Andrea.

"How was she?" Jonesy would ask, looking cute I would have to admit, though he was not just garden variety immoral, but well, slimy and gross.

"Young. You know how that goes."

"Pity," Lou would say again.

"You think she'll be all right?" Andrea might say, but more than likely it would be Jonesy because he didn't seem quite as self-centered.

"She'll have to be," Richard would say. "There's no way I'm going after her."

"You never do."

"You've got that straight."

"Besides," Richard again, "she's just a foster kid. Mother ran out on her when she was only eleven. Never saw her again."

There'd be no pity. There'd just be talk and thoughts that they could see why the woman bolted. And wasn't Charmaine just like her? Running away. Just running away. And they would say it like the supposedly compassionate enlightened ones they were, the people with all the good ideas and impeccably clean hands.

The farthest south I could travel on thirty dollars (I figured I'd better keep the other eleven for any unforeseen expenditures that might pop up) was Baltimore, Maryland. The bus stopped right at that nice lady's store next to the post office and I hopped on. I parked myself by the heater and tried to remember the songs Mrs. Evans taught me all those years ago when I was just a girl.

I felt old and jaded. Not prostitute, drug addict jaded like most folk think of the expression. But the world lost yet more of its wonder.

I began to doubt I'd ever feel at home anywhere. But I could make it on my own somewhere. Get a job, maybe waiting tables at the Texas Inn. Rent our old room from Mrs. Blackburn.

Nobody wants you to bleed all over their corn dog, Myrtle.

And I wondered how four years could be fast and slow all at the same time. I wondered if I'd ever get back to Lynchburg and realized no good reason for doing so popped up like some benevolent candle flame lighting the way. Lynchburg was dark and lonely, just like everywhere else.

So I hopped on the bus to Baltimore, my pockets filled with cocktail peanuts and pretzels and I hoped the YWCA wasn't too far from the Greyhound station. I didn't want to waste the money on a cab. Fifteen years old now, for I'd turned that age on the bus, completely on my own, I was wiser than I should have been.

10

I started watching skies when I began working at Suds 'N' Strikes Forever, a combination bowling alley/washateria in Dundalk, a Baltimore neighborhood. The day after I got off the bus, highly patriotic Frank Reasin and his wife Anita gave me a job at their bowling alley snack bar after I told them my story in selective bits and pieces.

Anita patted my hand. "I've heard how rough those foster homes can be. You can even stay upstairs at our house. All our kids are gone. Give me the number for your social worker and I'll make all the arrangements."

"Don't call, please. They'll just put me back into the system. Please, let me just work here . . . under the table. I promise I won't be any trouble."

Frank put his arm on Anita's shoulders. "I don't know. I'm not sure about this."

I turned to run away but Anita hollered. "Wait!"

I turned back around.

"You can stay. We can't have you running off to who knows where."

Frank nodded. "But only if you stay in our spare room upstairs so we can make sure you're all right."

"I won't be much trouble," I said.

He nodded. "I can tell that right up front."

Anita patted my shoulder. "You need anything, hon, you just ask."

I served up cardboard pizza and hot pretzels and heated up those Stewart sandwiches sealed in heatupable, crackly cellophane wrappers that steamed up inside as their innards—which might be grilled cheese, a hamburger (or "hamburg" as Frank would say), a cheeseburger, or a hot dog—came to life leaving a greenhousey layer of condensation I'd try not to dislodge as I opened the wrapper.

Nobody likes soggy sandwiches, Myrtle.

I told them I went by Charmaine, my middle name.

After the bowling alley closed at eleven, weather permitting, Frank and I sat in green-and-white webbed lawn chairs on the upper porch of their small green bungalow. He didn't know much about the stars, he just liked them.

Frank's girth resembled a farmhouse.

After about an hour he'd say, "You tired yet, hon?"

And I'd say, "Yeah."

"Well, I'll go on home now. Anita likes me to make sure you're okay before we nod off."

"I'll be fine."

"Kitchen's yours. You just fix anything you want if you get hungry. Just make sure you turned off whatever it was you turned on."

"Okay, Mr. Reasin."

He hefted off the lawnchair, comfy blubber rolling like sea billows and left with a hearty wave. Like Mrs. Evans.

And so I sat, alone and empty under the stars.

"A hedge of protection, Lord. A hedge of protection." I heard the voice of Grandma Sara in my head and the profound realization that God honored her prayers echoed the most beautiful sight in the sky I'd ever seen.

In a mildly cloudy sky, little dark puffs of cotton steamed like paddle wheelers across the dome of heaven there above the bowling alley. But the wind soon died. Behind two embracing clouds the moon slowly rose, hidden at first, and then, a fantastic white beam of light shone, a monochrome sunrise, a single ray piercing the night. My breath caught in wonder and surprise and I remembered that during the darkest of hours, God is. The moon continued to rise and the words of the song "Even So Lord Jesus Come" filled my heart despite my world of fear and turmoil, despite my race so hard in the running. Yes, Jesus, I need Your infilling, Your rich infilling.

So come, Lord Jesus, come.

Like the song says.

Oh, if He'd just pull me out of here, I would so appreciate that.

And I held my breath, waiting and watching, expectant and brave because if this was the day my Lord and Savior chose to bring me to that meeting in the air, that Jubilee of jubilees, I was ready.

"Come Lord Jesus, please!" my voice whispered in the still silence, in the spring air of a foreign place where the flowers didn't bloom as brightly and where I wandered in search of home. "Oh, please, Lord, come and get me now! I'm so tired. I just want to go home."

My heartbeat accelerated, fueled by a frenzied anticipation. Could it really be? Could this be the "crowning day when my Savior I should see," just like the song said?

And then I cried as the moon rose yet more, bursting from out of the clouds, brighter and brighter, clearer and brighter. And the words, "I am your way, your truth, your life, no man cometh unto you Father, Myrtle Charmaine, but by Me" stippled my memory.

Even at fifteen, that profound knowledge that He was enough permeated my brain, scratching the itches, soothing the raw places, and maybe it's hard to believe, but it was enough. It had to be.

Nobody likes a religious freak though, Myrtle Charmaine.

I mean if Mama objected to nosebleeds, how in the world could she even stomach a man dying on a cross, blood oozing from scarlet wounds into thirsty wood?

To this day I remember that sight, and I've searched the sky ever since, whether on the road or sitting out under the night stars at a rest stop holding hands with my Harlan and drinking vending machine hot chocolate. I've never seen anything like that sky, before or since, and some folks would call me crazy, but I know for sure that God did that just for me, proving in extravagant silence that He is with me always.

11

*J*esus never deserted me during that time on my own. Two weeks into the job, I began to choose my favorite denizens of Suds 'N' Strikes. Marg worked the main counter, the bowling doings on one side, the washateria on the other, her owl glasses missing nothing. Dave, the night manager on weekends never ceased to tickle me the way he'd act like a one-man SWAT team when he opened up the bubblegum machines to add more candy and prizes. I'm sure Mike and Ike would be proud to know they were so valued.

But my favorite regular at Suds 'N' Strikes didn't work at the alley, he came in every afternoon and his name was John Roberts. John Roberts always said, "Just call me John Roberts." Nobody ever asked why until me. He said, "Because that's my name."

John Roberts fell on his head when he was three years old and was never the same. That's what Frank Reasin said and Frank's known him since kindergarten.

John Roberts' mission in life was to teach the kids how to bowl. "Aim for the center of the lane! Shoot right down the middle!"

Some kids cried right away.

Others would smart mouth. "Hey, buddy, if I could shoot it right down the middle I would!"

Most tried to ignore him. But John Roberts refused to be ignored. A nice lady came in one day and I watched the whole episode from the snack bar. John Roberts approached her children, offering hints.

She smiled, tightening her dark blond ponytail, and I could tell right away she knew something peculiar flipped and tumbled within him. I poured myself an orangeade and settled in for the show. She allowed John Roberts to help each child through several turns and then, poor John Roberts went too far. He grabbed the little boy by the arm. "You're not listening! Down the middle . . . like this!" And he pulled the ball roughly from the child's arms. What a sweet little boy, I'd already decided, looking just like his mother with dirty blond hair and gentle, very round blue eyes.

That mother sprang to her feet. "Esteban, sit with your sisters." She marched right up the polished floor of the approach. "Look. I appreciate the fact that you're trying to help, but I don't yell at my children and maybe you'd better leave!"

Roar, lady, roar!

I clapped. I just couldn't help myself. "That's right! You defend your children."

John Roberts stayed away for two weeks. But that lady returned. Every Tuesday afternoon she'd cart in those kids, all with Spanish names, and they bowled while she did her laundry.

And so Luella Cuestas became my best friend in Baltimore. She invited me over to her little house for crabcakes one night and I found out her husband Claudio had died four years before, not long after she gave birth to Guadalupe, her youngest.

"I live on the insurance money and what I can make with my artwork," she said as she poured us a cup of tea after the kids went to bed. "It won't last forever, but it will last long enough until Guadalupe goes off to first grade and I can get a real job while they're all at school."

"Your kids sure love you."

"I know. There isn't anything I wouldn't do for them."

"That sure shows." I looked around her little home, an old prewar house painted pale turquoise blue on a narrow street. She'd taken me on a tour earlier. Two large bedrooms and one bathroom constituted the upstairs. A double bed and a toddler bed sat in one room, a set of bunks in the other. Downstairs a big kitchen and a living room filled up the first floor. I wouldn't call it "neat as a pin," a term Mama always used, but it smelled clean and flowery and signs of belonging dotted the entire dwelling like candlelight through a tin lantern: a leftover Christmas ornament made by a schoolchild hung from the kitchen chandelier, a sampler embroidered with each child's name overlaid a portion of wall above the kitchen door. It announced the mixing of cultures that originally formed the Cuestas household.

THE CUESTAS HOUSE

Isabel: my soul
Esteban: my heart
Guadalupe: my spirit

And all around the words little hearts and houses followed one another. The frame, nicked and battered, held it all together. Luella was that frame, I decided.

She painted murals all over her home and chose the least everyday colors I'd ever seen on her walls. Bright yellows, reds, purples, even parrot green in the upstairs bath!

I told her everything about myself that night. She swiped a tendril of limp hair behind her glasses and cried and cried. "Here I've been feeling sorry for myself for four years and look what you've been through!"

"But I didn't tell you this to make you feel sorry for me, I just . . . I . . . well, I don't know why I told you. I just did."

"God had you do it. God felt sorry for me. Oh, Charmaine, your nose is bleeding." She jumped up and handed me a clean, soft dish towel, just like Mrs. Evans.

That night I took note of God's utter resourcefulness realizing that He can even use a mother's desertion for someone else's good.

Looking at the stars from the roof of the house that night, I prayed I'd see how God redeemed it for me, I prayed that somehow—anyhow, somewhere, anywhere, someday, any day—I'd look back and say, "It's okay. I can see why it happened this way."

We all want answers, right? We all want someone to tell us our past pain made the present easier not only for others but for ourselves, that in the end it was worth it.

One more thing: thank You God I'm not one of those ladies who lost their husband before the children were raised.

12

I started really reading my Bible that spring there at Suds 'N' Strikes.

I can see Mama rolling her eyes right now. *Nobody likes to hear how God helps you, Myrtle Charmaine. They want a gutsy tale of self-reliance and strong-willed gusto in the face of adversity. Why don't you just keep God in the background where He belongs?*

Oh, hush up, Mama.

After I'd saved enough for busfare back to Lynchburg just in case, I started branching out a little in the spring. With my weekly paycheck of eighty dollars, I paid Mr. Reasin ten dollars for my room, another ten for my food down in the snack bar even though he told me that was "Ridiculous, hon! It's not like you eat all that much."

But I said, "Just take it, Mr. Reasin, have a little mercy on my conscience."

"Well, I'll take the money for food only because you insist, Charmaine. And only because you made it a matter of conscience. I believe in a healthy conscience. So what are you gonna do with the rest of the money? Because if you need any clothes or personal items, that

Kresge's down the street is the place to go. Good prices. Nice people there, too. My second cousin, Cass, works there."

"What I need is a used bookstore."

His eyes lit up. "You don't say? You like to read?"

"Yes, sir. But I need me a little Bible."

We sat up on the porch that Friday night, an overcast, swollen sky butting its gloomy nose into our conversation, making us look up at its girth at every imagined raindrop. Next door, steam from the dryers on the Laundromat side billowed up like cumulus clouds, its milky mass sucked up into the breeze of a hungry storm. I pulled my coat closer around my middle.

Mr. Reasin scratched his head. "It seemed like you had something deeper about you, Charmaine. I've got an extra one downstairs, or if you want, I'll get Anita to run you over to the Baptist Bookstore. We've got the four-year-old class at church next quarter and she's got to get some materials."

I added it up in my head. I had sixty dollars left over, just this week! No need for food other than at the snack bar. I wanted a new pillow as I'd left my real pillow in Vermont, and maybe a set of my own sheets, too. A new blanket could wait until next week. Summer clothes would have to be bought eventually, so I'd keep saving. I wanted to write to the Ferrises' and have them send me up my clothing, but figured a clean break was better all around. At fifteen, I had no right to be on my own.

Now I had no idea what Anita Reasin really looked like inasmuch as God made her because her look included a curly raspberry-colored perm, drawn-on eyebrows, blue mascara, penciled lips. She wore all manner of undergarment armor that showed its bumps of hardware through her tight, fine-print housedresses. The ladies at the Baptist Bookstore knew her right away.

"Anita! How you doing today?"

She set her purse upon the display case that supported the register. "Doing fine, doing fine." Except in Baltimorese it came out, "Doin' fahn, doin' fahn."

"I'm looking for some good stuff for four-year-olds and Charmaine here is looking for a new Bible. Charmaine is our new snack bar girl at the bowling alley."

The lady smiled at me through bare lips and cat glasses. "Nice to meet you."

Anita pointed to our right. "The Bibles are over there. You got any questions, I'll be at the Sunday school aisle over there to the right of all those choir robes."

I nodded, glad she didn't find some other lady to help me. This was the first Bible I would buy for myself, and some events deserve a little privacy and quiet. I wanted to hear as well as feel the air of the pages as I flipped them up near my face. I wanted to smell new leather and paper by myself, and I wanted to rub the little satin ribbon-markers against my own cheek without someone telling me not to.

Wouldn't Mrs. Evans have loved to have been here on this day!

The quietness of the store settled on me like Jesus' seamless garment and my eyes danced over the stacks of little boxes containing the most precious gold, the rarest of jewels, truly the pearl of greatest price. My very real need to travel light through this world centered my gaze on the smaller boxes, and I read the word "slimline." That sounded interesting. Sleek and easy to tote. And new! It said so right on the box.

I reached up and pulled down the first one I saw and when I opened the box and smelled that new Bible smell that delights followers of Jesus all over the world, even more than the smell of a new car, I'd wager, I knew I'd found it.

It was pink to boot!

I hugged it to my chest and told God "thank You." And I felt the breeze of the pages as I flipped them, smoothed the white satin ribbon against my cheek, breathed in the freshness of a newborn copy of God's Holy Word, and I let my sudden tears baptize the first page to which I turned. It fell down, down, splattering upon John 11:35, "Jesus wept."

So Jesus wept, too, right then, right there with me.

I suppose people in religious bookstores know when someone is having a spiritual moment and have been trained to leave well enough alone. I don't know this for a fact, but I've suspected it for years. Nobody bothered me as I sat Indian-style, alone on the linoleum-tiled floor, the gray speckles floating in and out of focus inside my waxing and waning tears.

I told Jesus, "You had a right to cry. You knew what a sorry old world this was all turning out to be. Such plans You All must have had."

The teardrops on the page glistened in the fluorescent lighting. I ran a hand over them smearing them into wet comets across the God-breathed, onionskin sky. Beneath the water the fine fiber buckled slightly and I tried to calm myself.

You see, I wish, just once, Jesus would just stand before me, take my hand and we could just have a good cry together.

Mrs. Reasin tiptoed up and laid a hand upon my shoulder as I sat there and dried my face. She didn't say anything, just gave me her warmth and stood there with her own eyes closed. And I knew she prayed.

That night it rained and Mr. Reasin locked up and went home without our usual closing-time chat. I flipped on the little milk-glass lamp, running my fingers over the tiny polka dots of glass and I settled comfortably onto my bed. I opened that Bible, the Spirit Wind blowing warm inside me. I read until I slept and I awakened to my darkened room, alone and happy, and realizing that God really had a plan for me and I'd best get on with it.

I needed to sing.

I needed to be back in church and I told Mrs. Reasin that the very next day. I hadn't been in church since Mrs. Evans had died.

"Can you all use some help with the four-year-old class, Miss Anita?"

"That would be nice, hon. We leave for church around nine in the morning. Want us to go?" She stood by the bowling-ball polishing machine. She polished a few of the house balls every day, which frustrated Mr. Frank because why waste the power on a house ball that is only going to get grimy anyway? But if you saw Suds 'N' Strikes and Miss Anita's house, it would make perfect sense.

"That'd be nice."

And so there I found myself among the four-year-olds, wiping noses, pouring warm Hawaiian Punch from the can, laying out butter cookies like the ones Mrs. Evans used to buy, reading stories and singing songs.

Mr. Frank and Miss Anita just stared at me with open mouths the first time I sang. And I smiled and shrugged. "Praise the Lord, is all I can say."

And the gift box in my throat glimmered and shone with the anointing of the Holy Spirit. I knew that and it frightened me because like my little King James Bible says, "To whom much is given much is required."

13

"Do I look okay?"

Miss Anita hugged me, and with that girdle, I swear it was like hugging a salmon, but I didn't mind. I'll take good hugs like that no matter what, and you can take that to the bank!

We stood in the hot-pink women's bathroom of the church. The choir, in which I now sung soprano, or alto, or wherever they needed a voice, began to line up outside the door. The self-conscious whispers of be-lipsticked mouths beneath the carefully made-up upper regions of the women's faces shuffled through the louvered vent plate at the bottom of the bathroom door.

"You look wonderful, Charmaine. I'm not sure why you felt you had to scrape your hair back though. I've been trying to get my hair to look like yours for years!"

"I didn't want to take away from the rest of the choir. This hair is loud, Miss Anita. People's eyes just go to it."

"Like moths to a flame!"

"That's truer than I'd like it to be, that's for sure."

We smiled at each other in the mirror.

"You'll do fine, hon. Trust me. And let's face it, the

people here at Holabird Assembly aren't choosy. If there's a blessing to be had, they'll find it sure enough."

And maybe some hands would be raised in the bargain, lifting up holy hands to the Lord. Now if only I didn't have to sing next to Mrs. Cox, because that woman couldn't carry a tune in a bucket, a bowl, or a box! Hopefully I could concentrate extra hard, especially before my solo part.

I felt like I did the first time I performed at E.C. Glass High. I can hardly describe the nervous blips that ran through all of me like mice in a maze, when we walked onto the platform behind the pulpit. I felt like my heart and my brain turned into giant rat wheels, and two mean little rodents scampered on them, running, running, their slender feet and paws going like pistons, their beady little eyes glowing red and saying, "You nervous enough yet, Myrtle? Huh? Huh?"

Then they laughed this little "weeee-heeeee" laugh that makes me want to stomp on them. Don't even get me started on what they were doing down there in my stomach.

To this day, after hundreds and hundreds of times up on stage, I feel exactly the same. It's different singing for Jesus than in school plays and on "live entertainment night" at Suds 'N' Strikes. Yep, after the solo that I am about to describe, Mr. Frank said, "Let's make Saturday nights a little classy at the alley." And Miss Anita fell for the idea like a ton of girdled Jell-O, bouncing with excitement at the idea. Once again, I was fitted for a gown, but this time, wooo-hooo, we threw taste to the wind! Miss Anita and I sure breathed a more common air than Cecile Ferris and I ever would!

Life was too short. Clothes could be too fun.

But thoughts of sequined gowns were yet to rise from the depths of my entertainer's heart that morning in church. A soulful sea of faces, Bibled laps and expectant hearts waited for a blessing.

I was glad that tongues don't sweat like hands do, further making singing in public even more difficult. But perspiration beaded on my forehead as the choir rose for the choral number. The piano player was Billy Noekowski, a bony, large-headed fellow with detonated black hair and ice-pick legs. His large knees reminded me of footballs. He pounded his way into the introduction.

I started into the first verse of "His Eye Is on the Sparrow." The choir ooohed and mmmm'd all around me as I sung louder and with more feeling than ever before. And I just wanted to sing and sing and sing and *sing* about Jesus. Because He was all I had, really, right then in my life.

All I had.

I tell you this. He's really all anybody has, and I count it a blessing I learned that so young. Because then everything else, all the people, places, things—the nouns of this world, and even the adjectives that describe them: big, nice, yummy, loving, breezy and all—are just filling in the pie!

Nobody cares about you and God, Myrtle Charmaine.

14

$\mathcal{L}$uella brought the kids over for my first night singing at Suds 'N' Strikes. In the women's rest room she applied my makeup. "I just got into Artistry makeup, Charmaine. I figure if I sell a little on the side each month, it may pay for groceries."

"Sure looks good, Luella."

Oh, Luella is so pretty.

Her girls, Isabela and Guadalupe watched, their large brown eyes absorbing their mother's every flitter and flick.

Anita Reasin entered one last time. "It's almost curtain time, hon! How do you like the dress? Comfortable? And are those shoes too high?"

"I love it. And the shoes are comfy as can be."

Well, as four-inch heels could possibly be.

Luella pinkied some gloss over my reddened lips. "You did a remarkable job on this gown, Anita. You should be proud of yourself."

Anita herself dressed up for the occasion. No housedress tonight! The black skirt and beaded sweater actually became her girth. She appeared heroic, a woman in charge of the place. "I am. I haven't sewn in years. I wondered if I could still do it. Well, anyway, you guys, Frank just taped up the final bit of tinsel on the new stage and we're ready to go."

I gazed at myself in the mirror one last time. I looked at least twenty-three or -four. "Are you sure this is okay?"

"I sure am, hon. I haven't been this excited in years. A lot of the church people are coming, too. You'll have a full house, hon."

And so my debut as a real singer occurred that night in May during my sixteenth year, over five years after Mama had left. I sang songs like "Sing," "Raindrops Keep Fallin' on My Head," and well all those Burt Bacharach type songs because Billy Noekowski had piano books for them. He played, banging away, his sparkly red bow tie that matched my gown vibrating with each chord pounded, or tinkled, or swirled.

I sang amid the sounds of tumbling pins, dryers, washers, pinball machines, and cheers from folks who got strikes and spares. I sang amid the fluorescent lights, the gleam of polished wood, and the neon beer signs. I sang amid the smell of popcorn butter and pink candy, pizza and National Bohemian. I sang under the warm air from the overhead heating vent and the smiles of those who knew me as that poor girl with no family.

And I sang better for all of it.

I know that now.

But I still don't know if the misery is worth the art. I did realize, however, that I would do all I could not to become like Mama. Work hard. Not be satisfied with my present.

We ended that set at the bowling alley with "Down by the Riverside." The joint really thumped, let me tell you.

Part Three

1

$\mathcal{I}$t's easy to see your life as a roadmap of sorts after the fact. Looking back now it made perfect sense I wouldn't stay at Suds 'N' Strikes Forever. I spent an entire year there singing. Mrs. Reasin showed me how to sew and Luella somehow managed to pass her eye for design on to me. And I'd be dishonest if I said I didn't enjoy my life there in Baltimore. Church with the Reasins on Sundays. Choir. Singing at the bowling alley and running the snack bar during the days. My nosebleeds stopped, too.

Luella and the kids invited me over for supper at least three times a week and those kids just loved me because I'd play Monopoly or Ants in the Pants with them as much as they wanted, which gave Luella time to have a nice long soak in the tub. "I haven't felt like a girl since Claudio died," she said. "Sometimes I get so busy being a mother I forget I'm even a woman at all."

So I learned to sew and that skill came in handy because I was always working on some kind of singing costume. A lime-green affair with silver beaded trim hugged my frame the night Bansy Pruitt entered my life.

Now Bansy resembled a human beanbag, a lumpy pyramid that began beneath a skull the shape of a gumdrop and continued to flare out in a downward flow.

He placed a tiparillo between his ribbon-thin lips, lips shadowed by a nose so small I wondered if someone had wacked it off in his childhood with a hockey stick or something. See, that northern, cold weather look hovered about him, categorizing his entire form as jowly, soft-sided luggage.

I hated his accent from his first word which was, "Yo."

Yo? What kind of a greeting was that? I could see "Hey" or "Hi" or even a nod and no word at all. But "Yo"?

"Hey."

I just finished my set. Old Billy Noekowski and I really grooved. We settled into our own artery, pumping rhythms and melodies together in a most biological fashion. I don't mean to be prideful, but I don't think anybody does a better rendition of "Smoke Gets in Your Eyes" than I do. And I sure did have them laughing with my irreverent interpretation of "Billy Don't Be a Hero," an eye-roller for sure.

Bansy smacked his lips. "Good singing, gal."

Gal. Oh, my lands!

"Thank you."

"What's your name?"

"What's yours?"

He sucked on the tiparillo. "I like your style, girlie."

At that moment, Mr. Reasin sidled up and spirited me away.

"Who is that guy?" I asked.

"Beats me. Seems a little shifty, but you can never tell."

"He reminds me of that Plumpy character in Candyland."

Frank laughed at that. "You know, Charmaine, you're exactly right."

2

I found out Bansy Pruitt's name the third night he showed up at Suds 'N' Strikes. By that time I began to get a little weirded out by the fellow, so I just walked my singing shoes right on over, placed my hands flat on his table and set, "So let me get this straight. You're here because you're doing laundry, right?"

"No."

"Then maybe you better march you and your tiparillos right on out of here because you're beginning to scare me."

I felt my eyes tear up because although I was a scrappy sort back then, confrontations scared me to death. The shadow of Mama still loomed. Loomed like a thin, mangy old cat with only one claw left, but a claw that, nevertheless, could scratch out an eye in a split second.

"Don't be scared, Charmaine. I'm here because I think you've got talent. Have a sit."

Have a *sit*?

"Where are you from?" I asked.

"All around."

"Not good enough."

"New Jersey."

I sat down.

"So what brings you to Suds 'N' Strikes?"

"I'm actually a location scout for a local filmmaker."

"Really?"

"Yeah. We may use the alley in a new film."

"What's it called?"

"*Bowl-O-Rama.*"

"*Bowl-O-Rama*?"

"*Bowl-O-Rama.*"

"What kind of a name is *Bowl-O-Rama*?"

He shrugged, driving his angel-food shoulders up into his neck blubber. "My boss is more than a little eccentric."

"I'll bet!"

"So you think the alley will do for this movie?"

"Yeah. You gonna bring your boss along?"

"Yeah, next week."

"When I'm singing."

"I'm thinking about doing just that. He'll like the strange angle. I mean who's ever heard of a Laundromat-bowling alley with live entertainment?"

I eased up a bit. "You can sure say that again, mister. Have you met the Reasins?"

"They own the place, right?"

"They sure do. And once you get to know them, you'll want them in your movie."

"Think they'd mind having one shot here?"

I shook my head. "They'd love something like that. They really would."

That night, a spring mist falling on the roof of the

bowling alley, Mr. Reasin and I sat drinking vanilla Cokes. During the previous summer we put up a big beach umbrella and a couple of lounge chairs. But now it sheltered us from the wet.

"Well, I'm letting them come make that movie here."

"You don't say!"

"Yep. Worked out a good deal, I guess. Not that I would really know if it wasn't. But it'll cover expenses and then some."

"So what are you gonna do when they shoot the film?" I asked. "Go on vacation for the month?"

"Heck, no! I'm going to be watching these scoundrels like a hawk. You know those entertainment types."

Well, no, I didn't really. "I know what you mean," I said anyway.

"Always looking for freebies even though they make more money than anybody these days."

I didn't know that either. "Still, it's gonna be exciting, don't you think?"

He shrugged his wide shoulders. "Let's hope it's not too exciting. But hey! You get to be an extra! Even have you singing in the background. That's got to make you feel good."

"That'll be fun. You think they'll get me a real Hollywood costume?"

"No way. Not those cheapskate s.o.b.s. If you want to look good you girls better come up with something on your own."

Me, Luella, and Anita designed a doozie.

When we hand-sewed the last sequin on the night before the scheduled shoot, we actually threw a party there at Luella's. The kids made a big pitcher of cherry Kool-

Aid. I brought some squirt cheese, pepperoni, and Chicken-in-a-Biscuit crackers. And Anita Reasin made her famous no-bake peanut butter fudge.

What a time! The kids pooped out long before we did. Anita left to marinate the chicken legs she was throwing on the grill for the Memorial Day party they were giving the next day. Teriyaki chicken legs! So Luella and I stood at the doorway to the older two's room. Isabel was a charming little beauty back then. Sweet nose, brown eyes, black bobbed hair, and big old, crooked teeth. In the bed next to her Esteban slept, his head of hair like a wild mane. Guadalupe slept in Luella's room in the toddler bed at the foot of her own double bed, her dark hair feathering like spin art across her cheeks.

"I feel so sorry for them," Luella said. "What kind of people will they be growing up without a father?"

I shrugged. If she wasn't making the connection to me, I wasn't about to remind her.

What kind of people would they be?

Empty?

Sad?

Scrappy?

Lonely?

Alone?

Wanting?

Scared?

Apprehensive?

Blue?

What kind of people would they be?

3

On *Bowl-O-Rama* night I almost didn't make it out of the ladies' room I felt so nervous and scared and bereft of talent, but Luella and Mrs. Reasin literally carried me out and when I realized my embarrassment at being forcibly delivered to the set would far surpass a flat note or, please Lord no, the inability to hit the high note, I said, "All right you two, all right!" And set my high heels upon the industrial strength, grayish-gold carpet. "Just give me a minute to compose myself."

So I leaned up against the faded white lockers and said a prayer in my mind that might have lasted two minutes if said verbally, but only lasted twenty seconds as the thoughts didn't really even get the chance to become actual words, just pleadings and emotions. Although, the words "help me" did manage to appear quite frequently.

I stood before the director, Bart Lake, and tried to listen to his instructions.

"Now you'll only be on-screen for a couple of seconds, but we'll want to shoot you for at least half the song."

Talk about a weirdo, this guy!

So I sang in my green dress, my red hair dressed almost in an Afro by the hairdresser on the set, my makeup completely overdone, not that I dared to say anything. And do you know they let me and Billy Noekowski do the whole song because Mr. Lake forgot to yell "Cut!" halfway through.

They all clapped when I finished.

And I bowed. Regal and queenlike, hair vibrating like a hive of bees, I bowed.

Now I've never taken drugs. In fact, given the circumstances of my life, I've emerged relatively unscathed as far as vices, thanks to that bunch of oddballs in Vermont. But acclaim is like a drug.

I felt their approval.

I felt their admiration.

And it covered my desperation like a combed sheepskin all the while snaring me like the purest powder of cocaine.

Bansy struck then, slowly inching his way toward me like a giant snail, secreting a trail of promised silver and maybe even gold.

"You don't need to be here at Suds 'N' Strikes, Charmaine. Bigger things await you."

Mr. Lake overheard. "He's right. Although, not much of this kind of singing going on these days, Bansy. You don't sing disco, do you?"

"I can sing anything, anytime, anywhere."

"Is keeping your clothing on a requirement?"

I gasped.

"I'll take that as a yes," Bansy said. "How old are you, anyway?"

"Nineteen," I lied.

"Twenty-one would be better." Mr. Lake reached into the pocket of his bowling shirt for a pack of Dunhill cigarettes. From what I heard from the crew, Mr. Lake liked to dress for each shoot to fit into his surroundings.

"Then I'll be twenty-one. Shoot, mister, with this much makeup on, I look twenty-five if I look a day."

Two weeks later, I found myself on a bus to New Jersey.

The same Greyhound station that welcomed me to Baltimore, bid me good-bye, along with Anita, Frank, and Luella.

But I had to keep movin' on. Just like the song says.

4

I first sang at a sorry old club in Atlantic City, after they legalized the casinos again. My first real live nonbowling alley gig and it occurred at some sorry old club with nothing but alcohol, some little round tables sprouting like mushrooms from a floor that looked completely capable of producing honest-to-goodness fungus. Of course, without a gambling license, that club was destined for a quick slope downhill and I slid right along with it.

That stupid Bansy man.

Mr. and Mrs. Reasin tried to warn me, but I saw film stars swirling all around my head like little Tinkerbells with wands trailing stardust, or maybe I should say *starlet*-dust.

I might have known better.

I suspect that some Divine protection was in the works at the Satin Dahlia as well as some Divine workings-in-general.

Maybe it was just dumb luck, Myrtle Charmaine.

The night that impacted my life the most as it now stands, years later here with Harlan and all, was a partic-

ular Friday night in June of 1977. I followed another act,
an act called the Gemstones.

One girl named Ruby, the other named Grace.

We went out for drinks afterward at a more respectable
club and that summer we lazied through the afternoons,
lying out on the beach. Well, I lay under an umbrella, not
only due to my pale skin but because in the city that puts
on the Miss America pageant year after year, I still didn't
have too much to be proud about with my bustline. I got
a view of Dorothy Benham who was to become Miss
America 1977, and was thankful I never had to stand next
to her because, let me tell you, my white trash roots
would have clearly shown! And not only that, she sings
opera. Opera always wins out over any other type of
singing on the singers' scales.

But the talking sure was good there on the beach with
Ruby and Grace! As girls do, we learned all about each
other the first day.

Grace lay in the sun, bronzing away. "I'm from a regular family, I guess. Got parts in the school plays and all
and tried Broadway, but the only job I ever landed lasted
an hour and led me to this gig. Ruby here's the one with
the story."

Grace turned over and fell asleep.

And Ruby went on. Foster homes, too. We connected
over that. But Ruby wasn't able to lock the door to her
room like I did, so Ruby eventually ran away and involved herself in all sorts of things, and all sorts of guys.
"I could tell you some tales about the kind of losers there
are out there. Makes you want to become a nun or a les-
bian."

I gasped.

Ruby laughed. "You are straight off the farm, aren't you?"

"You'd be surprised."

I told her my tale. But I told her Mama died. Even then, it wasn't anything I wanted anyone new in my life to know.

By mid-July the Songbirds took flight. I designed and sewed us some classy costumes and we found a couple of lower-order casino gigs. Together we rented a room at a boarding house and I held down the fort on nights that Ruby and Grace had dates. Shades of Vermont still lingered in that I felt too young and inexperienced to get involved in that sort of thing again.

Thank the Lord for that!

5

*W*hile Ruby never stayed out all night during our time in Atlantic City, Grace sure did. She'd pick up men after shows and we wouldn't see her again sometimes until the next gig. There Ruby and I would be waiting in the casino dressing room, costumes in hand. I've got to give it to her, though, she was only late once and Ruby and I covered beautifully with her alto and my melody going. We even decided that night that if Grace should ever up-and-at-'em we'd do just fine as a duo. We figured we'd add a couple of little dance steps if she ever did leave because we could do that sort of thing and Grace couldn't. We weren't talking major tap or jazz moves, just some dips and swirls like those girl groups in the '60s used to do.

But we knew we'd never kick Grace out and we knew she would never leave, because she needed people. Grace needed people to parent her, and Ruby and I didn't.

One night Ruby and I sat on the bed sewing sequins on the costumes I decided to make since December was coming. Little Santa outfits. Spangled and sparkling and something more out of a Christmas wine TV advertisement than anything to do with the real meaning of the holiday. I hadn't thought of the real meaning of Christmas for a while now.

"You know that 'people who need people' song?" I asked.

"Of course. Sappiest darn thing I've ever heard!" Now Ruby could take her beautiful features and contort them into the ugliest faces known to mankind when she felt deeply or had an opinion, which was a lot because Ruby was a thinking type of girl with rubbery type of skin.

"Those words make me think, though."

"What about? How sappy it is?"

"Oh, shush, Ruby. Think about it, 'people who need people are the luckiest people in the world.'"

"You think so?"

"Well, why wouldn't that be the case?"

"I don't know. But it feels wrong to me."

"So how would you write those lyrics?"

"People who love people are the luckiest people in the world."

"So, it's more of an 'I choose' type of thing?"

Ruby tied off the line of thread she'd been attaching the sequins with. "Definitely. It's on your own terms."

"Hmm."

"I tell you what, girl, I don't *need* anybody. And you don't either. And look at Grace."

"Yeah. Out with all sorts of guys, night after night."

"Exactly. That's a people that needs people."

I handed her the red thread. "I see what you mean."

"I'm insightful, Charmaine. You are, too. Lives like ours either wear you down to the bone or give you calluses, thoughts, lessons."

"You think Grace is wearing down to the bone?"

"With her upbringing, she's just starting lessons you and I learned by the time we were twelve, I'll bet."

I reached for the embroidery scissors and snipped off a length of white to begin attaching the fake fur to our little caps, à la *White Christmas*.

"So let me ask you a question, Ruby."

"Shoot."

"If we're so great, why are we sitting here sewing Santa-helper costumes and Grace is out on the town?"

"We choose, Charmaine. We choose to be here."

I shrugged. "Well, okay, I guess. Sounds a little hollow to me, though."

Ten minutes later, I threw down my handwork. "I'm tired of sitting around. Let's go out."

"Where to?"

"Who knows, Ruby? But we need to have a little adventure. Besides, I could use a little fresh air. This place is awfully small."

I swear a camper van had more room than that apartment.

"Well, all right. Just promise me we don't have to set foot in a club or a casino."

"That's an easy promise to make. Talk about the saddest places on earth."

We shrugged into our winter coats, locked up the apartment, and headed out toward the boardwalk.

"This is going to be a chilly stroll," Ruby said.

"I don't care."

"Me either, I guess."

"You know, Ruby, I always thought casinos were supposed to be fun places."

She sideglanced me. "Just come straight to the point this time, baby."

"Nobody sitting at those tables or at the slots ever smiles."

"You know, you're right. I never thought about it before. You're really something, Charmaine."

And I remembered Mrs. Evans then and how she'd always tell me exactly the same thing. I couldn't say I was really ashamed of my life at that time. Singing was fun, I didn't feel it was wrong. We sang clean songs, dressed modestly albeit with some flash and sass. But I knew I could do more with that gift box still sitting there in my throat. And did singing in casinos count as burying your gift in a napkin? Well, if it did, that napkin was most definitely a cocktail napkin.

"You ever think we could be doing more with our lives, Ruby?"

"All the time, girl. All the time."

6

*R*uby and I heard loud singing and stomping and clapping coming from a sidestreet off the boardwalk.

"What in heaven's name is that?" I asked.

"Sounds like revival to me, glory to God!"

"Oh, my lands, you tickle me, Ruby!" I tied my scarf more tightly about my neck. "Does that fit in with the definition of a club?"

"As far as I'm concerned . . . yes, if you define it by how likely you are to get hit on. But let's go in anyway. It's warm and there's no boozers."

We turned right, hopped down the stone steps and headed toward the music and noise. A couple of drunks wafted by like two old hamburger wrappers, balled up and smelling of yesterday's grease.

The older one wiped his runny nose with the back of his hand. "Ha! Ha! We did it again. Got the meal and didn't stay for the preaching!"

Oh, my Lord, the other one was a woman! I could hardly believe the soft voice that came out of her. "You're going to ruin it for the both of us, Glen."

"Shut your trap, Gina. Just shut it up right now."

And poor Gina did.

Ruby's eyes met mine. We continued toward what I guessed then was a rescue mission or something. So much for no boozers being present. A cross, outlined in bluish-white neon tubing swung in the breeze on rusted hinges. "Do you think they're married, those two hobos?"

"Beats me." Ruby shook her head. "Bet they've got kids all through the New Jersey foster system."

"Yeah."

"We're real people, Charmaine."

"Who, foster kids?" My lands, that was out of the blue for Ruby.

"Yeah. You know what I mean?"

"I guess so. Like there's kids, Jere and Gloria's kids, and Bob and Jean's kids, and Lou and Pete's kids, and then there's foster kids, like we're some big nebulous blob with kids' arms and legs sticking out?"

"Something like that, although I've always thought of it more like being in some black hole of a womb by the lady with the name 'Foster.' The Foster kids. They don't mean nothing to nobody."

"Amazing the difference an apostrophe 's' makes."

"All the difference in the world."

The light from the mission struck our faces.

"You ever want to get married and have your own kids someday, Ruby?"

She shook her head, then shrugged. "I don't know yet. What if I died or something after they were born? Then what?"

The music inside stopped.

"I want my own kids. And I want them to have an apostrophe 's' before their title of 'kid.' And I want them to have two names. I want it to be Charmaine and Ralph's kids or whatever."

"Ralph?"

"It's the first name that came to mind."

"Still."

"Ruby, that isn't the point."

Ruby curled her long fingers around the door handle. "I know, but couldn't you have come up with something a little more suave than Ralph right off the bat?"

"I guess not. My lands, here I was opening up and you start in on me."

She yanked on the door. "Let's get inside where it's warmer."

"You said it."

We walked inside.

Oh, my goodness! I saw the collection of misfits inside the large, unadorned room and I wanted to fall to my knees and weep, but all I could do was let the usherette, aged and smiling, dressed in a bright yellow Salvation Army-style uniform, lead me and Ruby to the front row of wooden folding chairs.

The music started up again.

7

*T*hank You, God. Thank You, God. Thank You, God.

I got to my feet there in the rescue mission, feeling the warmth of a rickety heating system that clanged a tinny merengue in direct opposition to the rhythm of the old hymn belched from an old organ. Under the pressure of the fingers of a man who reminded me of the cowardly lion, only thinner, "At Calvary" stuttered.

"Years I spent in vanity and pride," they all sang with conviction.

Vanity? Pride?

These people?

Now, me, I realized, could attest to both of these earthly attributes. Up there every day jiggling my hiney in time to Supremes' tunes. Pouting out Shirelle lyrics like I knew anything about what the songs said. And the Marvellettes? Don't even get me started. That "Mr. Postman" song gets me to this day. Because rest assured, after Mama left I felt like I lived for that man, hoping against hope he'd be bearing a maternal love letter.

Stop in the name of love.

Reflections of the way life used to be.

Baby love, my baby love.

Mama said there'd be days like these.

A piano joined in with the organ, and the man's fingers moved with the tenderness of the lover I hoped to have someday.

Ruby handed me a Kleenex. "Let's sit down before we make more of a scene."

"Well, at least the song is still going."

"I like it. Have you ever heard it before?"

"'At Calvary'? Of course! Who's never heard of 'At Calvary'?"

"Me."

"Oh."

"Come on."

We sat on old wooden fold-out chairs painted a chalky yellow. "You think these seats will hold us?" I whispered.

"It's worth the risk. Look there's a songbook on the floor." She picked it up. "What did you say that song was called?"

I told her.

Ruby turned to the song and her quilt of an alto wrapped around the notes and warmed them to perfection. I couldn't sing, so I let her do it for the both of us.

"You were made to sing gospel music, Ruby," I whispered, feeling almost prophetic.

Ruby just smiled, nodded, and kept on reading notes.

I remembered what it was like to pray as I sat there listening to Ruby sing. The hymns continued for ten more minutes. "Mansion Over a Hilltop." "Rock of Ages."

"Nearer My God to Thee."

Ruby's voice filled me.

The heating system seemed to say, "Come, come, come. Come, come, come."

"Nearer my God to Thee, nearer to Thee."

For some people, spiritual renewal comes on gradually like the flowers of spring. The crocuses of realization bloom. The daffodils of decision open up next. Then all sorts of blossoms burst forth. The white blooms of obedience. The red tulips of intimate prayer and finally, the roses of unending praise.

For others, spiritual renewal is like venturing into a hothouse in mid-winter, heaters at full blast behind a snowstorm swirling about the crystal panes of glass. The door opens, and more heat ventures out than cold swishes in with your entrance and you find yourself barely able to breathe in the vapors of blooming flowers. Hibiscus, tea roses, hyacinth, paper whites, lilies, and gardenias. Oh, the white pure gardenias that puff out breaths of sweet perfume from their gentle petals, rounded, sweet petals that expand when your head descends in shame and fashion a pillow, a perfumed, Holy bosom.

"Cast all your cares upon me."

"I will give you rest."

Oh, Jesus. Oh, Jesus.

My Lord and Savior, I am weak and weary.

I prayed for Him to let me lay my head upon His chest, to hear the beating of His holy Heart. I prayed that He'd fine-tune my ears. I gave myself back to Him.

"I'll give back the gift you gave me," I whispered.

Nobody wants your gift, Myrtle Charmaine, least of all God.

"Be quiet, Mama," I whispered. "This has nothing to do with you."

"What?" Ruby leaned over. A tear from her great brown eye splashed on my forearm.

I took her hand. "Ruby?"

"It's nothing, Char. Look, here comes the preacher man."

8

I never expected the preacher to be the same guy that had been pouring punch over at a side table as the singing was going on. In fact, I didn't really notice him, until the piano player stood up and said, "And now it's time for the preachin'! Reverend Hopewell?"

And that was it. The entire introduction.

Trust me on this one. We're a lot slicker these days, but not quite as dandy as that couple down in Charlotte.

The guy at the punch table straightened up, finished ladling the red mixture into a Styrofoam cup, smoothed his suspenders with shaking, flat hands, then grabbed a big brown Bible at the corner of the table. Now I mean really big, like the wee bit smaller cousin of the family Bible. Hardback, too.

"My, my," Ruby whispered and I held back the laughter.

"Must be serious about God's Word, Ruby."

"Either that or he's half blind and needs the big-print version."

Back then, I wondered how Ruby knew of the large-print version. Turns out there was one in the closet of her room in one of her foster homes, but I didn't ask right then because Reverend Hopewell thumped his Bible down on the lectern and stared.

He just stood there looking at the crowd and all I could think was how glad I was we weren't in our costumes or he might have thought we were prostitutes or something. But we sat there in our hats and coats looking respectable and his eyes alighted first on Ruby who nodded once like some wise old sagey person, and then they rested on me. I couldn't see the color of his eyes because of the peckish lighting there in the mission, not to mention it sprayed a general green glow everywhere, but they were rimmed by dark lashes that spiked out in isosceles triangles underneath his blondish brows.

Half his mouth lifted, then he looked down at the Book, slid a slender, nonmanicured hand over dark blond hair that seemed to be thinning before our very eyes, and cleared his throat.

"The man needs a hairpiece," Ruby whispered.

"Are you going to listen to the message or not?" I hissed.

"Okay, okay. I'll be quiet."

"I'd appreciate that, Ruby."

Then the preacher said, "Let's pray."

So we did.

And it was just like he brought us right up to God's throne and that he knew what was in our hearts. He talked about waywardness and loneliness and asked the Holy Spirit to comfort. He talked about sin and stain, and praised Jesus for His blood that washes it all away. He prayed for every one there, rich and poor, male and fe-

male, black and white, down and out, "and all ways in between dear Lord, because You know and love us all.
Amen."

"You believe that?" Ruby whispered.

"Believe what?"

"That God loves everyone."

"Of course."

"Oh."

The preacher cleared his throat. Oh, what a skinny
guy! Thank the Lord he didn't have a big old Adam's
apple or he'd have been stereotypical. His hair shone a
soft gold, fine and precious, and his eyes were kind.
That's all. Just kind eyes with dark lashes.

He'd slipped on a plaid sportscoat during his walk to
the podium. The shades of burgundy, gray, and green,
caught my eye, too. I realized the jacket was thin, close
to threadbare, with faded fibers bunched up too close in
some places, spaced too far apart in others.

I leaned closer to Ruby. "If he's like most preachers,
get ready for some fire and brimstone."

"Mm."

Then the preacher closed his eyes and prayed to himself for about ten seconds and I liked that although I wondered if it was for show like those swimmers and
Olympic athletes who make the sign of the cross before
competing, leaving you wondering if they really prayed
at all.

But his fingertips skated lighter than fairies' feet on
the slick surface of the lectern and they vibrated a little
like tender branches in a winter.

This nervous preacher was asking God to calm him. I

just knew that. For some reason, I was able to crawl into his head.

When he began his sermon, I did my own praying, because I knew that it wasn't an accident that I sat there, perched precariously on a yellow wooden fold-out chair in the middle of a sad little storefront mission in Atlantic City.

Then a fiery message gushed like a consuming lava river from the lips of the preacher who had been shivering in the winter of nerves only a moment before, a fiery message like nothing I'd ever heard before. But it wasn't the fire of hot coals or blowtorches. It was a cauterizing fire, sent from God to clean out the festering misery of the soul. See when a man is given a gift like Harlan's and he uses it for the Lord, you can believe him when he tells you God loves you and wants you to live a victorious life of faith. You can believe him when he says, "Choose you this day whom you will serve."

"God loves you! He's calling you to come. Won't you come today as brother Windsor plays the invitation?"

And he pleaded with the Holy Spirit to come and touch hearts and turn them toward the cross. And brother Windsor began "Just As I Am" and I sang, too, one of the only voices in the crowd.

"Do you know Jesus? Why not come and kneel at the altar and make sure you're going to heaven? Why not become His child?"

I turned at the touch of Ruby's hand on my arm. She cried and said, "Come with me, Charmaine. Will you?"

"Of course, Ruby."

Harlan held out a hand. "Now is the hour of your salvation."

And we knelt there together as Ruby prayed to have her sins forgiven. It really is like the song says. "Oh, precious is the flow, that makes me white as snow. No other fount I know. Nothing but the blood of Jesus."

9

$\mathcal{I}$n the back corner of the mission hall the preacher and Ruby sat in deep discussion. They leaned forward, knee-to-knee on two of the fold-out chairs, Ruby asking questions and this Harlan Hopewell fellow answering them, flipping through the pages of a much smaller Bible, looking her in the eyes, patting her arm, nodding his head, shaking his head. One time, I believe I saw a tear glisten on his cheek.

Having consumed about five cups of Hawaiian Punch, I read a flyer about the Harlan Hopewell Evangelistic Crusade once with each cup. The crusade consisted of the preacher, Harlan Hopewell, and the piano player, Henry Windsor, and the brochure said they met in seminary in 1968 where they started going to prisons "to spread the Gospel message that Jesus saves!"

I did the math. He was about thirty-one years old now and sure looked younger, like a gangly older teen. He hadn't lost that innocent earnestness of someone on the first round of dough-rising in the ministry. He didn't appear to have been punched down yet by fellow Christians, the air of pure intentions and calling puffing out with hopes and dreams. But I assumed that would come. Sooner or later, it always came. Unless of course, he stayed on the road and didn't have to deal with the same old complaining Christians day after day. According to the brochure, they'd been to every state below the Mason-Dixon line and east of the Mississippi.

Preacher Hopewell grew up in Chesapeake, Virginia, and Henry Windsor hailed from Greenville, South Carolina. A picture of the two of them in front of the High Point Theological Seminary sign gave me indication they'd been called to do exactly what they were doing, for behind them the motto, TELLING OTHERS IN SPIRIT AND IN TRUTH shone in gold letters. I guessed Windsor was the spirit and Hopewell was the truth.

I looked over at Ruby and Preacher Hopewell and realized this discussion would last a while. The old couple that ran the mission walked over to me on Hush Puppies.

The woman, in a plain, long-sleeved peach floral dress with matching belt, smiled and said with a soft, high voice, "They might be a while. Can I get you a cup of coffee?"

I shook my head. "No, thank you. I just drank so much punch I couldn't put anything else in!"

"I'm Loretta and this is Joe, my husband. We run this place."

"I'm Charmaine Whitehead."

I'd noticed the couple earlier in the evening, sitting in two chairs at the back storefront window where Ruby and the preacher now sat. The lights of the neon cross outside illumined their hoary heads, the lady's tarnished with yellow, the man's gradually getting darker the farther down it flowed from the top of his large head.

"How did you come into the mission tonight?" Joe asked, straightening his brown tie and hiking up his plaid pants by a belt with a huge brass buckle that said "Mack" with a bulldog looking out from between the legs of the "M."

"Ruby and I went out for a little walk after a night of sewing and came in to get warm."

"Good thing. Looks like the Lord had plans for your friend here."

Loretta nodded, turned, and poured herself a punch. "Isn't it wonderful? What about you, Charmaine? Do you know Jesus as your personal Lord and Savior?" I noticed the back of her hair was caught in a braided bun, a large braided bun, but the bangs were freshly curled and sprayed as stiff as feathers.

"I got saved when I was thirteen years old. Right in our kitchen."

Joe hiked up his pants again. "Well, praise the Lord."

"Amen to that!" Loretta said.

"How long you folks been here at this mission?"

And so these good people invited me back to their little apartment that consisted of a bedroom, bathroom, and a sitting area holding only two rose-colored recliners and a straight chair. Joe insisted I sit in his recliner.

"We've been here at the mission for the past twenty years. Were on the mission field in South America for twenty-five. We're Pentecostal Holiness, you know."

Well, I didn't. But it sure explained that big bun in her hair, but not his belt buckle! That seemed a little flashy for a Holiness type.

"But we wanted to come home, right Loretta?"

"That's right." Loretta reached beside her chair and

pulled out a lap desk on which some puzzle pieces and a magnifying glass rested. It appeared as if Joe had attached very thin molding around the edges to keep the pieces from sliding off. She placed clear pink reading glasses on her nose.

I set my purse on the floor. "How long has that vagabond couple been coming in here? The ones that left early?"

"They come every night. And they never stay," she said.

I leaned forward. "And yet you still let them come and eat? I'm so glad."

Joe just smiled. "Miss Whitehead, we're not the types to turn hungry people away."

"That's right, sweetie. We figure sooner or later they'll stay. It's not up to us to be picky about the rules when souls are at stake. God always provides enough food. And they're our own rules, so if we break them . . ." She just waved the magnifying glass.

An idea struck me. "Ruby and I sing in casinos. We have a little group with another girl called 'the Songbirds' and well, whether or not we should be singing in casinos and all isn't the issue, but what I was wondering is maybe I could come on Sundays and sing here. I don't have a home church yet, and, oh, I don't know, maybe you already have a singer and I shouldn't even be asking."

Loretta set down her magnifying glass. "Are you kidding me? We could use a little life, not to mention prettiness, here in this godforsaken place."

Joe cleared his throat, reached over and laid a tender hand on his wife's knee. "Actually, Miss Whitehead,

God's about the only thing we really do have. Sometimes Loretta gets discouraged. Sometimes it's hard to be here day after day."

I pointed to the doorway. "That Harlan Hopewell fellow has the right idea. Going from place to place. Almost a nomad for the Lord!"

"That kind of life appeal to you?" Loretta asked.

"Not really. You know, I'm nineteen years old," I lied, "and I've never really lived in a home of my own." I didn't want to explain. There'd be time for that. "Will you tell my friend Ruby that I'm heading back to the apartment and I'll meet her there?"

"Of course."

Joe and I stood to our feet. Loretta remained in her recliner. "Nice meeting you, Miss."

"Please, just call me Charmaine. Especially since I'll be back on Sunday."

"We'll be counting on it!" Loretta chimed and told me the service began at nine A.M.

Ruby and Preacher Hopewell were steeped in prayer, so I shuffled into my coat and let myself out onto the street, careful not to let the brass bell tinkle against the glass door.

I looked for the vagrant couple all the way home, but didn't see them. I thought about them and I wondered who their parents were. I wondered why I didn't end up like them. I wondered if someday, maybe I would.

But see, if I was on the other side of the microphone, holding onto it with all my might, ministering to others with notes and words, maybe I'd divide the chance of becoming just like them in half and then in half again.

Grace was still out when I arrived home.

Not that I thought she'd be there.

But in the mailbox sat a letter from Luella telling me all sorts of things about the kids, her artwork, and life at Suds 'N' Strikes. I couldn't understand for the life of me, just then, why it seemed so important to leave Baltimore behind.

10

*R*uby and I sang together at the mission that next Sunday. Harlan Hopewell gave the message to me and Ruby, Joe and Loretta, and the kitchen staff volunteers and the lady in the yellow uniform. It was a beautiful day, unseasonably warm.

"They tend to stay on the streets on days like this," Loretta whispered when I asked where all the homeless were.

After the message on the Prodigal Son that made me feel worse than I did before it was preached, we convened around one of the big tables in the large dining room.

Joe handed me a platter of turkey. "We always have a nice meal on Sundays. There's a benefactor who owns a food service company that supplies the meats here. Don't know what we'd do without him."

We filled our plates with Sunday dinner. And I caught Preacher Hopewell's eyes on me, and he smiled with a lanky sort of grin. I looked down and stabbed my pile of mashed potatoes.

"How long will you be staying here in Atlantic City?" Ruby asked.

"For two more weeks. Then it's off to Little Rock."

I turned to Henry. "You play a fine piano there, Mr. Windsor."

"It's even better when you two girls are singing to it. That was real pretty this morning."

"Thanks," Ruby said, and I swear she blushed.

"Thank you."

Preacher Hopewell looked at me some more. And I turned redder than my stupid hair that had blown to mammoth proportions on the walk over.

"Your message was beautiful, Preacher Hopewell," I said.

"Call me Harlan."

"Call me Charmaine."

Ruby smirked. "Call me anytime."

"Oh, Ruby!"

After we helped clean up the kitchen, Harlan suggested we all take a walk on the boardwalk. Joe and Loretta said they always take a nap on Sunday afternoons. Ruby said she'd already told Henry she'd help him work out new harmonies on "His Eye Is on the Sparrow," and so I said, "It's just me. Is that okay?"

"I've heard Ruby's story, but I haven't heard yours, Charmaine."

I put on my light jacket, and he shrugged into his worn sportscoat and we set out in the springlike weather. Thank the good Lord I was able to steer the conversation away from my story and onto Harlan's. Thank the good Lord he hailed from a normal family who lived in Chesapeake and owned a garage that specialized in brake work and lube jobs. "But we did everything else mechanical, too. I grew up underneath cars for the most part. We had long days, I tell you and we worked hard."

"Is your daddy still alive?"

He shook his head. "No. Died when I was in seminary. Got mouth cancer."

"Oh, my lands! Did he chew tobacco?"

"Yep. Never saw my father without something tucked in front of his teeth."

"What about your mother?"

"She's something! One of those happy people that roll with the punches. I've often said the woman for me will be that happy type like Ma."

"Sounds like a saint."

He laughed. "Oh, no. A temper went along with that, but they were only temporary storms, sometimes even like summer storms where the rain is falling and the sun is shining at the same time. My father worshiped her."

"Any brothers and sisters?"

"A sister named Bee who lives in Tennessee. She takes all my mail and calls for me when I'm on the road. And my brother E.J. who just got divorced."

"Oh, my!"

"Don't I know it. The woman he married was one of those sad-sack types that blamed everybody and everything else for her troubles. She was something. My brother couldn't do anything right and he tried so hard. Tore E.J. apart. Here he did everything he could for the woman, supported her, cooked, cleaned, did the laundry, took care of the kids, my mother did too—watched them during the day, and then *she* ended up divorcing *him*."

"Oh, no!"

"Yep. Got in with some crackpot psychiatrist who told her E.J. was 'enabling' her. Whatever *that* means. That she had major issues. Whatever that means. And she ditched him, leaving behind their two children, ran off to Virginia Beach and opened up an ice cream stand on the boardwalk. Says she's never been happier. 'All the fresh air and sunshine is what I needed, E.J. I just needed to be free to be happy. And you couldn't make me happy.'"

I couldn't help but chuckle at his mimicking voice. "I'm sorry, but you sounded so funny."

"It's okay. It's not your problem anyway, Charmaine. I'm sorry I'm going on about it, but you're so easy to talk to."

"I try to be openhearted."

"Ma is like that, too."

I smiled. "That's nice, Harlan. She sounds like a good woman."

He walked me back to our boarding house and stood with me by the steps that led up the side of the building to our floor. "I know you didn't want to talk about yourself, Charmaine. I wanted you to know that I knew. I didn't want you to think all I cared about was myself."

"No, not at all."

"Because people look at preachers that way, you know. And I guess it's deserved. But I'm trying not to be one of those. I'm trying to be a good, decent man."

I looked at him and knew something. I knew that my father was definitely NOT a man like Harlan Hopewell.

"You're going to be around for two weeks, then?" I asked.

"Yes."

"Well, maybe one night you can come hear the Songbirds over at the casino. You don't have to gamble or nothing like that!"

He laughed. "I'd like that."

"And you can meet Grace. She needs Jesus so badly, Harlan."

"We all do."

"I get scared for her, though."

"What nights do you sing?"

"Every night but Monday and Tuesday."

We made arrangements for him to come late Friday night, after the service at the mission. But I knew I'd see him before then. I knew that for the first time in my life I'd met a man who was capable of carrying my baggage.

I said good-bye and let myself into our little room. Grace lay asleep on her bed. The room stank. She'd turned the heat up full blast. I almost threw something at her.

Shameful. The girl was so shameful. How could she waste her youth, her beauty, and the love invested in her by her parents on dates for drinks? So far she'd been able to keep these dates at arm's length. Or so she claimed. But luck like that runs out sooner or later. At least I didn't wish that on her.

I continued working on the Santa costumes, sitting on the outside steps, sewing the final sequined holly leaves onto the hats. I fumed in Grace's direction and I despised her with such strength I hoped the girl would never wake up and do us all a favor.

Oh, Lord! I prayed, the thought sending fire of another sort of shame through my arteries and up to my head, causing it to bow further. I thought of the Woman at the Well again and how Jesus didn't judge her.

But the anger wouldn't leave me.

Grace woke up an hour later and scraped herself off the bed and down the hall to the bathroom where I assumed she retched up those free pretzels and peanuts.

I hurried inside.

On the bed, a large bloodstain sank into the bedding. I knew Grace had her period last week. Women's cycles always seem to get in sync when they live together and we were already on the same wavelength in the menstruation department.

Did she know?

Did she remember what had happened during her drunken stupor?

Had she been raped or was this something else?

I quickly stripped the bed, folded a towel in half and placed it over the stain on the mattress and pulled on fresh sheets.

Groaning, Grace entered the room just as I was finishing and fell into the bed. "Oh, Charmaine, I feel just awful."

"Go back to sleep honey. I'm right here. You'll be okay soon. Just sleep it off."

Had I done it? Had I protected her from herself?

Nobody can protect you from yourself, Myrtle Charmaine.

But I knew how things festered deep within the mind. Things the person who owned that very brain didn't even know existed.

See I've got my own demons. I know this. I know it right well and so far in the years since Mama left I've been able to somehow keep them quiet. But they'll come out someday. Or maybe somebody is going to drag them out of me.

There's a big demon and I am sure of it. But as of yet, I cannot put a finger on what it is. But he rules all the other ones, the smaller ones, the overt ones, the lying ones. And when he comes out, I don't really know if I'll be able to overcome him.

By the way, he looks like the mountain demon in *Fantasia*. Only he's purple.

It wasn't easy, I can tell you that. Anita and Frank ended up having to sign their permission for my marriage to Harlan before two witnesses and mail it to me. They became my legal guardians for about two weeks. And then I had to get a copy of my lease for identification. Oh, they get you coming and going in these government offices.

Harlan was mad, boy. He pulled me aside there at the marriage license office. "What do you mean you're only seventeen?"

"That's what I am."

"I thought you told me you were eighteen."

"I lied, Harlan."

"Don't lie to me, Charmaine. I can't take that. I can't take it that you won't trust me with the truth."

"Do you still want to marry me?"

I thought of our spring courtship, how I felt so safe with Harlan, so loved and cherished. We wrote letter after letter when he went away to preach. But home base became Atlantic City.

So we stood there in the mission and said our "I do"s

with Loretta sniffing right behind me and Ruby crying beside me. We invited all the bums in off the street for the reception.

Ruby joined up with the crusade not long after. And Grace "people who need people" Underhill swore at the both of us "up one side and down the other," as Ruby says.

Part Four

1

*W*e see all kinds of people at our crusades. Up-and-comers. Down and outers. To and froers. Over and underers. There's people that smell like roses. There's others that look like they haven't intersected with a tub in weeks unless it was some old rusted one they'd slept in at a junkyard. Lots of them have no home in which to settle down, and boy, can I relate. Call me "Mrs. Motor home Hopewell"!

You ever notice how many for sale signs really poke through lawns in your town? They spring forth from the earth like some sort of fungus. Seems like everybody is selling something. Especially houses. If there's one thing I inherited from Mama it's the want of a home of my own.

Winnebagos don't count.

No matter what anybody may tell you, they just don't count. Retirees' words don't count because they've already owned a home so they can't know how much a camper van doesn't count if you've already had a real place of your own.

First of all, they don't include Garburators. At least ours doesn't.

Second, they build the cabinets in the kitchen areas out of that particle board stuff, thin and unsubstantial. And if you try to paint them, I can tell you right now, it won't be long before all sorts of paint dandruff drifts down all over the place. Don't try putting border up around the top of the walls either. What a nightmare that turned out to be! Harlan rarely loses his temper with me, but that time . . . my lands!

I may sound ungrateful and I suppose I am, because after what happened with Mrs. Evans and then that Richard Lewellyn, I might have ended up homeless, a drug addict, or even a woman of the evening.

But I still dream about a place that when you slam the door it doesn't shake the entire living space.

It's been four years since Harlan and I married and I figure it's time I finally give in and learn how to cook. Now living in an RV can make that difficult, but with just the two of us, how big of an oven do I really need?

I almost burn the place down making cherries jubilee. Even had to sneak into a liquor store somewhere in Rocky Mount, North Carolina, for the sherry.

Harlan scratches his sparsely populated scalp in wonderment when I carry it to the dinette in the RV. Flaming away, the dessert scares him just as much as it scares me. He grabs the pan and throws it right out the door onto my new pair of rain boots.

Why me, God? Dexter boots! Seventy-five percent off the clearance price!

Now, I don't know much about much, but I do know this: no matter how bad things seem, there's always somebody worse off than you! And so when the apostle Paul said "Give thanks in all things, for this is the will of God in Christ Jesus concerning you," I think this applies to the negative as well as the positive.

Thank you, Lord, that I'm not a parapelegic.

Thank you, Lord, that I'm not pickin' trash in search of dinner.

Thank you, Lord, that I've never wintered without a good warm coat with a zipper that works.

Thank you, Lord, I've never had an evil uncle or Mama never brought home an evil boyfriend that abused me sexually or hung me in a closet because I breathed wrong.

Thank you, Lord, that, although I've gone hungry, it's only been because I'm dieting.

See what I mean?

So many true horrors abound, not ruined shoes and desserts, and we can either contribute to them or redeem them. That's what I view myself as nowadays. Motor home and all. A redemptress.

I like the sound of that. Although if the term goes abroad the women's libbers might say, "Oh, no, Charmaine, you're not a 'redemptress,' you're a 'female redeemer.'"

I'm still singing all these years later, and Harlan is preaching in Lynchburg at some revival meetings. Mid-July pounds us hard and, well, pass the deodorant and turn up the A/C is all I can say!

Harlan's meeting with the folks over at Oak Baptist, going over last-minute details, so I head up to River Ridge Mall to do a little shopping. Not that Lynchburg is the fashion capital of the world or nothing, but I find a cute little sweatshirt for Harlan's nephew at Thal-heimer's. I prefer to sew my own clothing as we're trav-eling down the road. I head out into the mall.

A girl cries on the bench near the fountain. So, me being who I am, I just walk on over to the Orange Julius stand, order a couple of Orange Juliuses, and hurry back over to the fountain before she can leave.

"Here." I hand her the drink.

And she looks up at me, distrusting first, then slightly amazed. She takes the drink, though.

"I'm Charmaine, what's your name?"

"Brandi." And then she sips, a strand of her dirty-blond hair catching in the corner of her mouth. She pulls it back and over the shoulder of her T-shirt.

"I saw you were crying and I just thought you might want something to drink. Crying always makes me so thirsty."

You know, I can keep talking and talking, and I fight against it all the time. So instead I just determine to sit there and sip along with her. I don't ask her what she cries about, though I am dying to know. I don't ask if I can help. Chances are I can't.

I'm not pretending this isn't awkward, either. I feel a little off-kilter.

"Did you see that cute little outfit in the window at the Weathervane?" I ask after figuring that babble is better than awkward this time.

"The yellow one?"

"Uh-huh. I just love these twinsets they're coming out with, don't you?"

"They're okay."

And we sit some more. I mean, after all, twinsets seem

a little old-fashioned now that this shaker knit sweater-stuff covers everybody these days. And with men's undershirts underneath! Watching these kids wearing their sweatshirts inside-out with men's boxers for shorts tickles me! Harlan and I have ourselves some good laughs over that one.

"You hungry?" I ask.

"No."

"Me neither. My appetite just goes right away when I'm upset. Well, anyway" —I sigh— "enjoy your drink. I was just in here to get my husband Harlan some new underwear and me some perfume and thought you looked thirsty."

She smiles. "Thanks for the drink."

"You need a ride home or anything?"

"I just live across Timberlake, behind the Hardee's."

"That's still quite a walk."

A group of guys over at the arcade steal her attention. Some dork-boy with a letter jacket stuffs half a candy bar inside his curled-under sneer and bellows, "Get over here now, Brandi."

She gets to her feet right away and then gives me an apologetic smile. "That's Brent. He's my boyfriend."

"Come on, Brandi!" he yells. "I said 'now'!"

I touch her arm and dig into my purse for my business card that says "Charmaine Hopewell, singer, evangelist, speaker" and my phone number, which is actually Harlan's sister's phone number, who takes our calls while we're on the road. Mrs. Evans's little songbird is sketched in light blue behind all the info. "If you ever need *anything*, call me."

And she takes the card and runs over to Brent the

Dork. He grabs the card, reads it, points to me, and laughs, making fun of all my red hair. But Brandi snatches the card away and buries it in the front pocket of her shorts.

That age is so hard to navigate. Mrs. Evans always knew what to do for sore hearts and that's one of those little things I cling to when I think about how Mama never did come back, how the weeks collected together to form months that ganged up into years until three pocket calendars had each one of their 365 squares Xed over. Three years. I stopped Xing then. I think about Mrs. Evans and how she availed herself to me and I choose to concentrate on that whenever I possibly can.

2

$\mathcal{I}$t's the first time I've visited their graves side by side. Patricia Jaffrey Evans and Sara Gray Jaffrey. Oh, Grandma Sara. I didn't know she'd died until I tried to find her in the nursing home. I imagine her eulogy, all the wonderful things her pastor had to say, how the people in the pews must have cried. I picture James and Francie, Stacy, and Mr. Evans sitting there listening. James would have been crying, Francie stone-faced. Mr. Evans would have been looking down at his hands or fidgeting with the flap on his suit coat pocket. And Stacy would have held me to her side as we both tried not to weep.

I lay a bouquet of red carnations upon each of their graves and I sang, "Home Beyond the River."

I'm not sure how long I sit there with them, their earthly husks buried deep into the soil. But the sunshine becomes a denser gold, the trees a darker green, and I know I'll see them again someday. And I'll thank them properly for saving me.

3

$\mathcal{T}$here are times when I lie back and gaze at the sky. Particular to no time of day, I choose rather to take my atmospheric thrills when the time is right.

Winnebagos actually aren't all that bad for sky watching, especially when Mel drives.

Sometimes, when Harlan prays in the bedroom cubicle at the back, Mel—our sound man and one of five people the Harlan Hopewell Evangelistic Crusade now employs—drives. He drives with as much attention as he tackles everything else. You should see him crimp wires, test mics, and coil the cords! A poetry of precision, our Mel.

His clothing, usually gray Dickies and a plaid shirt, bears the heavy, sharp markings of a hot iron. I'd bet fifty bucks he shines his rubber-soled wingtip shoes before each service and when he talks once in a blue moon, he says what he means and nothing more.

No wonder he never married.

Pity him.

Pity the girl.

And heaven help us, pity the children! Some folks are too good to have kids because the life for those kids could well fall into the "provoke not your children to wrath" category. Merely by existing with such precision and discipline, Mel George would be a stumbling block for his own offspring.

So when Mel drives I get to look all over the place with nothing to listen to but the hum of the motor, the bumps of the tar lines in the road, and sometimes Dr. J. Vernon McGee on the gospel radio.

I love that man. I love the way he asks my permission to speak there on the radio. "Now may I say to you . . . ?"

And me being who I am I always answer, "Knock yourself out, Reverend McGee!"

Now, if Mel's driving, this little smile stretches the right side of his mouth. If Harlan's driving, he laughs out loud and it is not a pretty sound, but I don't mind it.

Harlan says he's never met a funnier person. But I have to tell you this, Harlan makes me want to be funny. I never wanted to be before I met him. Sometimes I wish he'd take me a little more seriously, but nobody's perfect. Another lesson I've learned all too well! But he loves my sunny outlook and my smile. He says, "I can't imagine life without your smile. Don't ever change, Shug."

That's what he calls me, Shug. Another nickname for Myrtle Charmaine!

So far, I've been able to hide how hard it is for me to get out of bed and the blackness that every once in a while threatens to overwhelm me. I think to myself, "How much better can life get?" And the dragon stirs within, waiting for more happiness to be eaten upon his emergence. That is what I assume. I do hope I'm wrong.

Winter is especially grueling and many's the day I pretend I'm acting in a movie, that I'm playing the role of Charmaine Hopewell in *Her Everyday Life*, and the real me watches it all from her seat in a darkened theater.

4

*H*ow I wound up with my hair in this flour paste, I cannot say. I thought I was only making a cake! We're back in the Baltimore area doing a crusade up in Bel Air. Frank and Anita and Luella and her kids sure were surprised when Harlan and I came walking into Suds 'N' Strikes for some grilled cheeses and orange soda.

On the way to the church, I decided to make a homemade dessert, a real cake like Grandma Sara used to make. We stopped at the Giant supermarket, and picked up the ingredients listed in the magazine I bought. I figured, why not get started right away? Why wait until we settle down on our campsite?

And now here I stand with half the contents of the bowl dripping down from top to bottom.

"You all right, darlin'?" Harlan yells from the driver's seat.

And I start to cry. Doggone it! Why didn't I listen to him? He told me we'd be getting off the interstate and going down over hill and dale to the little church.

But did I listen?

Of course not.

"You like little cakes or big cakes with hair in them?" I holler back while sniffing away the tears.

Harlan pulls over, leads me back to the bathroom and washes my hair. I weep as he holds me in his arms, my hair soaking his Arrow shirt.

You can't do anything right, Myrtle.

5

I dial Bee Hopewell's number in Lebanon, Tennessee.

"Hello?"

"Bee?"

"Charmaine, I am so glad you called for messages. One just came in from a lady named Frances Evans. She said it's urgent. She said you'd know right away who she is."

Oh, my lands! Francie!

"Well, she left a number for you to call. Eight-oh-four area code."

"She's still in Virginia, then."

"I guess."

"How's my brother?" Bee asked after she gave me the number.

"Fine. Have you ever heard of Mathers and Minnick?"

Bee thought for a spell. Bee takes her time in the thinking department, flipping through her thoughts like skirts on hangers. But that's Bee for you. She takes an hour to eat dinner, which explains her heft. "Oh, yes! Aren't they those psychology guys?"

"Christian psychologists to be precise."

"Well, Char, let me tell you, as far as I'm concerned, all people need is Jesus to cure what ails them."

"That's what Harlan says. Hey, he gave me a Cabbage Patch doll a couple of weeks ago. It's the cutest thing! And since it wasn't around Christmastime . . . well, they're easier to come by now is all."

"Don't I know it!"

Yes, I'm twenty-two now. Too old for dolls.

After she reads me the rest of our messages and the tandem numbers I hang up the phone and debate on whether or not to call Francie back right away. They are all a sore spot with me by this time. Older, of course, and with families and all. Well, at least James and Francie have families. And I had to hear that through this crazy grapevine that actually included that awful Vicki Miller who is now married to the son of Lynchburg's richest people and doesn't that just beat all?

And yet, would I have felt better if she'd ended up married to a roofer, a janitor, or a bartender?

You bet!

My foster siblings never called me or tried to find me. Until now. So maybe they figured it was time to see if I made good. Although, maybe they knew because our picture appeared in the Lynchburg paper last time the crusade landed there.

I try not to list the realm of possibilities like I did with Mama, because, it seems silly to think that all four of them died.

But the kicker in all of this is something I have not yet divulged. I lied to Harlan. I lied about a lot, because there's a lot of difference between an orphan and someone who's been deserted by her own mother. I don't mind him feeling sorry for me, but the amount of sorry a desertion deserves is more than I can handle. That's the kind of sorry that the wounded person ends up consoling the consolee and that's just beyond my desires or capabilities.

Worse secrets have been kept, that's for sure.

I mean, I was a virgin when he married me. He should be thankful for that!

I dial Francie's number right away, my fingers feeling like melted ice pops. She picks up on the first ring, as though she has been waiting.

"Hello?"

"Francie?"

"Yes."

"It's Char— I mean it's Myrtle, Francie."

"Myrtle!"

She still sounds just like Francie.

"Why in the world did you go and change your name, girl! We've been looking all over for you for years!"

"You have?"

"Yes, we have."

Oh, Francie always could get irritated with me.

"Well, I'm sorry then."

"You should be!"

"It's nice to hear your voice now, though," I say.

Her voice warms twenty-five degrees at least when she says, "I sure know it."

"So you're still in Virginia?"

"Yep, over in Roanoke now. Got married to one of James's UVA friends. He's a pediatrician, which is quite handy with little Gloria, who's two-and-a-half and Travis, he's only five weeks and the cutest thing."

"Heavens, Francie, you've got your hands full! I'll bet they're cute!"

"Oh, they are!"

"This is so good talking to you again. How's everybody doing?"

"Well, Myrtle, not so good. You have no idea how glad I was to see that photo of you in the paper. We'd been trying to find you for another reason."

Her voice drops. Something is very wrong. "What is it, Francie?"

"Stacy died a month ago."

"Oh, no! What happened?"

"She had ovarian cancer."

"Oh, Francie. I wish I had known."

That autopilot of calm kicks in.

"I know. But that isn't the only reason I'm calling, Myrtle. Stacy had a child."

"So she married, too?"

"No. She went a little bit astray for a while, got pregnant, and you can figure out the rest of the story."

"How old's the child?"

"Two. A little girl named Hope."

"Who is she staying with?"

"With us."

"That must be terribly difficult."

"It is. And we'd keep her in a heartbeat, but that wasn't Stacy's wish."

"No?"

"No. She wanted you to take Hope if we could find you. It was a shock to us all, I won't hesitate to say, but there it was right in her will. She didn't have the nerve to tell us face-to-face."

"Well, being so sick and all."

"Oh, don't I know it. I'm not saying I blame her, Myrtle, just saying what happened."

"I'll have to talk this over with my husband."

Oh, Stace.

"I figured that. But the longer Hope stays with us, the harder the transition will be for her."

"I'll call you tomorrow. I'm sure Harlan will be fine with it."

"I knew you'd come through, Myrtle. You always did come through. Mama always said if there was anybody in this world that could rise to a challenge, it was you."

"She did say that? Mrs. Evans said that?"

"She thought the world of you, Myrtle."

"How's your dad?"

"Still living in that apartment. But he stopped traveling a couple of years ago. Opened his own children's clothing store out in that shopping center in Boonsboro."

"Really?"

"Yep. And you know Grandma died not soon after you left Lynchburg."

"I know. I went by the home the first time I came back to town and they told me."

"I'm sorry."

"Me, too. Her prayers have lived inside of me all these years, Francie."

"That sure is the truth. There were times I could almost see that 'hedge of protection' she was always talking about."

A great wail erupts in the background. "You'd better go put that fire out," I said.

"That's Hope. Gloria just bit her arm. Those two! 'Bye, Myrtle!"

And she hangs up the phone.

I stare out of the filmy glass of the phone booth and I remember Stacy. I assume she's right there next to her own.

"Harlan?"

"Yes, Shug?"

"Did I ever tell you about the Evanses?"

"No, I don't believe you ever have."

We lay in the section of the camper van we called "the loft." Harlan is just a real skinny guy and he's taken to wearing these new thin ties that the Chess King sells and they make him look even skinnier, if you ask me, not to mention straight off the set of *My Three Sons*. So you can believe me when I say it's easy for us both to fit on that bed that juts out over the driving area. Now, that, for your information is what makes this a Class C motor home and not a Class A. Class As look like buses; Cs resemble vans with a house piggybacked on it. Believe it or not, Melvin installed a skylight up here and we watch the stars a lot. All I can say is, "Thank You God we're not in that truck camper anymore." Talk about cramped.

Now, Harlan and I have never had much of a problem in the love department, if you know what I mean, which could be a little surprising considering that Richard-in-Vermont escapade. However, that was only one bitter mistake in a lifetime that may have had many. Not only that, Harlan is tender and treats me with such care, not rough and rowdy like Richard. And now that the sweat is cooling and we both feel like cats, I figure I'd best bring it up.

"Do you want to hear about the Evanses?"

"If it's important to you."

"They were my set of foster parents after I lost Mama."

"Were they good to you?"

"Oh, yes! Mrs. Evans was the best lady in the whole world."

"Was?"

"She died, too, when I was thirteen."

"Oh, Shug!"

See? This is why he doesn't know the whole story yet. Harlan feels other people's pain way too acutely.

He shakes his head. "I knew I was doing the wrong thing by staying silent. I knew I should have asked you to talk about your pain! Here you've been carrying this around and I could have helped lighten your load."

"Don't be silly, Harlan. You did lighten my load."

And there it all plays out, just like I knew it would, me comforting him. I hold him to myself as he says, "I'm sorry, Shug. I'm so sorry. I should have known. I should have cared more."

"Oh, Harlan, don't be ridiculous. You do care! Now let's get off this topic before I explode. I have some things I have to tell you. Hold on for a second."

Naked, I jump down from the bed, use the bathroom and stare at myself in the mirror for a while. How could I ask him to just suddenly bring a child into the ministry?

Aahhh! But the self-punishment he's doing right now

for not having the instincts he feels he should have had will work in my favor. Of course he'll let me keep Hope now.

Thank You, Jesus. The timing couldn't be better.

I climb back up into the loft and wrap myself beneath the quilt, next to his lean warmth.

"So why do you want to tell me about the Evanses tonight, Shug?"

He takes my hand and we continue to stare at the Plexiglas-covered sky. A dim reflection of our faces stares back—Harlan's long thin aspect with that Fred Astaire chin, me with my Irish smile and Transylvania hair. My ball-bearing breasts. His sunken chest. If any couple looks less glamorous after making love than we do, they must be one sorry pair! I smile despite the sad story ahead, the part where Mrs. Evans dies.

I cry again, because Harlan is the only person to whom I could ever confess my longing to tell Mrs. Evans of my love.

"I think she knows, Shug."

"I'm hoping Jesus passed along the information."

"I'll bet He did just that."

I pull the quilt up—the one Luella made us for our wedding present—around my shoulders.

"Anyway, my stepsister Francie called the ministry and I called her back."

"What did she want?"

"Stacy, she was the youngest sister, the one I shared a room with, died a month ago."

"Oh, no, Charmaine. Are you okay? I was wondering why you were so quiet today."

"It gets worse, though. Stacy had a little girl named Hope. Two years old."

"Poor thing. At least she's got her daddy."

"There's no daddy in the picture."

"Well, you can sure relate to all of that, then, can't you, Shug?"

I am silent.

"Talk to me, Shug."

"Stacy left a will, Harlan, concerning little Hope. She left her in my care."

Harlan is silent.

I don't know what to say. I want him to ask a question and any question will do because I'm not a choosy type, not after living half a childhood off cold egg sandwiches from the Texas Inn.

The silence of grief and the night impregnates itself with sleep, for me anyway. February night rolls over inside a freshly quilted blanket of dew and shuts off the sounds of all that is human.

A touch awakens me. Harlan's thin hand is gilded with the morning sun. He flips his fingers over my knuckles as glibly as he flips through the soft onionskin pages of his old Bible. I gaze out over the prickly cornfield beside the church.

"When do we go pick up Hope?" he whispers. His fingers travel to my chin and he parallels my face with his own.

"As soon as Forest Hill Church can let us go?"

"The last meeting is tomorrow night. Why don't you

call Francie and let her know we'll be down the morning after. We'll get an early start."

I raise my own flittering fingers through the thinning hair atop his head. "You're really something, Harlan Hopewell."

"No, Shug. You are."

"What made you want to take her on?"

"Her name. Can you imagine it? Hope Hopewell? That's a name that will make anyone smile. Especially you, Charmaine."

"Why do you say that?"

"You need somebody to belong to, Shug."

"But I belong to you." I nestle against his shoulder. I love this man so much.

"Not in the same way."

He is right. And I find it amazing that a man who truly knows so little about me knows me so well.

6

*H*onest to goodness, I swear if we owned a house, which we don't, we'd have to take out a second mortgage just for diapers! I make Harlan and the boys stop at rest stops all the time as soon as I change Hope because I refuse to travel all day in the RV with a soiled diaper.

I wouldn't trade my Hope for anything in the world, and most every mother I know says the same thing and rightly so. She took to us right away. Harlan loves her, too. "We've been sent a gift from God, Shug!"

And I agree.

The nicest thing I noticed about Hope right up front is this, she has Mrs. Evans's pansy eyes. I feel like God is giving me the chance to give back to Mrs. Evans all she did for me. Yep, pansy eyes and feathery, light brown hair that her satin ribbons use as a sliding board.

And do the people at the crusades love her? Oh, my! Sometimes if Hope is crying, I'll sing with her there on my hip. Our piano player, Henry Windsor, will even let Hope sit at the piano with him if both she and Leo, Grace's four-year-old, won't stay content in the nursery.

Grace Underhill is our resident, yet precious, as in "all God's children are precious" fly in the ointment. She sings with the crusade as well now. So there we'll be, up on stage singing and playing with the kids all around us and the folks out in the congregation thinking we're just regular folks after all. Just like them.

In all truthfulness, I think Henry likes having someone next to him up there. He's quite short, almost as short as I am. Dresses up in dark suits, shirts stiffer than Mama's gin, and hangs bright yellow ties around his neck— sunshiney bits of silk that light up a face filled with the joy of music. Henry and I love to perform together. And when I'm with him, I'm glad I'm short.

Now, I don't know much about much, but crusade people have much more in common with the circus crowd than they do regular, house-abiding citizens.

Tonight is a night like that. The Songbirds have been complete once again for several years now. I love them like sisters, well, Ruby anyway. Grace is more like that annoying cousin you feel so sorry for you can't turn away. But our voices blend like sisters' voices. However, I do believe the Songbirds are beginning to crumble and it breaks my heart.

So tonight we start with "Jesus Loves Me," a wonderful message no doubt. Ruby undergirds us all with her deep, African tones, and Swedish-rooted Grace lifts us up with her sweet high notes. And then there's me, in the middle as usual, doing the melody. I guess Mrs. Evans really knew what she was talking about all those years ago.

Ruby wears red like she almost always does and she stands to my left, tall and gorgeous, and smooth. Her butt protrudes beneath her gown, and so do her breasts and her tummy, but Ruby doesn't care. She always says, "I am woman, hear me roar!" and then she'll curve her thin, sculpted arms up into a bodybuilder's pose. The gown falls slim and straight, yet modest with a high neck and tight, long sleeves made of fine chiffon. After all, we sing to a pretty conservative crowd more times than not.

To my left stands Grace. We wear our autumn lineup of dresses. Grace is swaddled in goldenrod. The dress hangs tea-length, which she loves, and flares outward. Truly it reminds me of something that Rosemary Clooney would have worn in *White Christmas*. Oh, I love that movie! Matching pumps trace the outlines of her small feet. Grace sings with little hoopla, but her face shines the light of heaven, or at least that's the look she's going for. Grace will tell you singing with the crusade is a job and nothing more. "You two can feel called. I'm just a backup singer."

And here I stand in the middle, not because I want to be the star, but because if Grace gets Ruby's notes right in her ear she starts to sing the melody with me. I'm wearing orange. Now let me tell you, standing in between Miss African Sculpture, imposing and ready for the royal ball, and Miss Blond Junior Miss of the Universe 1973, I look like a little flame between two searchlights! However, my dress distinction is that I go shorter, the hemline at midknee. I never did that before the Songbirds met up with Harlan's crusade all those years ago. But he said to me, "You've got pretty legs, Shug. You need to show them off a little."

Out came the scissors, let me tell you! I love that man. I haven't had a nosebleed since I met him.

After "Jesus Loves Me," Henry ching-and-lings, and bring-a-dings his fingers up a key or two and ends up going right on into my most favorite of all the old songs, "His Eye Is on the Sparrow."

I know He watches me, just like that song says.

A lot of folks are jealous of a natural gift whether it be singing, drawing or writing, or math and the like. And even though I don't know much about much, when you realize that God gave it to you through none of your own doings, you feel it in the nerves of your teeth that He can just as easily take it away. And so you try harder. You try your best not to bury it in a napkin like the man in that parable did, and then God blesses even more. Now that's the joyful part.

Tonight Harlan and I lie in the little bedroom part of the RV, Hope crying like no tomorrow is in sight, refusing to be calmed, crying for reasons only she knows and I project all sorts of craziness. What if she's crying because she has something wrong with her brain synapses? And what if those brain synapse malfunctions just get worse and worse and worse? And what if, say when she's a teenager, she decides to steal a car because her brain synapses rob her conscience? And what if she ends up in a penitentiary, living through all those horrors only to end up in a fight with kitchenware duct-taped to her hand? What if? Times like these, a mother would gladly trade every last lick of talent she possesses for the certainty that her children will come to the Lord, walk in the light, and be a living blessing.

People think of me as a "singer." But in truth, I hope

that someday, years down the line, God will prove through my children, Hope and the ones He'll give us someday, that He gave me the grace to be remembered as a whole lot more than that.

7

$\mathcal{I}$ am sitting in the office of some bigwig music agent in Nashville, Tennessee. And when I say "bigwig," I mean big wig. This lady's hair puts mine to such shame it can only be as fake as her breasts, which stick out a mile. This cleavage is the kind that deserves some kind of geological status. The Marianas Trench.

That's her name. MaryAnna Trench.

It's all I can do to sit here without chuckling. I am afraid I have a look on my face that's disrespectful and condescending, sort of like what I imagine a famous novelist might wear when some well-meaning grandmother tells him her eight-year-old granddaughter is an author, too, because she wrote a children's book last week. However, it really is just a simple girl trying not to laugh.

I don't think, however, that MaryAnna Trench notices my expression because she's too busy looking through her desk drawer for her pack of smokes, thus giving me an even better view of MaryAnna's trench.

I wish Harlan sat with me now, because we'd be laughing ourselves a good one! On second thought, maybe I'm glad he decided to hold down Fort Hope. And Ruby's there, too. I've had the same conversation with her for three days straight.

"Sign on with me, Ruby. Come on! It'll be you and me, like always!"

"No way! I'm with you and Harlan because I believe in you all. But entering Southern gospel music officially? It's a white world."

"That's not true."

"It is true. There's a huge gap between Southern gospel music and black gospel."

I shrugged. What could I say? She was right.

"And can you imagine a black lady and a white lady paired up together in an official act? You never see that, Char. In gospel music or any other kind."

"But we could start a trend!"

"Un-uh. Not me. I'm not that brave. And you wouldn't be either if you really thought about it."

But she got me thinking. Music is such a segregated world. Whether gospel or not. There are black-girl groups and white-girl groups. Black bands and white bands. And very rarely do the twain meet.

Except for maybe KC and the Sunshine Band and they've been out of style for years.

MaryAnna pulls me out of my thoughts.

"I couldn't believe my fortune when I saw you at that crazy crusade," MaryAnna says, her sprayed black up do bobbing with the movements of her hands. "I couldn't believe I let Daddy drag me out to that thing." She's still poking through the drawer with a ruler now, pulling things from the back up to the front. "I thought I had an extra pack in here somewheres. I don't guess you smoke, do you, Mrs. Hopewell?"

"No, ma'am. Used to work in a bowling alley and had enough of it for a lifetime. Seems somebody was always lighting up."

"Good for you. Bad for me."

MaryAnna Trench's tissue has the gray look of stimulus-based malnourishment. Coffee, cigarettes, and alcohol, I bet, keep her moving, like some sort of diuretic-driven Mrs. Frankenstein. I want to ask her how many times a day she has to pee, but know that isn't a question for our first meeting, or maybe ever.

She slams the drawer shut and bites on her bare thumbnail, and I wonder if she'll call what she ingests "lunch."

MaryAnna blows out an exasperated sigh. "Okay, well, I guess I'll have to get through this without one."

Wonderful. My first shot at an agent and all she can think about is a cigarette. One thing good about growing up the way I did is that it breeds resourcefulness. "I've got an idea. Let's walk down to that Eckerd store there on the corner and we can talk on the way."

MaryAnna jumps to her feet, breasts jiggling like two molded aspic salads. She is very thin otherwise, which makes the breasts suspect. No butt. Celery stalk legs and a neck with napa cabbage veins and tendons. "Good thinking! Let's go." She grabs a handbag from underneath her desk. Not a purse. A handbag. Any woman will tell you there's a clear difference between the two.

"Do you sleep well at nights, Ms. Trench?"

"Hardly a wink. Why?"

"Just wondering."

She checks her face in the mirror by the door, a face grounded by a black V-neck shirt she probably bought in the toddler section to ensure that kind of fit. "Let me tell you this, Ms. Hopewell . . . hey, can I call you Charmaine?"

"Of course you can."

"Just thought I'd ask. Some of these singer types can be so uppity."

She shuts the door to her office, waves to the nice receptionist in one of those Michael Jackson red leather jackets, who showed me in and made me a cup of tea while I waited an hour past my appointment time.

"Well, I'm sure not uppity. I come from nothing, and I'm still nothing, Ms. Trench."

"Well let me just tell you, Charmaine, if you hire on MaryAnna Trench, you got an agent that works almost twenty-four hours a day for you."

Well, I'll be. Suddenly I wonder if Mr. Haney on Green Acres has taken over the emaciated, augmented body of MaryAnna Trench.

While walking to the drugstore, we talk about all the dead country music stars because, believe it or not, Ms. Trench keeps pictures of their graves in an album. If that isn't the weirdest thing I've ever heard I don't know what is!

The bell clanks against the glass door of the drugstore as we enter. MaryAnna is still talking. "The latest ones in my collection are Judy Canova and Junior Samples.

"Junior Samples died?"

"Yes. And not long ago."

"Always wondered how he came across that name. Must be a story there."

"Oh, the country stars have their stories."

"Don't we all?" I say.

MaryAnna, eyes bright with excitement, lays a hand on my arm. "Hard luck story?"

"You wouldn't believe it if I told you."

And MaryAnna grins. "Honey-pie, the buying public loves nothing more than a hard-luck story."

At that moment, I realize that the niggling little tickle inside of me, the one that said "You will be famous one day, Myrtle Whitehead," is whispering again.

I picture my Mama. I remember her prophecy of fame for me, her ill-conceived daughter. I remember a lot in this moment, reminded by MaryAnna Trench of my hard-luck story.

Hard-Luck Story.

Myrtle Charmaine Whitehead Hopewell's *Hard-Luck Story.*

Oh, my lands!

Maybe I should skip the singing profession and go straight to the biography.

"Would you mind if I made a quick call from that pay phone outside while you buy your smokes?"

"Not one bit."

I push my way back outside, my spiked heels clicking against the concrete. Hairdos mill above me, fringes and studs vie for attention and a few rhinestones sparkle at eye level. And cowboy boots and hats bob everywhere. As if any of these people wear these items of clothing for their intended purposes! However, the big hair makes me feel right at home, and smugness envelops me because mine is natural.

A man with boots pointier than Vicki Miller's head

hangs up the phone, gives me a little salute off the brim of his seventy-five gallon hat, and I smile.

Harlan, who's waiting for me at his sister Bee's house, picks up on the first ring. "Shug?"

"It's me. Listen I don't have but a minute." I tell him the entire hard-luck story angle. "Do you think it can hurt to approach it like that?"

"Well, I don't know, Char. I've never thought about stuff like that before. I can tell you it would be a great way to share the way God has turned your life around with His blessings."

"The best among them being you, Harlan."

Sometimes I even make *myself* sick.

"Well, I don't know about that, Shug. I think I'm the lucky one in the whole deal."

My goodness, I just love this fellow.

"I'm not going to sign anything today, Harlan. Just so you know."

"Whatever you do is fine with me, Charmaine."

MaryAnna Trench emerges, stepping onto Music Row and lighting up a Pall Mall right away. She French inhales, something I think I would learn to do if I ever became a smoker. But that would be death to my vocal chords, unless I want to sing like Kim Carnes or Rod Stewart.

She exhales. "Now what I need to know is if you want to take your career mainstream or Southern gospel?"

I try to keep up with her long legs. It is not easy. "I don't know. I never really thought about it."

"Think about it. It's important."

"Will I get on with the Gaithers if I go strictly Southern gospel?"

MaryAnna laughs and laughs and it reminds me of somebody starting an engine after it's already running.

The truth is, I love gospel music. It's in my blood, although I never once really heard Mama do more than hum. The thing about gospel, I guess, is if they find out the real truth about my life, that I've been lying all these years about Mama being dead and all, they'll forgive me. Right? I mean, isn't that what Christians do?

I guess it's just the changes that have occurred in my life lately, getting Hope, taking my singing career a step further, dealing with Grace who missed two nights at last week's crusade and came home smelling like a still, but I'm feeling extra weary, and a little blue.

It takes even more effort than usual to do even the most simple of things these days.

Better stick with Jesus.

"I'll go Southern gospel."

I need all the help I can get.

8

*S*ome women remember the year events happen by their hairstyle, where they lived, or what job they held. I remember by my clothing. Even now I still sit at the machine for a couple of hours a day as we drive in the motor home or park somewhere in a church lot or a campground. I still make all the costumes for the Songbirds. I can remember what year we sang at which church because I remember our dresses.

I'm still the same. Right now, I'm looking at MaryAnna Trench and thinking, "I am signing with my first agent and I am wearing a pair of purple designer jeans—50 percent off at Hecht's—and a white, frilly cotton blouse I made a few months ago.

Of course, MaryAnna's outfit tops mine completely. Her skeletal form is swathed in a caftan this afternoon. A caftan! I'm thinking I may just travel around the world via Ms. Trench's choice of outfit. Paris and all black the first visit. A caftan now. I won't be at all surprised if next time I greet her she's wrapped up like a caterpillar in a sari or wearing khaki and a pith helmet.

I can't quite imagine someone in a sari smoking Pall Malls, however.

"Just sign by all the 'X's, Charmaine. I assure you it's a standard contract."

And so I do as she says and the funniest feeling comes over me, like I am a candy bar at the movie theater, but I'm paying the customer to buy me and eat me, throw away my wrapper and forget about me by the time the last flicker of light has faded from the giant screen of silver.

I really wish I could afford a lawyer. But isn't that what agents are supposed to do anyway? Protect their clients from the record companies and whatnot?

"You do have a lawyer in-house?" I ask.

"Not in-house. But one who we use all the time."

"What's his name?"

"William Williams."

"William Williams?"

"Well, he goes by Billy."

I call Harlan who's over at Bee's as soon as I leave the building. "I'm by that Eckerd store."

"How did it go?"

I sigh, feeling silly all of a sudden. "I signed. Their lawyer is named William Williams. He goes by Billy."

And Harlan and I laugh and laugh.

"Don't worry, Shug. You'll do all right. You know that."

I wish I had his optimism. Lately, though, it's all I can do to even summon up the smallest bit of real enthusiasm. And I outright snapped at Grace the other day. I feel so testy!

Harlan says, "How about if we celebrate tonight? We're pulling out tomorrow morning for Greensboro."

"You want to go out to eat?"

Harlan and I hardly ever go out to eat. Evangelists rely on "love offerings" and let me tell you, born-again types are the most tight-fisted group of people you've ever seen. One time we had a church take out a portion of the love offering for the extra gas and electric it took to turn on the lights of the church for those few services not normally scheduled during the week.

"You know I love to eat out. Where do you want to go?"

"How about the Western Sizzlin'?"

"Really? Steak?"

"You know it, Shug. It's not every day a beautiful lady signs on with a real Nashville agent."

"That sure is the truth. Okay, I'm on my way home."

So I climb into Bee's little Mazda and make my way back to Lebanon. But I stop in at the Kroger for some Sominex. I don't know why, but I've been having trouble sleeping lately. I wish I could blame it on Hope, but to be honest, that child sleeps like a teenager!

Poor Harlan, too. My libido is down to nothing these days but I'm able to muster up some semblance of enthusiasm for his sake. And once we really get started, I do enjoy myself.

Nevertheless, when I step up into the RV and see Harlan standing there holding our baby, I smile. "Mama!" she cries and lunges for me. I drop the bag and catch her before she crashes to the ground.

Harlan picks up the bag and looks inside. "What's this for? You having trouble sleeping, Charmaine?"

"Just falling asleep, Harlan. I feel so keyed up nowa-days."

"Must just be the excitement of your singing career."

"Must be."

A big homemade sign is taped to a cabinet in the kitch-enette. knock 'em dead, shug!

I hug my husband, kiss my baby, and can't wait until morning when we pull out of here. I'll still be all curled up with Hope in the bed at the back of the van, feeling warm and sleepy.

I can't say I understand Harlan's drive to go around preaching like he does. But I can understand why he doesn't want to settle down. Still, he takes good care of us. I guess maybe I should be more like him.

I'd like to say I am one of those people in search of their father. But I'm not. Because I doubt Mama had any idea who my father was.

I suppose I could get all sentimental and imagine some fairy-tale scenario.

1. They were childhood sweethearts and he came to visit her at Randolph Macon, they succumbed to a night of pleasure due to the passion in their hearts. He promised his heart forever, slipping a ring on her finger, and on the way back to Suffolk he died in a tragic car accident.

2. He was an older man, a rich widower with an aching heart. He saw my Mama walking home from class one day, her books bumping slightly against her slender, youthful hips, and he asked her out. She

never really loved him, but she pitied him, allowing herself into his arms for only a short time. After that she told him it could go no further. She wanted to fall in love, you see, to feel that heady blush of a fully beating heart, but it never happened. She never told him about the pregnancy to avoid complications and the accusations from Lynchburg society at large that she only slept with him to ensnare him.

3. He was a dying young man with only six months to live. She sat at his bedside until the end, hiding her belly as it expanded to keep the failing invalid from experiencing yet more pain as his sweet young life faded away. But he knew. Yes, somehow he knew and as he died he said, "Take care of the child. Take good care."

Most likely, my father was none of those. Most likely he could have been one of ten subordinary people, and what child wants to deal with that?

9

$\mathcal{I}$t's the autumn of 1983, and Harlan, Hope, and I are headed to Suffolk for a crusade. Mama's hometown. So it's easy to imagine the butterflies I feel. No need to diet this week. I couldn't put more than dry toast in my mouth even if I wanted to. Only one time was I more nervous than this that I can remember and that was when *Bowl-O-Rama* began to shoot my scene. But when I compare meeting that eccentric director to possibly meeting my grandma Min, well, it's like comparing a deli-counter turkey sandwich on white hold the mayo, to a gooey cheesesteak sub, extra cheese, and fried onions, if you please.

I tell you what, I thought those Sominex pills would work. I am so tired of being tired. Lying there awake at night I do too much thinking. It's that simple. And when I do too much thinking, I hate to admit it, but I do miss Mama a little. Or I miss what Mama and I might have been, I guess. I definitely miss Mrs. Evans in the true sense of the word. Francie and I talk every couple of weeks now and that makes things hard. Daddy this and Daddy that, and James this and James that, and I feel like such an outsider, despite the fact that I'm raising Hope as my own. They all agreed she should call us "Mama" and "Daddy" because everyone has a right to have parents.

We'll adopt her soon.

Well, we are almost to Suffolk. This Route 58 is so boring that I've decided to lie down with Hope for a nap, not that I'll sleep, but I'm going through a list of ingredients in my head for the crème brûlée I'm going to make. After that cherries jubilee nightmare, I figure I need to give the whole gourmet dessert affair another chance. I'll get one of the boys to run to Food Lion later on.

Melvin's driving today because Harlan is sitting at the dinette going over his new series of messages entitled, "What's *Really* Eating at You?"

Lord, help us, but he's on this antipsychology kick right now. As if people don't think Christians are strange enough.

I draw Hope's little body close to mine, slipping my arm beneath her tender neck and cuddling her childish form into my own. She smells so good. Harlan got us a Rubbermaid tub to put in the shower stall for her baths. When we give her a bath he sits in the narrow hallway outside the bathroom door and I sit on the toilet with the lid closed and she splashes and plays. And you know, she doesn't even mind getting her hair washed? I thought all children hated getting their hair washed. One time, Luella told me about Esteban and how he screamed so much during his baths she dubbed them "The Bath of a Thousand Screams."

"How much longer, Melvin?" I hear Harlan ask.

"About twenty more miles, reverend."

Rain pings the tin roof of the motor home. I grieve inside because I know I will try to find my grandma and I know I will do it behind my sweet Harlan's back. This is something I must do without him because I couldn't bear telling him if Grandma's dead or doesn't want anything to do with me.

Harlan unknowingly heaps guilt upon my already loaded conscience when he makes his way to the back and curls up with "his girls," as he calls us with his particular brand of corny sentimentality. He whispers softly in prayer, so softly I cannot understand the words.

I pretend I am asleep.

I often wonder nowadays what ever attracted Harlan to me in the first place.

Route 58 unravels before us.

I look over at Harlan, asleep now beside me on the bed. His mouth gently sags to the side and a soft, whistly sort of snore blows from the gap. Hope's profile, sculpted with the smoothness of Ivory soap and about as lacking in porousness, steals my gaze, but not my thoughts. We've pulled into the church parking lot. Over the phone, the church was quick to apologize for being so new. Harlan told me about it after he first talked to them. "They said, 'We're not one of the old historic churches, Reverend Hopewell, but we do know how to praise the Lord here at Grace and Truth Assembly.'"

We laughed ourselves a good one.

"Not one of the historic churches?" I asked.

"That's what they said."

"Must be a stuffy old town, Suffolk." No wonder Mama wouldn't go back. Unless she did go back. Oh, dear Lord! What if I find her right there with my grandma Min?

I hear Melvin hooking up the electrical to the church and I peer out the small window at the back, relieved to see our motor home is parked behind the church. It's embarrassing enough to live in a motor home without being parked in plain view to all passersby.

"Harlan?" I rouse him. "We're here."

He opens his eyes but does not sit up. "What's the place like?"

I peer out again. "Not much. Little red-brick, country-style church. Looks like it was built in the fifties."

"That's new to these people?"

"I guess so."

He sighs. "How much money do we have left in the account for salaries this month?"

"About fifteen hundred dollars." I keep the books.

We have seven people on the crusade payroll now. Harlan and I, Henry Windsor, Ruby and Grace, Mel and his nephew Randall, who we never see because once he sets up our sound system and all, he heads off to the bars. Mel was hoping this stint with the crusade would go far in saving his soul.

Harlan sighs again. "I was hoping to get you a nice surprise, honey. But I think it's going to have to wait. Thought I could stow a little more away."

"It's a surprise you're *saving* for?"

"Yep. It's going to be real nice. But we've got to make payroll."

"God will provide, Harlan," I say. "He always does."

There, that sounds holy.

Harlan nods, kisses my cheek, and rises out of the bed. "Your desires can't be first in the pocketbook, Charmaine, but they are first in my heart. Do you know that?"

"I do. I do know that."

He sits back down and I curl up against him, my head on his lap. "I never promised riches, did I, honey? Did I lead you to believe we'd ever be comfortable?"

"Well, not in a financial sense. But I think we've achieved comfort of another kind."

He strokes my hair, really softly, over the top layer of hair because Harlan knows better than to try and run his fingers through my rat's nest. "And maybe heavenly riches? Can you be content with those rewards in the meantime?"

"They're the only kind I've ever had anyway, Harlan. I wouldn't even know what the other kind looks like!" I try to lighten it all up so he'll be at his best tonight. With Hope asleep there I can't make love to him to boost him up, not that I really feel like it anyway, so I figure I'll make love to his male ego and his sense of purpose. "We live for heaven, Harlan. I may not know much about much, but I know the difference between corruptible and incorruptible."

Just like my little pink King James Bible says.

And then I give his buns a squeeze to let him know we are in this together and we always will be. He laughs, like I knew he would.

"You don't get serious for long, do you, honey?"

"Nope. It embarrasses me."

"That's all right. It just makes me listen hard the first time."

"Pastor Hopewell?" It's Melvin's voice. "Pastor Chorey's in his office. You coming out?"

"Be right there."

Harlan quickly brushes his teeth, puts on a little fresh

cologne, and I watch him out the window as he strides toward the church.

"Melvin?"

"Yes, ma'am?"

Melvin stands outside the motor home. I speak to him through the louvered window. I can see the hood of his yellow rain slicker.

"I need a local phone book."

"I'll fetch you one."

"I need to get my hair cut."

"That's fine, Mrs. Hopewell."

"It's been a while."

He just shakes his head and hurries toward the church to do my bidding.

10

*M*ama didn't buy me many toys as one could well imagine. However, she did get me a Lite-Brite. I loved that contraption. I loved all the colors, even the clear pegs. Sometimes I'd do the snowman with little clear pegs, making snowflakes all around him. I loved the butterfly and the groovy flowers. I loved the house and sometimes made up my own houses that never, ever looked like Mrs. Blackburn's boarding house.

My favorite Lite-Brite creation was my own name. Mama said to me once, a smirk on her face, "Myrtle, you just have a thing for seeing your name in lights, don't you?"

I just nodded and said, "I guess so, Mama."

Now, I don't see my name in lights per se very much but every once in a while I do see it in those plastic letters they use on lighted church signs. And there it glows on the Suffolk church's sign. Ruby, who's driving me in the crusade pickup truck to get my hair cut in the vast metropolis of Suffolk, Virginia, says, "How come Grace and I never get our names up there?"

I bark out a laugh. "If you'd have been the one to marry Harlan, you'd have yours up there."

"Well, then, I suppose I ought to be thankful it's not. So what are you going to get done to your hair?"

"Just a trim."

"Charmaine, nobody in this darn crusade can afford a trim. So what's the real deal?"

I sigh. "Ruby, how can you *always* tell when I've got something else in mind?"

She points a finger at me, turns on the right turn signal and pulls out of the church parking lot. "You may call it 'something else in mind' but where I come from we call it 'being up to something.'"

Here is the chance to finally tell somebody the truth. I know I can trust Ruby, I just don't know if she wants the responsibility.

"You're hiding something, aren't you, Charmaine?"

I nod. "You want to hear all about it?"

"It's not an affair, is it?"

"Oh, my lands, no!"

"Is it some other kind of sin problem?"

"In a roundabout way, I guess."

"How long have you been carrying this secret around?"

"Good heavens, Ruby, do you want to hear it or not?"

"Okay, yes, I do."

"Then pull off the road down there at the Hardee's and I'll buy you a sweet tea and tell you the whole thing."

"I have a feeling I'm going to regret this."

"You can stop me at any time."

When we settle in the beige plastic booth with sweet teas for both of us and an extra large fries for Ruby, I take her hand. "I'm going to ask you this. Are you sure you want to hear this?"

She hesitates. "Let me ask you one question. Does this have to do with your parents?"

"My mama."

"Was she from this area?"

I nodded. "Might still be from, I don't know."

Her eyes round. "You mean your mother may be alive?"

"Yes, I do."

"You told me you were orphaned."

"I might be."

"But then again, you might not be."

"Right."

"Do you know who your father is?"

"Nope."

"Do you have a sister?"

"Not that I know of."

"Well, you do now. Tell me it all, honey."

I do.

It all comes out quite calmly, like I am telling her about a harrowing time in traffic, or maybe something even not that bad.

"She never came back?" Ruby asks, and she sips the last of her tea, that final gurgle at the bottom a hollow punctuation to my story.

"No."

"So you found your grandmother's address?"

I nod.

"Let's skip the hairdresser and drive by her house, Charmaine."

"Really? You don't mind?"

"Of course not."

She gathers her coat and bag, as do I. Then she turns toward me after she slips on her jacket. "You planned on telling me someday, though, right?"

"I did. I didn't know when, Ruby. I think I waited more for your sake then for mine."

Did I? Who knew?

And Ruby coughed away a tear.

Ruby grips the wheel of the crusade pickup truck, the one that hauls her trailer. "I left Grace in the travel trailer. I asked her if she wanted to come along but she just said 'no.'"

"She scares me, Ruby."

"Me, too."

"I swear she was high before the service the other night back in Emporia. Had those glassy-looking eyes and all."

Not to mention the slight odor of Vermont clung to her hair.

"I know she was, Char."

"You've known about this for a long time."

Ruby nods and turns off the road onto Freemason Street. "I told her I wouldn't tell anybody, but I wasn't into the hiding business either if she got careless. I tell you what, I've made up some of my own creeds for life and one of them is not to assume any responsibility for other's people's actions."

"Yeah, well, that's an easy enough creed to adopt for now. But just wait until you fall in love someday."

"Well, I'm determined that will never happen, Charmaine. Men may not all be alike, but they all have the potential of being alike."

Poor, Ruby. I won't tell her that love's heady waters become a most delightful and needful brew. That when it's right, its silks and satins turn not into sackcloth and ashes, but the most comfortable of brushed cottons. I've learned something along this path—people need to learn for themselves. I could talk until I'm blue in the face, spouting all sorts of advice until I'm worn out. But people are going to do whatever they wanted anyway. So I keep my mouth shut about stuff like that and usually go on and on about the inane.

Besides, nobody wants to hear about the intricacies and lessons of your life, Myrtle Charmaine.

You know, one time I heard that nephew of Mel's call me "shallow." Now he didn't know my ears were in close proximity, and I went back to the motor home and cried and cried until I realized that I do seem shallow, but that's only because I feel so deeply I could never begin to drag those feelings up to the surface much. After all, it would be like dragging a Chinaman through the earth and up to Virginia.

The thought of Grace destroying herself rips me to ribbons. You see, I met her parents once and they were the nicest people you'd ever want to meet.

Grace is Mama in the making, I tell you. And maybe that's why I find her so hard to stomach.

Ruby makes a right turn. "What number did you say it was?"

"Twenty-three-oh-six."

"There's Twenty-one-ten. Up two more blocks."

I breathe in.

"You nervous, Charmaine?"

"Yeah. Of course."

"But we're just driving by."

"But a house tells a lot about a person."

"That's the truth."

I mean, I should know, I live in a motor home.

"And what if Mama lives there?"

We pass the first block. Lots of old white or brick homes sprouted from the Southern soil, as if some old Civil War general threw seeds of a dying way of life before going off for the final battle.

They were probably built in the 1920s and I'm too dumb to know it.

Ruby shakes her head. "I don't think she's there."

"Why not?"

"Just doesn't make sense. Did she ever strike you as the type that would go running back home to her mother?"

"Never."

"So there you go."

"My stomach still feels sick."

Ruby slows down as we make it to my grandmother's block. "That should be it, third house on the right."

It sits on a small, narrow lot, plopped down between two bigger houses. "You think that was a guest house or something?" I ask.

"Looks like it to me."

"Huh. This isn't at all what I expected."

"What did you expect?"

"Well, Mama was so brash and sassy, I figured she was from the wrong side of the tracks."

Ruby stops in front of the house. "It's a modest little home. But this sure is a nice neighborhood."

"Maybe she grew up in that big house next door! Maybe they were really rich and then something happened and they had to sell that big house and move to the guest house."

Stop theorizing!

"Maybe you're right about that. Hard times can fall on anybody, Charmaine."

"I sure know that."

"Sounds like you had a weird childhood."

"No stranger than yours."

Ruby shakes her head. "No. Mine was garden variety tragic. Yours definitely isn't run of the mill."

"What if my grandma isn't playing with a full deck?" I only say that to add yet another cliché to the conversation.

"I don't see why that makes any difference at this point."

"I'd like to think she remembered she had a granddaughter out there somewhere."

Ruby thinks about that. "You're right. Now why do you think she never tried to find you?"

I shrug. "Don't know. Maybe she doesn't even know about me."

"Oh, that will be rich. What a reunion."

"Thanks, Ruby. That really makes me feel a whole lot better."

The house looks as if it was born to this world of antique homes sometime back after World War II. It appeared to be the Peter Pan of the neighborhood, refusing to grow up big like the rest of them.

"Kind of like a fairy-tale cottage," Ruby says.

"You think?"

"Sure. Can't you picture the seven dwarves poking their heads out of the dormers, and that entryway with the pointed roof?"

I examine it afresh. "You're right. It's actually kind of cute, isn't it?"

"I mean, if it has to be here among the behemoths, at least it's got its own peculiar brand of charm."

I nod. "I like it."

"Me, too." She drums her glossy nails on the steering wheel. Ten minutes pass as I get more and more nauseous. "How long we gonna sit here, Char?"

"I was hoping she'd come out," I say.

"Maybe the house is good enough for the first day. We'll be here four more days."

"That's true."

"Maybe anything more would be too hard to digest."

"You're right."

"Maybe we should come back tomorrow morning."

"Okay."

"Maybe you could call her on the phone."

"That's true."

"Hey, you never know. She might even go to that church we're at."

"I doubt it."

Ruby glances over at me. "Why?"

"This is a Methodist neighborhood if I ever saw one."

Ruby looks around and considers my statement. "You're right. Rich people don't really like to get messy and sentimental about God."

"I think tears of the Spirit embarrass them, don't you?

I mean think about it, it's not usually the well-dressed members that are coming up to the altar and throwing themselves on the mercy of God, is it?"

"No, you're right about that, Charmaine. It's that rich man and the eye of the needle thing, I guess."

I laugh. "Well, with the way things are going, that's one thing we sure don't have to worry about!"

"You said it, girl."

She pulls the gearshift from park into drive and we putter away in the truck.

"Maybe I'd do better to leave well enough alone."

"Maybe."

A light rain begins to fall. "But I can't do that."

"I don't blame you."

"Will you find out about your family, Ruby?"

"No."

I just nod. I mean, what can you say to that?

We drive about a mile before I get the courage to ask her why.

"Remember that day we went into the rescue mission off the boardwalk?"

"Sure I do."

"I found out something that day, Charmaine. I discovered the true definition of family. And those drugged-out people that neglected me and left me for days in my crib and only a bottle here and there, they don't fit the description. Do you know when social services came to get me I had a staph infection from the feces and urine constantly against inflamed diaper rash?"

"Oh, God, Ruby."

"I almost died in the hospital."

"Oh, Ruby!"

"So, no. Why would I want to find people like that?"

"Maybe you have a grandma, too, an aunt or some-body who'd care."

"If they cared they'd have found me by now."

The funny thing is, there's no bitterness in Ruby's tone. Matter-of-factness straight down the middle of her verbiage wrangles me more than any sort of rage might have.

She points to me. "I'll bet you anything your grandma doesn't know you exist."

"I don't know what would be better. Either one makes it horribly difficult for me to approach her. And if she doesn't know, how could I prove it to her? I don't look a thing like Mama."

"Maybe you look like your grandma."

"Lord help the poor woman if I do!"

Ruby shakes her head. "Did anybody ever tell you you were ugly Charmaine?"

"No."

"Then why on earth are you always so down on yourself?"

"Isn't it obvious?"

"Not really, girl."

"Well, if I'd been pretty and genteel and charming and all, Mama wouldn't have been ashamed of me. She wouldn't have kept me cooped up in that apartment and she wouldn't have left the way she did."

"Oh, Charmaine. That had nothing to do with it."

"I don't know."

"Oh, please. The woman was mental. It's the only explanation."

"Mental? My mama?"

"Of course. Why else would a woman leave her child like that?"

"You mean Mama was crazy?"

Ruby shrugs. "If the shoe fits."

"You know, Ruby. You love clichés, don't you?"

"So sue me."

We laugh and I think right then I'll take a trip to the library tomorrow and find out what in the world kind of mental illness would cause a mother to abandon her only child.

Mental?

Do I laugh now? Or do I cry?

11

$\mathscr{I}$ stare at the entry in the phone book. Harlan sleeps in the back. The little white alarm clock flips all its number tiles from 12:59 to 1:00 in the morning.

We had a wonderful service tonight. The Songbirds sang "Just a Little Talk with Jesus" and the folk got to their feet, clapping and shuffling around. Now, if Suffolk is as stuffy as I've been led to believe, obviously these people have chosen to break the mold! I sure do admire that.

Even Grace broke a sweat during the number. We went with the flow, I sure can say. Henry Windsor kept bringing us around for another chorus. And it's true, just a little talk with Jesus does make things right. I mean, it may not take away your problems, but it sure does help you get through them.

Although, sometimes I wish talks with Jesus would just take them right away. Wouldn't that be nice? Hi, Lord! And poof! 'Bye, 'bye cares and tears!

Why He didn't just create Heaven and us people in our glorified bodies and skip this whole earth phase is beyond me. I can only suppose He had His reasons and they're good ones. It's all anybody can suppose having taken that initial leap of faith.

I've heard people say, "Christianity has all the answers."

Well, as far as I'm concerned it doesn't. It just has the most answers. Because there are some things we'll just never know this side of glory. So we trust God's got His finger on the situation or we turn our back on Him and get all mad because He hasn't sat down with us and explained it in minute detail.

Even with my less-than-ideal childhood, I always knew God had better things to do than appease Charmaine Hopewell's curiosity. Not that He couldn't do that *and* get the other things done, too, Him being omnipotent and all.

See? This is why I don't get into deep theological discussions. It hurts my head. I'd rather be thought of as shallow. I really would.

Now Harlan's another story. You should hear him argue with the Calvinists!

I look down at my grandmother's name there in the phone book. "Minerva Whitehead." Well let's hope to goodness she was rich at one time because that's a name only money can redeem.

Minerva Whitehead.

Min.

She goes by Min. I know that much because every so often Mama would sigh and say, "I know exactly what your grandma Min would say about that!"

I begin to think up possible scenarios for my grandma living there in that little guest house.

1. She used to live in the big house, but her husband, my grandfather, whom my mother never talked about, gambled away all the money, or lost it on Wall Street (same thing according to Harlan). She sold the big house to pay off the debts.

2. She used to live in the big house, but then my grandfather got terminally sick and he had let the insurance lapse and they spent all their money on his insurance. When all was said and done, all my grandmother had left was the guest house.

3. Or, heaven help me, Grandma was just the housekeeper and Mama, the illegitimate offspring of the rich man, grew up in the shadow of the wealthy family in the big house.

I hope it isn't number three! Of all of those, dear Lord, don't let it be that. It's as bad as one of Ruby's clichés and I saw something like that in a movie with Humphrey Bogart and Audrey Hepburn, without, of course, the fornicating.

As another Virginia autumn rain begins to tap our metal roof, I realize none of those ladies at the revival tonight was my grandmother. Nobody that birthed a woman like my mama would dance down the aisles like these gals.

I had hoped she'd be there. I had hoped I would look out into the congregation and see my own face there, only it would be an older face with soft skin like waterlogged tree bark. The hair would be white and pulled into a soft, frizzy bun. But in the elderly department all I saw were twin sisters with salt-and-pepper poodle perms, a bleached blond beehive, and a greasy black *Little Rascal* girl hairdo.

None of them could have possibly been my grandma.

Oh, but Harlan was on fire tonight! Talking about problems that beset us. Talking about how Jesus is the answer. Not wine or strong drink, or affairs or drugs. Even unnecessary prescription drugs. I guess he figured he wasn't speaking to a bunch of heroin addicts.

Good thing my Sominex is over-the-counter!

The clock clicks again. 1:10.

Obviously the pills aren't working.

My lands.

I recall those sleeps of my childhood and just yearn.

If only I could feel like myself these days.

The silver writing embossed on the cover of my pink Bible shines blue in the light of the alarm clock, so I climb up into the loft over the cab, turn on the little desk light and begin reading, knowing I'll be asleep in no time.

Isn't that so sad? Satan, once again, has to get the last word, even if it's by giving you the sleep you really need. Anything to keep you from reading what God has to say. But don't you see, in the end God wins, because He's the one that loves us the most.

12

$\mathscr{I}$ finally got to sleep around
dawn last night. I really thought the Bible would put me
to sleep as usual, but the old Woman at the Well got in my
way and set me to thinking about things. First of all, I
figured maybe I better put *myself* in her place instead of
Mama all the time. That's a surefire way not to take the
message of the story to heart. And how many times do I
do that? Read the Bible and think about all the people a
particular passage applies to.

Absalom: Mama
Esther: Mrs. Evans
David and Bathsheba: Mama
Delilah: Mama
Dorcas: Mrs. Evans
Jezebel: Mama
Poor Mama!

So for the first time I think of myself there at the well.
I actually put myself into that woman's shoes and imagine closely what it must have been like. For some reason,
it's always summer in the Bible to me. So the air surrounding the stone well is thick and everybody's got hot

feet and dusty hems. I tell myself as I take my water jar down from some old rough-hewn shelf near my door, that I'll walk slowly so as not to drain my strength for the walk home with the heavy jar.

But as usual, I can't wait to sit and gab with some of the other town strumpets, so I hurry and for one of the only times in my life no one is at the well.

Imagine that. A big well, one that Jacob built, in the middle of Samaria, and no one's there. No chitchat today.

Wonder if the Woman at the Well had red hair?

Anyway, it's not hard to imagine it at all, me sitting on the lip of that faraway well, resting my feet. Woman like me live far away from wells I'll bet because people are scared we'll contaminate the water. I stare down into the water and see my silhouette against the reflection of a colorless, summer sky.

And why is it that the weather or season is hardly mentioned in the Bible? How am I supposed to know what month Adar is?

I gaze at the featureless outline and I think to myself, "What happened to you, Charmaine?" Of course, I doubt the Woman at the Well's name was Charmaine, but the scriptures don't say. One day you're a young girl with hopes and dreams, and then, you're sitting on the edge of a well, all alone, having had more men than you'd ever imagined.

Joshua.

Jeconiah.

Ezra.

Ananias.

Ehud.

All failed marriages.

How did you make a mess of five marriages? Why is it everything you touch turns to a mess? I want to throw a handful of dust into the water to take away my dim reflection, but I don't want to taint my own water. So I get to my feet and decide to draw out my water and get on home to Thaddeus. He's not the marrying type.

The ping of the rain on the RV's roof intensifies, drawing me out of my imaginings. That poor woman. Of course Jesus came when she needed Him, when she needed a good man. But what if I sat at that well and it was really me, Charmaine Hopewell, not me pretending to be the Woman at the Well? I'd sit there looking at my silhouette and I'd cry out. I'd see not a woman who'd squandered her life on men, I'd just see somebody who once had nothing much to squander but had suddenly been given riches galore. I could hurt a lot of people now if I decided to squander my life. Harlan, Hope, Ruby, and Grace, even Melvin and Henry Windsor.

Then Jesus would walk up to me and offer me His living water, right there at the well, and I'd drop to my knees and worship my Lord and Savior. Yes, I'd worship Him face-to-face, as I hope to do someday. Oh, Lord Jesus, just to see Your face is all I want.

Dawn just begins to blush the sky and I drift off, safe in the knowledge that I've been harbored in God's hand all these years. People may want this to be a tale of a girl who loses it all due to poor decisions, who drags her heart and soul through the mire of worldly living, who makes terrible decisions. But God doesn't always work like that. Sometimes His grace keeps people from making huge mistakes. Maybe it's because they've already received their fair share of pain from external sources.

I call willful sin elective pain.

Why should I elect to cause myself pain when there's so much of it that rains down without my goading? However, I'd be lying if I said I wasn't always waiting for a twig to snap beneath my feet.

Then again, I guess I don't really deserve God's favor from my own merit. He gave the land of Canaan to Israel despite the fact they were, as He put it, "a stiff-necked people."

I guess that's good news for me.

Harlen awakens me at 9:30, Hope sitting on his lap there on the bed.

"Shug? You okay? You were sleeping like the dead."

"Just couldn't seem to get myself going. I tried and tried to get out of bed earlier, but just couldn't. My goodness, I think this traveling is beginning to get to me. What I wouldn't give for a night in a regular bed!"

Harlen smiles. "The church ladies are giving you a luncheon at eleven-thirty. Remember?"

I raise a hand beneath the bedspread. "I forgot. Can you pour me a Diet Coke? Maybe the caffeine will help me get going."

"Anything you want, sweet thing."

They sit me and Ruby and Grace at the head table with Mrs. Chorey and the deacon's wives. "No, no, no, ma'am, you don't have to bother yourselves with the buffet line," a younger woman in a denim jumper and a rust-colored turtleneck with two oak leaves embroidered on the collar assures me. So they load up plates of fried chicken, Smithfield ham, ambrosia salad, seven-layer salad, broccoli cheese casserole, and potatoes au gratin.

Iced tea, too. Loads of sugar. Southern tea, which, in my opinion beats all others.

And no plastic forks for these gals. We eat with stainless on plain, serviceable china plates. I notice a nice kitchen in the back of the basement and I think to myself for the first time ever, "If Harlan and I ever have our own church, I want a nice kitchen with real cutlery and plates."

Peanut-butter pie for dessert.

They don't make peanut-butter pie better anywhere than Suffolk, which is the peanut capital of the world, after all.

That reminds me. I might seek out the recipe and try it out on Harlan. Last night after the meeting I made some chocolate junket and put it in the fridge. I'm going to give some to Hope this afternoon as a little treat. Mrs. Evans used to make junket for me as a treat.

Mrs. Chorey leans over to me after I put a bit of ham in my mouth. "Look at them. They're a nice bunch, these ladies."

I swallow. "Yes?"

"Oh, yes. Now, lest you think I'm a regular Pollyanna, I've been in churches where nothing I did was right no matter how hard I tried, but these people, they're special."

I'm glad to hear that. "What do you think the difference is?"

She shrugs. "Spiritual maturity. Several large, close families in the midst. Who's to say?"

"Every so often we come to a church like this. Usually they're small and humble."

"I know. Can't say many of the high falutin' types come here to Grace and Truth."

The time has come. "There's a woman in this town my mama knew. I was wondering if you knew of her."

"What's her name?"

"Minerva Whitehead. Lives over on Freemason Street."

She taps her chin. "Name sounds familiar, but I can't place it. Definitely doesn't go to church here. But if she lives on Freemason Street that might explain it!"

"Oh, she lives in one of the guest houses, I think."

"Then I'm surprised she hasn't found us!"

We laugh.

"She doesn't know me, but she knew my mama very well."

"Is your Mama all right?"

"Oh, she died when I was eleven."

"I'm sorry."

"So you see, meeting this woman—"

"I understand. Let me ask Tanzel over there after lunch. See the pretty lady with the gray curls in the burgundy sweater? She's the church secretary and knows everybody in town."

"I'd be grateful." I lay a hand on her arm. "Please don't tell my husband, though, Mrs. Chorey. My grief over my mama worries him, and I hate to worry him."

"Oh, my dear. I understand about how a preacher's wife protects her husband from all sorts of things."

"If we don't, no one else will."

"You're a real peach Mrs. Hopewell."

When she called me that, I wanted to cry.

We sit in the church office drinking tea. All sorts of framed funny sayings are hanging on Tanzel's walls. Things like, I HAVE ONE NERVE LEFT AND YOU'RE STANDING ON IT.

She smiles. "The ones about menopause are taped in my drawer!"

I feel a kinship with her right away and know I'll come back to this place every time I'm in this area.

"So you want to know about Mrs. Whitehead?"

"Yes, ma'am. Minerva Whitehead. You know her?"

"Oh, yes, I sure do know Min Whitehead. Went to Sunday school with her for a while years ago. She was my son's sixth-grade teacher."

"She was a teacher?"

"Still is. But now she teaches fifth grade because she said she didn't want to move up to the middle school. She's the elementary type."

"Really?"

"Oh, my yes. You should see Min with children. She's always been everyone's favorite teacher."

Not at all what I expected. "Has she always lived in that house?"

"She and her husband bought it back after the war. They're not from here." Tanzel leans forward. "She's from . . . *Florida*."

"Oh," I whisper. "Is she the type that would mind if I dropped in?"

"Not at all."

"What about her husband? My mama never mentioned him much."

"He died of cancer about four years after their daughter was born. Her name was Isla. She was always a strange one." She leaned forward. "Left years ago and hasn't been back since."

My heart fell. Maybe Grandma Min knew as little as I did about the whereabouts of Mama. But now I knew, at least, I wouldn't be running into Mama. I wouldn't just be showing up at her abode with a big-haired, big-toothed "Surprise!"

"How strange was this Isla?"

"Some folks just seem like they're not with you, even when you're two feet from them."

That sure described Mama.

"Had a lot of boyfriends, too. Very promiscuous. Not that her mother knew the extent of it. But, well, my daughter always filled me in on the high-school gossip. I think she broke Minerva's heart. She'd disappear for days at a time."

"I can't imagine having to deal with that."

Tanzel reached into her drawer and pulled out a ledger, then slid a pen out of the holder at the corner of the desk. "I think it hardens you after a while. I mean, you love them, but you have to decide whether or not you're going to let that love kill you or make you strong, if you're going to go on living, or not."

13

I really thought Grace had gone on the wagon, but she fooled me. She'd only added to her repertoire. I don't blame Ruby for not telling me. She keeps my secrets, too.

Ruby has been trying to get me on antidepressants for the past few years and so far I've resisted. Harlan's content to believe I'm "just not a morning person." Besides, with his message of "What's Really Eating You" and his brother E.J.'s experience with the psychiatric realm, I'm trusting God to deliver me someday.

It's a light depression, I'm sure. I mean, I do eventually get out of bed, and I read that depressed people get very snappish, and I'm not a snappish person at all. At least not much, and only at Grace. So I must not have a bad case.

I think Grace must deal with something like depression, too. When I first started making costumes for Grace she was a size eight. Now she's a four. Which I am, too, but I'm short. Grace is 5'8".

I still love Grace like my cousin as I did years ago, I just now love her as the cousin who's a screwup. If that sounds harsh, well maybe it is. But obviously somebody should have been harsher with Grace years ago.

The real icing on the cake to this situation is that Grace's parents wait for my calls to tell them that their daughter is all right. Isn't that rich? I have to call some-one *else's* parents, me, the girl who has none, to let them know their daughter is still alive. Of course I lie, lie, lie, and tell them she's fine.

I've ranted at Harlan. "Why? Why do I do this?"

"You don't do it for Grace, honey, you do it for her parents."

"Still."

"I know, sweetheart, I know."

"Will she ever wake up to herself?"

"I don't know. But that's not our concern."

"It will be if she disgraces the ministry, Harlan!"

"How in the world can Grace do that?"

I don't know the answer to that. But I'm sure it isn't out of the realm of possibility.

"Well, I shouldn't lie, though. At least we can agree on that."

"You're right. But I'm not going to pretend I can't un-derstand why you do."

We've had this conversation so many times it makes me sick. And still something inside me tells me not to let Grace go, to hang in there for her parents, if nothing else. If I was honest, I'd realize it was more, I'd realize I was assigned to Grace as surely as I'd been assigned to sing.

What a pain!

Oh, Lord!

I lay Hope in the bed for a nap, grab a can of Diet

Coke, and walk over to the girls' trailer. I knock. "Grace? You there?"

"Come on in, Charmaine."

I do. She sits at the dinette with a glass of clear liquid. "Hey Charmaine, I'm just having a glass of water. Want some?"

I know it isn't water but I play along.

"No thanks. I brought my soda. Where's Leo?"

She points to the bed at the back of the trailer. He lies in a lump on the bed, shoes still on his feet, face in need of a good wipe. Four years ago Grace, who swore she'd never sing gospel songs and fled Ruby and me, showed up at one of our crusades with a newborn. Little Leo. "Grace."

"Don't say it, Charmaine."

"Don't say what?"

"Oh, come off it. You know."

"Look, you can drag yourself down this path you've chosen. But what about your boy? Doesn't he deserve better?"

"Yes, he does. Better than this two bit *crusade*! Better than traveling around in a trailer and singing in tasteless, homemade costumes. I've ruined my life and I'm taking a baby along for the ride. Yes, he deserves better. Feel good, now?"

She is talking about my life, too, only I don't think it's so bad. "So what can I do?"

She grates out a laugh and I see a deadness in her eyes that hasn't been there before, as though a precipice has been tumbled over, finally, after all this time. And I am surprised that it took this long, really. "You already do everything for me but drink my drinks and sing second soprano."

"Am I keeping you with us?"

"Yes. But only because I don't know where else to go."

"You can always go back home, Grace."

She lifts her glass and sips, looking so much like Mama I feel my skin raise at the chill. "Maybe I will someday."

I look back at Leo's sleeping form. "Do you want me to care for Leo for a while? Let you concentrate on straightening yourself out?"

She only nods.

"Have you thought about going someplace to dry out?"

She nods again. "But I don't know where."

"There's a place up in New York State, it's just for women. But it's a Christian place, Grace. I can make the calls."

"Do whatever you have to do, Charmaine. I'll cooperate."

I sigh. "Let me know when Leo wakes up. I'm going to go make a chocolate cake. Maybe he'd like some with a glass of cold milk."

"He'll sleep for a good two hours more."

"Just let me know."

But Grace says nothing else. She just reaches into her pocket and pulls out a pack of cigarettes.

I see her puffing out behind the trailer a minute later and think, I am watching a living tragedy. I wonder if God will lift her up out of the miry clay and set her feet upon the solid rock.

I mix up the batter for the cake, put it in the oven to

bake, and run into the church. Ruby sits at the piano playing like no tomorrow. "Ruby?"

"Yeah, Char?"

"Can you go sit in the motor home for a few minutes? Hope's asleep and I got a cake in the oven. I just have to make a couple of quick calls."

"Sure thing."

I sit down in front of Tanzel's desk and ask her if I can use the phone.

"Of course, honey. Is it a private matter?"

I nod.

"Go on down to the kitchen. There's an extension there and nobody will bother you."

"You sure you won't pick up your line and listen in?" I joke.

"I'm not promising a thing!"

I call the home for addicted women and explain Grace's situation.

Twenty minutes later I pack her things and ask Melvin to carry the sleeping Leo to the motor home and lay him on the bed next to Hope. Then I drive her to the train station for an express north.

When I return, I awaken Leo from his nap, bathe him, put on a fresh pair of pants and a shirt, and show him the loft of our motor home. "This is your bed now, sweet boy. You like being up high like this?"

He nods effusively.

Melvin builds a little railing right away and by the time we finish the service tonight, it is securely installed. At twenty-three years of age I am the practical mother of two children.

Leo doesn't even cry for his Mama that night. He eats

another slice of cake and flinches every time I put my hand out to stroke his full, sweet cheeks, or smooth his soft blond hair.

I pray Grace will make it to the home. I even bought her a bottle of Seagram's to make sure she had no reason to get off the train.

You know, I really have to wonder about life sometimes.

14

Today one of the deacons and his wife took us to Shoney's for a nice lunch, and now I am resting before Ruby and I begin practice for tonight's service. We're singing "Beulah Land" and that newer song, "I Want Jesus in My Life More Than Anything." Of course, we lead the music with Henry Windsor and tonight is Gaither night. How the folks love to sing those Gaither tunes, and I don't blame them. Tomorrow night is "Life Is Like a Mountain Railroad." I just love that song.

Without Grace's high parts we'll have to do a little adjusting, I guess, especially when we simulate that train whistle.

But, I feel close to sleep now as I lay next to Hope here in the back of the motor home. And I look down and see her little body there, her eyes closed in slumber. She's so pretty this little one. Her eyes move beneath her lids, which is really pretty odd-looking but nonetheless amazing, and I know she's dreaming about something. I can see the pulse beat in the artery in her neck, so strong and rhythmic and real. The human body never ceases to astound me.

Now it confounds me how living, moving beings just walk about as self-propelled machines. We don't plug ourselves in, and once we're older and we don't have mothers stuffing food in our mouths, we fuel ourselves. It's not like a car that a human has to put gasoline into.

As I said, a real miracle.

I wonder if a time existed when Mama ever laid down next to me and stared at me while I slumbered? How I wish to Jesus I could take for granted that she did. I wonder if her mama, Grandma Min, stared down at my mama, Isla Jean Whitehead?

It's a hard thought because I believe I know the answer. As wonderful as our bodies are, they are also terrible and mysterious and things go wrong. Fine-tuned things like our brains. I picture Mama's brain now and I see this shriveled-up, sick thing sitting there in her skull.

Mentally ill.

I went to the doctor earlier today. I know my life is good, but I can't shake the feeling it isn't. The Sominex isn't working and I think of Harlan's brother E.J. and figured that maybe if his wife had just done something not so drastic when she first realized she had a problem, that maybe all that stuff wouldn't have happened. I told him about my sleeplessness, my tiredness, and how angry I could get at Grace sometimes.

"Do you ever cry for no reason?"

"Not really. But I do get the urge to throw things against the wall every once in a while."

"Do you?"

"Throw things? No, sir."

He gave me a test where I answered all sorts of questions like, "Do you ever feel those around you would be better off if you were dead?" to which I answered "no." But despite that, he tallied things up and said yes, I was depressed. "I thought depression was more extreme."

"Not always. People have their own way of manifesting symptoms."

I nod. "What if you just give me a better sleeping pill? Maybe if I get more rest that will do the trick."

So he does. And I am glad because I sure don't want to get on some awful medication. I'll bet Harlan's happy mother didn't take a pill her entire life!

He suggested counseling, too, but with my life of traveling hither and yon, I know that is impossible. And while I can hide a bottle of pills in my Tampax box, I can't hide a weekly visit to a shrink. And after the damage that psychiatrist did to Harlan's sister-in-law, well, I'm a little reticent, and who can blame me? Mama never trusted doctors either.

Two more days and our time in Suffolk will come to an end. We hit the road on Thursday and head down to Atlanta. Or "Hotlanta" as they say.

Oh, my lands.

Ruby is in hog heaven now that the travel trailer is her own. We boxed up the rest of Grace's things and stored it in a corner of the utility truck that carries speakers and such. We'll drop it all off at Bee's when we go by that way. Ruby already put up new yellow curtains, bought a new spread for the bed and a new lamp. It looks like a real little home in there now. All that space for one person, and then there's four of us in the motor home. I don't blame Ruby, but what I wouldn't kill for a little ranch home somewhere. It could be brick or just siding. I wouldn't even ask for shutters as long as I could walk across floors and not always down aisles.

But guess what? Harlan agreed to get new carpet for the RV and he said I could pick whatever color I want. I never could get all the mud out from that gravedigger night. He asked me to just hold off for a few months until our finances strengthened a little. So I'm going with plum. And Ruby and I are going to reupholster the dinette and van seats, too! Won't Melvin have a fit? I can look into his mind right now and see his thoughts. I can see him thinking biblically. "Talk about casting your pearls before swine. And purple? How can a decent man drive in a purple seat?"

He won't say anything though.

I sit at my dinette imagining the possibilities. I'm going to try putting up border again, the adhesive kind, and some mirrors to give the illusion of space. I had the idea of installing a ceiling fan in the bedroom area and Harlan looked at me askance. "What're you trying to do, Shug, decapitate me?" So there went that idea. That's okay though, because I'll tuck it away for later when I want something else and I'll be able to say, "Well, I couldn't get that fan I wanted so I thought this would be a good second."

Ha.

I love our womanly tricks of the trade. And you know what? Some of these things just come naturally. I know this because Mama sure didn't teach me.

Hope and Leo sit on the bench across from me. Leo's coloring and Hope's shoving crayons in her mouth. But Leo's in his own little world and doesn't seem to mind. In fact, he takes the cornflower crayon from her pillowy fist and starts on a sky. He's got potential, I do believe. I wonder if Grace ever noticed?

I gaze at his little head, the straight cap of blond hair swinging slightly as he bears down on the crayon and practically digs a blue pond into the paper. I gaze into his little head and I see myself there. I see a small child with a drinking mama. Only at least my mama made sure I was clean. I have to give her that.

"Leo?"

He looks up and nods.

"You doing okay these past couple of days here with us?"

He nods. "Uh-huh."

"Would you like another piece of chocolate cake?"

"Uh-huh."

Shoot. Why did I offer that? Now I'll have to give Hope some and she insists on feeding herself and I'll be giving her yet another bath today! So much for trying to get a glimpse of Grandma Min this afternoon. I'd better get a move-on soon because tomorrow is the last day.

15

Tonight it's "This Old House" and "Suppertime." Now that "Suppertime" song always makes me want to cry. Those gospel songwriters and their mamas! Makes me wonder if I should pick another genre of music to sing.

MaryAnna Trench called me today. Some man down in Atlanta wants to hear me sing for something he organizes each summer called "Gospelganza." Next summer it will be Gospelganza '84 and they travel all over the country. Talk about good exposure. When I told Harlan about it, he just shrugged his shoulders. "Well it can't hurt to check it out, Shug. But don't get your hopes up too high. There's crazy people everywhere."

And that sure is the truth.

What a day today is. I love weather for some reason because although it's always changing, it rarely does something other than what you're used to. Weather is like God, always unexpected, but never completely unpredictable. 'Course there are times when a cyclone hits, and it catches you unawares. It's violent and swirling and moves like an army catching anything that's not nailed down to the earth. And God's like that too sometimes, only it's not about being nailed down to the earth, it's about being nailed down to the Kingdom of God. Today is one of those autumn days that have been dropped in a toaster for just a spell. Not much else has changed, the air still feels thin with October and smells of leaves and smoke. So I slip into my yellow sweater, strap the kids in their car seats, and head on out in the truck over to Freemason Street. I've already decided I'm not going to go and see Grandma Min, but I am going to try and get some clues as to who she is and to see if this is the house my mama grew up in.

Hope, in the middle of the truck bench seat, already looks like she's falling asleep. Praise God! What a morning! This child is turning into a pip. Getting into everything. I wonder if I was like that. Leo just looks out the window. The nice thing is that he and Harlan have always had a shine for one another. I wish I had taken some more time with him before Grace left. Now, I just am not sure what to do for him.

But my heart couldn't be more full for the little fellow.

I ride through the Hardee's drive-thru and get myself a Diet Coke and Leo a Sprite. We just smile at each other. I pull away and utter a prayer for Grace and in the same space of brain wonder how she could not see the value of this little boy.

What a great night's sleep I had last night! That prescription sleeping pill beat the over-the-counter variety. This may just be the answer. And maybe Harlan's right. In his sermons he says we're so quick to seek our own methods of healing and redemption, that we're too slow in falling at the Savior's feet and giving it all over to Him.

It's 3:15 and I am hoping I catch my grandma coming home from school. But as I pull up, I notice a car already sits in the driveway. It's a dark blue Escort.

And so I begin to look for clues. All the curtains are lined so I can't tell if frilly pink ones hang in the upper, dormered windows. I figure if a girl grew up there, surely there'd be pink, frilly curtains at one of the windows. The garden has been mulched this autumn and the bushes trimmed, but not in perfect shapes. And then the warm breeze blows and I notice it sitting there in the backyard. A rusty old swing set. I see my mama swinging there, dangling her legs, all alone, for she never spoke of a sibling. And I see Grandma Min checking at her from the kitchen window from time to time. And Mama is just lonely.

It is a lonely house.

What has Grandma Min been thinking all these years? How sad did Mama's choices make her?

I can't believe Grandma Min was the abusive type that pushed her daughter from the house. I mean, she is a schoolteacher. So what happened to drive Mama to Lynchburg?

I just need to do this. Just go on up to the house and knock on the door. I picture myself doing so in my mind's eye, which is always a good first step. And so I decide that if I don't do it now, I just may never, and we're leaving town tomorrow night.

I pull the truck into the drive.

"Now Leo, just sit here a minute while I go ring the bell. Try not to wake Hope. You know how she can be."

"Uh-huh."

I check my hair in the rearview mirror, freshen up my

lipstick a little, turn off the engine, and roll down my window.

I should have told Harlan. He'd be here with me now. He'd run interference or something. Maybe he'd even go up to the door and tell Grandma Min the entire tale.

What if she is really a bitter old woman who wanders around inside her little house? What if she really doesn't want to know about me?

So I breathe in and set my feet on the brick path.

Bitter old women didn't spread mulch and trim their bushes, did they? Bitter old women didn't keep the swing set around, did they?

But I'll bet bitter old women did buy lined draperies.

I step onto the landing and ring the bell before I could talk myself out of it.

A long slim window lines either side of the dark blue door and I see someone peer out the right one. A white brow lifts, her florid forehead knits, pale blue eyes widen then disappear. Locks click as they are disengaged.

The door opens and there she stands, my own flesh and blood. She wears a plaid skirt and a dark green turtleneck and her white hair is cut short and boyish. "Can I help you?"

How do I start this? Why didn't I think up a good starting sentence. "Are you the mother of Isla Whitehead?"

She pales.

"Are you Minerva Whitehead?"

"Yes, I am."

"I'm your granddaughter, Myrtle Charmaine."

She shakes her head in bewilderment. "What?"

"I'm Isla's daughter. She named me Myrtle Charmaine

and always called me Myrtle, but a few years ago I decided to go by Charmaine."

She remains silent.

I expect her to ask if this was some sort of joke, you know, like they always do in books and movies and stuff. But she just stands there with her mouth open. My nerves jangle like silver charms. Should I offer proof? I open my purse and pull out my driver's license. "See here? Charmaine Whitehead Hopewell."

"You're married?"

"Yes, ma'am."

I can't even begin to gauge what she must be thinking, but the color returns to her face. She looks at the picture of me on the license and then back at my face.

"I know it's not very good, but I just get so nervous in front of those motor vehicle cameras. Why, when Mr. Reasin taught me to drive and took me to get my learner's permit they had to take five shots before they got one of me with my eyes open."

I don't know what else to do but fill the empty spaces with my babble. No wonder God had the people of Babel disburse. He probably got tired of hearing all their noise. Just like I am tired of hearing mine. But still I go on.

"I'm here in the area just until tomorrow. Mama mentioned you from time to time—"

"She's still alive?"

I shake my head.

"Oh, no!" She jams her hand against her mouth.

"No, I didn't mean 'no,' I meant I don't know! I don't know whether she's alive or dead."

Grandma Min turns away, walks over to the steps in

the center hall of the house, and sits down. I follow her inside. "You said your name was Charmaine?"

"Yes, ma'am."

She bows her head. "And your maiden name was Whitehead?"

"Yes, ma'am."

"So you're mother wasn't married?"

"No, ma'am."

"I'm sorry for you then."

I don't want to tell her that isn't even the worst of it, so I don't just then. I'm hoping there will be time for that. "I know this is a shock."

She sits there with her head bowed, still clutching my driver's license. I pull out my little calling card that has Bee's phone number and replace the license with it. "I'm sorry. I shouldn't have come here, I guess. But well, you being family and all . . ."

Grandma Min starts to cry and I don't know what to do. "Good-bye, then, Mrs. Whitehead."

I leave the house, hoping against hope that someday she'll call that number.

16

*M*ark is the Rodney Dangerfield of the gospels. People go on and on about the book of John, not that I blame them. Matthew, well, he was an apostle and gets a good deal of exposure from the pulpit. And Luke, the physician, wrote such a beautiful account of the nativity, and anything written to someone named Theophilus must be good. But Mark? You just don't hear too much about Mark.

But I've been reading there and I do believe I found a new female Bible hero. The lady with the issue of blood. I'm not quite sure what an "issue of blood" is, but it's a woman so I figure it must be she's bleeding vaginally. Can you imagine having your period for all those years? Twelve years?

That poor, poor thing.

Too bad Mrs. Evans wasn't there to comfort her.

I think I'd have spent all my money on doctors, too, so I cannot blame her there. In fact I can't find anything to blame this poor woman for, not like the Woman at the Well who slept with all those men. I admire her for stepping through the crowd like she did, for falling on her feet, for reaching out and touching His hem. I don't think I would have had her courage.

Harlan preached on this passage the night before. Now sometimes my husband can be a little bit forthright about things and this current series, "What's *Really* Eating at You," has given me food for thought, pardon the pun.

Ha.

He talked about how we're looking for a pill to cure everything. Don't I know it! And darn that sister-in-law of his who hand-delivered this bone for Harlan to pick.

He said, "We need to be bold in our faith! Not rely upon man. Do I hear an 'amen'?"

And of course, all the men amened.

"We need to step forward in the crowd, we need to kneel, yes, we need to kneel!"

"Amen, brother!"

"We need to kneel at the feet of the Savior. We need to grab hold of the hem of His holy garments. We need to want His power enough to do that, amen!"

"Amen!"

"Hallelujah!"

"We need to grab hold."

And he reaches into his pocket and wipes his brow. "Yes, we do," his voice quiets and he leans forward, the silence of the building suddenly deafening. "Grab hold of that hem. Grab hold of that hem."

His voice intensifies. "Grab hold of that hem!"

He shouts now, "Grab hold of that hem!"

The ladies in the front start chanting, "Grab hold of that hem. Grab hold of that hem. Grab hold of that hem." And since it was an Assemblies church, I hear a couple of people speaking in tongues.

Harlan continues, now in full sway. "Jesus says 'Come to Me all ye that are heavy laden and I will give you rest! Take My yoke upon you and learn of *Me* for I am meek and lowly in heart and ye shall find rest for your souls! Rest for your souls!'

"Are you sin-sick and weary?"

He claps.

"Are you laid down with the cares of this life?"

He claps.

"Have you a sickness that you've tried to heal? Have you spent money on doctors? Have you been disappointed by the workings of man on your behalf? Are you ill in body and soul and nothing anyone ever does heals your ailments?"

He claps twice. "Lay them down! At the feet of Jesus! Lay them down and lay yourself down while you're at it, beloved, and grab the hem of Jesus! Grab that hem!"

Henry Windsor begins to play and the group works itself up into a frenzy.

"You've been trying! You've been trying to dig yourself out of the miry clay. Give Jesus a turn! Grab hold of that hem!"

I felt the Spirit fill me, telling me to grab hold of that hem. Grab it Myrtle Charmaine Whitehead! Now is the hour of your healing.

From what, Lord?

Grab the hem, Myrtle Charmaine.

What hem, Myrtle Charmaine? What a bunch of crackpots!

Oh, Jesus.

Now is the hour of your healing, Myrtle Charmaine.

Suddenly, I came to. I was on the floor and Harlan stood over me, fanning me with Sunday's old bulletin.

"Honey, you okay?"

But I couldn't speak. All I could do was cry.

Now, a day later, I am sitting at the dinette, rereading the Mark passage as Melvin drives us away from Suffolk. It is midnight. Harlan is always exhausted when we pull away. I tell him he doesn't have to help Mel and the boys load up, but he insists. So he's asleep in the back of the motor home. Little Leo is asleep in my loft. He has a little nose whistle that is so cute. I can hear the pace of his breathing and I am comforted.

We are heading back west on 58 where we'll hit I-85, then head on south to Atlanta. Melvin and Randall slept all day in their truck camper so they'd be fresh to drive. I'd hate to have their schedule.

So here I sit. I took my sleeping pill and I'm pulling a Martin Luther of the mind on myself and wondering why I have such little faith. Didn't the Spirit say I was healed and yet I swallowed that pill anyway.

Of course you did, Myrtle Charmaine. You think you're so spiritual.

That's not true, Mama! I'm a struggler like everyone else.

So I pray in the dim light of my little lamp and I watch the lights go by. Not many of them out here. And I am glad God can see me. He knows I took that pill and in a strange way that comforts me. Imagine how horrible life would be if we could hide things from God.

I called Bee's this morning and no messages came in. I called her this afternoon and still nothing.

17

I wonder what that demoniac did when he went back through the Ten Towns, as it says in the book of Mark? I mean, first of all, people were probably pretty scared of him to begin with even though he was clothed and cleaned up. Crazy, they said about him, I'll bet.

"That guy is crazy!"

Then he shows up, after being healed by Jesus as this normal guy. Imagine that. One day he's more animal than man. The next he's experienced the touch of the Divine and is probably more fully human than I'll ever be.

Nevertheless, he went to the towns.

Too bad it couldn't have happened like this for Mama. Too bad God didn't just reach out and perform a miracle.

The bad thing about meeting Grandma Min is that now I know she doesn't know a thing about Mama's whereabouts, even though Mama is probably dead. I'm thinking that maybe I can find Mama now that I'm a little older. Of course, I don't have a lot of money for a private detective.

I figure I'll send away for a D.C. phone book and call

hospitals. Maybe they saw her years ago when she went up there. Maybe they have her on record. Maybe they can tell me how she died or where she ended up.

Maybe they can tell me something.

❧

"Bee?"

"Oh, hey, Charmaine."

"Any messages?"

"Nope. None today."

I hop back up into the motor home and we are on our way from Spartanburg, South Carolina, and back on I-85 toward Atlanta.

Melvin fixed me up a way to put my sewing machine on the side table and anchor it to the wall so it doesn't slide around. I just sew and sew on the road. Right now Hope is strapped in her car seat at the dinette and Leo sits belted in. They are listening to a Robin Hood tape and looking at the picture book together. Leo tickles me. Hope kept grabbing the book so he unbuckled himself, got a lollipop out of the kitchen cabinet under the silverware drawer, and gave it to her.

It worked. They're looking at that book so nicely now. That boy's so smart!

Harlan, sitting in the captain's chair next to Melvin's, swivels around. "How's the dress coming?"

I take the pins out of my mouth. "I'm not sure. Maybe I should have gone a little more plain Jane."

"For an event called 'Gospelganza'? You must be kidding me, Shug. I think magenta with orange trim will knock 'em dead!"

"You do?"

"Oh, come on. You're the prettiest thing going."

I smile and he smiles and swivels back to study from his concordance and reference books. The smiles stays on his face all the way around.

To tell you the truth, after only one day I'm already tired of being the one to rush and get the messages from Bee. I'm going to tell Harlan about Grandma Min tonight.

Harlan was able to get a church to speak at in Atlanta. It may not be much money, but it should go far in helping us. Thank You, Lord, the church in Suffolk reached out their arms of generosity. We not only made payroll, but Harlan told me yesterday his surprise is around the corner! "Pretty soon we'll really be living, Shug!"

I can only think it's going to be a house. I imagine we'll settle around Tennessee near Bee. And that would be fine with me. I'm not going to be picky, either. As long as there's walls I can paint, I'll be one happy camper.

I am about to audition right here in Atlanta. MaryAnna Trench meets me on the steps to the auditorium at Kennesaw State College.

"Oh, Char, you look great! Where did you ever find orange high heels?"

"Lottie's in Greenville. Half price."

I don't hug MaryAnna. She's not the type of person who inspires hugs and I'm a huggy sort so what does that say?

I must admit my magenta dress is wonderful. Full skirt, '50s style, an orange sequined belt, and a jacket with orange lace that falls from the elbow length sleeves.

Nothing like anything you'd ever find in the department store, I can tell you that! Harlan thought a hat would add the finishing touch but we couldn't find one to match so I made a bow for my hair.

"You ready?" MaryAnna flattens her own full skirt. Only hers is plaid and she actually wears a tam. The pom-pom on top nods back and forth, mimicking her own movement as she mimics mine. Scotland forever!

"Harlan's parking the truck. Then we can go in."

We made camp yesterday at a KOA near Cartersville. The boys are going to do routine maintenance on the equipment this week and Ruby will baby-sit when I need her. Melvin built a campfire last night, so we sat around and sang some of our favorite songs. It's times like these that bring us members of the crusade together. We really are a family.

Even now Ruby watches the kids in her travel trailer.

I know I said I would tell Harlan about Grandma Min last night, but I haven't yet. I think if this audition goes well, I really will tell him tonight. That way at least we'll have had a good day behind us.

Great. They've got the lights going and everything in this place. I can't even see the guy. I didn't meet him beforehand. His assistant said, "Just get out on stage and start to sing."

Henry Windsor begins the opening strains of "This Old House" and I do my best not to clear my throat. I opt for a big grin and a wave of my hands as I begin.

We really go, Henry and I. Of course, this song is made for a quartet, but we take a different spin on it. I sing it bluesy-like. Like nothing I've heard before. And Henry just goes with it. I sneak a glance over at the piano and he's swaying like Ray Charles! And we begin to feed off each other's energy. Our sways unifying, our souls flowing in the same groove and I am stunned for a moment, blinded by the lights, the sound and the stream of notes.

I am in ecstasy. If I was a man I'd be guilty of having a mistress, I'd have sold out to a different love, my heart given over to another lover.

The song lasts ten minutes if it lasts a second. By the time we finish, both Henry and I are covered in sweat. I reach into my skirt pocket and pull out the handkerchief I keep handy during every concert. We wipe our brows in tandem.

18

A day later MaryAnna bursts
into the motor home where we are consuming chicken
salad on potato rolls. "You've got it! They want you on
the tour this summer!"

I turn to Harlan. "Oh, Harlan! I can't believe it!"

"Congratulations, Shug!"

We hug. The kids clap their chubby hands.

"You need to be back in Atlanta in mid-May for prac-
tices. They'll be forwarding your song selections as well
as tapes with the orchestration after Christmas."

I jump a little. "Whoo-hoo!"

Harlan unfolds to his feet and kisses me. "Now this is
cause for celebration! I say we poke into the savings a little and have us a steak dinner!"

"Okay!" I hug him to me tightly.

MaryAnna says, "Not too much steak, Charmaine.
You don't want to pack on the pounds between now and
then!"

"What?" Harlan pulls back. "This woman is perfect in
every way."

My agent shakes her head. "You two are too much. If

you weren't my client, Charmaine, you'd make me sick. But as it is, a client with a healthy marriage is much easier to manage than someone who not only wants representation, but a marriage counselor, too."

"You been married before?" Harlan asks.

"Four times. I could write a book on marriage."

Harlan and I look at each other and don't say a word.

"How about some lunch, Ms. Trench?" Harlan shows her a seat.

"No, thanks. But I'll sit with you."

Under her watchdog eye the chicken salad I'd made earlier turns into sawdust. "I'll just get myself another Diet Coke."

"Good girl, Char."

I want to growl at her.

It's five P.M. and I stand in line to use the phone at the campground. Why there's a big line at this time of day this time of year at the KOA in Cartersville, Georgia, is beyond me, but there you have it. I can't get my mind off Grandma Min. I figure she actually may not call the number. She actually may write a letter, which is what I would probably do. It would be hard to get all your thoughts across well in a phone call, but in a letter, that would make all the difference.

So the first guy talking on the phone had problems with the hitch on his RV. He said they've been towing a little AMC Hornet on the back.

The second guy ordered a pizza.

And right now a lady goes on and on about her grandson Carl to, I presume, her sister.

Carl this. Carl that.

Oh, my lands.

I find out Carl walked at ten months, said his first words at eight, and I'm sure this poor lady has heard this all before.

I clear my throat.

She doesn't turn around.

I thank God that at least I don't wear those ugly thick-soled shoes like the ones she's got on. And those brown elastic-waisted stretch pants are just an eyesore. Kind of like the clothing equivalent of the industrial part of a city the main interstate always runs through.

I hope Bee is home.

Finally Granny Brown Pants hangs up, turns and displays a set of "Miracle Ears." She smiles like a sunbeam as her eyes meet mine and I feel so bad about criticizing her like I did.

"Aren't you just the prettiest thing?"

And I feel even worse.

"Thanks, ma'am."

She slides on by.

I pick up the phone and dial Bee's number.

"Hey, Bee. It's me."

"Hey, Charmaine."

"Any calls?"

"No. Just some mail."

The phone feels hot and hard in my grasp. "Anything interesting?"

"A bill from the propane company, two invites to speak. One's a church in Richmond and the other's in a town called Mount Oak."

"I've heard of it."

"There's also a personal letter for you."

"Oh, yeah? Who from?"

"No first name. Last name is Whitehead."

I try to breathe but feels like my lungs have filled with Cheez Whiz.

"Char?"

I manage a breath. "Sorry. Got something stuck in my throat."

"You okay?"

"I'm fine. Listen here's the address of the church Harlan is speaking at this Sunday. Just forward it there as soon as you can."

I give out the information.

"You got it, Char. I'll put it in the mail right now."

I don't know how long I've been sitting here under the picnic pavilion. Someone's fired up their charcoal grill somewhere and pretty soon campfires will glow. I wonder what Granny Brown is cooking tonight?

My life is at such loose ends. My career is moving forward, but where to? I'll be receiving a letter from my grandma soon, but what does it say? And Mama? Well, that's one loose end destined never to be sewn into much of anything. And then there's Leo and Grace.

I head back to the phone and dial the number of Grace's rehab place.

She never arrived.

Doggone it! She never even arrived!

I run back to the motor home and pick Leo up in my arms.

"Hey!" He squirms. "It's too tight!"

But he settles in soon and my tears baptize us into a new life for the both of us.

⬿⬿⬿

Tonight is the night of reckoning. I have to tell Harlan about Grandma Min, because most likely he'll see her letter at the church before I can intercept it. I'll only raise his suspicions if I offer to get the mail first.

Oh, my lands, he's been talking about hairpieces lately! But that's another story altogether.

We're still at the KOA as Harlan doesn't speak in Marietta until Sunday. The pastor there is an old friend of his from the seminary days and when Harlan called after we finished up in Suffolk and offered his services, he just said, "Praise the Lord! After the corker I gave them last week, the congregation and I need a vacation from each other."

"What did you speak on . . . tithing?"

"Yep."

And they laughed so hard I had to find out what all the commotion was about.

Melvin's got a campfire going again tonight. It's chilly. I cocooned the kids in heavy sweaters and they're sitting out there bundled together in a quilt. The pool is, of course, winterized, but I've been staring at it a lot while I'm here. I don't know why.

The depths are strangely inviting. But then, they always have been. Heights are, too. I'll never forget the time the Evanses took us all for a climb up Crab Apple Falls in the Blue Ridge. I wanted to jump down the rocky face of the falls. In fact the urge came onto me with such vigor, I clung to Mrs. Evans's hand.

Fire doesn't do that to me, however. I steer clear of it, not because it invites me into its furnace, but because I can't imagine the pain if I threw myself inside. I guess being burned alive is my biggest fear. And yet it's so beautiful to gaze upon.

I'm sitting next to Harlan. I swat the side of his leg. "Let's go to the camping kitchen and make a big bowl of popcorn for everyone."

"Why not just make it in the motor home?"

"I'd like to take a walk with you."

"Well, why don't we just take a walk?"

"Okay. But what about the popcorn?"

"We can make it in the motor home when we get back."

"Okay."

Now see? Why do I always have to make up this other excuse? Why didn't I just say, "Let's take a walk, Harlan?" That's all it would have taken. And now he knows I don't just want to walk.

We slip away. The kids are getting drowsy and Ruby just waves us on letting me know she'll slip them in bed. But I'm hoping our talk won't take that long. I'm hoping that he'll understand.

We set our feet on the path toward the tent section. There are only a few hardy tent people set up. You have to admire the tent folks.

All day I've been analyzing the reason I've never felt comfortable telling people Mama deserted me. I wondered if it was that I didn't want their pity. And then I came to the conclusion that everybody likes a little pity once in a while. Those books that have everybody crying, "I don't want your pity!" are just plain goofy. Everybody likes some acknowledgment of their suffering. Now you don't want people fawning all over you, but a little sympathy every once in a while does a body good.

I wondered if it was the fact that saying she was dead was a tale completely encased in itself. Mama died, I went to foster care. That's pretty simple. Not a lot of explanation necessary with that tale. I know, I've been saying this long enough to know. Not many people ask how she died and when they do, I let them off the hook by saying, "It was such a long time ago, don't even ask how she departed!" Most people want to think the worst, so I let their imaginations replace their inquiries.

But I know why I did that now, why I've always hedged this portion of my past, and it feels good to have finally nailed it down in my own mind. I believe I've told people Mama was dead not only because I wanted to believe it myself, but because I didn't want to arrive at the conclusion that only a crazy person would leave her eleven-year-old child for two weeks. What kind of mother would do that?

Do I believe Mama loved me?

I can't even answer that. So much so that it isn't even an issue because it's too painful and I can never know.

So how in the world can I just tell the world that my mama left me and never came back? How can I throw that information out there when I cannot even begin to understand the "why" of it myself? Bottom line, Mama left me. The fact that she stayed away is secondary. Ruby is right. Mama was crazy. She belonged in the halls of an institution other than motherhood.

"So what is it you wanted to talk to me about, Shug?"

"How did you know I wanted to talk to you?"

"You're not exactly the-walk-in-the-woods-type of person, Charmaine."

I squeeze his hand. "You know me way too well, Harlan."

"And that's the way it should be. That way I can say I love you completely."

Oh, my lands. He's said this many times before, and it wounded my heart those times, too. Well, at least it provided a good segue.

Now or never, Myrtle Charmaine, but I don't really see why you have to do this in the first place. It's family business and he's not family.

"Well, there is something you don't know about me and that's what I wanted to talk to you about."

"Should I be sitting down?"

"Probably, but let's keep walking."

"You talk better when you're moving."

"I know."

"You know, Shug, you should just dive on in anyway. If you think about what to say you'll torture yourself."

"Okay. Well, here goes?" I laugh a glassy laugh. "My mama may not be dead."

"But—"

"Let me get it all out, Harlan!"

"Okay, okay."

"I'll just tell the story real fast."

And I do.

"So the letter is coming from your Grandma Min soon?"

"Uh-huh."

"Shug, would you have ever told me if you hadn't felt you had to?"

"Well, I didn't actually have to now, Harlan. I could have just pretended my grandma finally found me after searching for me for years. I could have thought up a dozen things. Or I could have done my level best to have just hid it all."

He nods. "Okay, that's fair."

"I want to go see my grandma again. I want to go by myself."

"What about the kids?"

"I'll take them with me. It's only Tuesday. You really don't need me until next Monday when we arrive in Mount Oak for the crusade there and that's only three or so hours from Suffolk. If I could take the motor home, you could bunk up with Henry in the little trailer."

"But you don't even know what that letter says, Charmaine. For all you know she could be telling you never to come around again."

I hadn't thought of that. And why I didn't think of it already must say something, but I don't know what it is.

"Just promise me you'll wait until we get that letter, then you can go for as long as you need. Ruby can cover for you."

"She sure can."

So we decide that then.

And I feel a lifting of my soul. I hate hiding things from Harlan. But I'm finding that my initial instincts about him were right. He is more than equipped to carry my baggage. Letting him may be the truly difficult act.

See, this conversation isn't over. Not by a long shot. We'll be talking about this for weeks and months to come. Harlan will come up with all sorts of possible scenarios, and I'm sure they'll be nothing new. I'm sure I'll have already thought of them, and then some. And it will be like being covered in skin boils and living in a salt mine.

But I did the right thing. I may not know much about much, but I know I did the right thing.

19

Harlan and I sit in a Cracker Barrel with his pastor friend, Tony Sanchez. How a guy named Tony Sanchez ended up in Marietta, Georgia, still remains to be seen and I was more than bowled over when I met him a few minutes ago and he had a thicker Southern drawl than I do.

He's real nice. Youngish like Harlan, expanding around the middle, and he pulls out a string of pictures of his two girls. He's thinking about leaving his church because they care too much about the building. I listen to their conversation as I sip my Diet Coke through two straws and butter up saltines as fast as the kids will shove them in.

I look at those crackers and think about having some myself, but after MaryAnna Trench's remark, I'm being really careful.

"How long they been acting like this?" Harlan asks Tony.

"Ever since I got there. I thought maybe I could whip them into shape, and I've been preaching on what ministry really means until I am blue in the face, brother."

"So how long you giving them?"

"Another year."

"Well, I gotta hand it to you. You seem to know when a situation is hopeless."

"Maybe it's not hopeless. Maybe I'm just the wrong guy."

The waitress sets down our order. I looked at the side salad and bowl of chicken noodle in front of me and shook my inner head. Then the words that have been in my mind lately about this whole weight-loss thing echoed once more. "It's your job to look good, Charmaine."

Not that it'll do much good, Myrtle.

Now why is that? What can't you be up in front of people and look like a regular human being? Look at Sandi Patty! She's done just fine that one. 'Course, I'm a good singer but I ain't no Sandi Patty!

Actually the soup isn't bad.

Harlan says, "I have to say that sometimes life on the road gets grueling. But at least I don't have congregational problems."

Tony points his fork in the direction of Leo and Hope. "But you gotta be thinking about those little ones, brother. How old is that boy?"

"He'll be five this spring."

"He needs to be in school."

Harlan nods. "I know. We were thinking about home-schooling just for a couple of years. Until we find out where God wants us to settle."

Where God wants us to settle? Oh, my lands. I felt hope and disappointment mingled. On the one hand, Harlan does want to settle down someday in the not too distant future. On the other, that means his surprise is NOT a house.

Or maybe he is just saying this to throw me off.

That would be just like him!

Leo eats like a dream, picking up his ham biscuits just fine. Hope's only remedy is to spray him off with a fire hose.

As we walk to the truck and Tony to his station wagon, he calls out, "Forgot! Here's a packet that came from your sister, Harlan. Let me get it out of the car."

Dear Charmaine,

Forgive me for what happened the other day. It all just came out of the blue, so to speak, and I couldn't take it all in. I'm sorry you left so quietly the way you did without me at least summoning up the strength to thank you for finding me.

Your mother and I lost track of each other before you were born. We never really did get along though I've got to say we both tried to iron out our differences in our own unique ways. But how does a butterfly and an ant find common ground? That was Isla, a true butterfly. And yet at times she could sink down to the depths of despair over so little. I never knew what to do for her but I tried everything. I want you to know that, Charmaine. I want you to know that the reason she's disappeared has nothing to do with you. I know that better than I know my own name.

I could write an encyclopedia the way I feel right

now, but I think I'll spare both you and I and not do so. I do want you to know, however, that I'm happy you're alive, Charmaine. And if I had known you were in existence, I'd have done my best by you. I don't know what the condition of your heart really is by this time after all these years, but I'm hoping the fact that you saw fit to find me means that maybe there's room for a lonely old woman. I have so many questions. And I guess you do, too.

So here's my number and I invite you to call me anytime. You can even call collect because Frederick left a good pension and the house is paid off and my expenses are almost nil.

Your Grandma,
Minerva T. Whitehead

I look over at Harlan who's doing his best not to watch me as I read the letter in the Cracker Barrel parking lot. "She wants to see me, Harlan!"

"Oh, Shug." And he hugs me.

Hope claps.

I'm nervous and excited and all sorts of things. And I am actually driving the motor home. I'm just hoping I don't have to back this monster up!

I called Grandma Min the night before. The conversation felt a little strained, but no more than I expected.

"I was thinking of coming on up tomorrow. The crusade can spare me this week. It would be a good time for me to get away."

"All right."

"I'm bringing the children."

"You've got children?"

"I do." I didn't feel it was the time to explain just how I happened to acquire Hope and Leo.

Poor Leo. My heart breaks afresh for the little guy. Imagine having Grace for a mother. Harlan called several police stations on the line northward and they said they'd put out an alert or something so that the towns along the train route would be on the lookout for Grace. So far, we've heard nothing. Yet another missing person in my life.

So Grandma said there was plenty of room and staying until Sunday would be fine.

Doing my level best to avoid a travel pickle, I pull the motor home into the parking lot of a truck stop in Gaffney. "Let's use their bathroom, kids."

I plan on making lunch in the RV but why use up our store of water if we don't have to?

In the bathroom a young woman asks me for some money. "You need something to eat, honey?"

"Yes, ma'am."

"Well, hold on a second. Let me finish up with these kids. What's your name?"

"Penny."

"Okay. That's my motor home out there. I'm just about to make lunch and you're welcome to join us."

If she is an addict she'll refuse.

"That would be great. I haven't eaten since dinner on Tuesday."

"You traveling?"

"Yes, ma'am."

"Hitchhiking?"

She nods. "I know it's dangerous, but I had to get away."

"You're a runaway."

Fright skates across her glistening brown eyes and she begins to turn.

"No wait! I won't turn you in. I just want to hear your story."

So now lunch is over and Penny, the kids, and I are back on I-85 heading toward Charlotte. Praise the Lord, He's giving me an opportunity to spread His love. There seems to have been fewer of those times than usual lately and my role as redemptress has taken a backseat in these trying days of digging up my past.

But no matter. It just shows that God hasn't chosen to stop using me, sleeping pills and all, and I'm thankful.

I get in a few words about the gospel. After all, I am an evangelist's wife. She nods and says, "I grew up in Sunday school." So I keep my mouth shut until Charlotte where she thanks me and gets out.

I can only hope some people are having compassion on Grace right now.

Too many loose ends, Myrtle Charmaine. You've got too many loose ends. Not that I expected any different from you.

20

Grandma Min hugs me tightly and says, "You're so real. Such a real person."

I know exactly what she means so I say, "I thought I was alone in the world, too."

And that pretty much says it all, and we understand. We eat supper amid all the antiques I failed to notice the first time I entered her home and she gives the kids some presents: coloring books and crayons and some blocks. The dishes, from her collection of antique china plates, still need doing so we get started.

Grandma hands me a tea towel. "Here. I'll wash and you dry."

I say that's fine.

We work in silence for a while, but it doesn't feel too awkward, only as if we're both lost in our own thoughts. We're almost on the pans when Grandma asks, "You want to try and find her, Charmaine?"

I shake out the tea towel. "Yes, I do. But I doubt she's alive."

"I've been figuring that, too, but a mother has to hope. A mother is never supposed to give up until there's a body." Her voice sounds calm yet her eyes are anything but. She wipes the back of her hand over her forehead, leaving a streak of dish suds.

"Where do we begin?" I say and I wipe off the streak with my dish towel.

She doesn't recoil. She acts as if having your face wiped is the most natural thing in the world and it is in this moment that I know all is well between us. It is in this moment I know that I am her granddaughter and she loves me, even though she doesn't know me, simply because of that.

I am changed.

"Tell me everything you know."

And I do. The second time in less than a week.

Now why is that? Why does life sludge along like a molasses river and then suddenly you're being swept out to sea?

The kids are asleep. Grandma Min made us pork chops with gravy, sweet red cabbage, brussels sprouts, and rice for dinner and they ate like crazy. Well, not the cabbage. Or the brussels sprouts. Or much of the pork chops for that matter. But they loved the rice and gravy!

"I'm really not much of a cook," I feel led to confess as I pour the hot water into a waiting teapot. "I wish I wasn't the Hamburger Helper-type, but I am."

"Don't apologize. Judging by that business card of yours I'd say you've got other talents. I love that little songbird on there."

We smile at each other. I tell her all about Mrs. Evans. I tell her about Richard Lewellyn and the trip to Vermont.

Now, I've never shared that with anybody. But this is my grandmother, one of the people whose blood flows in my veins and that means something.

How can I describe Grandma Min? Since our arrival yesterday, all during the beginnings of our search today, I've been watching her. Obviously if there is insanity in the family as Ruby insists, it must have skipped this woman. Talk about wise and calm and giving. Yet I naturally wonder if these aspects of her came after Mama left, due to the lessons learned. But it certainly isn't something I'm going to ask.

First of all, she likes the kids and admires me for taking them in. I can't help but feel so good at that. Having your own relative admire you just fills your soul. Family approval is new to me and now I can see why kids that don't have it strive for it their whole lives. I've asked her all sorts of questions and never once has she said, "Don't even ask!"

I'm trying so hard to recognize something of Mama in her, but so far I can find only physical characteristics. She shows me a wedding portrait of her and my grandfather.

"Oh, my lands!" I say. "You and Mama favor each other so much!"

"We sure did look alike. But she took after my sister. Rachel had that wild streak, too."

"What happened to her?"

"Ended up committing suicide when she was fifty years old."

"No!"

"It was horrible. And she meant to die. This wasn't one of those warning things. Blew her head off with a shotgun." The words were spoken dispassionately but I knew better.

"Do you think that maybe Mama committed . . . ?" I wince. This was a scenario that had never entered my mind.

Grandma Min takes my hand. "It's what I've supposed for a lot of years. I didn't want to think that, but I couldn't help but remember Rachel."

"Were you the one that found her?"

"Thank God, no, even though she was living here with me at the time. The gas and electric man did."

For some reason that seemed so sad.

We sip on our tea and sit in the small kitchen, the windows black against the autumn night. A heavy breeze shakes the panes in their grid, a slight clacking sounding in our ears. I love gusts of wind as they seek you out through the smallest openings of the house, whistling your name.

Grandma pours a little more into her cup from the pot that sits between us. "Remember in my letter I told you that your mother's disappearance had nothing to do with you?"

I nod.

"I want to tell you something about Isla. She started exhibiting the symptoms of a manic-depressive early on. Eight years old, in fact."

"My lands!"

"It's in our genes, Charmaine."

"What about you, Grandma?"

"Nothing so far. I get a little blue now and again, but it always passes in a day or two. What about you, Charmaine?"

"I deal with depression, I think."

"You think?"

"Uh-huh. Right now I'm just on sleeping pills. I can't bring myself to get on medication."

"You should consider it."

I rest my chin in my hand. "Would it have helped Mama?"

"It did help her. But she always went off of it. She was stubborn that way."

I tell her all about Harlan's messages.

"I think he's talking about blaming real sin on other things," Grandma says.

"Maybe. But how rich would it be that he says this stuff and his own wife is popping pills?"

"You make it sound so vulgar, Charmaine."

"Isn't it? A little?"

She nips the delicate handle of her cup between two fingers. "No."

I get the feeling she's not going to explain further. But she says, "If it helps, it helps. All I know is that your mama was a different person with some help."

I tell her about Harlan's sister-in-law and her therapeutic life in Virginia Beach.

"That explains it then. Most people have a personal reason for being adamantly against things. I can't say I blame him for feeling the way he does."

"Me, neither."

"Well, you could at least talk to a doctor about it and see what he says."

"It doesn't really matter much anyway. I couldn't afford it, and how would I hide the expenditure from Harlan even if I could?"

"I'd get it for you, Charmaine. I would. But in the meantime, while you're here, you can sleep as late as you want."

"Thanks, Grandma."

"You know, even if this stuff wasn't in the family, you'd have a lot of reason to be depressed. I'm surprised, after all you went through, you didn't go over the deep end."

That sure is the truth.

We are silent for a while as Grandma finishes the crossword puzzle she began this morning. I'm thinking about this revelation regarding Mama and amazed at how Ruby nailed it. I am equally amazed I missed it. I was a child, though, and I guess my views of her failed to grow up as the rest of me did.

"I was sorry to hear the initial investigation years ago turned up with nothing."

I nod. "They were thorough. Even the hospitals turned up empty." I had called my social worker from days of yore earlier that morning and she told me the entire story.

"Well, when people want to be gone and stay gone it's easy enough to do."

See, it's okay for Grandma Min to say words like those, because we both bear the brunt of Mama's ways. From anyone else it would sound callous.

"Where do we look next?" I ask.

"I guess cemeteries. Get death records and all."

"How do we do that?"

"I have no idea."

So I know what tomorrow will hold.

I reach out for Grandma Min's hand. "Well, at least we're not going through this alone."

She squeezes my fingers.

"Grandma, why didn't you ever try to find her?"

"It wasn't the first time Isla disappeared. And Isla never liked me. I couldn't imagine what it would be like if I suddenly showed up."

"But she was gone so long."

"I know. I had heard from her once while she was in Lynchburg. And, Charmaine, I was scared to find out why I hadn't heard from her in so long. The days turned into months and so on and so forth. I can't explain it any deeper than that. Sometimes a mother just doesn't want to know if she's certain enough the news is bad."

"Then why now?"

"It's time to know. There's two of us needing it. Not just me anymore."

"You really think she's dead, don't you?"

"I do."

"So do I."

"Well, Charmaine. At least it will close some doors when we find out."

"But it's opened up others, hasn't it? I mean, we're here together, Grandma Min. You and me."

That night I slept in Mama's old room for the second time. I'd gone through her yearbooks and saw someone involved in the more creative type of thing: drama club, art club, school plays, choir, the glee club. But all that stopped when she hit her junior year. And I knew suddenly why Mama sat there and cried that night I sang "Away in a Manger," and it felt good to know.

"Do you think she died of illness, or foul play or natural causes?" I ask the next morning as we clear the breakfast dishes and the kids watch Sesame Street in the next room while they color.

"I've always thought of Isla as a victim, Charmaine. I guess I always will. Whether she was a victim of her own devices or someone else's remains to be seen."

Her words are tidy. Her expression is not.

After the dishes are finished, Grandma begins calling the offices of vital records all up and down the eastern seaboard. I'm sure there must be an easier way to do this, but if there is, we don't know it. We're not detectives.

I watch the kids and look through photo albums.

Mama was a cutie pie. Her little heart-shaped pale face framed by dark hair pulled back in a headband. Saddle shoes, sweaters. Ballerina pictures. Piano recitals. Softball and gymnastics. Vacation at Disneyland, the big national parks.

Strange that there are mostly pictures of Mama and Grandma. No big family gatherings, nothing like that.

"I heard from Tanzel over at Grace and Truth that you're originally from Florida," I holler in after I hear her hang up the phone with New Jersey.

"That's true."

"Did you lose contact with your family? I don't see any other family in these pictures."

She appears at the door.

"So to speak."

"What happened?"

"I was excommunicated from the family if you want to know the truth."

"Why?!"

"I married a Christian man."

"What's so bad about that?"

"They're Jewish."

"You're *Jewish*?"

She raises a finger to her mouth. "Shhh. Don't want this whole town to find out." She smiles.

"Then I'm—"

"A quarter Jewish."

"Oh, my lands!"

"Does that dismay you?"

"Oh, goodness no. It's nice to know you're one of the chosen people even if only a quarter of you is."

I figure I'm in for a lot more surprises like this.

"What about Grandpa's family?"

"His parents died when he was little. Raised in orphanages and the like until we met. They were Irish. He had red hair just like yours."

"So we have more than a little in common that way, he and I."

She nods. "You favor his mother quite a bit, Charmaine. He only had one little picture of her made just before she died."

Oh, well. So much for getting a big ready-made family out of all this. "Looks like it's just you and me, then, Grandma?"

"That's about it. You disappointed?"

"A little. Not in you. But I always pictured something really different. Lots of aunts and uncles and all."

"I can't blame you there."

"So how're the phone calls coming?"

She waves a hand, mouth curling down. "I hate the government. They all want requests in writing. I'm getting down the addresses and I think that will be our next step. Writing all these letters."

"Well let's just write one and I'll make copies of it down at the stationery store then handwrite the addresses in and all. You got a typewriter? I can get started on that while you make the rest of the calls."

"It's there in the underneath part of the secretary." She scribbled down something on her notepad and ripped off the paper. "Here's Isla's social security number. You'll need that. You can just set the typewriter up on the dining room table if you'd like."

So I begin the letter.

It all suddenly seems so strange. Just two weeks ago I'd been riding along in the motor home doing my thing. Sewing costumes, singing, taking care of Harlan and Hope, worrying over Grace, and missing the folks in Baltimore. And now here I sit trying to find out whether or not Mama is dead and I have a Grandma and a little boy to take care of, too.

But I do believe that God is lurking about, waiting to show me His glory. This situation has sailed in too fast and furious to count as just a mundane happening in an already extraordinary life.

It is Sunday afternoon. Grandma took me to Lutheran church and everybody seemed glad to meet me. We ate lunch together at the Virginia Diner and now we hug by the motor home parked on the street outside her house. We're both small and the hug is perfect.

We are the same size. And I keep looking for all sorts of things we have alike. We both wear size five shoes and our fingernails grow out of their beds in the same squarish shape.

"You be careful now, driving that big thing all the way to Mount Oak!"

"Oh, I will. The kids are finally asleep back there so I'm hoping I can make it the whole way during their nap." I lean forward. "I gave them both a little children's aspirin to aid in a good sleep."

"Call me and let me know you got there safely."

I think those are some of the most beautiful words I've ever heard.

We don't cry. I'm not much of a crier and I guess Grandma is cried out after all of these years. But the sun seems to shine a little brighter.

"You can call Bee's anytime and I'll get back to you within a day."

"I'll remember that."

I thought of the packet of request letters we'd taken to the post office on Saturday afternoon. "As soon as you hear something—"

"I'll pick up the phone."

"Okay." I want to say "I love you, Grandma" but maybe it isn't yet the time. "'Bye, now!"

And she kisses my cheek and I kiss hers and when I drive away, I feel there is a little more of me along for the ride.

21

I've been redeemed by the blood of the lamb!" Oh, we are singing like there's nothing but tomorrow and this congregation is really jumping at the Port of Peace Assembly of God of Mount Oak.

Now this is worshiping. This is praising your Creator. This is rejoicing in the Lord!

And this is what I have been created to do.

I grip my microphone and Ruby and I slip into harmonies on the second verse, her deep alto supporting my thinner voice. God made our voices to go together. Sometimes I can't tell where mine ends and hers begins.

I forget about everything else at times like these.

See, a lot of people think that someone like me, up in front of folks singing and performing, are doing nothing *but* performing, that we are up there singing for ourselves and conscious of nothing *but* ourselves. But that's just flat out not true. I sing before the throne of God, the gift box in my throat pouring forth the light of praise.

If you could crawl inside my mind while I praise the Lord this is what you'd see. You'd see a multitude of people of all colors, shapes, and sizes to your right and left and in front. And you'd know they were behind you, too. Before you, you'd see a giant throne, and pillars aglow. The line of pillars recedes so far into the distance that you cannot see their end and they curve, so it seems, into infinity. Now, in my mind the throne reminds me of the Lincoln Memorial but that's only because man hasn't seen nor heard of the wonderful things God has prepared for those who love Him.

I see lots of white, but I see color, too. Vibrant purples, of course. And scarlet and saffron and cloth of gold. Midnight blue and lapis lazuli blue. Amber and emerald. And the colors are clear and perfect and a praise in and of themselves.

I stand there amid the throng and sing because I am made to sing. Now, some people can't understand how heaven will be so great if all we do is stand around singing. Harlan doesn't believe everyone will be in that eternal chorus. He thinks some will have other jobs to do, jobs that they love, jobs they were made to do. He thinks that some of who we are and what we enjoy here on earth goes right on up to heaven with us and is used for God's glory there, too. He thinks this is just a training ground.

I like that.

I am made to sing. Therefore I take comfort in the fact that I may just make it to the vocational heavenly chorus. I may get to sing for eternity and that would be bliss indeed.

So when I am up before a congregation and we're singing "I've Been Redeemed," I really am not completely there up on stage. I'm surrounded by gemstones, gold, and the glory of God and the people before me are a most celestial throng and we are offering up a sacrifice of the praise of our lips to He who sits upon the throne.

Harlan's hands are over my eyes. "Okay, Shug! Keep walking." We amble slowly down the hallway of Port of Peace Assembly and the time has finally arrived for my big surprise.

I'm thinking now it may be a surprise party of some sort. I doubt if it's jewelry. Harlan's not the type to even think of something like that.

The doors to the church open in front of me and I feel the nip of November air caress my cheeks. My shoes thud on the asphalt. I'm trying not to get too worked up. But I do know it's big. Is it a new car maybe? Something cute to tow behind the motor home?

"Okay now, Shug, get into the truck."

I do.

He ties his bandanna around my eyes.

"Harlan, this is freaky."

"No, it's not. You'll see. I can't wait to see the look on your face when you see what I've got cooked up for you!"

"Where are the kids?"

"Ruby took them first. They're waiting for us there."

Can it be?

What else could this be?

It is a house he's driving me to. I just know this. A new home. Real walls and sturdy cabinets. Square rooms. Not just an aisle running down the middle.

"How long is the drive?"

"Just five or so minutes."

Oh, good. It would be nice to be so close to this church. I mean, if we're going to settle in Mount Oak, then this is the house of worship for me.

I hear gravel crunch as Harlan turns off the main road. He brakes, stops the truck, turns off the engine, and then comes around to help me out.

"I feel so shaky, Harlan."

He chuckles. "Oh, Shug, I can't wait for you to see this. It's what we've needed for a long time. Especially you. I know you've been cramped in that motor home."

"Oh, Harlan!"

I can't wait to see the house.

"And it's luxurious inside, too," he says.

"Really?"

"But I'm not saying nothing else. I don't want to give it away. Just a little further. Okay, now stop."

I feel him working the knot of the bandanna free at the back of my head. "Now keep your eyes closed until I say." He shouts, "Ready y'all?"

"Ready!" a chorus of voices responds, and I hear Leo's and Hope's in the throng. Oh, they must be so excited.

"Charmaine Hopewell, here is your new home! Open up!"

I open my eyes.

"It's a Class A, Shug!" Harlan's voice fills with happiness and before my eyes I see a large motor home that looks like a bus. How many times on the road we passed those and I thought, "Looky there. That's traveling in style."

A motor home.

Another house on wheels.

"I think I need to sit down, Harlan."

"She's so surprised she can't even stand up!" he hollers to the gang.

Ruby runs forward and I know I am as pale as lace. "Come on in, Char. This is the prettiest thing you've ever seen!"

No, it isn't.

I may not know much about much, but I know another motor home is not the prettiest thing I've ever seen.

"She's in shock," Harlan says and he puts an arm around my shoulder. "Aren't you, Shug?"

"I am," I manage to whisper.

And they usher me inside while Harlan gets me a glass of ice water. "It's even got an icemaker, Charmaine!"

An icemaker.

"Charmaine?" He suddenly sees me. "Are you all right?"

He couldn't know how disappointed I would be. He couldn't know because I've never said a thing. "I'm fine, Harlan. I just need a minute to get over the shock."

After all I've been through, I roll with the punches probably better than most. I drink that glass of water and take a look around my new home. Done in shades of blue I say right away, "It's so peaceful in here, Harlan."

"That's what I thought, Shug. Now hold tight and let me take you on a whirlwind, grand, twenty-five-cent tour!"

The bedroom at the back has sconce lights on the wall and some real closet space.

"The mattress there is decent. And I'll get a foam

square cut to put with the sofa bed so it's even more comfortable."

"How long has this all been going on?"

"Since well before Suffolk!"

"And I never knew."

He points to the dinette. "Sit there, Shug. Isn't that comfortable?"

"It is."

"And look at this table and the cabinets. Real oak laminate!"

"It sure warms up the place."

He knocks on the table. "Sturdy, too."

"Seems to be lots of storage."

"Oh, you wouldn't believe it. Not to mention all the room we'll have underneath now."

"Are we self-contained?"

"Would I settle for less?"

Oh, Harlan, dear Harlan. I love you so.

The tour continues and in the bedroom, I turn around and fold his arms around me. "I think I can handle living here."

"So I've got your approval?"

"You mean you haven't already bought it?"

"Well, no. I've made the preparations, but the owner agrees I can back out of it if you absolutely hate it."

Now's my time to say something, something about taking the down payment and putting it on a house. But then he'd know. Harlan would know that the life we now have just isn't enough and I can't do that to him.

"I say let's get it."

He lifts me up. "Oh, Shug. We've got us a good life, don't we?"

And I have to agree with him. Because life can be so much worse. Believe me, I know. It's something I have to remind myself of everyday.

Why?

Why do I have to remind myself?

I decide to call a doctor. Life shouldn't be an internal struggle, a continual convincing that all is well when it surely is.

I wait until nobody is around inside the church office and call a Dr. Braselton. They take me right away. I tell him of my struggles, he shakes his head and pats my hand and says, "I'm writing you out a prescription."

I drive to the pharmacy and wait for them to fill it. I buy a Diet Coke at the gas station, position the Tofranil on my tongue, and I swallow.

Part Five

1

$\mathcal{H}$arlan lifts his glass of tea. "It's time, Shug, don't you think?" He sips.

I ruffle my Leo's carpet of hair. It has thickened up so these past few years! The once light blond cap is a dark, dirty blond now. He truly looks related to Harlan. "I don't think I'm doing right by Leo in homeschooling, Harlan. I've known that since last year. And second grade is coming up this fall. He needs to be in a school."

Imagine me, the high-school dropout, homeschooling.

Leo hugs me with his stick arms. Now, I can only tell you this, I never thought I could love a little guy the way I love this boy. Affectionate doesn't begin to describe Leo. It's as if our hearts kiss one another all day long, even when we are apart.

Hope's a busy bee. And we are much alike, always going strong and smiling. Oh, my, but she can be a hardhead! I like that about her. I like the fact that she chooses her battles and fights to the death.

And has the Tofranil been great. I truthfully *feel* like the person I used to *act* like before. It's worth the dry mouth it gives me. I just keep a cup of ice handy.

We sit now at the dinette in my Class A motor home, Harlan, Leo, and me. True, the RV disappointed me a few years ago, but I've learned to appreciate this place. Ruby's made the Class C her own and Henry and Melvin are in the travel trailer. Russell, Melvin's no-good nephew flew the coop shortly after Grace did and we hired two brothers from Alabama fresh out of electronics school who take the truck camper. Everybody moved up when we got this thing, which made the entire deal a little more acceptable for me.

Oh, Harlan's become almost a celebrity! His crusades on getting right with the Lord and not relying on psychology and pills has been freeing people all over the South! My favorite quotes from his sermons are these:

1. "Man needs to be saved from his own wisdom as much as from his own righteousness, for they produce one and the same corruption." That's by William Law, whoever he is.
2. "But the true God hath this attribute, that He is a jealous God; and therefore, His worship and religion, will endure no mixture, nor partner." Sir Francis Bacon.

And I know Francis Bacon is right. People are looking to man for the answers when God has them. Counselors are resorting to psychotherapy instead of good advice from the Bible. I know Christians are hurting themselves and each other and Jesus is the answer.

Just like the song says.

Of course, I'm still taking my medication. I tried to get off it after a year, but fell right back down into the depression. At least now I know it's a physical problem, not a spiritual one. Harlan still doesn't know about it.

Yes, I am torn. I believe his message, and surely my walk differs from Harlan's talk. I save up money here and there from the household expenses each month, buying less meat, more pasta, and as much generic as I can, to pay for my medication and doctor visits. Grandma Min helps when I need it.

Sometimes, though, I hear Harlan make it all sound so easy and I long to tell him what it's really like, that it isn't what he thinks. I want to tell him, but obviously I can't. He's so bold and healthy. I wonder if there's ever been a time he thought he was going out of his mind.

Anyway, the crowds love it. We're getting all sorts of letters of deliverance, and Harlan gives God all the glory.

Over the last few years I've been a hit at Gospelganza. I was sold on performing for the masses from the very first concert. We've also had a regular itinerary of churches that ask us back year after year, usually for the same basic week. In spring we can count on being in Macon, Americus, Birmingham, Huntsville, Jackson, Pensacola, Ft. Meyers, Jacksonville, and Chattanooga. In fall we can always count on the folks in Suffolk as well as Chesapeake, Lynchburg, Richmond, Farmville, and Charlottesville. We do a lot of North Carolina in the autumn and the winter too, which makes Mount Oak, set right on the border of North Carolina and Virginia, right in the hills, a great place to settle down. We sort of settled here anyway.

Port of Peace Assembly welcomed us as their own after that first visit and invited us to park the RVs on their lot whenever we have some free days. That's where we are now.

Port of Peace sits right in town. All sorts of churches inhabit this town, but no other Assemblies churches. We even know the folks at Bill D's Restaurant now and although I cannot vouch for their biscuits and gravy personally, thanks to MaryAnna Trench, my agent, dictator and dietician, Harlan put on at least twenty pounds.

Although two of those pounds come from his new toupee, I'm sure. I offered to give him half of my hair and that just tickled him. "One redhead in this family is enough, Shug."

To be honest, it gets to me just a little. Why should Harlan get to wear a toupee to make him feel good about himself, and I shouldn't pop a little pill into my mouth once a day? That's hardly fair.

Hope, five years old now with very long wavy hair and the worst, yet cutest case of knocked knees you've ever seen, runs up into the RV from a long stint on the church playground. "I'm done playing for now. Can I have something to drink?"

"Sure, honey." I stand to my feet and pour her a glass of Kool-Aid. I grab myself a Diet Coke. "Where's Leo?"

"He's in the church with Melvin."

"What are they doing?"

She rolls her eyes. "Redoing the sound system in there . . . again."

"Those two. Like peas in a pod!" I turn to Harlan. "See what I mean? Leo's the mathematical technical type. I couldn't do him justice. I can barely multiply fractions."

Harlan agrees. After all, Melvin's been teaching the boy math for the past two years and I may not always be able to rely on Melvin. "And we can also put Hope in the church preschool."

"Preschool? Harlan, she's old enough to go into kindergarten next year."

He pales. "Is that so?"

"It is."

And the picture of a bird clutching a ringing alarm clock in his claws flies across my mind's sky. Naturally, it's a little bluebird. The purple Fantasia dragon flies up behind him and wants to eat him, but I just shove that demon lizard right back down where he belongs.

Hope drinks down her Kool-Aid. "I'm going down to the nursery to play with the toys."

"This would be a good life here, Harlan."

"You up to being a regular old pastor's wife?"

"Harlan, I could never be a regular old anything!"

"I thank the Lord for it."

"Bee?"

"Hey, Charmaine."

"You won't believe it! Harlan's taking a church!"

"Oh, my!"

"I know. We just agreed at a meeting with the board not ten minutes ago and he's going to be the senior pastor here at Port of Peace. We're going to buy a house!"

We both holler into the phone.

Bee yells to her husband Robert. "Hey, Robbie, Harlan's settling down!" Her voice softens. "Well, I got to tell you, I won the bet!"

"What bet?"

"I bet Robert that Harlan would settle down well before the age of forty-five and I was right."

"Congratulations. I'm glad you were."

"So what about the kids, they excited?"

"Yep. Leo, you know how sweet he is, says, 'Mama, I loved having you for a teacher, but I think it will be fun to go to school.'"

"I love that boy."

"Isn't he the sweetest thing, Bee? I find sweet little notes from him all the time in the cutest places."

Harlan rounds the corner into the lime-green church office.

"I'm talking to Bee, baby."

"Did you tell her?"

"Uh-huh."

He grins. "Can I talk to her?"

"Sure thing!"

I hand him the phone. I can hardly believe this is happening. I've looked forward to this my entire life. "Can I find out about a real estate agent?"

"I'd be shocked if you didn't. Yes, I'm here, Bee," he says and I am off and zooming like one of those fancy race cars, only I am purple!

The church secretary, none other than Miss Tanzel from Suffolk who took the job here a year ago after I informed her of it, nabs me as I fly down the hallway. "Charmaine?"

"Oh, hey, Miss Tanzel!"

"Got a phone call. From that Mizz Trench lady."

Oh, my lands.

Tanzel leans forward, pressing the receiver into her thigh. "I don't like her. She's pushy."

"I know."

"You watch out for that one. I don't trust her."

I take the phone and cover the receiver with the palm of my hand. "Tanzel, could you ask Mr. Plummer if he knows what real estate agency I should go with?"

"Be glad to." She leans forward and whispers. "I've got to tell you I'm tickled to death you all are staying on here. That last pastor's wife . . ." She rolls her eyes.

I laugh and take my hand off the receiver. "Hey, MaryAnna."

"What took you so long?"

"What's up?"

"BrooksTone Records wants to see you!"

"They already called?"

"Yep. Apparently after hearing what we sent them, they sent a scout out to that gospel festival in Amarillo you did a while ago. And BrooksTone is a good label, Char. This is no two-bit Christian thing."

"I thought they were a Christian label."

"They are. Just not a two-bit one."

"So when do I leave?"

"They want to see you at the beginning of September. And behave yourself. We want a good deal."

"You think we'll really get a good deal?"

"A nice little chunk is what I'm going for, Char. They can afford it. And you know how the crowds love you."

I never know what to say to statements like that.

She continues. "And your little homespun tape sells like crazy at the concerts. I told them your sales figures and they were thrilled. You're a sure thing, Char."

"But can they do better for me? I mean, I won't make nearly as much per tape now if all I get is royalties."

I hear MaryAnna's lighter click. "True." Puff, puff. "But you'll be in stores and they'll get you into mainstream record stores, I think. I mean Farris McCord is one of their artists and I heard that song "Always My Father" on the regular country station here in Nashville several times last week. You'll get airplay, Char. We need that. And let's face it, I get paid off your royalties on these deals, sweetheart. Got to make this worth my while."

True. "Well, let's negotiate and see what happens. We can always turn them down if we think that's right."

Judging by the pregnant silence, I can tell MaryAnna doesn't like that, but right now, that's just tough. "Look MaryAnna, I've got to go house hunting."

"House hunting?"

"Yes. Harlan's taking a church here in Mount Oak."

"He's taking a church?"

"Yes. Are you not hearing what I'm saying the first time around?"

"It's just a shock, Char. I mean, you get so much exposure at those things."

"But the crusades aren't about my exposure, MaryAnna."

"Well they should be!"

Here we go again. MaryAnna and I have this conversation at least twice a year. "No. It's about ministry. I don't know why you can't get that into your thick head. Maybe if you actually came to one you'd understand."

She laughs with scorn. "I wouldn't be caught dead in a church."

"I know, I know, I know. Why did you take me on in the first place then?"

She hesitates. "I needed a client."

"A client?"

"You heard me."

"You mean you didn't have *any* other clients when I hired you on? You *lied* to me?"

She hesitates again.

"Oh, come on, MaryAnna, you're halfway into the confession, and after all this time, you might as well go all the way."

"No. I had no other clients."

"Why not?"

"None of your business. You're doing fine. We've turned into quite a team these past few years. So now don't start nosing around into my personal life."

"Oh, my lands, MaryAnna, you take yourself way too seriously."

"You don't know what it's like to be me."

"Boo-hoo. Did your mother abandon you when you were eleven?"

"Well, no."

"So stop the pity party." Watch, her skeletons include cancer recovery, spousal abuse, and a runaway child.

I hate myself just then. I don't know why it is that some people touch my heart to its core, and others leave it cold. And what right do I have to differentiate from one person to the other? It's hardly something Jesus would do.

"I'd better let you go find that house."

"It's a home, MaryAnna. I'm finally going to be able to go home."

Her voice warms as she says, "I know, Char. I'm not sure what I was thinking."

"Me, either." I laugh. "You can be really difficult

sometimes. You know that? I mean, I'm the artist. I'm supposed to be the temperamental one and I'm the one fighting to be heard."

"You're right."

"No wonder I'm your only client."

"Well, you're not anymore, you know."

"At least there's that, then."

"I'll try to be a little nicer."

"Good. 'Cause I've completed my three years with you, you know and we've never signed anything officially that I have to keep you on."

"You're coming through loud and clear, Char. You don't have to beat me over the head with it!"

It was as close to an apology as she had ever come. "Don't worry about it. Hey, why don't you come to Mount Oak when we're all moved in?"

"I may just do that."

As if that would really ever happen. "MaryAnna, I don't know what your problems are, and I'm sorry for making light of them like I did."

"No, it's okay. I'm a wallower. I'll be okay."

"You sure?"

"Yeah, I'm sure. I've lasted this long haven't I?"

"You don't sound sure."

"Okay, Charmaine! Let it go!"

"I just want you to know my ears are good at listening."

We say our good-byes and I turn to Tanzel. She shakes her head in disbelief. "Remind me not to cross you unduly."

I wave my hand. "Oh, that! That's just the way MaryAnna and I communicate. If I didn't do that she'd walk all over me!"

"She that type?"

"She's more than that type. She's the prototype of that type!"

She puts her reading glasses back up on her nose. "So I'm right about her, then."

"Probably." I lean over and rub her upper arm. "I'm so glad you're down here now, Miss Tanzel."

"Me, too. Hey, why don't you all come over to my place for dinner tonight after you've looked at houses? We can go over the flyers together and I can tell you what to look out for."

"Okay. That will be nice."

"You go on now. How about six o'clock?"

"We'll be there."

"Anything your kids hate to eat?"

"Everything. If you make a side of macaroni and cheese, they'll be all set."

"Do you spoil them?"

"I guess I do."

I guess I have to, if only to prove things to myself.

We only have so much money and it isn't much, so we're limited as to what the real estate agent will show us. I don't want to see anything even a few thousand dollars above our price range. See, any old thing will do right now, and I want to keep it that way. I don't want to get the yearns before I've stepped even one foot over the threshold of my very own home.

I've blamed so much of who I am on my lack of roots,

so I am feeling a bit of trepidation. What if we move in and a few months later, it's not enough?

The agent, a stick-bug of a woman named Gina Kraft, pulls her car up to a brick rancher. It's long and unadorned.

"Are you sure this is in our price range?" I ask.

I look down at the sheet describing the property. They called it a "handyman's special." I know that's the cute way of saying "this thing needs work."

2

*I*t took me all of August to convince Grandma Min that the school system of Suffolk doesn't need her there but that Port of Peace kindergarten and preschool sure does! She's due to pull in the drive in her little navy blue escort this afternoon. Harlan will be following her in a U-Haul truck. She said, "I've got to bring my antiques with me, sweetie. That's not something I'll even negotiate on."

Needless to say, we have no furniture to speak of so I said, "Sure, Grandma! That would be great."

Oh, the house, the house! I just love my new house. My check from Gospelganza provided us the downpayment we needed. The prices in Mount Oak are so low! So we moved at the end of August into that first ranch I viewed, four small bedrooms, a living room and a country kitchen with this little den area off to the side. It's kind of plain looking right now. No shutters, not much shrubbery, a chain-link fence around the backyard, but I've got plans!

"God will take care of you!"

Just like the song says.

The yard's big, though, with a little swing set the old owner left up because their kids outgrew it and they were just as glad not to have to dismantle it before they moved.

But Melvin offered his services and Miss Tanzel says she's handy with a paint brush, so between the two of them, with Harlan and I taking orders and doing what they say, we'll have this place in shape in no time. Already it's looking better and the plumbing works, too!

And it's mine. This little place is mine.

So stick that in your pipe, Vicki Miller, and smoke it! I'm no longer boarding house trash.

My favorite part of the house is the little alcove in the living room. Perfect for piano. Maybe I'll find a second-hand one like Mrs. Evans used to have.

The first room we've painted is Grandma Min's room. It's actually the master bedroom, but I figure she's come from having a house all to herself, whereas we're coming from an RV so one of the lesser bedrooms feels palatial to Harlan and me. I can't wait to see what she thinks. Her bedroom is the color of freshly bloomed wisteria and Miss Tanzel and I pasted up a border with cascading wisteria blossoms. I found a white eyelet bedspread at Walt's Mart and curtains to match.

Walt's Mart.

That never ceases to tickle me. Mount Oak isn't big enough for the real thing, I guess, so this fellow that goes across the street to the Baptists, opened up a store about a quarter the size of the real thing. But it's all we've got at this point and I do love the bedspread.

I peer out in between Grandma Min's curtains and see Hope and Leo playing in the yard. Still no biological baby of our own, so I'm figuring God's completed our lit-

tle family without our help. It seems mental illness runs
in the family, so why perpetuate a weakness like that into
yet another generation? I don't blame Him for nipping it
in the bud with me. I mean, all things work together for
good, don't they?

I grieve over this in secret. I so wanted a baby from my
own body, and yes, I do look on Leo and Hope as my
own, but I'd be lying if I said I'm disappointed Harlan
and I are barren.

Why is this? Why do people who have no business
bearing children get pregnant at the flick of an eyelash,
and good people with loads of love to give inside the
walls of a good home, can't conceive?

That's one of those God ways I can't even pretend to
understand.

And yet those barren couples, with their desire for
children, are sometimes blessed to make a home for any
old child. Any old child will do. And any old child will be
loved as much as anyone.

Isn't that wonderful?

Too bad Mrs. Evans died. Too bad Mama didn't give
me up for adoption and so have given me the chance for
a normal life.

Grace calls a couple of times a year and refuses to tell
me her whereabouts. She's proud that Leo's doing so well
and I always say, "You should see him for yourself,
Grace. You should let him know you're still there."

Believe me, I of all people know how Leo must feel.
But at least he was young when Grace left. "He calls me
'Mama' now, Grace," I said during our last call.

"He does? And you let him?"

"What else was I supposed to do? It's better for him

that he feels that connection with *somebody*." It's hard not to get mad at Grace during times like these. I've never met a more selfish person in my entire life.

"I'll come back someday, Charmaine. I really will."

Now I don't know much about much, but I do know that Grace won't ever be back for Leo. And I don't know how much longer I can go on lying to Grace's parents. And for that matter, I don't know why Grace's parents are so willing to go all these years without talking to their daughter. No wonder she's like she is.

Unless, of course, they are like Grandma Min. But that can't be because Grace at least cares enough about them to let them know she's alive.

Poor Leo. They don't even *know* about him!

Lord, when you next see Mrs. Evans, tell her I'm try-ing hard. This is the way I can tell her that I loved her, to try and be just like her. At least God sent me Mrs. Evans to offset some of the damage Mama did. And if I'm not thankful for that, then shame on me.

"Grandma Min!" Hope yells and runs over to her as she climbs out of her Escort. Harlan's already pulling in and climbing out of the U-Haul truck.

"Hope!"

Grandma leans down and hugs her. Grandma's not the type to scoop up kids and whirl them around. Grandma's not so showy like I am. I'm an amusement park of affec-tion. Grandma Min's more of a beanbag chair.

Hope tugs on her plaid skirt and drags her back toward the swing set. Grandma rolls her eyes in my direction and says, "Well, at least I know who's the boss around here."

Harlan pulls Grandma's trunk out of her backseat. "That sure is the truth."

I grab the two remaining satchels and head into the house behind him. We set Grandma's things on her bedroom floor. It's hardwood. Don't ask me from what kind of tree. We haven't done it over so it looks kind of like some giant took a bath in our house and left the soap scum behind.

"Harlan?"

"Yeah, Shug?"

"Just let me hug you."

"Okay. I'm all for hugs."

"I missed you last night."

I love the feel of my husband. He's tall so my head rests right on his breastbone, and I hear his heart. And I know his heart and his knows mine. "Thanks for letting her come live with us."

"Are you kidding? We've got us a built-in baby-sitter! Not to mention some furniture to sit on."

"Well, I'm going to make a pitcher of iced tea."

"How about that icebox cake you told me about last night? You think it's ready yet?"

"Uh-huh."

I am still on my dessert quest. The icebox cake is the family favorite by far because I don't have to turn a single dial on the oven or the stove, nothing flames, and there isn't a single ingredient capable of sloshing over the side of the mixing bowl.

"I love that cake, Shug. You sure are a fine cook."

We laugh and laugh.

Now I don't want it to be mistaken that I think Harlan's perfect. He's not. He can be a bit hardcrusted when it comes to his views. I'll be honest, I'm really not so sure about what he says in his "What's *Really* Eating at You" sermons. I've read up a little on mental suffering, due to Grace and Mama. I know some people just have wild streaks and there isn't anything you can do about it, but I also know there's more to it than I'll ever realize. I'm not some smart medical type, but I'm trying to understand, even if it's just a little.

Having achieved what I'd longed for all my life, I can honestly say I'm not disappointed. Waking up in my bedroom thrills me every morning.

We sit at the kitchen table. Well, Grandma Min's kitchen table, actually. The cloth, an orange-and-white checked goodie, is another special from Walt's Mart. Two-ninety-nine with matching cloth napkins in a brown check for fifty cents a piece! It's looking like autumn around my home.

My home.

Thank you, Jesus.

Oh, and the china she brought! I feel like I am living high off the hog these days. From RV, particle-board furnishings straight to fine antiques. The inside of this place is quickly becoming the home I always dreamed about. Elegant and fine.

The kids are down for the night. They haven't wanted to sleep in their own room and who can blame them after those years of sleeping together on the dinette of the RV? So I put both twin mattresses in Leo's room as his is a tad larger. I plan on checking out yard sales and buying lots of toys cheap and we'll make Hope's room the playroom.

I just checked on them and they looked like angels. Worn out like me. I felt too tired to give them a bath and they were just as glad. I think they would have fallen asleep in the tub!

"Anybody want a cup of tea?" I ask.

"That would be lovely." Grandma looks up from a teacher's magazine that holds pictures of some of the cutest bulletin boards I've ever seen. Grandma's all moved in, her things put away, and life has settled into what I guess it will be for years, saving for those little shifts we all experience now and again.

Harlan nods and lifts a finger. He's weary, already getting the dirt on some of the problems we've inherited at Port of Peace.

One of the elders thinks if you don't show up on mulch day, no matter how much you do in other areas, you're not pulling your weight. He's mad at half the church.

The nursery staff is in an uproar over an eighteen-month-old biter whose mother drops him off on Sundays. Two people are threatening to quit unless he's asked to leave. Three people are threatening to quit if he *is* asked to leave.

"We're all the Jesus that child may ever know!" says the children's minister. And I agree with her, but I'm keeping my mouth shut. I've already decided I'm keeping my mouth shut about everything I possibly can.

And at the pinnacle of our troubles teeters the disagreement as to who they'll hire to put new railing on outside and whether spindled or Chippendale would be more appropriate.

My lands.

However, a lot more good things than bad things go on

at Port of Peace and I try to remind Harlan of that every day.

They hired Henry Windsor on as the new music director. And Melvin, already employed by some sound system company, runs all the equipment on Sundays.

I fix the tea as Harlan and Grandma talk about the class she'll be taking at the preschool. The pre-k class. She's excited. Buzzing around the rim of my brain I hear that sweet, geriatric twitter, that youthful, high sound that makes me wonder what she was like as a youngster.

Harlan doesn't know we've been searching for Mama these past few years. I think he's always wanted to assume she was dead, for my sake. He never brings it up unless I do, which surprised me, and I almost never bring Mama up. All these years later I still don't talk about her much. Now that I'm a mama, with a mama's heart and soul and a mama's way, I sometimes even allow myself to hate her. Sometimes I hope she really is dead. Even if she was a schizophrenic. Or manic-depressive or whatever disorder she suffered from. I've tried to read a little about everything. I do know she was *not* an agoraphobic! A lot of symptoms overlap, and it's hard to remember what she was really like. I was only eleven years old and kids seem to accept things as normal that are hardly so. I cannot diagnose her any more than I can diagnose what ails the lady in the checkout line.

So, yes, maybe I should feel more sorry for her than I do. I probably don't really wish she was dead. But with my heart so sore from being tossed back and forth all of these years, I wish Harlan's easy explanations worked for me. I need to remember my mama was a victim. But that doesn't make the memories of her mistreatment of me any less painful. In fact, it makes it worse because there's nobody really to blame, is there? Nobody to focus my now unjustifiable rage upon, nobody to take responsibility. And here I am, wounded, yet feeling sorry for my attacker.

If that doesn't feel like a case of eternal heartburn, I don't know what does!

I set down the pot and some mugs onto the table. We fix our cups, milk and sugar for Harlan, just milk for Grandma, and nothing for me.

Everybody's tired. We sit in silence and that's okay because that's what families do.

I am struck suddenly with the realization that I am living in a house with four other people. My flesh and blood grandma, my husband, our adopted daughter, and our foster son. I remember Ruby talking years ago about that adjective our son bears. "Foster." And I do believe that the next time Grace calls I'll ask her what she thinks about Harlan and I becoming official parents.

Leo George Hopewell.

I like that.

I think Leo will, too. Hopewell is a much nicer name than Underhill.

Harlan excuses himself after finishing half his cup and I know he's going back to do his evening Bible devotional. He's been reading Spurgeon's *Morning and Evening* every day ever since I've known him. I'm more of a *Daily Bread* kind of person. One verse, a short paragraph, a poem, and a prayer. Now whoever thought of that was a genius. It even keeps the attention of someone like me.

Grandma scrapes off her glasses and rubs the shelf of

skin beneath her eyebrows with the pads of her thumbs. "Oh, me. I'm tired, sweetie."

"I'm so glad you came down here, Grandma."

"So am I, Charmaine. You're my sweetie."

Oh, the love I feel just now.

"Tomorrow I'll take you over to the school. I can help you set up your room if you'd like."

Her eyes light up. "Oh, I've got plans. You handy with a stapler? I've got to put up my bulletin boards by next week."

"But school doesn't start for two weeks."

"I'm an early bird. Remember, what else have I had to do for the past two and a half decades?"

I see her point.

I have to ask the question. "Any more news?"

She shakes her head. "Just more dead ends. We're never going to find her on our own."

"That's what I'm afraid of."

"You want to hear what I've been thinking?"

"Uh-huh."

"What if we hire a detective?"

"A private eye?"

"That's exactly what I mean."

I sip my tea and look down. "Aren't they expensive?"

"I've lived frugally and selling the house helped, too. And now that I'm living here with you and Harlan, my expenses are even more limited."

I nod. "You got any idea who you're gonna get?"

"I do. He's from Richmond. He's coming down to Mount Oak next week to meet with me."

"Where?"

She shrugs. "I don't know. He's going to call when he gets into town. You got any suggestions?"

"How about Bill D's Restaurant?"

"That's what I'll tell him."

A private eye. I am amazed. Of course I wondered about doing something like this years ago, but I knew it was something Harlan and I could never afford.

Poor Grandma Min. Most old people spend all their savings on their health, but it appears Grandma is still forced to give all she has for a daughter who never gave a fig for anyone.

As I said before.

3

I am so excited. You should
see this BrooksTone Records place! Marble and chrome
and leather chairs. The receptionist, with a black, arsty-
type dress—very New York—and a French twist with
some tendrils hanging around her pale face, is so polite.

"My name is Charmaine Hopewell? I have an appointment with Carl Bofa?" I am whispering. I don't
know why. Maybe it would echo too much in here and I'd
seem like the Podunk singer I am. Why did I think coming here was a good idea? What was MaryAnna thinking?
Me ready for a real record deal? In this high-class, high-
powered world?

Her switchboard lights up. "Just a moment, please."

So calm!

I mean singing in front of the folks that come to concerts like Gospelganza is one thing, but coming to
Nashville to a big record company like BrooksTone? I'm
an idiot.

She works those buttons like it's a typewriter, saying,
"BrooksTone Records . . . one moment, please," "Brooks-

Tone, please hold," and "Thank you for holding, how may I direct your call?"

She's more polished than Reverend Robert Schuler.

"I apologize for the delay."

I wave a hand with nails lacquered much too red if hers are any indication. "Oh, things always come in droves, don't they?"

"They absolutely do."

They absolutely do. Now I would never have said it so fine like that! I would have said, "They sure do!" and then blabbered on about all the times that it had happened to me.

Wonder if this gal gives deportment lessons in classiness? Right now, I sure do wish Cecile and Clarke Ferris had rubbed off on me more.

"I'll let Mr. Bofa know you've arrived. Why don't you have a seat on the settee?"

The settee? It looks like a leather couch to me.

I am out of my league here. I'm so far out of my league I'm in a different sport altogether. It's like a softball player from Podunk, U.S.A. trying out for a Stanley Cup hockey team.

Even the decor tells me this.

Where there aren't windows there are gold records and posters, cover art and paintings by Mr. Bofa. Now, I don't know much about much, but these paintings look like something Hope would do. I can't even tell what they are!

I have no idea what color the walls really are.

Gray maybe?

Does it matter? Probably not. I'll never see this place past today anyway.

"Ms. Hopewell?"

The soothing voice accompanies a light touch on my shoulder and I open my eyes.

I'm sure my face matches my hair. "I can't believe I fell asleep!"

"It's all right. A lot of people do. It's the furniture."

"Very comfy!"

Why am I shouting everything?

"Jay is ready to see you now."

I look at my watch. "I've been sitting here for an hour?"

"Yes, I'm sorry. We've had a delay in the scheduling."

"No, no. I wasn't complaining, I just can't believe I fell asleep for that long!" I whisper, "Was I snoring?"

And she laughs her true laugh and I can see the girl behind the image. I like her. "Yes, but nobody came in."

"Oh, good! Promise me if I do that again you'll wake me up!"

"I will."

She smiles into my eyes this time. She has nice eyes, a grayish-green mossy kind of eye with a deep blue rim. Eye-of-the-storm eyes.

We are sisters and I know this because when she turns around, her tag at the back of her neck is turned out and there's a runner down the back of her panty hose.

"I'll show you back."

I grab my purse. "Thanks."

Her heels click a lower tone than mine as we negotiate the black marble floors. She's much taller and therefore heavier than me. And now I can see that the dress beautifully hides a nice-size derriere. Good for her. I'll bet she's not living on Diet Coke!

More art, more records, more posters.

Wait a second!

Jay? Who's Jay?

"I thought Mr. Bofa's first name was Carl?"

"It is. You'll be seeing Jay Spentser first. He's our artists relations guy."

"My first line of defense?"

"Exactly. Use him for all he's worth. It's why they pay him five times as much as they pay me."

Oh, that was indiscreet. Good, then.

She shows me to an opened doorway. A pair of white sneakers, the boat kind, glow from beneath the kneewell of the desk and a preppy-type guy wearing a pink Izod shirt stands to his feet. "Charmaine Hopewell! I'd recognize you anywhere."

"I hope that's good," I say.

"It sure is. It pays to stand out in this business."

The receptionist smirks. "Don't let him fool you."

And we say in unison, "He says that to all the girls."

He winces at the receptionist. "Thank you, Ella, for your support." He sounds like those cute Bartles & Jaymes guys in those funny commercials.

I smile. "You sure know how to make a girl feel good about herself."

"It's my job."

"I'm Jay, by the way."

"Ella told me. Good to meet you."

We shake hands. What a cutie pie. Freshfaced, blond, was quite possibly a tennis pro in another life if you believed in other lives. But he must be a golfer judging by the paraphernalia. Golf clubs, golf shoes, golf ice bucket, golf tumblers, golf pictures, golf books, and a mechanical bank where a golfer putts the penny into the slot.

"Have a seat. Would you like something to drink?"

Ella steps forward. "Soda or coffee or tea? We have whatever you'd like."

"I'd like a Diet Coke."

Ella backs out and says, "You be good now, Jay!"

Jay sits back down and rocks back in his leather desk chair. "Ahh, a Diet Coke, huh? That's a good girl."

"A girl's gotta do what a girl's gotta do."

"And nowadays it's hard to get away with being a big singer."

I smile. "There are some."

"Yep."

"But I don't have their voices."

He taps the desk. "I like a girl who knows her limitations. But it's not about just the voice, it's about the attitude and of course, the ministry."

My ears perk.

He leans forward, eyes earnest. "We may be fun and games here at BrooksTone, but to me it's about more than the bottom line. You really sing to the soul when you're up on stage."

"You've seen me?"

"Who do you think got your foot in the door here?"

"Well, then, I should thank you."

"No need. I felt like the Holy Ghost was whispering in my ear."

"You feel like that, too, sometimes?"

"No doubt about it."

Well, my, my, my. I guess Christians come in all

shapes and sizes. He just seems too normal to have the Holy Ghost whispering to him. I mean, he's wearing a polo shirt and jeans.

Ella arrives with my Diet Coke. "I'd love to stay and chat, but the phones will go crazy."

"'Bye, Ella," I say.

And we smile into each other's eyes once more.

One thing for sure, I am at home with these people. Now I guess Mr. Bofa will be another story.

"So, what questions do you have, Charmaine?"

"Tell me about BrooksTone."

He does. And I learn that it was bought out by the big entertainment conglomerate, Kinglee Enterprises, last year. "Of course, they brought in new managers who care only about the bottom line."

I shrug. "Business is business, I guess."

"But does one really have to compromise their intended mission?" he asks.

"I sure hope not." I lean forward. "What is your intended mission?"

"To further the gospel while building up the artist him- or herself." He leans forward. "But I want you to know I am here for you. I'm determined we'll always put the artist first and foremost."

I'm not sure whether to believe him or not. But I guess I'll give him the benefit of the doubt.

He looks at his watch. "Well, ready to go meet the big guy?"

"The big guy?"

"Just a pet name."

I guess a pet name like "big guy" can go either way.

"Let's go then. I might as well get this over with."

He escorts me farther on down the hallway and we stop at the end. He points to the left.

Double doors and a stainless steel nameplate that says, CARL BOFA, VICE PRESIDENT looms, yes looms, before me.

He knocks and a muffled "Yeah!" sounds from within the obviously hallowed chamber of the vice president.

"Carl? This is Charmaine Hopewell."

"Charmaine! Come on in! Thankya, Jay."

My lands, his accent is thicker than mine. I'm surprised he didn't say "Howdy-doo!"

Jay shuts the door and I wish he hadn't.

"Thanks for seeing me today, Mr. Bofa."

"Don't be so formal, call me Carl. The music business is very informal."

"Formally informal?"

He points to me. "I like your style, darlin'."

Darlin'.

Now I am once again unsure. I mean "darlin's" can go both ways, too.

"Have a seat on the couch."

Naturally he has a corner office and it is walled with smoky windows on two sides. The other two support more records, more posters, and, guess what, more art. And there are photographs he has taken as well. Now that I see his office I understand his art. Lots of extreme close-ups of segments of cowboy hats, spurs, and the like.

A conversation area sits in the far corner. Now I must say I am a bit surprised because this office is nothing like the lobby. It is comfortable and warm and even has a gas fireplace going in the corner.

"Did you have a hand in decorating this place?"

"Yep. I'm an old cowboy at heart."

I can sure tell. Little sculptures of men on horses dot the room. The couches are brown, worn-looking leather and there's even a saddle on a stand in the corner near the bar, which looks more than stocked. This surprises me, too. Even though it is a Kinglee subsidiary, BrooksTone is still a Christian record company. I don't say a word, though. Not at this point. Probably not ever.

And does it really matter in the long run?

Now is not the time to answer that.

"So you love gospel music?" I ask as I sit down and cross my legs at the ankles like Mrs. Evans taught me years ago.

"I do."

"Who're your favorites?"

"The Cathedrals."

"I love them! Who else?"

"Vestal Goodman."

"I love the Goodmans. Think I could get away with using a hankie?"

"Darlin' with that hair, you've already got yourself a trademark. If you sign on with BrooksTone, the first thing you'll do is make it even redder!"

He makes me think of Gomer Pyle, but smart.

And why did they name that character Gomer? Gomer was a girl in the Bible!

Carl reaches out and runs his fingers through the left side of my hair. I am stunned. His fingers catch in the mess. "Ouch!"

"Sorry, sugar. You are a cute thing. The folks are going to love you!"

"They already do." I steer him back to the business at hand. You'd be surprised how many strangers reach out and touch my hair. "You know I've sold twenty thousand tapes of my own at Gospelganza concerts, don't you?"

"I sure do."

"So what are you going to do for me that I can't do for myself?"

"Well, that depends on how far you'll go to succeed."

"You won't find a harder working singer. I'll even come down and do background vocals for you. I'll sing anytime, anyplace, and anywhere and you can take that right on down to the bank!"

Blabber, blabber, blabber.

"So you'll work hard. Do whatever it takes, eh?"

"Yes, sir. You won't find anyone more willing to go the extra mile than Charmaine Hopewell."

"By the way, darlin', what's your middle name?"

"Charmaine."

"Your first?"

"A girl's gotta have her secrets."

He winks and leans forward, opening a drawer in the coffee table. He removes a cigar that's laying on top of a Penthouse magazine.

Oh, great. A porno freak. This is just my luck! I pretend I don't notice it.

Get out! Get out! Get out!

Sometimes women have these moments where we see it all. We see the past as it is, the present as we think it is, and the future as what it could be if we keep our rear end right where it is.

I see myself black and blue in some emergency room and I don't know why. I see a young redheaded girl traveling south on a bus in the winter wilds.

Those images attack me.

And I push them away. This is my big break! I say to them. My big break. We can fix up the house so it's sweet and charming. I'll buy Harlan a new car like a Buick or an Oldsmobile, something real nice and comfy because he's so tall. The cute outfits I could get for Hope swim their empty arms in my mind and I see *her* there, the angel baby. And Leo, well, I can put that little smart guy in a good private school like that Nansemond place in Suffolk, only it won't be in Suffolk because I'll always keep my babies right here with me.

If Mr. Bofa gets dangerous, I'll just run out and that will be that. But I don't want to jump the gun, do I?

"I like you, Charmaine."

"Thank you."

"So what else can you offer BrooksTone?"

"Well, you haven't answered my question, Carl. What can you offer me?"

"Would you like a tour?"

"Yes, I would."

He escorts me out of his office and back up the hallway to Jay's. "Jay, give Charmaine a tour. Introduce her to folks."

"Sure, Carl."

Thank you, God! I'm getting out of this cowboy shrine.

I am amazed. The art department is beautiful. "We do most of our album art in-house," says Jamie, the art director who's dressed more like an accountant on his day off.

The sales and marketing folks couldn't be nicer.

Everyone's so nice.

So why do I feel so itchy inside?

4

*O*h, my lands! What a nut! He reminds me of some Southern writer-type there in his light colored suit and black tie. His hair is white and longish and honest to goodness he's a cross between Colonel Sanders and Samuel Clemmens! Samuel Phlegmmens would be more like it. His cough rumbles more than a pack of Harley-Davidsons.

But he's black. And he's a Northerner. Two cigars peer over the front pocket of his suit.

His name is Dovey. Nathan Dovey. But, "Don't call me 'Nathan,' don't call me 'Mr. Dovey,' because I won't answer."

And I say, "Fine by me, Dovey."

I want so badly to call him 'Lovey Dovey,' but Grandma paid him to come down to talk to us and I sure don't want to waste her savings.

We lay out everything we've done, which is mostly government agency and records stuff, because obviously we haven't been able to go gallivanting around the country on a flat-out search.

He writes the details down left-handed, his bony

knuckles reminding me of mushrooms with little brown caps. He writes quickly and with a beautiful, flowing hand over the pages of a small spiral notepad with a light blue cover.

Sometimes you just never know.

"Did your mother ever mention your grandmother?"

"Sometimes."

"What did she say?"

I look over to Grandma then back at Dovey. "Well, I don't know if I want to say."

He must understand because he speaks respectfully to Grandma Min, the ashy, potato-brown skin around his eyes creasing with sympathy. "This may be painful. But it may increase my chances at finding your daughter." He pats her hand and right away I think to myself, I love this man!

I shrug, trying so hard to cage in Isla's attitude, to bar in her disrespect with my own softened words. "She just . . . well, there were times when she thought she did things differently than Grandma might have and she'd say, 'Wouldn't your grandma Min have a fit?'"

Grandma reaches for her handbag, shakes her head once, twice, then returns the bag to the floor. She clears her throat and takes my hand. "Go on ahead and tell these things, sweetie. I know it's really not you saying them."

I nod. Normally I'm not at a loss for words, but this is different. Isla's actions become more and more reprehensible with each drop of love for my grandmother that fills my heart.

"Did she ever mention your father?"

"No. And she wouldn't let me ask about him."

He turns to Grandma. "I noticed you didn't mention

this in your letter. Do you have any idea who Charmaine's father is?"

"Judging by Charmaine's birthday, Isla was already pregnant with Charmaine when she left Suffolk."

So she didn't go to Randolf Macon Women's College then? Oh, my lands. And why do we have to talk about my father, anyway? Obviously he was or is no better than my mother.

I feel just now as if my heart has grown a toenail on one of its curves and someone yanked it off down to the quick.

Grandma grabs my hand. "Isla had been seeing a young man who worked at the Planters factory. He met her at one of the restaurants in town where she waited tables. He was all right, I guess. He loved her a lot more than she loved him."

"What was his name?"

She squeezes my hand. "David Potter."

David Potter.

"David Potter." Dovey writes that down. "Will I be able to contact him?"

That sure is the question. I picture a young, thin man. Shy. Working in a peanut plant, whatever people in peanut plants do. Sandy hair. Bright blue eyes rimmed with black lashes. Bright blue eyes made brighter by pretty Isla Whitehead.

She shakes her head. "David died just after Isla left Suffolk."

Well, at least I didn't have to have my hopes raised for too long. But five minutes of wishful thinking might have been nice instead of five seconds!

"Are his parents still living?" Dovey asks.

"Well, his mother is. His father died about ten years ago, I'd guess."

"Do they know anything about Charmaine?"

"I don't know. I don't know them all that well. And I didn't know about Charmaine until *she* found me."

"Did you tell Mrs. Potter she had a granddaughter?"

Grandma Min drops my hand and whispers. "No." She turns to me. "I'm sorry, Charmaine. I just couldn't. I didn't want to share you with them. And I figured, maybe there'd be so much pain for them. And we don't really know for sure, do we?"

I press her hand. "This will save for later, Grandma. It's okay."

Dovey writes some more. "Still she might have heard from your daughter. I really should follow that lead."

I ask, "Can you do it in a way that it won't give things away?" Right then, I want to preserve Grandma Min's heart and our way of life.

"Of course. 'Discreet' is my middle name."

I smile. "I thought it was just Dovey."

He laughs. "Good one. Anything else?"

"Well, she did have lots of boyfriends. I believe she was a loose woman." I *really* didn't want Grandma to hear that, but she didn't look at all shocked.

"You remember any of their names?"

"Uh-huh." And I list them off. "Except there was one more, the man she went off with when she left Lynchburg. All I know is that he was from Washington, D.C. I never knew his name. She just called him 'that man,' really tenderly, too."

"Do you remember what kind of car he drove?"

I nod. "But they never came up with anything back all those years ago."

"Don't worry about that. The police say that all the time because they don't have the time to follow every lead. You never know. It might be something they've missed."

"Okay. It was an old Cadillac, black, with fins. In really good shape. D.C. plates."

"You think if I found a picture of it you'd be able to identify it?"

"I'll never forget that car as long as I live."

Funny, I hadn't thought about that snazzy man's car in years, but there it sat in my mind, glistening and black and daring and yet rude and pushy. Almost pulsating with the hate I felt for it. I hated that man, too.

See, it's like this. I always thought of Mama and figured she must have had really terrible parents to have done what she did. But now that I know Grandma Min, I know better. Yes, she was mentally ill. I know that now. But she chose to go off her medication and that was, pure and simple, selfish of her.

She had a daughter!

Why couldn't she take the pills for me, at least?

That purple *Fantasia* dragon is waking up inside me and I can only hope that when it opens its mouth and spews fire in a circle all around, we all won't blacken, curl up, and disintigrate.

Dovey pockets his notebook. "All right, then. I'll get started. I've got other clients so this may take a while. But if she's still out there, I'll find her."

"I haven't seen my daughter in over twenty-five years. If I have to wait a while longer, well, that's what I'll do."

He points to me. "What about you?"

"I don't have much of a choice, do I?"

"Why do you want to find her?"

"Just to know."

I feel a hardness petrify my own gaze and Dovey knows. Dovey knows I hate Isla Whitehead. "It won't make the pain go away," he says. "I've been in this business long enough to know that knowing doesn't always make things right."

I smooth the table with my hand. "But it makes things what they are. And right now, I don't even know that."

He nods and taps the tabletop with the fingertips of his left hand. "All right then. I'll call you as soon as I know something. Try not to call me all the time for details. I call when I have some new information and not before. Continual updates are expensive and you two seem too sensible to need mollycoddling."

Grandma and I look at each other and shrug. "That's fine, Dovey," she says. "We'll just go on as usual and try not to think about things too much."

"That's the best way to go about it, ladies."

5

$\mathcal{I}$ love October. I love the way the air breathes. I love the smell of people's fireplaces going. I love the metallic taste of apple cider and the fastidious blue of the sky.

I love spring even more.

But October is here and I'm loving my new life.

Nashville is a pretty old town. I'm riding down luxurious Belle Meade Boulevard in a limousine. "It's not the best way to get to the studio, but it's one of the prettiest," the driver says.

The leaves are ignited as though made of the money people in these parts must burn on whims I've never even considered.

They're all here. Italian villas. Colonial mansions. Tudor fortresses. Gated Greek palaces. Stone, brick, wood, you name it. I love the tiled roofs.

The driver says, "This is *the* street to live on around here. Lots of artists and execs. I'm not sayin' there aren't other nice places, but there's a regular who's who here."

But you know, I'm surprised right now. Because while I admire this drive from my hotel in Brentwood to the studio at BrooksTone on Music Row, I realize this life will never be mine, that when I married Harlan I said, "No" to riches, and that it's fine.

I have other riches.

People God has sent me.

I used to be alone, you know. I don't come by these thoughts easily. The road to this point had a lot of broken glass along the way and the fact that I can still walk is only by God's grace.

If I could be spirited into these houses and see nothing but people getting along and loving each other the way we do, I might be jealous. But I doubt I'll find that behind 98 percent of these walls. I really do.

"Can I use this car phone?" I ask the chauffeur.

"Of course, Ms. Hopewell."

I call Harlan. Things are fine.

Tanzel comes on the phone and tells me about this mix-up between the music director and the children's choir leader. "But I straightened it out!"

As if that was ever in doubt.

I call Grandma, but remember she's at school.

I call Ruby. She's decided she's taken a shine to Henry Windsor!

I make a firm decision just then, to be more like Ruby and just decide things. So that is what I do. I make a decision.

I call Grace's parents before I can change my mind. If I give myself time to think about it, I'll never do it. I tell them the truth.

It's abrupt. I know. But it's right.

"I can't cover for her anymore. I'm not even sure where your daughter is."

Ruby would be proud of me. I tell them almost everything I know. All except for the part about Leo's existence. How can I? What if they come and take my little boy, my little roller-skating, dinosaur-drawing, huggy-kissy boy, away from me? I couldn't bear it.

"Why didn't you tell us?" Mrs. Underhill asks.

"I promised Grace not to."

"But we relied on you, Charmaine."

"And Grace relied on me. Maybe you all should keep family business exactly that."

And I hung up the phone after a quick, "'Bye now."

I know it's not a way to tell someone their daughter's a drug addict. But for the life of me, I couldn't summon up the strength to do it any other way. They deserve to know. Grace doesn't deserve anything else.

The buildings become more intensely gathered the farther into the city we drive. I purposely push Grace from my mind. This is my day. This is my day.

We pull into the parking lot and I am so excited. When I signed the contract Jay said, "Now a lot of artists have their own studios they use and producers they like to work with and they just send the finished product here. What are your preferences?"

I wanted to guffaw. I mean, I am so professional! "Just point me in whatever direction you want," I said.

So here I am. Ella's showing me back down the hallway that Jay took me down last month.

"I'm kind of nervous."

"Don't be. I've heard your other tape. It's wonderful."

"You think so?"

"Of course."

She's wearing ivory today. No panty-hose runs, but part of her French twist is falling down at the back.

"Trust me, Charmaine. Jay's got a good nose for this sort of thing. He wouldn't have brought you in if he didn't think you could deliver."

"What about Carl?"

"Carl doesn't care about BrooksTone. He was sent here by Kinglee because they wanted him out of their hair."

"Really? How do you know?"

"This is a small community, Charmaine. Word gets around."

She shows me in and we start. They've already picked out a bunch of old favorites for me to sing, the arrangements have been done, and all I have to do is sing what's on the sheet music.

Now that I can do.

One song is an original.

"We thought we'd give this songwriter a shot, Charmaine," Jay says. He's been sitting with me in the studio the whole time and I am glad.

The song is perfect. Soft, sweet, and all about Jesus. It's called "Ten Thousand Lilies."

"I think this will be your hit," he says.

And I believe him.

"Do you think we'll have this all done in two weeks?"

"I sure do. All the accompaniment tracks are laid down, and besides, you're a natural."

Are people in this business always this flattering?

The gang and I just finished a swanky dinner at Merchants. My two weeks are up and I'm basically done. I'm sharing a limo with Carl because he lives in Brentwood where my hotel is. Not the horsey guy I thought!

"So what do you think, darlin'? You like BrooksTone so far?"

"I love it."

I'm trying to look out the window as much as possible. But I'm having a hard time finding the balance between being rude and yet still seeing the sites of Nashville.

Plus, I don't want to connect with him on any level.

"Good. We like our artists to be happy. You happy, Charmaine?"

"You mean happy with the recording sessions or happy in general?"

"In general."

"Oh, yes, sir. I sure am. I love my husband and my children so much. They're the most important thing to me. More important than even this stuff, Carl."

"Still, you do seem like a gal that knows what she wants and how to get it."

"Thank you."

"You know sometimes we take a BrooksTone artist and put all the Kinglee muscle behind her. The marketing, the distribution. Everything."

"Really?" Oh, my lands.

"I think you've got potential for a broader market. You've got such . . . appeal."

He runs a hand over my hand.

I pull it away.

"Phil, take the long way back to Charmaine's hotel."

"Yes, sir." The chauffeur puts up the divider between the front seat and the back.

"Look, Mr. Bofa—"

"We're back to that? Come on, Charmaine, call me 'Carl.'"

"What's going on, Carl?"

"Nothing that hasn't gone on before, I can tell you that."

What do I do? I'm stuck in this car. "Let's not take the long way home."

His hand reaches out. I slap it away.

He reddens.

He slaps me.

That quickly.

Right across the cheek.

Oh, God.

He rips my shirt.

I can't scream. I want to, but my throat fills, bloated with fear.

I lash out again. Fists curled.

He punches the side of my head, right on my ear.

Now I can scream.

Phil slides the divider down a tad. "Everything okay, sir?"

"Keep driving!" he screams.

"No!" I yell.

He jams his hand over my mouth and whispers in my ear. "You be quiet, darlin', or your future is as good as gone." He says, "It really is okay, Phil. Charmaine just pulled a muscle if you know what I mean."

Phil laughs and the divider returns.

I bite Carl's hand.

I pray.

I feel my panties being torn down and I kick out as hard as I can.

God, get me out of this.

His pants come down.

I thought I had known fear before.

But he isn't ready to perform. I am one percent relieved even as my heart speeds up yet again at the rage flipping in his eyes.

He decides to just beat me up now that his intended weapon has lost its aim, now that he has no hopes of anything.

God, just let Phil stop the car.

Please.

Fists fly from both of us. I am able to remove a high-heeled shoe and I swing it across his face, landing it on the tender spot of his cheek.

He roars, grabs my arm, and slams it back against the door.

"Stop the car, Phil!"

The divider goes down.

"Stop the car!"

"Yes, sir!"

The wheels have not stopped turning and I am on the street, scrabbling to my feet and running for my life toward a Waffle House.

Harlan jumps to his feet when they return me to my hospital room after surgery. Carl broke my arm and ripped tendons.

"I drove as fast as I could, Shug."

He kisses me.

I am safe.

"I won't leave you again, Harlan. I'm sorry."

I start to cry but force it down allowing only a single sob to escape.

"Go ahead and cry, Shug."

"I can't Harlan."

"Then don't, Charmaine. You don't have to do anything you don't want to do."

"Can you climb up on the bed with me? I think I just need to feel you here."

He does, his big feet in their big wingtips looking clownlike and awkward. And so safe.

I think I will fall back asleep before I look in a mirror and see the bruising. I think I need just a little more time before I see the extent of the damage.

"Harlan?"

"Yeah, Shug?"

"I fought as hard as I could. He never penetrated. Nothing even touched down there."

He cradles my face in his hands. "Charmaine Hopewell, you're really something. But then, I've always known that about you."

"I love you, Harlan."

"I love you, too."

And he does. Oh, Harlan sure does. And it is in this that I seek my rest and find it.

Not long afterward a nice detective lady from the Nashville police department comes and talks to me. She asks me if I'd like to press charges and I say, "Yes, ma'am. I surely would."

I'd like to see Mr. Bofa and his *sofa* put away for a long, long time.

Harlan caresses my face. "You're a fighter, Shug."

"Wish I didn't have to be."

"I admire you, Charmaine. I still can't believe a woman like you would have a man like me."

6

*B*ring it right on over here!"
Harlan points to the corner of the living room. A white
cable with a pointed end sticks out from the wall. Just installed. Cable TV!

Isn't technology just a wonderful thing? I lie on the
couch still nursing my arm and my bruises. And am I
jumpy these days! I've dipped down a bit emotionally,
but I really don't want Dr. Braselton to up my dosage. I'll
get through this.

The deliverymen deposit the set on the $39.99 Walt's
Mart TV stand Harlan already assembled. Two hours
later the cable man comes and hooks up everything. He
shows us how to work the box on the top of the TV and
hooks up the VCR, too, so we can use the remote. Can
you imagine? You can just tape things off the television.
I've always wanted to really get into soap operas and
maybe now I can.

But which one should I choose?

Definitely not one that has anything to do with hospitals. Not after what I've just been through. But I'd like
one with lots of rich people who have nothing better to do

than slam doors, whip around quickly during an argument, and plan society galas that help the homeless.

Take it from me, though, homelessness comes in many forms.

I wonder if those rich people on Belle Meade Boulevard are really like that?

The kids jump around talking about a network named Nickelodeon and this show called *Pinwheel* they watched over at Tanzel's house when she baby-sat them.

Harlan fixes the service men some iced tea and they drink it down gratefully, their big Adam's apples bobbing in their throats. And then, after they leave, he pulls out the remote, juggling it from one hand to the other, eyebrows rising and falling. "Shall we take her for a spin, Shug?"

"I wouldn't stop you." With my good hand, I pull my blankets up to my chin. "Grandma? Wanna come in a see the new television set?"

She hollers in from the kitchen where she's browning meat for the sloppy joes. She's been a real peach during this recuperation time. "I'll be right there. Go ahead and get started without me."

It's funny how she's blossomed since the moment I first saw her. A closed mum turned into the sunny bloom of Autumn. I just love her so much. I've forgiven her about the father thing. I have to. But I do plan on scouting out Mrs. Potter's house if I'm ever in Suffolk again.

See, I've got to think of it this way. Me suddenly showing up on her doorstep may give her a heart attack or something. Talk about "out of the blue." I mean, it was one thing for Grandma Min, because she was my mother's mama. But this Mrs. Potter lost her son over two decades ago, a nice kid who worked at a peanut factory, and all of a sudden his daughter shows up?

That might make even a perfectly healthy person have a stroke and I have no idea what state this poor woman is in. I mean, she's already lost a child and that's the worst thing anyone can go through.

Harlan flips through the channels slowly, a big grin pulling his face apart at the seams. I watch him instead of the TV but then realize this is a new stage in our lives. We are the family living in a brick ranch house with cable TV, so I take heed of the screen in front of me.

"Harlan! Stop! Stop right there! Is that that MTV show?"

"Oh, my."

"Who is that man?! And what have they done to his hair?"

Harlan's eyes go buggy. "And what in the world does 'the union of the snake' mean?"

"How should I know?"

"Those are the craziest darn words I've ever heard." Harlan looks disgusted. "They don't even make any sense."

"Who *are* those guys?"

Grandma Min walks in, drying her hands on her apron. "Oh, that's Duran Duran."

"Who on earth?" I ask.

"Actually they're not the cat's pajamas anymore. But they were hot tickets a couple of years ago."

My mouth falls open. "How do you know about this stuff, Grandma?"

"I taught sixth graders for years, sweetie. I've always been up on the latest pop idols."

"Well, my lands." I point to the screen. "This calls for popcorn 'cause this is even better than the circus!"

"I'll make it, Shug! We'll have us a good old time."

Harlan's been trying to wipe out Mr. Bofa's attack ever since it happened. And I guess the pictures of that night will fade eventually. But maybe not.

But I've lived through worse for a long time now.

Still, I'm jumpy and skittish and I look over my shoulder a lot when we're out because a man like Carl Bofa could pop up anywhere, waiting to get me back.

I hope they throw the book at him. I'm not looking forward to testifying against him, I can tell you that. But I will because I've made up my mind to do just that.

7

I've turned into a regular night owl, thanks to the TV in the house. David Letterman tickles me to no end! That space between his teeth makes him naturally humorous. Kind of like what my hair does to me. And I don't know why dropping items from a high window makes me laugh, but it gets me every time!

I'm lying in bed in a Nashville hotel room. This place has a king-size bed, a microwave, a minibar that I'll tell you right now I'm not taking a thing out of because that stuff costs as much as it would at a kiosk by the Smithsonian in Washington, D.C. or out at Forger's Creek, that new Christian resort near Roanoke. Whooo-eee. They charged two dollars for a Diet Coke by their pool!

I did a Gospelganza concert at Forger's Creek last summer.

I love swanky hotels. A coffeemaker rests on the sink not three feet away from my toilet. I'm not about to make a pot of coffee in *that* thing tomorrow morning! You know, they say you should keep your toothbrush eight feet away from the toilet? I can't even begin to imagine the germs on that coffeepot.

And I'm not all that germ conscious!

My final recording session, laying down some finishing touches and an a cappella version of "Blessed Redeemer," went well today at BrooksTone.

Carl, of course, is gone. And all his artwork, good riddance. The walls aren't gray, they're taupe.

I'm tired but I call home anyway. "Harlan?"

"Hey, Shug. How'd it go?"

"Good."

"Any problems?"

"Not one. The staff actually gave me a standing ovation when I walked in. Even the Kinglee people."

I hear him clapping. "I think that's fine."

"I kind of doubted that Carl was well liked, but you never know."

"That's the truth, Shug."

"Anything new, Harlan?"

"Grace called."

"She did? Did she say where she is?"

"She's in Atlanta."

"Really?"

"Yep. I was surprised she admitted where she was."

"When's she coming back? Did she say?"

"No. She asked about Leo and I told her he was in second grade and doing well."

"Did you tell her he's a real whiz with numbers?"

"I did. Again."

I'm sure he rolls his eyes just then.

"What did she say, Harlan?"

"Nothing much. Something like 'That's nice to hear' or something like that."

"How did she sound?"

"Crazy. You know Grace."

The room blurs as he answers and I picture Grace tying her arm with a tourniquet and then sticking a needle about eighteen inches long into it. I picture it going straight through her arm, lodging into the table and pinning her there for life. "Did you ask her if she's still using?"

"Yep, I asked her and she said 'yes.'"

"Well, at least she's honest."

"Not that it's getting her anywhere."

"We need to get her some help, Harlan. What about your old friend from college? That nice fellow we had lunch with all that time ago?"

"Tony Sanchez?"

"That's him. He lives down that way, doesn't he? Can't he check things out?"

"I'll give him a call."

"How're the kids?"

"Fine. Hope took a road map in for show and tell and pointed out all the states she's already been to."

"Oh, that's cute."

"Leo's been assigned the funniest book report. They have to take a pumpkin and make a character from their book out of it."

"That's cute, too."

"Your grandmother said she'd help with it."

"When's it due?"

"Next month, when you'll be singing for that big concert in Louisville."

"I'll try and get as much done as possible with him beforehand."

He chuckles. "Yeah. But you know how those school projects can creep up on you."

Isla never once helped me with a project.

"I promise I'll help him some, Harlan. I just have to."

His smiled wafts over the wires and he says, "You are a real peach, Charmaine."

I'm glad now that I told Harlan about Mrs. Evans and how she called me "Peach." Now he sometimes does, too. Harlan's so sweet.

Some people think peaches just grow on a tree. But I know they are carefully tended and the sweetest ones are shown the most care.

I want Leo and Hope to be peaches. I really do.

8

$\mathcal{I}$ am experimenting with the hair painting kit I bought at the IGA. The girl on the box wears the cutest cap of curly hair. I'm tired of red, red, red, and nothing but red. They give you this little plastic brush with black bristles and you mix up this white goop and just paint stripes on your hair. I figure I need real pizzazz so I'm painting on really big stripes. Grandma is doing it for me because my arm still hurts too much to lift it high. The cast is off though and I say, "Hallelujah!" You can't know how annoying casts are until you've been in one for eight weeks.

"Shug! Come in here and look at *Jesus Alive!* with me."

Jesus Alive! is one of those television shows that have a bunch of popular Christian guests and the hosts, Peter and Vinca Love, sit and chat, and pray and prophesy and all. I know their last name seems fake or at best contrived, but I had a Sunday school teacher named Sue Ellen Love so I know it's an actual last name. Whether or not it's *their* actual last name, I can't say.

I even met them when I sang at Forger's Creek, their

multimillion dollar conference center, resort, and golf club in the Shenandoah Valley.

And you should see that place at Christmastime.

Now Vinca is flamboyant in a very odd way. If I'm Las Vegas, she's Montana. Cowboy boots and huge skirts with as much material as you'd find in a bedsheet. And yet she wears her long brown hair pulled back in a tidy bun at the nape of her neck. She was nice to us Gospelganza folks, make no mistake about it, but she seemed hardened in a way. Not a bad hardened, more of an imperviousness. She's also had diabetes since childhood, which has probably done more to build her into a woman of God, a woman who knows what's important, than anything else. She's from high society Richmond, I think I heard.

Peter is one of those rugged cowboy poets. Grew up on a ranch in Wyoming, traveled the rodeo circuit for quite a while, and even starred in a few westerns back in the sixties. He wears the ranch garb and looks mighty fine in those jeans and boots and hats.

Mighty fine, ma'am.

But Harlan will have to accept the fact that those two can keep while I see to my hair. Shoot, they're on that network of theirs at least four times a day anyway.

"Oh, Harlan! I'm in the middle of something."

"Well, your loss. God must really be blessing these people. The studio is completely full and they just took a camera outside and showed the line going around the building for the next show's shooting in a couple of hours!"

"We're almost done painting my hair. I'll come in

while it sets." I turn to Grandma, "What do you think about those people?"

She shrugs. "I think it's a little goofy. Not like the Lutheran people I'm used to! Although she's close. But I mean, 'Ropin' in souls'? What's that supposed to mean and don't you think it's a tad odd?"

I shrug. "I guess. But they seem to really love the Lord."

"I still think they're odd."

We finish up and tidy the bathroom. I'm very attentive with my home and rightly so. And Grandma's right with me. I figure I must have inherited that gene from her.

Harlan's got a space heater near the couch as the furnace went up last week. Doesn't that figure? Thank goodness we're in the South and it's only November. He pulls back the quilt he's under and I slip down next to him. "Watch the hair Harlan, that's bleach. You'll ruin that shirt for sure if it gets on it."

I turn toward *Jesus Alive!*, trying to keep my hair from touching anything. "Oh, I love that old Cowboy George guy on there."

"Did you meet him when you were up there, Shug?"

"Yes. And he's the cutest thing! Seems like he really loves the Lord."

We watch awhile as they sit there and laugh and joke. Vinca is her normal hilarious, sarcastic self, lambasting Peter like she always does. All in fun, of course. Peter sits back and admires her and he's always telling how much he loves her. They really do seem like lovebirds.

I fold my legs up underneath me. "They're just so much fun, aren't they?"

"Yep. And think of how many people they must reach for Christ, Shug."

"That sure is the truth. And all over the world."

"Now me, I'd just be happy reaching the South in general."

I am not about to ask what that means because I don't want to know. If that man thinks I'm leaving Mount Oak so he can go back to evangelizing every man, woman, child, dog, and cat, he can think again.

I got Grandma Min to tell me everything she knew about my father. It's funny, as in odd funny, what happened to me after I found out he had a true identity. For so long I've listed the possibilities in my mind. But for so long, I wittingly turned my back on him. It was my choice.

Then the choice flew away from me.

But that's not right. The choice was never really there to begin with. No wings. No bird. Nothing.

All I could do was grieve.

And I did. I grieved through the opening of school. I grieved through the first turn of the leaves all the way through Halloween at which time I allowed the kids to trick-or-treat for the first time all the while wearing a ghost costume myself so no one would recognize me as the preacher's wife over at Port of Peace. (Although how many ghosts have their arms in a sling?) Leo went as a ghost, too, because he wanted to be just like me. Hope wore a clown outfit with makeup thicker than Ronald McDonald.

And the grieving settled into acceptance eventually.

And here I am now knowing more and wishing I could know yet more. Wishing I could know the man himself. The man who never knew he had fathered anything, much less Isla Whitehead's illegitimate brat.

From what Grandma says and judging by the one snapshot she has of him, I think he would have done right by me. I never once thought of the real scenario. In all my musings I never once thought my father was a factory worker who was crazy about my mother and would have laid down across the railroad tracks only Isla just used him and when she got caught bearing his child she chose to get the heck out of town rather than give him the privilege of fatherhood.

And doesn't that beat all?

Isla the user.

Makes me not so mad at all those men that used her. Maybe she deserved a little payback for what she did to David Potter.

The picture of him rests on my bedside table now in one of Grandma's antique silver frames. He is wearing jeans rolled up at the cuffs, loafers, a leather belt, and a plaid shirt. His hair is blond and is combed to the side and Grandma said I have his mouth. I think so, too. It's unmistakable. That alone is enough for me to claim him as my own. With Mama's reputation he might not have been my father. But I'm choosing differently.

She said he loved to sing. In fact that was how he and Isla met, in the school play. *Arsenic and Old Lace*. He played the guy who thought he was Teddy Roosevelt and the next year he won the starring role in *Oklahoma*!

I wonder how many guys Isla used before poor David? Grandma Min said, "I tried to tell her that David was a nice boy. That he really loved her. That he didn't deserve to be treated like that."

"How did she really treat him?"

"Oh, she'd go out with him when it suited her. But she stood him up all the time. She'd go out with her girlfriends or she'd pretend she had a headache. He'd buy her the sweetest little presents, too. I'm sure he spent half his paycheck on her."

At least. How much did young men in peanut factories make?

"I never once accepted a gift from a young man," Grandma said. We sat outside in lawn chairs, watching the kids on the swing set.

"Me, neither, Grandma." Unless I count the winter boots from Richard Lewellyn. But they were a necessity, so I don't think they count quite as much.

She turned to me then and she smiled. "You know, Charmaine, somehow, you managed to take after me."

"And thank the Lord for that!"

Amen. I do thank the Lord for that.

I stare at the mailbox in my front yard and I wonder if Isla has a mailbox now or if she has a pine box.

I wonder about a lot of things now that the last leaf has fallen and life still feels swollen and expectant. Come to think of it, maybe I am pregnant. Maybe I'm pregnant with a missing mother, a dead father, and a black hate. And what's that mess gonna look like when it's finally born?

The purple *Fantasia* dragon?

Oh, my lands. Get a grip, Charmaine.

9

$\mathcal{A}$ million and a half lights you said?" I can hardly believe my eyes.

Grandma Min shuffles through the glossy brochure. "Yes, that's what it says."

Harlan's eyes are popping out of his head. "Look at this place, Shug!"

Forger's Creek.

Forger's Crickkkk!

Of course, I sang here in the summer and heard about the Christmas display, but now I am seeing it for myself and all I can say is, "My lands!" We ooh and aah our way down the main thoroughfare called Damascus Road.

Is that cute or what?

Grandma thinks it's corny.

The buildings are camplike but sturdy. Lots of logs and stone and glass and the heads of the streetlights look like they're wearing cowboy hats.

I have a feeling I may get sick of this Western theme before the weekend's out.

"Can you imagine it, Shug? Can you imagine building an empire for the Lord like this?"

No, I can't begin to imagine, but I just say, "God has different callings for different people, Harlan."

See, now *that* is a good answer. Spiritual, but filled with hidden meaning! I am proud of myself.

He gets silent, which means the message sunk in.

Well, good.

Tanzel agreed to keep the kids for us while we take a couple of days here in Roanoke. Tomorrow we're going to watch a taping of *Jesus Alive!* Now people have told me that I am Harlan's Vinca Love. Isn't that cute? I tell you one thing, I wish I had nice teeth like she does. And I take too much off people. With Vinca, it seems like she'll give you the shirt off her back, but if you push her too far in other ways, watch out! I know this because when we taped the Gospelganza show here at the resort, I saw her slam out of their home, yelling, "This time you have gone too far!" before shutting the door.

Well, you know the media types. They were probably interviewing her or something and asked an inappropriate, nervy question.

Harlan pulls the station wagon up to the Grand Lodge entrance. Now after staying in nice hotels with my singing and recording, I've gotten used to seeing luxury cars lined up for the valet to whisk away to some unknown lot. But here it's different. I see another station wagon like ours, an old one with the fake wood on the side. Rickety Buick sedans and Econoline vans populate the parking lot. Yes, I see a Mercedes or two, but regular old, everyday cars fill the lot.

As we make our way to the front desk, around one of those long cars with long horns on the hood, I say to Harlan, "This is a nice place for regular folks to come. You can give to a ministry, feel good about the tithe, and then have a nice vacation every year to boot."

They've jumped onto the Jim and Tammy Faye Bakker time-share wagon.

"See Shug? It is a good ministry."

"I never said it wasn't, Harlan."

"Well, you've just never been sold on this sort of thing."

"TV preaching?"

"Uh-huh."

I shrug. "I've just never thought much about it, that's all. I mean, we couldn't even watch much TV until recently."

I'm desperately trying to steer this conversation in another direction, pretending I have no idea what he is getting at. I don't want my husband to get up there behind people's household television screens, his long, tender face watching the world as they suffer, work, and play.

Truth is, TV preaching seems like an easy way to fulfill the great commission of going ye into all the world, and that's where I choke. *Is* there an easy way to fulfill such a calling direct from the lips of Jesus? *Should* it be easy?

I just don't know.

When Jesus said, "The harvest is plenteous, but the laborers are few," did He have empires like this in mind? This doesn't seem much like labor to me. How can it be? And I'm trying not to be critical, just inquisitive. I have more questions than ever after looking around me here in this place, after looking through Harlan's eyes, and I feel bad. But Mrs. Evans and Grandma Sara always told me that questions are almost always a good thing.

I look about at the lobby. Now this is one classy joint. In a Western sort of way, naturally. Chains suspend dozens of chandeliers made of deer antlers (poor things!) above our heads. Give me faith, Lord! Let's hope whoever ordered those chains didn't cut corners.

A stone wall, bigger than a church, houses a fireplace I could walk into. I can see into two other rooms through that square inferno: the main restaurant called Wyoming's, which, I hate to say, is way out of our budget, and the library for Mountaintop Members of the Forger's Creek Founder's Club.

Oh, it's all cushy in there, like something an English lord would have if he was a cowboy.

So much for that verse, "Neither Jew nor Greek, bond nor free, but we have all been made to drink in one body." I guess money counts around here.

Now that snake Carl Bofa would just love it in here. In fact, over by the entrance to the family-style restaurant called Cowpokes, two of his paintings hang. I turn my back on them.

"I'm just going to walk around here in the lobby while you check in," I say to Harlan.

"Go ahead, Shug. I'll meet up with you in a minute."

"Grandma?"

"I'm right with you."

But I can tell Grandma is still quite skeptical. She doesn't want to say anything because she's a Williamsburg, Virginia, brass-sconce type. I know she finds this decor gimmicky at best. I love it, though. It's warm and friendly.

Must have cost a mint! But as these two are always

saying, "Christians deserve the best, too! Why should we accept second-class blessings from a first-class God?!"

"Look here." I point down to a discreetly placed plaque on a leather sofa and I read, "Given by Joseph and Delia Waters. Isn't that nice, Grandma? People just put this stuff in here so the ministry itself didn't have to pay for it."

"Good tax write-off, too."

I bop her on the arm. "Oh, Grandma, you tickle me to no end."

Harlan's arm slides around my waist. "Hey, y'all. Isn't this something?"

Stars dance a ring-around-the-rosy inside his pupils.

"Wanna hit the little mall?" I ask.

Grandma nods. "This place just sort of reminds me of Disneyland's Old West part, doesn't it?"

"Only smaller," I say.

Harlan squeezes me closer. "But maybe not for long. Look how the Lord is blessing now. This all is just waiting to explode!"

"I just saw on TV the other day that plans for an amusement park are in the works as well as a big, outdoor concert setting. It will seat ten thousand people." Hopefully they'll have me sing there someday.

We enter the mall area from the lobby, content to leave our bags in a corner of the lobby. As Harlan said, "What kind of Christian would steal something from a brother or sister in Christ?"

Oh, this place is too cute. "Look Harlan, a beauty parlor! Pretty Mares All in a Row. Isn't that the cutest thing?" I turn to him, laying a hand upon his arm. "Can I make an appointment, honey? Please?"

His gentle smile fills me. "Of course you can, Shug. What about you, Grandma? You up for a haircut?"

She runs her fingers through her short hair. "I need one badly. But I'm not sure I trust this place."

I laugh. "Well, if we get butchered we get butchered together."

"All right then. I'll bet if I had a ponytail, they'd do great braids."

Laughing, we walk into the salon to make our appointment for tomorrow morning.

I tug Grandma's sleeve. "Isn't this exciting?"

"You deserve a little pampering, sweetie."

A permed hairstylist runs over on red pumps stuffed over bobby socks. "You're Charmaine Hopewell, aren't you?"

My eyes bug open wide. "Yes, I sure am. I'm sorry, but . . . well, have we met before?"

"Oh, no, ma'am. I go to Gospelganza every year when it comes to Winchester. I've got your tape. I just love you!"

Oh, my. Nobody's ever run up to me outside of the concert setting before. I'm so stunned. My mouth drops. Grandma snickers softly but takes my hand. I come to. "Well, what's your name, honey?"

"Georgie May."

"It's a pleasure to meet you, Georgie. You do a good cut?"

She leans forward and whispers, "The best here in the shop if you want to know the truth."

I turn to the receptionist. "Then put me in with Georgie."

"Me, too," says Grandma Min. "She seems believable to me."

Harlan watches all of this from the side, shaking his head and smiling. In fact all three of us are smiling like insipid jack-o'-lanterns.

"Can you sign the tape cover for me tomorrow? I'll be sure to bring it in. I just love that tape."

"All right, I'd be tickled to do that." And that's the truth. I've signed lots of tape covers at concerts, and each time I write my name I can hardly believe it. "I've got a new one coming out this spring."

"Oh, yeah?"

"From a real record company."

"No kidding? That's great! You here to sing on the show?" she asks.

"Oh, no! I'm sure I'm not even close to being in this league."

"Of course you are, Mrs. Hopewell. You sing like an angel. You have the prettiest voice I've ever heard."

Oh, my lands.

So I just smile and pat her hand. "We'll see you tomorrow morning at eight o'clock."

As we walk into the mall she yells, "Hey y'all, that was Charmaine Hopewell!"

"Charmaine who?"

"Who's that?"

"Hopewell did you say?"

"Never heard of her."

Now that is more like it.

"Looky there, Shug, you're famous."

"Oh, Harlan. One hairdresser in Forger's Creek, Virginia, does not render a girl famous."

"I don't think you give yourself enough credit."

"I don't have to. You do it for me."

He kisses my temple. "I guess I have to be honest and say that if you did, I may not find you so sweet and sexy."

Harlan hardly ever uses the "sexy" word, so I turn and kiss him back and I'm thankful that we got two rooms instead of one. Let's hope Grandma Min turns her TV up real loud tonight! We haven't made love since Carl Bofa.

My lands.

I realize right then that I feel so much older than my twenty-five years.

Grandma walks in front of us, the twinkle lights on all the trees illumining her pathway.

"It's just so pretty in here, Harlan, isn't it?"

"It sure is, Shug."

Grandma turns. "Look! A china store! Oh, my. Those are beautiful teapots in the window."

"I've heard Vinca loves china," I say. "Go ahead on in. We'll be there in a minute."

I turn to Harlan. "Let's sit on a bench for a second okay?"

"All right."

So we sit on a bench between two sparkling ficus trees. "Just promise me one thing," I say.

"What is it?"

"Promise me you won't dream of this when you close your eyes."

"You know me too well, Shug."

"You're right. This isn't you, Harlan. This isn't me. This isn't us."

"You think this is wrong?"

"I just don't think it's us. There doesn't need to be two Peter and Vinca couples out there."

He is silent.

"Honey, this isn't our style. We're down-home. Really down-home. Look at all this stone and glass and pewter and brass. For heaven's sake, we shop at variety stores."

"But they started out that way years ago, Shug."

Though Vinca is from society and Peter's family owned a large cattle ranch, they did start small, going on the evangelist circuit and even sleeping in their car for months on end. They never do pretend they're better than anybody else. I have to give them that.

"I don't begrudge them this, Harlan. Look how happy it's making these folks. But this isn't for us."

He is silent again and I let him be. After five minutes of watching people go by I can no longer stand it. "Spill it, baby."

"Spill what?"

"You're not telling me something."

He sits back and slips an arm behind me on the bench. "You're right."

"So let me have it."

"We've been at the church for four months now, right?"

"Uh-huh."

"And I'm feeling that wanderlust again to get back out on the road."

"Oh, Harlan, no! Please don't ask me to leave Mount Oak!"

"I'm not. Listen, Shug, I've got an idea."

"Harlan!"

"No. Please. Just let me say everything and then you can get upset."

I have to laugh at that and he jumps on it. "See, Shug? You're not as upset as you think you are."

"Stop telling me what I am or not, Harlan." I try to sound as serious as I feel. He deserves that. We all do.

"Okay. The church wants to start televising its services."

I dip my head. "The church?"

"Well, me, too. But just on cable access. John Patterson is donating the cameras and the equipment we'll need to tape the programs. See, I'm hoping this will curb that wanderlust, Shug. You know I'm not happy if I'm not preaching to the multitude."

"So it'll be the Sunday services?"

"Yep."

"And that's all?"

"For now."

"Harla-a-an."

"Well, I've got to be honest, Shug."

"And they want me to sing, right?"

"Right. It would be good for the show to have you on. I mean, look Shug, here's a hairdresser in Virginia who knows who you are. And with that BrooksTone record coming out in the spring, that will be wonderful for the show."

Dear Lord. "What's it going to be called?"

"*The Port of Peace Hour.*"

"Sounds like the *Port-O-Potty Hour.*"

"Shug!"

"Well, Harlan! This is an awful lot to spring on someone in the space of two minutes!"

He puts his arms around me. "I know. But I didn't know how else to do it once you asked me to spill it. I've been trying to break it to you for weeks."

"And you were hoping that coming down here would help me see the potential of a television ministry?"

"I guess so. Yes."

"Oh, I see the potential all right. But maybe not the potential you see, Harlan."

He doesn't ask me what I mean, and I don't have the heart to tell him.

Harlan looks around like he's at the Ritz or something. "Look at this bedroom, Shug! A wardrobe thing and everything."

"It's an armoire, baby."

"Darn. I don't see a TV."

"Look inside the armoire."

He pulls open the doors. "Well, would you look at that? There's the TV! Have you seen anything like this before?"

"In Nashville when I went to record."

The hotel room isn't nearly as high-end as the lobby and the mall. However, it's neat and houses good, oak furniture, pretty quilts, and a clean bathroom with little soaps, shampoos, and lotions.

The coffeepot is not by the toilet, thank the Lord.

I look through my luggage just to make sure nothing was taken in the lobby, and sure enough, "It's all still here."

"Did you think it wouldn't be?"

I shrug. "You can be too trusting sometimes, Harlan."

Excitement stutters inside me. I sit in my studio seat and when the music and lights go up I am transported back to Suds 'N' Strikes, back to that first moment of glory when the crowd belonged to me.

The *Jesus Alive!* gang files out smiling and waving and I understand exactly why they do what they do.

Harlan sizzles beside me like one of those glass balls with all the electric waves wiggling around inside it.

Much to my surprise I am pointed out in the audience by Peter himself. "We'd like to welcome Charmaine and Harlan Hopewell today to the show. Charmaine is a big hit on the gospel music concert circuit."

I can see which camera has us in its eye, and I wave as the audience claps. I figure that hairdresser let them know, and I am glad I had her do this pretty curled updo this morning.

Vinca stands and claps, smiling. "Come on up and sit with us, won't you?"

"Good idea, Vinc!" says Peter and he extends his hand toward me.

I turn to Harlan.

"Go on, Shug!" His eyes glow and I know he loves me so.

I turn to Grandma and she smiles and nods.

They settle me right next to Cowboy George who puts his arm around me and gives me a sideways hug.

"I love having impromptu guests," Vinca says. "I hear you have a new album coming out, Charmaine. Would you like to tell us about that?"

So I do.

Oh, the folks at BrooksTone won't believe this.

Peter takes his wife's hand comfortably. "Now, I know this may put you on the spot, Charmaine, but we have a fine band, and I hear your rendition of 'His Eye Is on the Sparrow' is one of the prettiest things ever to hit an eardrum."

"Will you?" Vinca asks.

"With pleasure."

So I sing, and the band follows me perfectly.

We have dinner with them that night in a private dining room in Wyoming's. Vinca's flowing skirts are made of a gorgeous gold brocade and she wears a black velvet bolero vest. I feel so short and typical.

Harlan shares his vision for *The Port of Peace Hour*.

"Whatever we can do to help!" says Peter.

Vinca leans forward and places her hand over Grandma Min's hand. "I realize we're not everybody's cup of tea." She looks at Harlan and me. "You'll reach people with the gospel that we don't have a hope of finding."

Grandma smiles. "May I tell you that I loved your china shop?"

"I knew it!" Vinca claps. "You are a china fanatic, too, aren't you?"

And they suddenly whisked off to Limoges and all sorts of places that they have both loved for years, and most likely their mamas did, too.

~⋙~

On the way back to Mount Oak Harlan says, "A lot of people need deliverance, Charmaine. If we can provide some peace of mind, some grace to someone out there who may never get it otherwise, that would be a good thing."

"So that will still be your angle? The 'What's *Really* Eating at You?' thing?"

"It's the message I've got to tell. But how about if I simply call it a message of deliverance."

"But what if you're wrong, Harlan?"

He shakes his head, confusion shorting his gaze. "Shug, are you okay?"

"Yeah. I'm okay. You're okay."

He laughs at my joke. And when I fail to laugh back I want to gag.

10

    I grip the phone. "Grace, come on home."

Why did I say that?

"I can't, I just can't."

"I'm going to tell your parents where you are. They already know you left us."

"Where am I, Charmaine?"

"On the street. I don't know which street. But I'll find out. My guess is you're still in Atlanta."

She is silent.

"I'm right, then?"

"Yes."

"What's it gonna take, Grace?"

"Nothing. I'm never coming back."

"Just carry my number in your pocket at all times, Grace. So when they find you rotting in a Dumpster they'll call and I can tell your son his mother is dead."

She is silent.

"He stopped asking about you this summer, Grace."

I hang up on her sobs and I hate myself. What more can I do? I'm raising her son. I'm doing all I can.

"Leo?" I call his name out the kitchen window. It's December 26, 1985 and he's having a good old time out there in the carport on the pogo stick we got him for Christmas.

"I did twelve in a row, Mama!"

"That's wonderful!"

"Melvin said his record is twenty four hundred and thirty-six!"

"You'd better keep practicing if you want to beat him."

"Oh, I'll beat him all right!"

I put that call in to Tony Sanchez myself. He tells me he'll get on it first thing in the morning. "If she's on the streets of Atlanta, Charmaine, she's as good as found."

I decide pogo-sticking might be a good thing just then. I decide I'd better do a lot of pogo-sticking and the like because you just never know when that pogo stick will be stolen right from beneath your feet.

Ruby and I walk around the local IGA. She pushes the cart because she injured her knee while running last week. Ruby is so athletic and toned these days.

We shop for ingredients to make a large-scale batch of tuna casserole. In the winter, each church in Mount Oak volunteers to house the homeless for a week at a time, turning our fellowship halls into a shelter after six P.M. We offer a hot meal, warm blankets, and someone to talk to. I've looked forward to this for weeks and it's finally here.

I am still at a loss regarding Grace and I tell Ruby this.

"It's not your problem, Char."

"But I've got Leo, so I think it is."

"Then what you need to do is stop lying to Grace's parents."

"I did. I told them I hadn't seen Grace in a while."

She is surprised and I don't blame her. Ruby's known me for so long. "Do they even know about Leo?"

I shake my head. "No."

And doggone it, Ruby knows my fears because she says, "You're scared if they find out about him they'll take him away from you."

"Bingo, Einstein."

"Hey now, don't be hurtful."

She's right. "I'm sorry."

"I forgive you."

I stop the cart in front of a tower of Pepsi, seventy-nine cents for a two liter bottle. "I don't know what would happen if I lost that little boy. We're all he has."

Ruby visibly buttons her lip.

I ramble on for her, "Other than his grandparents."

Oh, the irony of the situation is stunning.

"Why do you feel you have the right to hide Leo from his family?"

"Loyalty to Grace?"

"Come off it, Char. You and Grace never really fancied each other."

"That's true. I just love Leo so much, Ruby. On the one hand, I know what's best for him, that I'm the best thing for him. On the other hand, I know what it's like to have your mama walk out on you and I don't want him to go through that."

We continue walking.

Ruby lays a hand on my arm. "Of course, you could be

like that stupid white girl, Scarlett O'Hara, and think about it tomorrow."

"I have a feeling I'll end up being dumber yet and put it off until at least next year."

"Come on, Char. Let's go look at nail polish. That always cheers you up."

Nail polish? My lands. But I don't have the heart to pretend Ruby's anything other than right on the money.

Good old shallow Charmaine strikes again!

"Ruby?"

"Yeah, Char?"

"You okay still with singing on the show?"

"Of course."

"Okay, just checking. I know how you feel about TV preachers in general."

She laughs. "It's for Harlan. You know I adore Harlan."

We continue shopping, chitchatting about this and that, relying on our love for one another.

"How's Henry?" I ask.

Ruby smiles. "It's moving quickly. I wouldn't be surprised if there's a wedding come June!"

We hug right there by the stand up freezers. And I watch the reflection of our embrace as I gather strength.

Part Six

1

*S*pring is almost over. The cherry trees have dropped their pink snow upon our temporarily succulent lawns and the daffodils waved a brown, translucent good-bye a while ago. I should know. Surprisingly enough, a bunch of them popped up all over our yard. Right in the middle of the yard, too. Grandma Min dug up bulbs for days. We got a little secondhand rider mower and it's the funnest thing I've ever driven. I mow that lawn twice a week if I'm home to do it. In fact, the three of us adults fight over who gets to fire up that mower.

The Port of Peace Hour is a hit all across the South!

We really do have Peter and Vinca Love to thank. I've been on their show every other week since Christmas. I file out there with the rest of them to sit on the couches and I wave to the crowd.

Harlan is beside himself. "Twenty stations and counting!"

I'm excited for him and sick for me. But my album debuted two weeks ago and the first pressing is already gone! Talk about feeling like the blessings of God are falling all around. Showers of blessing.

Just like the song says.

People write to our show like crazy, telling about deliverance of all kinds. Telling about getting back to the Bible and actually listening to it for a change. Telling about the healings that have resulted. Broken lives repaired, torn relationships mended.

We even started a twenty-four-hour-a-day help line for counsel straight from the Word. Tanzel's in charge and doing a wonderful job. Some professional Christian counselors even volunteered to man phones. They give advice straight from God's word. And then there are the older and wiser folks who have seen it all, lived it all, and can listen with a wise ear.

Isn't that what counseling is anyway? I'm not sure why there's such a big uproar about this sort of thing. I think maybe Harlan's beginning to see that God sometimes speaks through other people. Just as long as you don't use the word "psychology."

His brother E.J. is dating a nice girl now. Divorced, too. Bee says she's a sweet thing.

I am scheduled to sing on *The PTL Club* for the second time, the first being after I started appearing regularly on *Jesus Alive!* and on *The 700 Club*, too! Those publicity fellows at BrooksTone have taken that ball and run with it! They said they haven't ever had an artist do this well straight out of the starting gate.

Hallelujah!

Grandma and I head to the fabric store. There's just nothing like a fabric store in my estimation. It is literally the world at your fingertips. Silks from China and Japan, woolens from Scotland, and cottons from India.

Grandma and I look at scissors. She said it's time I treat myself to a decent pair.

"What do you think of these ones, Grandma?"

I heft a pair of Wiss scissors.

"They're wonderful scissors, sweetie."

And they come in their own, velvet-lined, beautiful box. But I'm not going to say that because Grandma is more worried about the blades, I'm sure.

"Oh, yes. These cut fabric like it was butter."

They'd better. Imagine spending fifty bucks on a pair of scissors.

"But it's worth it, Charmaine. Good tools last, too. You'll never need another pair."

"Well, I'm sick of orange handles, I can tell you that."

I place them carefully in the red plastic cart and we move on to fabric. I need some new outfits for Gospelganza and my own Ten Thousand Lilies tour.

I finger a length of purple leopard-print cotton. Now this will make quite a sarong. "Do you think this would be too wild to wear on *Jesus Alive!*?"

"Not one bit. People find you so endearing, sweetie, you can get away with more."

Endearing.

That's the word everybody uses to describe me. I mean, that's nice, but I can think of a lot of other adjectives that would denote more of a presence.

Witty.

Charming.

Intelligent.

Insightful.

But there's me. Good old endearing Charmaine Hopewell. Then again, maybe that's why my music hits a true chord with folks all over. Maybe it's better to be loved than respected. I'd rather not have to choose, though.

Dovey called us the other day. He said he's checking mental institutions now in the search for Mama. Grandma cried all night and I got scared. I wonder how much of that still lives inside of me?

"Charmaine? It's Tony Sanchez."

"Tony!"

"It took some doing, but I found her."

"You found Grace?" I put my hand over the phone. "Harlan! Tony's found Grace!"

He runs in from the bedroom.

"Tell me what happened?"

"I think she was out of town for a while. Or went underground or something. You never know with addicts. But I've got a friend who runs a rescue mission downtown, Jamal Weaver. He's been keeping a lookout for her ever since you called me. Nothing, until this morning. She wandered in for a meal."

"So where is she now?"

"Down at the mission. They're arranging to get her into a rehab place not far from here."

"She'll never go."

"I'll escort her there myself. She wants to go. I'm not sure what has happened since she talked to you last, but she says she's ready to get her life together."

How can a person be so happy and so sad at the same time? I look at Leo watching TV.

"Thank you, Tony. You've probably saved her life."

"Anyway, I'll have the home get in touch with you. It's one of those Christian homes for women only."

"Good. That sounds like it may just be the ticket."

I plaster Leo to me tightly after dinner. We sit on the couch as he does his math homework. He lays his head back against my shoulder, feet up near his rear end as his legs support his folder.

Oh, this sweet little boy. My sweet little boy.

I hear some voice within say, "I love her, Charmaine. I love Grace Underhill."

And I say back, "But what about my heart? Isn't my heart worth anything?"

How does a woman go about her day when her day is spent in front of thousands of adoring fans. Fans? Oh, my lands. I just prefer to think of them as listeners. How does she smile and wave when the little boy she's come to love as her son is more dear than ever, when that child's mama is getting better, when that child's mama will come and take him away? How can she smile when what's best for her isn't best for everyone?

We now have a singing ensemble on the show. *The Sounds of Peace.* I know that's a direct rip-off of *The Sounds of Liberty* on Jerry Falwell's *Old-Time Gospel Hour*, but I'm not all that creative and no one could think of anything better.

It could be a lot worse.

My concert tour starts on the first of June. I'm booked

in some of the bigger Assemblies of God churches and some state fairs and gospel fests. Of course, I'll be with Gospelganza, too, and guess what? I'm taking our old RV on the road so I can keep the kids with me.

I keep getting this picture of Marilyn Monroe on the USO tours as she walked onto the stage just waving her hands to all those GIs. Blowing kisses and smiling. But instead it's me. And I'm not sexy. Or voluptuous. Or blond. Or that beautiful, for that matter.

Okay, maybe I should just change the image altogether because that one depresses me!

Speaking of depression, I saw Dr. Braselton yesterday. He's a nice enough man but he says I really should be getting exercise and eating better. "All that caffeine from those Diet Cokes isn't helping you get off medication, Charmaine. And wouldn't you like to get off the medication eventually? You don't have to be on this stuff forever, Mrs. Hopewell."

Well, of course I'd like to get off it! But who has time to exercise? And no Diet Cokes? My lands, a pill is a whole lot easier, even with the incessant dry mouth I have. And how can I find time to exercise with all my singing engagements? The invitations have been coming in one after another.

So many letters have arrived since the album debuted. I can't even read them all anymore. I've hired Tanzel on in the evenings to help me with my correspondence. She writes the letters and I read them and sign them in between phone calls and sewing my costumes and baths and meals. I actually bought six yards of purple silk yesterday for a two-piece pants outfit to wear on *The 700 Club*. I'm thinking I'll truly make purple my signature color.

I enjoyed my time down at Heritage USA.

Heritage Yooo Esss Aaaay!

They treat their show guests first class all the way. And don't you know Tammy Faye cried the entire time I sang "Ten Thousand Lilies." And she smiled into my eyes. She's as short as I am, so it was nice not to have to look up. I felt like there was one person in the world for that space of time that understood me, and it was Tammy. Now I don't guess she and I will ever be friends and hang out and eat French fries at McDonald's together. But that's okay.

I am sitting at my sewing machine, threading it with purple thread for that sarong I'm making. I set it up here by the sliding glass doors in the den so I can watch the kids play and Grandma garden. The flowers around our house look every bit as pretty as the ones she planted in Suffolk. Grandma makes things grow.

Harlan comes in the room. "Well, Shug. I've got great news!"

"More stations?"

"Even better! We're going to be on the TBN network! They saw our show on the Loves' new network and want to get in on the act, I guess."

"Oh, my lands!"

"Now, it'll be at one in the morning, but you've got to start somewhere."

"Still. Nationwide!"

"That's right."

He pulls me from my chair and folds me into his arms and I am so happy for him. Then he looks at me in horror. "What about this summer?"

"What about it?"

"You'll be on the road most of the time. What are we going to do about your musical numbers?"

I shrug. "I don't know. Record a bunch of them beforehand?"

He claps twice and points at me. "That's the ticket! You're so smart, Shug. Just a savvy thing you're getting to be."

Savvy?

Myrtle Charmaine Whitehead, the nosebleed queen?

I wondered then how many years it would be before I looked in the mirror and turned away at what I saw.

"I think it's wonderful you're getting a real signature look about you, honey. You and purple go together so well. It's kinda like Vinca Love and her big skirts."

I picture Vinca and wonder if she ever sits back and thinks, "Who is this man, Peter Love, and does he bear any resemblance to the man I married? Any at all?"

I can only pray I don't feel that way about Harlan ever. I can only pray that these worms of doubt that crawl around my heart every so often when I see him rant and rave on stage will not worsen with time.

Sometimes his fervor embarrasses me.

After sunset, Grandma comes back into the kitchen. Sarongs are simple so it's already half finished. She sits at the chair opposite my sewing machine. "I just saw a terrible news report."

"Oh, no. What happened?"

"Apparently, Peter Love's pilot got killed going in to rescue a missionary family in the Sudan."

"How?"

"Peter got word that the lives of this family, the Dallards I believe they called them, were in imminent danger. Anyway, he asked his pilot, Mack Something-or-Other—it sounded Russian to me—to go in and get them out."

"That's awful. Did his plane crash?"

"No. That's the worst part. He got to them and the villagers put him in a car with the Dallards and set the whole thing on fire."

Oh, dear Lord! "Oh, Grandma! I don't ever remember meeting him. Was he married?"

"Yes. She works at Forger's Creek. Runs the pool and spa, they said."

The whine of the machine stirs the evening air around the table. Hope and Leo have been down for over an hour now and I'm glad they don't have to hear this story.

2

$\mathcal{D}$ovey sits in front of us at Bill D's. We are right in the front window. Grandma Min and I are scared because on the phone two days ago he said, "I don't want to tell you this over the phone."

I never knew private eyes were so caring.

He's wearing the same sort of suit as before. A bow tie of blue and red stripes tops the mother-of-pearl buttons lined like Christmas lights up his front. I'd bet my life they are tuxedo buttons.

He reminds me of the bow-tied politician-type today.

I hear a toot and look outside, peering between the branches of a blossoming cherry tree. I wave to Ruby as she passes by in Henry's new little Pontiac Firenza. A large green Impala, the color of an iguana, zooms by next.

We order some drinks. Coffee for Grandma, Diet Coke for me, and Dovey gets a butterscotch milk shake.

Grandma lays her hands flat on the table. "So tell us."

"I found her. She's still alive."

Grandma's hand flies up to her mouth and she gulps down one big sob.

I am stunned.

She is alive.

She is alive and she left me and she never came back. SHE NEVER CAME BACK.

I can do nothing.

I am heavy, I am light. I'm numb, I'm keen. I'm enlightened even as I am plunged down into a foreign darkness. I am Myrtle again. Just stupid old Myrtle with big teeth and ratty hair.

Dovey sits patiently as we react. I realize, looking at Grandma, that she isn't capable of doing anything. I realize it is up to me.

"Where did you find her?"

"In Crownsville, Maryland."

I remembered the folks in Baltimore talking about Crownsville. If somebody did something crazy they'd say, "Next thing you know they'll be carting me off to Crownsville!"

I say, "So she's at the . . . ?"

"I'm afraid so."

"What's Crownville?" Grandma manages to say.

I put an arm around her and pull her close. "Grandma, Crownsville, Maryland, is home to a mental institution."

Her hand returns to her mouth and she sobs more.

"But Grandma, we thought this might happen."

"I know. I know," she mumbles into her hands.

"What condition is she in? Do you know what her diagnosis is?"

"Paranoid schizophrenia."

Oh, Lord.

"Grandma, do you know what that is?"

She nods. "It's what my sister Rachel probably developed before her suicide. She was never diagnosed though."

"Can we visit her?"

Dovey reaches into the inner breast pocket of his suit and pulls out a business card. "Here's the card of the clinical director of the hospital. He said to give him a call anytime you want. He was very helpful."

Grandma asks. "Will you call for me, Charmaine?"

"Yes, Grandma. I'll make the call for both of us."

I have a nosebleed later on.

And I thought I had come so far.

3

The phone rings. At this point in my life it could be so many people: Harlan, Tanzel, BrooksTone, the doctor at the mental hospital who I called yesterday and hasn't yet returned my call, Ruby, the folks at Forger's Creek, and I could go on. I remember those days at the bowling alley when no calls ever came in for me.

"Hopewell house."

"Charmaine?"

"Grace."

She sounds normal.

"Hi, Charmaine."

"Hi, Grace. Where are you?"

"Still at the home."

"Really?"

"Yeah. I'm doing well."

"I'm glad for you."

"I've a month behind me. Only eleven more to go!"

"Yep, eleven more." Eleven more. "You coming back here, then?"

"I'm not making any plans yet. One day at a time and all."

"I guess that's what they say."

"It helps knowing you're taking such good care of my baby."

Your baby? He's my baby. You left him behind and you've never come back.

I can't say "I love Leo *like* he is one of my own" because Leo and I have more in common than a mother and her biological child could ever have. Love Leo like my own? Leo is my own. Leo is me.

"They treating you okay there?"

"Sure. I get a little tired of all the Bible stuff, but if it works, hey, who am I to knock it?"

"You never know. Maybe you should rely on God to get you through."

"I'm trying. But it's like anything else, Char. Baby steps. You know."

"Yeah, I guess so."

"Can I speak with Leo?"

"Oh, honey, I'm sorry, he's at a friend's house."

"Oh. Well. Maybe another time?"

"Of course."

"I'd better go."

"I hope you continue to do well, Grace."

"Thanks. See ya, Char."

"'Bye now."

I lied. Leo is in the next room painting a picture of a jet plane.

Harlan deserves to know all about Mama. "What's *Really* Eating at You" or not. He is my husband and I love him. And he loves me. This I know.

I put the kids to bed hours ago. Grandma reads in her room. She loves Mary Higgins Clark. I'd love to be a reader like that.

Harlan's already laying in bed and he's reading, too. His books are the nonfiction types, though. He got reading glasses last week and he looks so cute in them.

"Harlan?"

He lays the book on top of the covers. It's entitled *Old Testament Exegesis*. "Hey, Shug. You coming to bed?"

"Uh-huh. But I need to talk to you."

"Okay. You all right?"

I nod. "It's about Mama."

He takes off his glasses and lays them on the book. "Come sit here with me then."

I climb in bed, put my arms around him, and rest my head in its place atop his heart. I can't see him this way, which is good. "We found her."

"Alive?"

"Uh-huh."

He tightens his arms around me. "Where is she?"

"In Maryland. In a mental institution."

"Oh, Shug."

"I know."

I tell him everything. I tell him everything.

Mama's illness and how she acted when I was a kid. My depression.

Everything.

He deserves to know he's been preaching while a hypocrite wife stands next to him singing and acting all spiritual.

"So, you married a nutcase, I'm afraid," I finish up.

"Oh, Shug."

He is silent for a few minutes and I don't know what to say. So I just ask, "Are you mad at me?"

And his arms squeeze me even tighter and I feel his lips on my hair and not long after a single tear splashes on my forehead. "I'm not mad," he pushes out between a swollen throat. "I'm not mad."

For days now, Harlan has been very quiet. He has to get used to the news, I know. I don't blame him. I told Grandma he knows everything and she is relieved. "Harlan's too nice a fellow to keep in the dark, sweetie."

In truth, I feel a great relief. I finally opened up my baggage for Harlan to see and inside, beneath Harlan's loving gaze and even his pity, the purple *Fantasia* dragon shrank to the size of a child's toy. Not that he'll ever go completely away, I guess, because I do believe I'll struggle with all of this for the rest of my life. Telling the truth is never easy. But the load is lighter and Harlan's hand is next to mine on the handle. More to the point, he's been right there with a dish towel every time my nose has bled this week.

Maybe he doesn't need to be strong so much as absorbent!

Ha!

Funny, I thought deliverance from the purple dragon would be different than this. I thought it would be bigger and grander, for some reason. Unless this isn't the dragon. I mean, dragons are who they are, whether you recognize them or not.

I'm sitting in the den working on some play clothes for Hope. She's so active, always climbing and running. I've decided some matching shorts and sun shirts will be just right this year. She tans so easily.

Kindergarten blossomed her. She's turned the corner from toddler to little girl and we have so much fun these days. Of course, she's outside on the swing set right now. Sitting on the top bar.

She scares me, sometimes, but I hate to tell her "no." Harlan registered her for gymnastics this fall and I have to give him credit for seeing her potential. He's like that. Always seeing the possibilities.

I begin to sew in the waistband on a pair of striped seersucker shorts as Harlan sits down in the lounger beside my table. I bought the chair for him for Christmas because he deserves to put his feet up at the end of the day. But this evening, the sun still golden on the horizon, he sits on the edge of his seat. "Shug?"

"Yeah, baby?"

"I've been thinking about things."

"Me, too."

"I think it's time for me to change my message."

What? " 'What's *Really* Eating at You?' "

He nods. "I need to broaden things. I feel like I've been this magnifying glass that hones in on people's sins ninety percent of the time and offers the solution ten percent."

"I'm not sure I understand. Doesn't the Bible teach against sin?"

"Yep, it does. It also teaches about other things, too. I

guess what it all comes down to is this, Shug. I've really neglected the scriptures."

"But you know the Bible from cover to cover."

He looks out at the kids, then turns back to me. "Truth is, Shug, it's gotten easy. I've been recycling the same material for a couple of years now. I've gotten lazy and irresponsible to my calling."

"Oh, Harlan! That's not true. You're the most dedicated man I know."

"But I'm a preacher of God's Word. God never told me to be so lopsided about it."

I shrug. "I suppose."

"So anyway, I'm taking this summer to really devote to study."

"That's good."

He looks down. "This is hard for me, Shug."

"I know that, baby."

"Anyway, I'm sorry."

"For what?"

"For the fact that you've suffered alone all this time."

"That wasn't your fault."

He takes my hand. "Yes it was. You should have been able to come to me with anything."

"But I didn't want to burden you, either."

"See? I always talked about how happy and fun you are. And then all that talk about my sister-in-law! I never gave you a chance to reveal your hurts. As I said, I've been doing a lot of thinking."

"I'm sorry I didn't trust you with my problems."

"Me, too."

"I guess we both are at fault."

He sighs. "Maybe. But we can only change ourselves."

"I'm going to visit Mama as soon as school is out."

"I want to come."

I shake my head. "I think this is something Grandma and I need to do alone."

"I guess you're right."

"But hey, it will give you several days for nonstop study."

"That's true."

"I'm going to need you badly when I get back, baby."

"Good. I've needed you to need me for a long time now, Shug."

I push down on the pedal of the machine. "Harlan, I want you to promise to tell me if I start acting like I'm going crazy. I really do. I don't want to end up like Mama."

"You're really something, Charmaine Whitehead, and you're the least crazy person I know."

Harlan kisses me on the cheek, then leans back in his lounger and falls into a soft sleep. I gaze at the crescent of his lashes.

I fall in love with this man a little more every day.

School is out. I have about two weeks off before I get in that RV and start my summer tour. The crickets still scratch and the early mist still hovers over the lawns of the neighborhood. The sky reminds me of the rainbow sherbet the kids have recently taken a shine to.

I load everyone into the station wagon. Ruby sits in the passenger seat next to me. Grandma Min sits in the back with the kids. Still groggy, they lean against their pillows and eat Cheerios from a Baggie.

Harlan leans in, pats my knee and says, "Ready?" He looks back at Grandma, too.

She nods, and I say, "As ready as we can be, I guess."

He smiles, his skin crinkling at the corners. "You'll be fine, Charmaine. I know you will."

He kisses me softly, with all the tenderness he holds.

A minute later we back out of the driveway and Harlan stands there waving, alone on the cement pad.

Ruby lays the map across her lap. "You are taking I-95, aren't you?"

"Oh, sure. I don't want to dilly-dally. We have less than a week."

Grandma's hand grabs the headrest behind Ruby. "And you're sure your friends in Baltimore won't mind us staying with them?"

"Of course not! It'll be fun. Luella says she has plenty of room."

Oh, Luella. Married for three years now and living a good life with a prosthetics manufacturer in Harford County. Six bedrooms, a pool, and a membership to the country club that she's never once taken advantage of. And she's opened her own small gallery now, too.

See how life can turn around on you?

But she's still Luella and I'll bet her house, which she tells me is painted in all sorts of wild shades inside, is nothing like the houses of the ladies at the country club.

I'm figuring about seven hours for the drive. Finding a gospel music station, I tell everybody to settle in. The kids color, Grandma Min looks out the window, Ruby adds up the mileage as we go, and we sing along together with the radio.

I remember when I first got MaryAnna as my agent.

"Ruby?"

"Yeah, Char."

"Do you ever regret not signing on with me? I mean, we could be doing all this together."

"Not one bit. You know I never live with regret. I count the costs up front."

"And now you and Henry are together."

She grins. "Oh, baby."

"Two more weeks!"

"I know. Girl, I cannot wait."

Ruby's hanging on to her second virtue and Henry, who blushes at the word "bra," is essentially fine with that, but I'm sure he takes a lot of cold showers these days with the wedding so close. At least that's what he told Ruby the other day.

I'm missing a concert in Savannah for the wedding, but I haven't told Ruby that, and I'm not going to. She's a "the show must go on" kind of lady.

We stop for an early lunch at a Cracker Barrel near Fredericksburg and stock up on candy for the kids. Around two o'clock I pull the car into Luella's new driveway! A semicircular driveway.

Of course I got lost three times trying to find the darned house.

She runs out before I can even climb out of the car.

"Charmaine!" she screams, her skinny arms waving around, her upper body sealed in an embroidered chemise. She's barefoot, toes painted silver running beneath a flowing red gypsy skirt.

I leap out of the car. "Luella!"

We embrace.

Oh, my lands. This is so good. I feel like my nubby Velcro self has been rejoined with the soft side.

"Oh, Luella, I have missed you!"

"Me, too, Charmaine. Me, too!"

And in two seconds we are back to those times in Dundalk. I, a deserted runaway, she a freshly grieving widow, but time kept marching on in every place but our hearts.

This will be a nice place to come back to after going to Crownsville.

I introduce everybody.

Luella says, "The kids are still in school. So you can see them later."

"I'll bet they've gotten so *big*!"

"They have, Charmaine. Isabel has a boyfriend and is going to Towson State. Esteban still loves gymnastics and we think he'll be getting a scholarship, and Guadalupe is always singing. In church, at school. Everywhere she can."

That warms my heart.

She ushers us into her house.

"Luella, I feel like I'm in a palace."

"Oh, don't! People don't clean their own palaces."

Grandma Min asks, "You clean this place yourself?"

"Sure do. My neighbors think I'm crazy, and I guess I kind of like that image around here. Talk about a boring bunch."

Ruby nods. "Just tell me you've got a Jacuzzi tub

somewhere and we're *all* set. You all won't see me for the next three days."

"You're covered, Ruby. Three Jacuzzis and a hot tub."

"Hallelujah!"

"I'll show you guys to your rooms and you can rest until supper." She turns to me. "Charmaine, Frank and Anita will be here by five. We're going to barbecue out by the pool."

Oh, this is old home week. A nice, wonderful mote of sweet to go along with the bitter plank tomorrow will bring.

❧

There they are! Anita still wears her poodle hair cut and Frank's belly is still expanding. His hair is white. They wave, the skin beneath their arms flapping in the breeze. I wonder if I've ever seen anything more beautiful in my life!

❧

Dinner now over, we sit around the iron table by the shallow end of the pool, one of those natural-looking type of pools with stone surrounding the water. A waterfall, lots of greenery. It is like sitting next to paradise.

Grandma Min went to bed with a mystery book she found in the library. Tomorrow weighs heavily on her. Ruby is in the hot tub inside the screened porch. Isabel has taken all the kids to the arcade at the mall, and I am sitting with my Baltimore family.

"We've been watching your show!" Anita says. "I'm so proud."

"Well, you all gave me my start."

Frank loosens his belt. "That's what I said, but Anita always says that God was looking out for you and I shouldn't take any credit whatsoever."

"He was, and is. But you can pat yourself on the back a little bit, Frank. How are things at the bowling alley?"

"Better than ever. We added ten pins a few years ago to keep up with the times," Frank says.

Anita nods. "Best thing we ever did."

"I still have the little Bible we bought together that day, Mrs. Reasin."

"You read it much anymore?"

"I try to. Some days, well, you know how it is."

"I sure do, hon."

Frank sighs. "I still go up on the roof every now and again and sit in our lawn chairs, Charmaine."

"I'll bet they're rusty."

Anita waves a hand. "They are. But he refuses to take them down. You weren't with us long, hon, but we couldn't love you more."

They leave around ten and Luella and I sit at the pool talking until one A.M., long after the kids have come home and gone to bed.

We talk of womanly things: children, husbands, our sex lives, and low-fat snacks. I almost feel normal.

4

$\mathcal{W}$e walk in between the center space of four tall, white pillars. The Crownsville State Hospital is brick. I'm sure this has to be one of the original buildings because it has that old smell to it, that musty air no amount of disinfectant can erase. How long has Isla breathed this air? And why?

I finally allow myself to ask that question.

What event finally pushed her over the edge, rendering her unfit to navigate her own boat in humanity's sea?

⬿

"She's been in and out of this place for years," Dr. Luca, the clinical director, says as Grandma Min and I sit with him in the cafeteria. He is skinnier than a flagpole on a toy ship. He's on his lunch break and to be truthful, I'm glad we're talking here because both Grandma and I are less likely to cry. Despite his objections, we insisted we talk here. Perhaps for our own sanity.

But who wants to think a thought like that in a place like this?

"Can you give us some of her history?"

Dr. Luca opens a sandwich he brought from home. It's cut into two large triangles. "Are you sure you want to talk about this here?"

We nod.

"She's been in and out since the summer of 1971."

The summer after she left. I catch my breath. "Really?"

He nods. "Of course, things here at the hospital weren't what they are now. The programs were inadequate."

"Where was she living in between?"

"I'm not sure. We were so understaffed until about six years ago. I'm afraid we can't give you the complete picture."

Grandma leans forward. "But she is treatable?"

"Somewhat. From what I gather, she responded to medications for quite a while."

"How long has she been here this time?"

"For eight years."

Oh, dear Lord.

Grandma grabs my hand. "Why so long?"

"She's no longer responding well to medication or therapy. At least enough to live on her own."

"Is that possible?" I ask.

He nods. "Unfortunately, it is. These places would be empty if all it took was a drug."

I sit back against my chair and sigh. Grandma just stares at me for a little while. Dr. Luca opens his thermos and pours some weak, black coffee into the red screw-on cup. "We didn't know she had family or we would have contacted you, of course."

"Of course," says Grandma. "I'm not surprised she didn't mention us."

My heart swings like a pendulum. When it stops swinging, what will straight down feel like? I have no idea and I know I've never had an idea.

"Would you like to see her?"

"Is that all right?" I ask.

"Certainly. She's been in a flat state for a while now. We're wondering if she'll come out of it at all."

"What's a flat state?"

"It's a severe reduction in emotional expressiveness. No facial signs or normal emotions. Social withdrawal. When she does speak it's in monotone. She'll go for days and do nothing on her own."

"Will she feed herself?" I ask.

"Yes. When the plate is set in front of her."

I turn to Grandma. "Well, that's good!"

But Grandma is ripped in two, like a paper doll.

"She's enrolled in the training programs, and she does cooperate when given orders," the doctor continues.

"She was a waitress when I was little."

He just nods. "The medication does help insomuch as it keeps her from a state of psychosis."

"Psychosis?" I ask.

"Delusions. Hallucinations. Paranoia."

I lean forward. "She used to talk about her association with the Queen of England when I was little. And she'd gaze out the window a lot. I never knew what she was looking for."

"Probably royal guards out to get her," Grandma says, the lines of her face folding into deeper grooves.

When he finishes his sandwich, he shows us back to the ward giving us a brief history of the hospital. How it was built in the early part of the 1900s for insane people of color. They desegregated it in the late '40s but white individuals really didn't start coming there until the early '60s. He wasn't sure why.

"I haven't been here all that long. Moved in from Cincinnati last year."

I'm not sure why he feels the need to fill the silence, but he does and continues on as we walk down several different hallways. "For a while there in the fifties they sent the criminally insane here with the other patients, some of whom just needed a nursing home and nothing more. There were all kinds of riots."

It is so easy to picture riots in this place. A creepy aura born of violence remains despite the improvements and I think about that demoniac in the Book of Mark, how Jesus just cured him—snap—like that!

He did that spiritually for the Woman at the Well, too.

As I pass patients in various states, I pray for each one because you can never tell what God has in store for these folks. Maybe it's something wonderful.

Maybe.

Oh, shut up, Myrtle Charmaine. You're an idiot and you always have been.

Dr. Luca leads us into an activity room where people sit around on chairs or shuffle along the linoleum floor. I don't see Isla Whitehead anywhere. The television displays an old rerun of *Facts of Life*. Now, those girls always seemed perky, but, my lands, they look positively fast-motion compared to the doings of the room.

Plants sprout up in all the corners. They're trying to make it homey, here. I've got to give them that. An orderly keeps a watchful eye.

"Hi, Greg," Doctor Luca greets him.

"Hi, Doc."

The doctor points to a woman sitting on a couch, staring up at the screen and ushers us over. "Isla, you have visitors."

And she turns toward me. I barely recognize her. She is heavy now and prematurely gray. Her hands roll over one another in her lap. Her eyes are just as blue. They are bland.

Oh, Lord Jesus.

"Isla, it's your mother and your daughter, Charmaine."

"I used to go by Myrtle," I whisper quickly.

"It's your daughter, Myrtle."

She stares through both of us. "Oh, hello. Thank you for coming to see me today."

Grandma takes her hand. "Hello, Isla. We've been looking for you for a long time." Her voice shakes.

"I've been right here."

"Yes, you have."

Isla pulls her hand away. "Excuse me, I think I'll watch my show now."

Dr. Luca says, "I do know she likes to garden."

"Can she do that here?"

He nods. "We've given her a patch right outside these doors. Would you like to see it?"

He shows us over. Grandma gasps. "It looks exactly like my late spring flowerbeds at home. I've always done them that way."

Grape hyacinth and some burgundy pansies decorate the brown tapestry of dark soil. No weeds peep above the chenille earth and all is raked in perfect, symmetrical swirls.

We turn back toward Isla. She still watches the show,

and I see miniature Blairs and Tooties jiggle and boogie across the slick surface of her corneas.

Oh, Isla. What happened to your sweetheart face?

So we sit with her, not knowing what else to do.

"Grandma, did Mama get nosebleeds a lot?"

She shakes her head. "Not that I remember, sweetie."

"It's obvious she has to remain on medication and continue receiving therapy," says Grandma.

We are driving home to Mount Oak. The car is quiet. There's no gospel music playing and everybody else is asleep.

I don't know what I was expecting from Isla. I thought at least the sight of her own mother and daughter would bring out something from her. We went back three days in a row and still the same, polite response.

I am hollow. I have a mother, yet I don't.

Questions remain unanswered and now I know I'll never find out what really happened to Mama. But I know she responded to treatment and still failed to return. Not only is that a bitter pill, it's a bitter pill the size of a wrecking ball.

"I'm more frightened than ever, Grandma. What if all this starts happening to me?"

"You can't worry about that, Charmaine. And be thankful. Your mama had symptoms of mental illness way before your age."

"But my depression."

"It's under control."

"With medication."

"True. But Isla always went off her pills. I guess she played with fire once too often. Oh, Lord."

"I can't tell you how much of a fraud I feel, getting up there and singing while Harlan tells people just like me that God will deliver them. Do you think that's true, Grandma? Do you really think it's all a spiritual problem?"

"Not in your case. We can see that now."

I think I'll be asking myself that question for the rest of my life.

I picture Mama sitting there in the chair, watching television. "Will I end up like her?"

"I doubt it, sweetie. I really do."

"I guess that's all I have to go on at this point."

She takes my hand and we continue down the highway, away from Crownsville, with Isla's condition digging into our minds.

Grandma pulls out a little book of crossword puzzles she bought at the gas station. "Want to help me do this thing?"

"Sure Grandma."

But Grandma doesn't really need my help. She's just being nice.

5

*W*e moved her.

Mama now resides at Broughton Hospital in Morganton, North Carolina. It's beautiful there. Bright. Cheerful. Historic. We drove Mama down at the end of July. She made no protests.

I believe my prayers for grace are being answered because I'm finding that I do care for her in a very divorced way. I don't want her to suffer the same as I don't want a stray cat to suffer. And maybe that's exactly what Mama is, nothing more than a stray.

Now I am back on the road for the final round of touring this summer and Grandma Min is with us. This is my own concert tour, not Gospelganza. "Ten Thousand Lilies" has topped the Christian music charts and has sold four hundred thousand singles. Most of the money is going to Broughton Hospital. I guess I'm doing it for Grandma Min. She doesn't deserve to lose all her money on this, and Harlan's salary more than covers our expenses at the house.

She drives out there once every two weeks for a couple of days. I'm not sure what's going to happen once school starts again. We both agree that Mama cannot come and live with us at this point.

Maybe someday?

I don't know. I have to think of my family. What kind of home would that be for the kids? The obsessive tendencies Mama has would drive them crazy.

Tap, tap, tap. Tap, tap, tap. All along the outline of the car window. The entire way from Crownsville to Broughton.

Aaaaaahh!

I've become quite good at driving this RV. And as the miles stretch between Mount Oak and Tyler, Texas, where my first concert is, I think a lot about the Woman at the Well. And I wonder if she really knew how lucky she was to have met Jesus before she lost her mind.

Grace is almost halfway through her program. She hasn't yet told her parents about Leo and thank goodness, they've stopped calling me now that they know where she is.

But I have to wonder why she hasn't said anything? Is it because she's really not planning to come get him after she's well?

I sure hope so.

He's asleep right now in the bed in the back. Looking forward to school, he's been reading lots of books. Now they aren't real advanced-type books, but he enjoys them and that's all that matters.

Just yesterday he said, "Mama, how come you never read?"

And I said, "Because I just can't sit still for that long."

He laughed. "You said it, Mama. You're really something."

How many times has he heard Harlan say that? I can't begin to guess.

I wish I could give Harlan a son of his own.

6

That lawyer ripped me apart on the witness stand. But when someone's got as much scar tissue as I do, you can only do so much damage.

Remember how endearing I am?

Well, it worked in my favor that day. And when they flashed pictures of my injuries up on the screen, little me, and there was Carl Bofa, Big Guy himself, sitting over there, they pretty much realized that I spoke the truth.

Afterward, when I sat in the courthouse canteen trying to stop shaking, trying to stop a nosebleed, one of the prosecuting attorneys, a scrappy young man who looked perpetually surprised he made it to the right side of the tracks, said, "You're lucky to have escaped with the injuries you received, Mrs. Hopewell."

"You mean he's done this sort of thing before?"

He nodded.

"Why couldn't you say that?"

He sipped his coffee. "The judge ruled it inadmissible."

"Why?"

"Because he was acquitted the last three times."

I still shook there in that yellow plastic chair on that late August day. The humidity pounded fists at the windows, keeping me inside, though Harlan had pulled the car up twenty minutes before.

When we pull up into the driveway I ask Harlan if he would mind taking the kids out for ice cream. "I just want to sleep, Harlan. I just want to forget about today for a little while."

"I'll do that, Shug." He leans forward and kisses my cheek. "You get some rest."

Long after they've left for Bill D's, I stare at the stuccoed ceiling. I rise from the bed, root through my underwear drawer, and pull out my old bag of toenail clippings.

I was alive then. And I am alive now. So I walk to the bathroom, get out the clippers, and make sure there's evidence of that fact.

I drop back into the depths the day after the trial. Of course, it had been coming. I could feel it for days. That otherworldliness, that suspicion that I had flown away somewhere—but maybe not, maybe it was just hormones, or too much Diet Coke, or maybe, just maybe, I had a right to be depressed.

Watching the world through emotional mucus, weighed down by the hairballs of the mind, I call Dr. Braselton. I like him. He asks a few pertinent questions, keeps the pills coming, and that's fine.

"He *just* had a cancellation, Mrs. Hopewell," the assistant says. "Can you come right in?"

"Yes!"

The thing about the drops now is that each drop seems deeper than the one before it. So what is the bottom point? Will I get to a drop that is so low I move down to some other disorder? Is that what happened to Mama?

Dr. Braselton, who really looks more like a gym teacher than a doctor with his crew cut and potbelly, takes me right away. "When's your next trip, Charmaine?"

"Two weeks."

"Good. I'm upping your dosage a bit. Hopefully we won't have to switch you to something else."

I can only hope, but I swear I know better. "Is this normal? Do people switch medications?"

"Yes, they do."

"What can I do in the meantime?"

"Get off that Diet Coke. Start eating for heaven's sake."

"But nobody wants to see a fat singer."

"That's not true. And you won't get fat. You'll just get healthy. You've got to start taking responsibility for your own depression, Charmaine. Pills are only half of it."

I don't know what to say.

I know the medication will kick back in soon. I'll pretend I've got the flu until then.

I fill the prescription at the pharmacy, and on the way home stop at the IGA and buy some steaks, baked potatoes, and an apple pie.

I won't be Mama.

$\mathcal{I}$'m feeling so much better now. I'm more like myself than I have been in months. I'm eating better, laying off the caffeine, and taking little morning strolls with Harlan. I'm not yet on an all out fitness kick.

Well, we figured it out! The kids are back in homeschool, thank the Lord for Grandma Min who agreed to resign from the preschool to teach Hope and Leo. They all travel with me when my gig is within driving distance and we can take the RV. I've had to lay some ground rules because I found out people out there will take whatever they can get. If I can't take the kids I'll only be gone for two nights. If I can, the sky's the limit, providing I'm home on Sundays to sing for the show.

And *The Port of Peace Hour* is going strong! Harlan's well-rounded approach is making us more popular than ever. He studied hard this summer, I have to say. And I admire him so much.

Our Christmas special a few weeks ago was seen at prime time on all the big Christian satellite networks. Letters with donations are pouring in. We've been able to buy time on lots of stations. I never knew how generous people could be.

When Mama said all those years ago I had the markings of fame, she was exactly right. Sometimes I don't know what to do with it, though. I get a little embarrassed at all the accolades and the clapping and cheering. But the people I meet are so nice. Although some of them can get a little too attached. They look at me and just want to touch me, as if that simple act will bless them.

My Lord and Savior is so good to me. And He's given me this opportunity to tell everybody I know about Him.

A new record is done and will be coming out next month. We're on a one-a-year track. And soon, the Dove Awards will arrive. I'm up for two Doves, best new artist, and best female artist for 1986. Now if that isn't something, I don't know what is. See, I don't know much about much, but what I do know is that God can take someone like Myrtle Charmaine Whitehead and create good.

8

*B*rooksTone sent me the dress I'm wearing as I sit here backstage waiting for the Dove Awards to begin. I'm singing "Ten Thousand Lilies" tonight, before this entire, illustrious crowd.

It is one thing to sing to congregations and concertgoers, but it is completely another thing to perform in front of singers, the majority of whom are better, more famous than I am. I told Mama about it all on my last visit to the hospital and she smiled. A vacant, empty smile, but still, it was the first time for it and I guess I saw a hint of the face that gentled and shone when it beheld that big Christmas basket waiting outside our boarding house door all those years ago.

"I done good, Mama," I said as she turned her face away.

I can't say all this has happened to me through sheer ambition and determination. But I do believe I've been swept up in a tide I'm more than capable of swimming against. I suppose, inadvertently, that was the gift Mama gave to me the day she left.

At least she'll never know how much I once hated her.

But that hate is gone, replaced by not so much love as pity, regret, and sadness.

Poor Isla.

But it's my time to shine.

I walk out on stage in my high heels, the silk of my purple sequined gown sliding against my skin, and I wave and I really do feel like Marilyn Monroe, just for a moment.

The familiar strains of the music begin and I sing the words that have become so dear in the hearts of so many.

"Ten thousand lilies, ten thousand roses, ten thousand grapevines, ten thousand trees."

The crowd claps and I am lost. I'm back in the bowling alley, back in the clubs, back in churches all over, I am back in the world I was created to inhabit and I am fed by the people before me, the music behind me, and the song within me.

"I magnify you, Jesus, for You've loved me so." I finish the final chorus, my voice softens and my heart is full. I always feel like crying now. And sometimes I do.

But not tonight.

I blow kisses to my family, sitting there on the fourth row in their fine new clothing and I exit the stage. Several Christian music bigwig performers congratulate me, kiss me on the cheek, and say, "Well done."

I smile and return to my family.

I would say that singing here tonight was enough, but my stomach is in knots at the thought of the awards coming up. I shouldn't want to win this bad, but I do.

I didn't win.

I am back in Mount Oak licking my wounds. I sit in

my lawn chair by the swing set. Grandma Min plunks down a chair beside me.

"Still feeling sad?"

"Yes, Grandma, I am."

"Well, I don't blame you. The bigger they are the harder they fall."

"Well, I'm not all that big, but the fall still hurts. And if you say, 'It's an honor just to be nominated' I'll send you packing!"

We laugh.

The kids play in the dirt near the swing set.

"At least BrooksTone is still happy. The new album releases in a few weeks and they're putting 'Dove Nominee for Best Female Artist' right on the cover."

"Well, that's good," she says.

"A lot of good's come out of it. I'm almost booked solid through August."

"Fine by me. I love schooling the children."

"I know you do, Grandma. I don't know what I'd do without you. And I love having you with me on the road."

"You have quite an entourage, sweetie." She smiles and picks up her basket of garden tools. "I'm going to go cut down those tulips. They look peaked."

And such is my life. Traveling, singing, being with the kids, trying to do my best by Harlan, Grandma, and Mama. I'm still taking my pill each night and feeling all the better for it. But days like these cannot go on forever. I've lived many extra years in my short lifetime, enough to know that.

Part Seven

1

I never thought this life would become old hat but it has. I miss my lazy daytimes with the kids. We're always driving to one concert appearance or another. And for what?

Ministry, yes. That is true. If I didn't sing, use my little gift box there in my throat, I'd be wasting who I am. I realize not many people can sing like I do, and that is not cause for pride for me, rather it is cause for sobriety and honor.

And you can take that to the bank.

I do this for Mama's care, too, I guess. Until we get everything figured out with the state—who'll pay what and how much—I'm footing the bills at Broughton.

Isn't it strange? She did nothing for Grandma and me and we're using ourselves up on her. I can't pretend to understand why I'm doing this.

It's hard to believe it's been almost a year since my first record debuted.

I sit alone in my hotel room at the National Religious Broadcasters Convention here in Washington, D.C. I'm singing at the banquet tonight thanks to the recommendation of Vinca Love. What an honor to be asked.

Although I only flew in a few hours ago, I've already heard the buzz about Reverend Bakker and I am stunned. I've heard tell that he had an affair and paid the woman to keep quiet. Jessica Somebody. I don't remember her last name. The buzz is that Jimmy Swaggart is going to try and take over the *PTL* empire.

What will happen to them I don't know. Some reporter from Charlotte is all over it. If it's all true, then I can hardly blame the fellow. But if it's not, then shame on him. I've never liked reporters much. Too pushy.

This whole thing saddens me and I feel deceived. Nobody likes feeling deceived. It gets their hackles up. So if my reaction is any indication, I can't imagine what their faithful supporters are going to feel.

But he was so nice! And poor Tammy Faye! I can't imagine what she is feeling right now. I loved being with them when I sang on their show. We laughed and we cried and we fellowshipped.

I just pray all this isn't true. I just pray we'll find out in a few days that it is rumor and nothing more.

Grace is almost finished her therapy. She stayed on a couple of months extra. Maybe she's scared. But she says she's going to work there a while to help other women coming in. "I want to make sure this sticks, Charmaine, which is why I think I need some additional time."

I said, "Please take it, Grace. You know we'll take good care of Leo. Are you relying on God for help now?"

"I'm trying. It all still embarrasses me, to tell you the truth."

Outside the street below me lies cold and gray. Washington in February can be so bleak. Some puddles of snow grace the dirty sidewalk and the curb, and I watch as a Rolls-Royce drives by on its way to the parking garage. It swerves as a lady with a rusty shopping cart enters the street. Jumping the curve, it leaves dirty tracks on what was once a pristine blanket slipped down from heaven.

The phone rings.

"It's four-thirty," the front desk lady says.

"Thank you."

I had tried to nap, but couldn't sleep.

I paint my lips one more time and make sure my dress isn't ganged around me in a twist. I've had to let all my dresses out now that I'm eating like a normal human being. Harlan says I'm downright sexy and I feel womanly, too, now that I actually have hips and a tiny bit more up top. And now I can eat corn and put a little butter on it.

I'm early. Ninety minutes left before I go on. So I turn on the news.

The scandal is all over the place and it's all the anchors can do to keep from cheering with glee.

This whole industry, this whole religious broadcasting business was due for a shake-up. Nothing lasts forever, does it? For the life of me, I just can't picture Jesus up on TV begging for money.

God have mercy.

I am guilty. God have mercy on me, too.

I will say nothing, I decide. If the press asks me to comment there will be no comment. I can't afford to.

The meal is delicious. Hotel fare, but at least green beans almondine or ratatouille didn't show up on the plate. I listen to the introduction for myself and just smile, hoping against hope there's no broccoli in my teeth. I got so involved in a conversation with this television station owner from Kansas that the time flew by and I didn't get to go brush my teeth like I had planned. I turn to the lady beside me, a senior in college scouting for a job upon graduation. I grin. "Any broccoli?"

"You're free and clear." But she looks amazed nonetheless.

I ascend up the steps to the platform, pick up the microphone and nod to the sound man. I switched accompaniment tracks when I heard the news. It was supposed to be the upbeat hit from my new album called "You Shine." But, knowing what was going on out there in everybody's heart and mind, I felt it was time to get back to some basics, maybe remind us all why we're in this odd life of Christian broadcasting and entertainment to begin with.

I feel dirty and disgusting as the opening strains of "The Old Rugged Cross" begin.

And I sing and I remember and I hope against hope that I will possess the heart of Jesus through this whole mess because right then I realize we are about to descend into something unprecedented, something dark and of our own making. The purging has begun, Jesus is clearing the temple of the money changers, He is lifting high His cross and saying "Follow me."

"On a hill faraway," I sing. "Stood an old rugged cross. The emblem of suffering and shame. And I love that old cross where the dearest and best for a world of lost sinners was slain.

"So I'll cherish the old rugged cross till my trophies at last I lay down. I will cling to the old rugged cross and exchange it someday for a crown."

The music dies down after the fourth and final verse and, a capella, I sing the chorus to one of my favorite songs, "Blessed Redeemer."

"Blessed Redeemer! Precious Redeemer! Seems now I see Him on Calvary's tree. Wounded and bleeding, for sinners pleading, blind and unheeding, dying for me!"

Doggone it! Why this? Why now? Christ spilled His blood, Divine blood, and we have mixed it with our own sinful excrement and smeared it on His very cross and pronounced it not only good but holy.

2

$\mathcal{T}$he scandals are everywhere. And *Jesus Alive!* is no exception. Grandma Min summarizes the article from the *Richmond Times Dispatch* for me as I make my morning tea.

"It basically says that Peter Love sent that pilot over there into dangerous territory because he wanted him dead."

"You're kidding me?"

"No. He was having an affair with that man—Mack somebody's—wife."

"The lady that runs the pool."

"That's her. She's pregnant, too. And it's not Mack's baby. He wasn't able to sire children."

"Poor Vinca."

Grandma's mouth turns down. "I guess so. I'd be shocked to death if she didn't know about the affair."

I shrug. "It's hard to know these things, Grandma."

She sets the paper flat on the surface of the table. "Mark my words, sweetie, they're coming after you and Harlan next."

"Why would you ever think that? We're a couple of nobodies."

She shakes her head. "The article says they're investigating everybody associated with the ministry."

I think of all the times I sang on their show. "But I'm just a singer."

"A singer whose husband has a television show."

"Maybe you're right."

"I hope not."

"Me, too."

I set a teabag in a floral cup and wait for the water to boil. "Do they mention uncovering anything else?"

"Unfortunately, yes. Apparently they were dishonest in their solicitations for donations. They'd say they were going to use the money to help people starving Lord knows where and then only give a tiny percentage of it away. They'd keep the rest."

"Oh, my lands."

"Terrible. So here you think you're sending in a hundred dollars to feed starving children in third-world countries, and just a few dollars actually gets there, if any sometimes. Not to mention they oversold their time-shares just like at Heritage USA."

"And here I was singing on that show week after week."

"Just goes to show you even the most discerning of people can get snowed under."

I roll my eyes, thinking of the beautiful restaurant I ate at, the Olympic-size pool, first class all the way. "I feel sick."

"So do I. I was almost fooled by those people."

"What about personally?"

"They took huge salaries."

A toupeeless Harlan enters the kitchen, still in his robe and slippers. Grandma hands him the paper and he reads, leaning against the counter. He shakes his head every so often and sighs in between.

He finishes and looks up.

"Grandma thinks we're next."

He nods. "We are. They've already started talking to people around Mount Oak."

"Who?"

"I think he said he was a reporter from the *Washington Post*."

"Oh, great, Harlan. The *Washington Post*?"

Oh, my Jesus.

"I'm making a call to them this morning," I say. "If they want to know about us, they can come straight to the source."

3

Thy will be done" is a tough prayer to pray and really mean it. Jesus prayed that, and ended up crucified. Now, that hurts my heart to think of Him hanging there like that, in such agony. He sacrificed everything even bearing separation from His Father on that dark Friday.

How He must be grieved.

Vinca Love left Peter and returned to her family in Richmond. Peter's been on all the talk shows trying to repair the damage, but he invariably ends up blaming Vinca for all the problems in their marriage, from their infertility to his infidelity.

I thought even he'd be above that. It makes me sick.

But oh, my! The people crawling out of the woodwork. Although, that's not fair. Because some of their allegations are more than allegations. They ring truer than the bells of St. Mary. Construction workers were asked to put down their gear, move to the side while Peter gets on and says, "We've had to stop work until the funds come in."

One of those construction workers was someone Peter

led to the Lord in the old days when he had a prison ministry. He walked off the job that day.

I don't blame him.

The first interview I am granting will take place today. It's true. The *Washington Post* has already interviewed a bunch of people in the ministry behind our back. Tanzel told me.

Tanzel hears everything.

The doorbell rings on this March day. A week ago Jim Bakker resigned as the head of *PTL* and in the meantime Jerry Falwell is stepping in so Jimmy Swaggart can't do a hostile takeover. Who knows what the truth is? It makes my head hurt. And now the entire world has read of the excesses and we're all asking the same questions. Who could follow Jesus and screw people like this?

Maybe that sounds harsh. But it doesn't deserve a nice clean verb, in my opinion.

As expected, Harlan and I have been lumped into the entire mess. I guess I should have been a little less flamboyant with my dresses. Already I've read some op-ed pieces on the entire mess, and they've targeted my hair and purple outfits. "Lavishly awful," one woman said. "To think she's put out money like that for such tasteless garb." Viewers don't know I sew them myself. Maybe Harlan shouldn't have been so forthright about the whole "What's *Really* Eating at You?" business either because they've sure zeroed in on that even though he revamped his message almost a year ago.

We set ourselves up as easy targets and didn't even know it. I feel like a couple of cartoon characters.

My car was keyed in front of Bill D's.

Last night our house was egged.

Can't they see it's just a little house with a rusted swing set in the back? Don't they know there are kids living inside? And a grandma?

The phone calls have been so mean.

I pray that's all the backlash we'll get. I don't know how much more blood I can lose through my nose!

It's why I agreed to today's activities. To set the record straight as far as our ministry is concerned.

I have an appointment, an interview with that reporter from the *Washington Post*, a person I knew years ago, a person I ran away from years ago, the first person that made me think of myself as a woman.

I open the door and I see those lapis eyes that are now hemmed in by tiny crow's feet. That thick head of hair looks just the same.

Ten years fade to nothing.

"Charmaine!"

"Richard. Come on in."

Richard Llewellyn stands on my porch steps, wearing khaki pants, a white broadcloth button-down, and a loose blue-and-gold striped tie.

"Would you like to sit here in the living room or back at the kitchen table?"

He looks all around him. "How about the kitchen table? Then I can write more easily."

I show him through the living room and back into the kitchen. I bought a pretty lavender cloth for the spring—$5.99 reduced from $7.99—and the place is scrubbed clean as usual.

"This is cheerful," he says.

"Thank you. It sure beats life on the road. Although, sometimes I think I'm back in that RV more than not."

"Yes. I've been following you for quite some time."

"Oh, yeah?"

"I saw an ad for a Gospelganza Festival a long time ago and there was your picture. Different last name, of course, but there's only one person that looks like you and is named Charmaine."

"Hey, you were the one who suggested I go by Charmaine. That was the best thing I ever did."

Well, sort of. Harlan might differ with that.

I'm trying to charm the snake but I don't know how good of a job I'm doing.

He asks me questions about singing in Gospelganza, my albums, the church, the *Port of Peace Hour*. And we actually have a good time! It amazes me what can happen when people are mature enough to put the past behind them.

The time just flies by and I realize we've been sitting here for two hours. So I figure it's time for me to start questioning him a little bit.

"Are you married, Richard?"

He shakes his head. "You know me, Charmaine. I'm not the settling-down type."

"That's for sure."

"I'm actually a little surprised you agreed to see me after all that went down in Vermont."

I shrug. "That was over a decade ago. I've made out okay. It got me out of Lynchburg and for that I am thankful."

"You're something."

"That's what I hear." And I smile into his eyes, realizing with thankfulness that I really had left that part of my life behind me. How freeing.

He fills me in on Clarke and Cecile whose life sounds exactly the same as when I left and, "What about that gang at the cabin?" I ask. "Whatever happened to them?"

"The guys started a computer company together and Lady Andrea went back to England."

"Guess she couldn't slum it forever."

"Nope."

"Oh, Richard, even though we didn't leave on the best of terms, this sure has been nice!"

He's drinking a cup of tea and I'm slurping on Diet Sprite, my new drink of choice, since it doesn't have caffeine. "It has. Can I give my aunt and uncle your regards?"

"Please do. I hope our running away didn't affect them."

"Not at all. Only that you were their first and last foray into the foster care system."

"They really weren't cut out for that kind of life."

"You're right."

Harlan comes home from church. "Hey, y'all."

"Harlan, this is Richard Lewellyn, from the *Washington Post*."

Harlan extends his hand. "Well, good to meet you, Richard."

They shake.

"Ready for our interview? In light of what's been going on with the televangelist scandals, I'm hoping you might lend some clarity to the issue."

"I'd be delighted. Hey, it's almost six. What do you say, Charmaine? How about if Richard stays for supper?"

He shakes his head. "I really don't want to impose."

I bop him on the arm. "Of course, you won't impose.

Grandma's got some chicken stew in the Crock-Pot and all I have to do is throw in some extra dumplings."

Harlan hangs his key on the key hooks I screwed into the side of the kitchen cabinet. "You'll kill two birds with one stone. I mean, a man's gotta eat."

Richard laughs. "All right. You've convinced me."

I get up from the table to finish preparing the meal. "Well, I've got to say, in all these years I never pictured *this* scenario!"

Richard says, "Me, either. I thought you'd hate me."

I look at him, mustering up all the frankness I can. "Well, now, Richard, that wouldn't be very Christian of me, now would it?"

He smiles and looks me in the eye. And I remember that night at that big house in Lynchburg. I recall those eyes, that smile, and the way he made me feel, so grown up and alluring. I remembered how I thought he could do no wrong.

"How are you holding up under all the backlash?" Richard asks us as I set out supper. He leans against the counter as Grandma and I flurry the food onto the table.

I set down the green salad. "I don't know, Richard. It's hard to read all that about people you've trusted. I've tried to live a good life, be nice to folks, raise my kids as best I can, and then to read about myself in the local papers like I'm some sort of singing clown . . ."

"It hurts her terribly," Harlan says.

Richard nods, his fingers tapping on the fronts of his khakis. "I figured as much."

"Hopefully you'll be able to help straighten things out, Richard," I say.

He smiles.

Grandma lays out the last glass of soda. "Well, everybody, let's eat! Kids!" she hollers. "It's suppertime!"

Two hours later, after the best blueberry cream cheese pie I've ever tasted (I am a much better dessert cook now that I actually eat them myself), I walk Richard to his little black Volkswagen.

"Before I forget, I've got something for you, Charmaine." He leans into the backseat and pulls out a parcel. "When I told Aunt Cecile I was coming down, she sent this for me to give to you."

"And I've got something for you." I reach into my pocket and pull out four ten dollar bills. "It's the money I took from you all in Vermont."

"I can't take that, Charmaine."

"Please, Richard. I need you to."

So he shakes his head and does as I ask.

We say our good-byes and off he goes.

Well, if this all isn't just the limit! I'll be honest, I can use the encouragement, and maybe this will help us and our ministry in the process.

I take the parcel into the house. Inside rests my photos of the Evanses. I touch Mrs. Evans. Slide my fingertips along her cheek and chin. Smile into her pansy eyes.

I miss her so badly sometimes I want to crumble.

A family picture with me next to James is next and I smile. Yep, those were the days.

And finally, wrapped in layers of newspaper, my plate, Grandma Sara's willowware plate. Down the center a fissure snakes and as I lift it from the box, it breaks in two, the left side tumbling to the floor to brake into—I count them—six pieces. Seven in all.

The wall clock ticks and I watch the minute hand

move around as Grandma and Harlan clean up the kitchen. I barely realize it when Harlan picks up the pieces. I feel his movement. I hear his breath, but I am lost right now, rolling around in something I cannot name.

4

 $\mathcal{M}$ ama?"

She is gardening and she looks peaceful here with the earth beneath her grasp, the sun highlighting the white strands of her hair. Although she is bent down on her knees, her spreading behind resting on her heels, she looks like she used to in basic form. I remember her sitting like that as she'd go through the under-the-bed boxes in our room, sorting through clothing, folding and refolding.

She turns. "Oh, hello, Myrtle."

"Hello, Mama. Whatcha doin'?"

"Digging."

A paper bag of bulbs rests beside her. "You going to plant these?"

"Yes."

"Are they lilies? Tulips?"

"Irises. Mother brought them for me."

She turns back and continues her task. I am watching a robot, I think. A blood-pumping, nerve-shooting robot. She is here, but she is not.

"It's almost Easter, Mama."

"Did you get an Easter dress, Myrtle?"

"Yes."

"Good. A girl should always get a new dress for Easter."

"Why, Mama?"

She continues digging.

"Do you like it here?"

"They're nice."

"I'm glad."

I want so badly to ask her who wasn't nice to her in the past, but I cannot. I'm scared she'll descend further into the bowels of her mind.

Where are you, Isla Whitehead?

Don't even ask, Myrtle.

"Mama, what happened to that snazzy man from Washington, D.C.?"

There is quiet in the garden. A swelling silence that fills my heart with emptiness

"Don't even ask, Myrtle."

But the words are not Mama's. They are my own.

I should have known better.

Maybe Mama's just ill. Maybe nothing bad really happened to her. Maybe she's just a hapless victim.

Maybe it doesn't really matter in the end. At least not to me.

I stop at a pay phone on the way home and call Ruby. "Well?"

"It was positive!"

"That's great, Ruby!"

"Girl, I am so excited."

"Congratulations. To Henry, too. I'll bet he's on cloud nine."

"I told him an hour ago, and he's already looking at car seats."

"So let's see. Your last period was a month ago and it's the end of April—"

"I'm due near the end of December."

"A Christmas baby!"

"Isn't that exciting? You know, I sing about Jesus, but I have a hard time emoting like you do about Him, Char. But it's fitting isn't it? A new life for me. A healed life. And then this gift from Jesus. This baby. And around Christmas, too."

"I guess He wanted to make sure you got the message."

Ruby laughs.

"You deserve a little baby of your own, Ruby. You really do. Hey, gotta get back on the road." I don't want to provide a downer moment for her by calling attention to my own barrenness here on the phone. I was hoping the weight gain would be the answer. "I'm taking you to Bill D's for a butterscotch milk shake tomorrow night at seven o'clock!"

"I'll be there!"

Oh, Ruby. Your own little baby. It will be a beautiful baby.

It's eight P.M. as I pull onto our little street. Cherry Tree Lane. Isn't that the cutest thing? I love my neighbors. There are several with children around the ages of Leo and Hope and some older ladies for Grandma to associate with. They've started a club that meets every Tuesday for supper and cards. Life is good here on our street. It's quiet for the most part and lined with regular folks. We have a welder, a town policeman, three brothers who run the hardware store over on the town square, a hostess down at Josef's, the only gourmet restaurant in town. And then there are the card ladies and us.

I can't believe we've lived here for over a year and a half! Even when we moved in, I figured we'd be here a year, tops. Harlan surprised me with this one.

The neighbors have been wonderful during these hard times, keeping a watch on our house. We haven't had any vandalism for a while and every time a negative letter to the editor appears, someone always cooks a meal.

Tonight our house hovers there in the plum twilight, but it seems to be growing out of a huddle of cars bleeding from my lawn onto the street. People drink coffee and lean against bumpers. Some lady sits in a folding chair.

Something is very wrong. I honk my horn. The crunch of my tires on the gravel street warns their ears of my approach. All snap to attention.

There are vans from TV stations, too.

Let me through.

Something is very wrong. Something more newsworthy than my hair.

TV cameras focus their unblinking eye on me.

Had the vandals gone too far this time? Did they throw more than eggs? Did they harm someone?

Harlan? Leo? Hope?

They flock around my car like black fowl. And I honk my horn again.

NBC, CBS, ABC.

Where are my babies?

Harlan?

Let me through.

Unable to gain even two feet of progress, I stop the car and get out. They enfold me like piranhas on a carcass suddenly thrown to the depths.

"Let me through!"

A microphone is stuffed in my face. "Mrs. Hopewell—"

"Let me through!" I push my way into the mass, slapping away microphones. "Harlan!" I scream. "Harlan!"

The front door opens. "Shug!"

"What's happening?"

Harlan flies off the porch, pushing reporters and camera people aside like they are pickup sticks. "Shug!"

"Harlan!"

"Reverend Hopewell, do you know where the monies from your wife's record deals have gone?"

He advances toward me and Harlan shoves him away. He rocks off his heels, falling backward.

I feel his hand grab my arm and he pulls me through the throng. "Get back! Get back!" he hollers. "Get away from my wife!"

A *Washington Post* is shoved into my face.

"What do you have to say about this article, Mrs. Hopewell?"

"Come on, Shug. Let's get you inside."

After that shove, the crowd parts and there's Grandma Min holding open the screen door. "Come on in, sweetie."

"Where are the kids?"

"They're fine. They're in my bedroom watching a video."

Harlan shuts the door behind him.

"What's going on, Harlan?"

"Oh, Shug. That reporter friend of yours from the Post."

"Richard Lewellyn?"

He nods, looking out between the blinds. "None other. He's betrayed us."

"No!"

"Yes. I have no idea how he found out these things but it's all there in black-and-white. Your mother, Broughton, your record money going to pay for her care. And of course, my 'What's Really Eating You' message to make us look like hypocrites."

Grandma Min ushers me to the kitchen. "Let me get you a soda."

I nod. "I was hungry before I got home. But not anymore."

Harlan enters. "They're not going away. I thought surely they would leave once they realized you wouldn't talk to them."

"You have a copy of the article?"

"Yep. It was delivered by courier this morning."

"Can I read it?"

"I think you'd better."

"But he seemed so nice, Harlan. Didn't he?"

"You think everybody's nice, Charmaine." He turns to go into the living room.

"Harlan? Are you mad at me?"

"Of course not! We're in this together, Shug."

I turn to Grandma Min. "Did you read it?"

She nods.

Harlan comes back in, handing me the paper. "Here you go."

"Will you sit here with me while I read it?"

"I will. Let me put on the kettle. I could use a cup of tea right now."

It starts out so nice, telling of our humble little house, the quaint meal from the Crock-Pot, kids playing outside on the swing set.

In fact there's a picture of Hope and Leo right there. Naturally I signed a consent form, thinking surely, after the fun time we'd had, that the article would be all good. I didn't even mind his barb about all the antiques so much. After all, they are Grandma's, not mine.

Then he continued on, talking about *The Port of Peace Hour*, Harlan's hard-line stance on psychology. There is a cute picture of the singers on the show and uplifting quotes from people who we've ministered to.

"I stopped blaming my past and going to every shrink in town for answers. And I started reading my Bible and my life has been healed. Just ask my family."

"Prayer! Talking to Jesus in prayer has been the greatest therapy I've ever had!"

"The Hopewells saved my life!"

And then the other quotes begin. Things we'd never heard about.

"My son went off his medication due to the Hopewells' advice and he eventually committed suicide."

"My daughter and her husband stopped marriage counseling and she ended up in the hospital from his abuse. She's planning on going back with him once she's released."

"If the Bible didn't say we shouldn't sue a brother in Christ, I'd do it."

I feel twice as much air fill my mouth as it drops open at the next bit of my life. "The fifty thousand dollars Ms. Hopewell has received in royalties is nowhere to be found in the family accounts. The money has been traced to a mental hospital in Broughton, North Carolina, where Ms. Hopewell's mother, Isla Whitehead, is institutionalized for a disturbing mental illness. Although the fact is not well known, Ms. Hopewell has been undergoing treatment for depression for many years."

Finally, Richard Lewellyn cast his net of doubt on one more area of my life. In the portion where he interviewed Bansy Pruitt, that lardy man who scouted me at Suds 'N' Strikes, I find out I'd engaged in sexual activity to further my career, which cast all manner of doubt on the conviction of Carl Bofa.

Oh, Jesus.

Harlan is in the living room, looking out the window. He turns around and walks back to the table. "They're starting to leave now. Guess it's getting too late to hang around."

"Harlan. It's not true. I didn't sleep with that man."

"I know you didn't, Shug."

I stand up, put my arms around him, and rest my head on his heart.

5

$\mathcal{A}$ registered letter arrives
two days later as Grandma Min and I school the children.
The words within sting me like a wave of pepper over my
eyes and I drop the paper to the floor.

"What is it?" Grandma asks.

"It's Grace's parents. They're suing for custody of
Leo."

❧

I see it all on the news that night. Grace, with her family all rallied around her, looks so vulnerable. "I just want
my baby back is all," she says. "I've always wanted to be
a good mother to him and now I have the chance."

"Have you asked Ms. Hopewell to return your son?"

"Repeatedly," says Grace.

"My daughter fell on hard times, sure," says Mr. Underhill. "But we would have kept Leo with us. That
Hopewell woman called every month for years and never
even told us he existed."

And Grace remained mute. Crying and blubbering.

I call the only lawyer I know, the prosecuting attorney

who handled the Carl Bofa matter. He tells me I don't have a chance, not against the biological relatives who are more than capable of handling Leo's upbringing. "You can fight it, Charmaine, but I've got to be honest with you, I don't think you'll win but I'll recommend someone up there for you if you want."

I can't fight this battle. I pick up the phone and call the rehab home Grace was staying at. "Is Grace there?"

"No, I'm sorry. We don't have a Grace here."

"Grace Underhill?"

"No, I'm sorry, we have no one by that name."

"Did you ever?"

"No, I'm sorry."

"Well, if you hear from this nonexistent Grace, tell her Charmaine is trying to get in touch with her. Tell her I'll fight for Leo with every last breath I have."

The kids and I pull into the driveway from a trip to the IGA.

"Come on y'all. Let's get inside and I'll start supper."

"Okay, Mama," says Leo and I look back at him and we smile into each other's eyes like we always do. He winks. My lands, he's a good winker.

I grab two bags and hurry up the walk to unlock the door.

"Hey!"

Leo's yell turns my head. And I see them there, Grace and her parents.

"Stop that!" he yells.

I drop my bags and run toward him. But they beat me

to him, pulling him by his spindly arms. "No!" I yell, putting my arms around his waist.

Mrs. Underhill pulls at my waist from behind but I hold tight. "No!" I cry. "No!"

I'm holding fast. Poor Leo. "Hang on, baby," I say. "Mama's not going to let you go."

"You're not his mama!" Grace shouts.

I hold tight.

"Hold tight, Gracie," Mr. Underhill says. "I'll take care of her."

A second later his fist makes contact with my jaw. I cry out, my hands automatically seeking my face as they rip Leo from me and make for their van parked across the street as fast as they can. He screams and I cry and say, "I love you, son! I love you."

Grace shouts at him. "I'm your mama, Leo."

"Mama!" he wails again and she shoves him inside the van.

Hope sobs beside me. "Leo! Leo!"

Screaming, I run to the van and pound on the door with my fists as it pulls away. "Stop!"

But Mr. Underhill steps on the gas and has turned the corner before my cry of despair rises from my heart and into my throat.

Wailing and sobbing, I crumble in the middle of the street.

When would enough heartache be enough?

Hope sits next to me and crosses her legs. "Mama."

"Hopey." I pick her up into my arms as we watch the empty street and weep.

6

Grandma Min pokes me. "Get up Charmaine."

"Grandma, I'm just so tired."

And I am. I haven't felt this way in so many years.

"Let me just sleep in for another fifteen minutes."

"It's already noon."

What Grandma doesn't know is that my medication ran out weeks ago. I thought I'd see if Harlan was right. If maybe I didn't have enough faith. If maybe I could lick this depression thing on my own, just me and God.

Not that God has been all that hot to me lately. I almost resent Him as much as I used to resent Mama. And the kicker is, I still believe and don't doubt that He sent His Son, but boy am I doubting His ability to look out for His children.

If God's the only father I really have, I'd say He's done a miserable job in sheltering His child. At least I did better by Hope and Leo, and they aren't even my own.

So why try? I think I'll just follow God's lead and let everybody I love suffer and wonder what the heck *I'm* doing. Hey, Hope will survive. And all these trials will make her stronger. Isn't that right? Isn't that what I've heard all of my life?

Good then, Hope. Get strong. You'll be all the greater for it someday. And hopefully you'll be able to look at God and thank Him for the fact that I failed.

Maybe I should just stay in bed for the rest of my life and let the world think the worst.

I sit myself up just a tad, reach to the side of the bed, and grab my photo box and all the notes Leo ever wrote to me. I can't even bring myself look at them, but holding them in my arms seems to be enough to get me back to sleep.

Grandma stands at my bedroom door with her hands on her hips. "No more, Charmaine."

"No more what?"

I hear the birds outside in the apple tree. It lost its blooms long ago and the leaves are no longer tender.

"I'm not bringing your meals in here anymore, not that you eat them, and I'm not taking care of Hope, either. The summer's here and she can walk over to the church and to Harlan if she needs something."

"Where will you go?"

"I'm going to Broughton. I found a retirement community there with all the stages. Apartment living through nursing care."

"I'm sorry, Grandma."

"I can't live like this anymore, sweetie. Did you expect me to raise a crazy person then spend my last years caring for her daughter?"

I don't know what I was thinking, honestly. Not much. I'm so heavy on the chest. So full in the eyes.

Grandma sighs and turns away from me.

"God give me a little strength," I whisper. "I'm not asking You to make it all better, or it all to go away, because I know better than to believe You'll answer that prayer. Just help me to go after her now, just this time. Just this once."

I know she's not leaving right now. I have just a few more days to gather the strength.

Oh, Leo.

Poor Harlan is trying so hard. He had my medication refilled and brings it to me every day but I refuse. "Just a few more days, honey, and I'll go back on if I can't kick it by then."

I stare at the wall. There is another way, I know. And lately I've been wondering which method would be the easiest. There are no pills left in the house to swallow. No guns. Only cooking knives and a bathtub. I think that's truly my only option. I'll have to make sure Hope isn't the one to find me.

Harlan enters the room. Daylight fades. "I'm taking Hope to Tanzel's now, Charmaine."

That will make things easier.

"I can't keep Hope in this environment. Please Shug. Tell me what I need to do to make you better."

My world slips away before my eyes and in the end I see myself alongside Mama, making swirls in a garden that is a mirror image of hers.

"Call Dr. Braselton. He's been caring for me since I moved here to Mount Oak."

"I'll get the phone book."

"I'll have to go back on medication, Harlan."

"I wish you would."

"I couldn't kick this thing on my own. I tried."

I did it for him. But I don't tell him that.

"Well, now you know, Shug. Now you know you've got to do this."

"Why did God make me like this?"

"That I can't answer. But if you want me to tell you about all the wonderful parts of you He also gave, well, I've got all day."

And he does just that, pill in one hand, water glass in the other.

7

Soup from my husband's hand tasted better than anything I can ever remember.

I look back at that day a month ago and I see a nail-scarred hand. If a better explanation is out there, I don't know what it is, so I'm sorry.

Harlan began quite a parade to get me back out into the world. Luella came down with the Reasins for an entire week. Ruby stayed a night or two. Then Francie Evans drove down with her brother James. Tanzel was over every afternoon with the funniest little poems and inspirational pieces that had me laughing like crazy.

We walked every morning, Harlan and I, down Route 44 through the country, we took drives and watched folks go about their lives and he didn't allow me to read any papers or watch any television. He created a healing cocoon for me and I felt loved.

Seeing all those people who touch my life in such a short time span made me see I am blessed. And I guess that's the hardest part about the battle of depression, seeing things for what they really are.

I am sitting on my lawn chair now, the summer dew

still wet on the dried, heat-addled grass, and I sing to myself, knowing this battle will be with me for the rest of my life, but knowing I don't have to fight it alone. It won't be easy, I know this, but I finally don't believe I will end up hand in hand with Mama, with two swirly gardens and nothing but television.

I believe God healed me of that a long time ago.

8

$\mathcal{D}$ana Collier, interviewer extraordinaire leans slightly toward the camera, the lights of the studio sending sparks through her frosted pageboy. "Along with our celebrity features, we have a special interview planned for this evening's *Hot Topics*. More when we return after this."

The red light on top of the camera dims and Dana turns to me. "You're doing all right, Mrs. Hopewell?"

I nod. "Please call me Charmaine."

"I will. And you, Reverend Hopewell?"

"I'm just fine, thank you."

When the *Post* failed to respond within a day to our request for an interview, Harlan called the network and they jumped at the chance. So here we are, sitting on a plum couch, Harlan and me, our fingers intertwined. Hope and Grandma are having lunch and a trip to FAO Schwarz during the taping. New York City is the place for me, let me tell you! It's as kooky and nonstop as I am.

Dana lays a quick hand on my knee. "I just want to thank you for giving me the exclusive on this. This whole thing has been such a mess, I think it's good for America to know at least one televangelist is sincere and human."

"Human." I laugh. "That would be us."

"Now I'm going to ask what sound like hard-hitting questions to appease the viewers' sense of vengeance about all this. They won't know I know your answer already, so it will give you the opportunity to respond with the truth. Understand?"

"Perfectly, Dana." Oh, brother. If I found out this woman was made of plastic, I wouldn't be at all surprised.

"It's a show." She leans close to me, all confidential-like. "For all of our self-righteous seriousness in this business, we know if we don't give the viewer what they want, we'll be out on our ear."

I'll bet you say that to everyone.

Harlan smiles. "It's kind of that way with TV preaching, too, you know."

She points to him in a salesman way. "I hate to admit it, and if you say I uttered these words, I'll lie and say I didn't, but there's not that much difference between the two of us, is there?"

"Three seconds, Ms. Collier!"

Dana sits up straight. "We're back with our guests, televangelist Harlan Hopewell and his wife, gospel singer Charmaine Hopewell. Welcome to *Hot Topics*."

We nod our thanks and smile. "Good to be here, Dana," I say.

Dana gives a background on the televangelist scandal, dragging up Bakker and Falwell and Peter and Vinca. "And on the outskirts of all this, another scandal developed, far less known than the Bakkers and the Loves, but just as disillusioning to folks all over the South. Mrs. Hopewell, you've come here to set the record straight?"

"I have."

"I have before me quite a list of allegations regarding the *Port of Peace Hour* in regards to Reverend Hopewell's messages against psychiatric help for mental illness. Are these true?"

"Yes, they are," says Harlan. "Now some of them we've followed up on personally."

"You did?" Dana acted surprised. "Can you tell us about it?"

"Well, several of the allegations were found to be true. Unfortunately there isn't much we can do to help them, other than offer up any kind of comfort we can. And we do try, don't we Charmaine?" He turns to me.

I nod. "I've already traveled to all their homes. Some have offered forgiveness when we've asked, one hasn't. But I can't say I blame him. Losing a loved one isn't something easily accepted."

"Did this man lose his wife?"

"His sister," Harlan says.

"Anybody try to take this to court?"

Harlan nods. "Just one. The ministry wasn't held liable because we weren't offering medical advice, just spiritual counsel."

I put a hand on his knee. "And to Harlan's credit he never expressly told anyone to stop existing treatment."

Her eyebrows raise a tad. "Really?" But she lets that go, thank the Lord. Time is probably running out. "Well, what about the other allegations?"

Harlan sits up a little straighter. "Completely false. We investigated them thoroughly, willing to help out, and found that the situations were utterly fabricated, or the person in question had never even seen the show but had been sick for a very long time."

Dana shuffles her notes a bit. "So this puts quite a damper on your overall message then, Reverend Hopewell?"

Harlan nods with his calm, gentle smile. "Absolutely not, Ms. Collier. It defines it." He turns serious. "I'm sorry for what happened. I don't want anyone to think that I don't pray for forgiveness, that I have walked away feeling justified for every word I've preached. I grieve for these four families, and I pray for them, and they all know they have only to call and we'll be there. But I'd like to think we've come through this all a little less judgmental, a little kinder, a little more predisposed to grace."

"Speaking of Grace, Ms. Hopewell, can you tell us why you kept Leo all of those years without telling her parents?"

"I don't want this to come off as cruel against Grace, so I won't go into detail, Dana. Grace and I had an unspoken understanding regarding her folks about Leo and her lifestyle. I knew exactly what I was supposed to say when I called them every month to update them on their daughter. She wanted me to say as little as possible, but enough to ease their minds. They're good people, the Underhills, they just don't have all the facts."

"Do you miss him?"

"It's something I'll never get over."

If I cry now, like I feel like doing, it will cheapen my feelings, so I bite down on my lip and relish the pain I'll cherish forever. I had Leo for a time, and for the rest of his life he'll bear the stamp of my love.

"I miss my son, Ms. Collier."

"I'm sure you do."

She turns toward Harlan. "Your wife suffered from depression and yet you continued to preach your antipsychology message, is that not right?"

He nods. "But not for long. It was Charmaine, my beautiful, bubbly wife who's always been so faithful to the Lord and has always loved Jesus so much, that God used to convince me that I'd been going at it a little too strong."

She arched a brow. "So people aren't responsible for their sin?"

"Of course they are. But sin and sickness are two different things. And God's grace covers them both."

"It covers everything," I say.

She's not too pleased with this line, I can tell.

I lean forward. "It's like this, Dana. Maybe some of us rely on medicine to fill in the missing piece of our relationship to God, to cover up our sins, but maybe some of us just have things that are wrong with our brains. But God's bigger than that, too. Who am I to question the ways He chooses to heal?"

"Finally, Charmaine, there was a great mystery surrounding the profits you made from your record sales. Now granted, this was personal money, not ministry funds, but I'm sure the viewers are curious as to where this was going. First of all, your house is filled with expensive antiques."

"They're my grandma Min's. She was frugal for years and saved every penny she could to buy those things. She's one of those antique nuts!"

Dana twitters. "So you have an inherited taste for the finer things then?"

"Well, no—"

"And who can blame you? Isn't it true that you spent the first several years of your marriage in a motor home?"

"Yes, that's true."

"So being surrounded by these gorgeous antiques must be quite the experience."

"They're just Grandma Min's. I like them, but they're hers, not mine. Everybody has that one thing they love." I squeak out a chuckle that sounds more like a soft cry for help.

"What about your clothing?"

Here we go again. "It's a little known fact that I am quite a seamstress."

Her eyebrows raise. "I didn't know that. Did you make that suit you're wearing?"

"I sure did."

"Goodness, that's beautiful!" She reaches forward. "Real silk?"

I shake my head. "I wish!"

She laughs.

All this comes across as real, but I can hardly imagine this lady putting on a homemade anything.

"So your money wasn't being spent lavishly, was it?"

Finally! "No. I was paying for the care of my mother at Broughton Hospital. She's a schizophrenic and she deserted me when I was eleven years old. I only found her last year."

The interview continues and I am tired.

"Schizophrenia? What was the reunion like?" She looks so concerned.

"As one might expect. No emotion on her part whatsoever. But she's being well cared for now, closer to our home, and Grandma Min can go over and visit her daughter on a regular basis." I grab more tightly to Harlan's leg. "It's hard for Grandma."

"So mental illness runs in the family?"

"It appears so."

"Do you ever worry that your own mental illness will pro—"

"I think we're done now," Harlan says. He points off the set. "That man over there is counting down and there's only five fingers left."

Dana reddens and turns to the camera. "More *Hot Topics* after this."

Finally, our bit is over. Dana says a quick good-bye and hurries off the set.

An assistant producer ushers us back to the green room and thanks us.

And that is it.

"Well, if this isn't anticlimactic I don't know what is," Harlan says, stuffing his hands in his pockets.

"It was over before I could breathe!"

We stare at each other. And stare.

Harlan rubs his chin. "Hmm. I don't know, Shug. I feel kind of odd, don't you? Let down a little?"

I nod. "It just goes to show us Harlan, we really are a couple of nobodies, aren't we?"

And we laugh and laugh.

"Let's go meet Grandma and Hope."

Epilogue

We've been back on the air for years. I've reached the ripe old age of forty-two and Mama lives with us now. We waited until Hope was a little older. Thirteen, actually. And Hope is strong. She handles the situation beautifully. Grandma Min is spry despite her age, as if I doubted she would be, and has discovered the joy of bus trips.

I found another great dessert a few years back that even Mama can make. It's called a "dump cake" and all you do is dump cans of fruit, layer butter and sprinkle in uncooked cake mix. We all love it. Hope makes one every time she comes home from college to visit. Even my own children, one girl and two boys, can make it.

My nose still bleeds every once in a while, especially when Mama has a downturn or I'm planning to go into the studio to record. I wish to goodness they'd change the decor there at BrooksTone.

The Port of Peace Hour now lives up to its name. We do all we can to give peace to folks who don't know why life is so hard. We don't have the answer to that question, but we know there's some comfort along the way. And if that isn't good enough, well then, there's nothing else I can say.

My daughter Victoria calls out, "Grandma Isla is singing again!"

I know what it is and I smile. She's been singing "Good Morning Merry Sunshine" for a while now.

I've learned to join in as best I can.

should Grace have been allowed to take back Leo? Should Charmaine and Harlan have fought to get him back? Why or why not?

11. In *Songbird*, where was God's grace most evident?

IF I HAD YOU
by Deborah Bedford

Nora Crabtree has long since given up on her wayward daughter. When Tess turns up pregnant and begs for help, the last thing Nora wants is to get involved again. When Tess leaves, though, the Crabtrees have no choice but to bring this motherless baby into their home. Nora believes God is giving her the chance she prayed for—to right mistakes from years before. She pours all the love that Tess rejected into this new child. But when Tansy Crabtree vanishes on her walk from the bus stop, Nora and Tess must struggle with a relationship they thought had died years ago—and with the question of what is best for the little girl whom they both want to love. And Nora discovers that God may answer more prayers than she ever bargained for.

Available June 2005